SEVENTH SON

ALSO BY MIKE BARON

SEVENTH SON

MIKE BARON

WOLFPACK
PUBLISHING
— EST 2013 —

Wolfpack Publishing

701 S. Howard Ave. 106-324
Tampa, Florida 33609

wolfpackpublishing.com

Paperback ISBN 978-1-63977-188-2
eBook ISBN 978-1-63977-187-5
LCCN 2023951077

SEVENTH SON

SEVENTH SON

CHAPTER 1

BUSHNELL

At three p.m. on a gray November afternoon, Brascum's Brew Pub was mostly empty. The long, low dark brewery was the end cap on a strip mall that included a pet store, a liquor store, and a Qdoba. Josh parked his Chrysler in front, got out, and zipped up his leather jacket. Water lay in puddles from the first snow of the season.

Josh looked around, trying to guess the client's car: an F-150, a Tesla, and a Prius. Jerry Bushnell had sounded exhausted on the phone when he'd set up the meeting. Bushnell said he was coming from Milwaukee. He said he was a veteran. Had to be the F-150.

Josh entered the brew pub, stopping to let his eyes adjust to the gloom. The polished mahogany bar dully reflected soft lighting from industrial sconces. Josh looked up. Ceiling fans, ducts, and an open ceiling. Eight round tables lay between booths on both sides. Two young exec types sat at the bar talking in hushed tones. Otherwise, the pub appeared to be empty.

A man rose in the last booth on the right. He was slight, balding, with glasses, and wore a V-necked sweater over jeans. Tentatively he raised his hand.

"Mr. Pratt?" he whispered hoarsely.

Josh went over and stuck out his hand. "Mr. Bushnell?"

They shook. "You can call me Jerry. Have a seat. Would you like something to eat or drink?"

"I'll have a ginger ale."

Bushnell squinted. His glasses needed cleaning. "Didn't figure you for a ginger ale guy."

"How did you hear about me?"

"I read about you in *The Horse*. I'll be right back."

Bushnell went to the bar and returned with a glass of ginger ale, a shot of whiskey, and a mug of beer. He set the glass in front of Josh.

"Thank you. Do you ride?"

"Uh, no. I used to. I had a Ducati when I was in the Army but they shipped me out and I hadda get rid of it. That was a long time ago."

"How can I help you, Jerry?"

"I want you to find my brother's killer."

"Your brother was murdered? I'm very sorry to hear that. When did it happen?"

"June 15, 2012."

"That's over ten years ago. Did the police investigate?"

"Yeah. Didn't find shit. He was stabbed thirty-nine times."

Bushnell's shoulders hunched in grief.

"Breath in, Jerry. Breath in. Straighten your back and

draw it down to your abdomen."

Eyes shut, Bushnell arched his back and did as he was told.

"Now let it out in a controlled stream through your nose."

After each deep breath, Bushnell loosened. He opened his eyes. "I'm sorry. It just eats at me. Nobody gives a shit. I served in the Army but I got a medical discharge and somehow I don't qualify for benefits. I live in a shit basement apartment in Milwaukee with no windows. I have bed bugs. My sight is going."

He slammed the shot and took a long draught of beer.

"Did you drive here?"

"I took the bus. Then I took an Uber."

"Jerry, that's terrible about your brother, but I don't work for free."

Bushnell checked all around. He'd chosen a seat by the wall in the back so no one could sneak up on him. He reached beneath the table and pulled up a leather and green canvas backpack that had been around. "My family has always served. My old man served in the Gulf War. My great-great-grandfather Nathan served under Brigadier General Robert Granger. He fought at Tunnel Hill. His best friend Roderick McCauley served under John Bell Hood."

"Why didn't they serve together?"

Bushnell put his fingers on the table. "Because they were on opposite sides, duh."

"I see. I should probably read more. Which was which?"

"General Hood was marching north to invade Tennessee. The Union army drove them back. Nathan was a captain. He was among the first Union soldiers into Hood's camp. He found this after Hood folded camp. I don't know how he got it, but it's been in the family ever since. It is the only thing of value my family ever left me. My sons hate me. My ex-wife hates me."

Josh held his hand out. "Show me."

Bushnell carefully pulled a file folder from his backpack and unwrapped the string around the button. He pulled out a cardboard/plastic sleeve sandwich, held shut with jumbo rubber bands. Bushnell removed the rubber bands, pulled out a mylar sleeve and laid it in front of Josh.

It was written in neat cursive on yellowed linen paper.

October 26, 1864

Dear General Granger,

I regret that I am unable to send reinforcements at this time, as every able bodied soldier has been assigned to General Sherman, for his assault on Atlanta. Nevertheless I have the utmost confidence in you, and urge you to hold the line. Should Hood invade Tennessee, he will have opened a second front and will force us to split the Army of the East. I would put one of your Kentucky sharpshooters up against any greycoat.

Yours,

Lieutenant General US Grant

"Where'd you get this?"

"Don gave it to me."

"Is this for real?" Josh asked.

"You are the first person outside the family to see this. I've examined Grant's signature and handwriting. It's real. Do you have any idea how much a letter like this would fetch at auction?"

"No. Why don't you sell it and move out of your basement apartment?"

"I don't know how to sell it."

"Would you like me to help?"

"No. I want you to find my brother's killer. He was stabbed thirty-nine times."

"Where was he killed?"

"Right in front of the stage. Right in front of Cheap Trick."

"Give me a date and address."

"It was at Summer Fest. June 15, 2012."

"Did your brother have any enemies?"

"No. Everybody loved him."

"Were you there?"

"I was in Afghanistan. They gave me compassionate leave. I never went back. Now I can't collect benefits."

"Do you have a picture?"

Bushnell rummaged around in the backpack, pulling out a vinyl folder. He opened it up. A much younger Bushnell, with hair, smiling goofily as another man, presumably his brother, had him in a headlock and was delivering a knuckle rub. Pale color photo of much younger brothers sitting on a striped cloth sofa between a crew cut father in a sweater vest and glasses on the left, and prim mother, knees together, slacks and sweater on the right.

"My father's a piece of shit. He walked out on us when I was fourteen. Don was twelve."

"Would you like me to find you someone to talk to? Like a pastor or something?"

"I want you to find Donnie's killer."

Josh sipped his ginger ale. "What are you going to do if I don't take the job?"

"Keep looking, I guess. There's got to be someone who will help me. I served my country. Did you serve?"

"No."

They sat in silence for a minute.

"Let me at least put you up for the night, get you a ride back to Milwaukee."

"I don't want your charity. I want you to find Donnie's killer."

Josh tilted a hand. "What else I got to do."

"Does that mean you'll do it?"

"Listen. Here's what I'll do. I'll look into it. If, at some point, I figure it's a dead end, you can pay me for my time. Here's my card."

For the first time a gleam of hope crept into Bushnell's eyes. "That would be great. Great. Listen. I want you to take the letter with you. Put it someplace safe. I can't be draggin' it around."

"Why would you trust someone like me? You don't know me."

"I read about you in *The Horse*. You're a biker. You've got the biker's code. I can tell by the way you talk to me."

Josh sighed. "All right. I'll keep it safe. Give me your phone number. In the meantime, let me put you up at a motel and take you back to Milwaukee."

"Why would you do that?"

"To show my appreciation. Thank you for your service."

CHAPTER

2

O'MALLEY

Major Donald Bushnell had served two tours of duty in Afghanistan, from 2005 to 2009, earned a Purple Heart and Distinguished Service, was honorably discharged in 2009, where he returned to Milwaukee and opened a handyman service. Don had a reputation for quality work. He could lay tile, fix the plumbing, build a fence, install electronics, and was soon in demand among the gentlefolk of Morgan Heights, Alcott Park, and Wedgewood. He drove a new Ford Transit painted in his distinctive livery, a happy plumber in coveralls and Green Bay cap with a plunger over one shoulder, a toolbox in hand.

Josh printed out pictures. Across the street, the Lowrys had company. Lights and laughter tinkled down the long driveway. Josh looked down where Fig laid her snout on his thigh. She whined. Dinnertime. He leaned over and kissed the dog on the top of her head.

"All right."

Fig capered around barking and wagging her tail. Josh went into the kitchen and pulled out a grilled chicken breast from several days ago and gave it to her. He put on a jacket and walked across the street to the Lowrys. He went in through the open front door, living room filled with faculty in tweeds and ties drinking cocktails and talking politics. Louise, a handsome fiftyish in an ecru cocktail dress smiled and came over.

"Would you like a drink, Josh? Are we being too loud?"

Josh laughed. "You're never too loud. Listen, I have to go to Milwaukee tomorrow and I was wondering if you would keep Fig for me. I don't know when I'll be back."

"Fig is always welcome here, Josh. I'll be home until around eleven. Just bring her by before then."

George and Gracie, the Lowrys' schnauzers came wagging their stubby tails. Years ago, Josh had recovered them from a biker gang that had snatched them as training bait for their pit bulls. Josh had met his girlfriend Ray at the Lowrys'. They were the best neighbors he ever had. Some guests glanced over. He looked out of place.

"Okay. Is seven too early?"

"No. We're early risers. Won't you stay for a drink?"

"Can't, Louise, thanks. The game is afoot."

"What are you doing Thanksgiving? We'd like you and Ray to join us."

"I think we're going to her parents. She's going crazy trying to get her new play ready."

"What new play?"

"*Drunk Octopus Wants to Fight.*"

"Seriously?"

"You know I have no sense of humor."

Josh was up at five, went for a run with Fig, their breath condensing in the cold morning air. A hot hatch Honda with huge negative camber passed, blatting like a wailing baby. Josh returned, showered, dropped off Fig, and drove to the Magnuson Grand Madison, a sleazy hotel near the Ho-Chunk Casino on the East Side, to pick up Bushnell. The Grand Madison was the type of motel that had little signs in the room listing the costs of all appliances: television, clock radio, iron. In case you were tempted to take something.

Bushnell was waiting in the lobby wearing the same clothes he'd worn last night with his backpack on his lap. He stood as Josh entered and headed toward the front door.

"Thanks for doing this. You didn't have to do this. You don't know me."

"Don't worry about it."

"Did you put the letter in a safe place?"

"It's in a safe."

They got in the car, Josh returned to the Beltline and drove counterclockwise until he reached Interstate 90. They headed into the sun. Josh wore sunglasses and pulled down the visor. Bushnell dug around in his pockets and pulled out sunglasses with a yellow plastic frame, like something a child might wear.

"Do you know the precinct that investigated your brother's death?"

"No. But I talked to the detective. I have his card."

More digging, a cloth billfold. Bushnell looked through a stack of grimy cards and pulled one out. Detective Shawn O'Malley. They passed Lake Mills and Delafield. Bushnell talked non-stop. His kids hated him. He had no friends. Bed bugs were eating him alive.

"Sometimes I wonder what's the point. I have nothing to live for. I should just die."

"Knock it off," Josh said. "You go to church?"

"No."

"Wouldn't hurt. Go to the nearest church. Talk to the minister."

"What's the point?"

Bushnell lived on West Concordia in Borchert Field, a seven-story brownstone. Josh pulled to the curb. Next to the three-step front entrance concrete steps led down to a windowless steel door. "I live in the basement."

"I will report to you as soon as I learn something, no later than two days."

"Thank you." He sniffed. "You're the first person who's been nice to me in I don't know how long. Everybody hates me."

"Knock it off."

"Excuse me?"

"Attitude. I'll be in touch."

Bushnell got out, slung his backpack over one shoulder,

and slouched down to the basement. Josh headed south on Forty-Three, then east on Ninety-Four, to the waterfront. Every June, Milwaukee put on Summerfest at Henry Maier Festival Park, just south of downtown. Josh pulled into the park and around to a parking garage. Josh parked on ground level. There were only four other vehicles in the garage. He sat in his car and phoned Shawn O'Malley.

"This is O'Malley. Leave a message."

"Mr. O'Malley, this is Josh Pratt. I'm a private investigator from Madison. I'd like to ask you about a murder you investigated thirteen years ago. Please call me back. Thank you." He left his number.

He pulled on a dark green and gold watch cap, locked the car and walked north toward the inlet, looking at Milwaukee's gleaming skyline. The US Bank Center, Northwest Mutual, solid, square shouldered Midwest types in gray suits, the art museum that looked like a cyborg nun. A concrete path ran around the inlet. Josh went down some steps and walked north, past gulls and pelicans. He came to a wooden bench. *Jason E. Holland, Beloved Father, June 9, 1930, January 14, 2020.* He sat, gazing out at a handful of sailboats battened down, canvas covered. They'd have to be pulled soon. The lakefront froze in winter.

His phone buzzed.

"Josh Pratt."

"Mr. Pratt, this is O'Malley. What's this about?"

"I have a client who wants me to find out who killed Don Bushnell on June 15, 2012."

"Is it the brother?"

"Yeah. He been bugging you?"

O'Malley chuckled. "I'll tell you what I told him. Cheap Trick was playing. Ten thousand people. drunk, high, God knows what. Listen. I got to take a call."

"Can I buy you a beer when you get off?"

"No. But I'll give you fifteen minutes. I'll call you back."

The phone went dead. It was cold on the bench. He returned to the parking garage, slid behind his wheel, opened the glove compartment and pulled out a Yakima Henry Western. He dozed off. The phone woke him.

"Josh Pratt."

"O'Malley. Meet me in fifteen minutes at Sweet Diner, 39 E Chicago St. Can you do that?"

"Yes, thank you."

CHAPTER

3

JAYCEE

Sweet Diner was an upscale café just south of St. Paul near the river, in a quasi-industrial marketplace housing Adidas, Perry Ellis, and Christian Dior. Josh found a place on the street, passing a Milwaukee patrol vehicle at the curb, a massive SUV with battering rams in front and back and a light bar. He went in through the street entrance and around to the diner, which had its own interior door. A man in a gray trench coat sat at the window sipping coffee, phone on the table. Josh went over.

"Thank you for seeing me, detective."

"Have a seat. You want coffee?" He looked to a young woman in a white shirt and tight gray slacks clearing dishes, and made a pouring motion. "Maggie, when you get a chance."

Josh sat. "I met Jerry yesterday. He found my contact info on the internet."

"One reason this case remains in my mind is because Jerry won't leave it alone. I feel sorry for the guy."

"Me too. Told me he was a veteran."

"He is. I checked that out. Dishonorable discharge."

"I didn't know that. I don't know if I'm spinning my wheels. I looked up what I could find about Don Bushnell. Served two tours of duty in Afghanistan, came back here, built a business."

"It could have been any random nutso. I'm sorry to say, murders are up every year. With this defund the police crap and the city council looking over our shoulder, it's a miracle anyone remains on the force."

Maggie returned with a big white mug of coffee.

"Thank you."

"You want a cruller or something?"

"Do you have breakfast sandwiches?"

"Egg, cheese, bacon on English muffin."

"I'll have that, please."

They watched her go.

"Were you there that night?"

O'Malley nodded. "Yup. Busy night. Seven arrests for possession, one for assault. And the stabbing. I was at the north end of the park. The stabbing happened in front of the Pabst Stage, which is at the south end. We heard about it seconds after it happened and swarmed the area. Lots of eye witnesses. It was a big Black guy. It was a small White guy with a nose ring. It was two teenagers in hoodies. I got finessed into taking the case. There was no video in those days. I've covered hundreds of homicides and there are two reasons this one sticks with me. One. You hate to let one get away. Two. Brother Jerry has been stalking me for four years. Phone calls. Shows up at the station. We all sort of understand that he's had a rough time, and we respect him for his service. I wish I had something to tell him."

"Who was playing?"

"Cheap Trick."

"So if I were to pursue this case, I'd be wasting my time?"

"I didn't say that. You're private. You can spend all the time you want on this case. We're understaffed and over-loaded. I have to clear four cases a week."

"Could I see your notes?"

"Sure. What's your email?"

Josh reached for his wallet. Maggie set a white bone china dish before him with the breakfast sandwich. It looked good.

"Go ahead."

Josh ate the sandwich. "Did Don have a family? Anybody I can talk to?"

"Yeah. Wife, and two children, a boy and a girl. Let me dig that up."

He pulled out an electric notepad and leaned it against the condiment box. He poked and scrolled. He turned it around. Wife: Jaycee Bushnell. Children: Max and Sam, with their birth dates. Max was now twenty-two, his sister Sam nineteen. Josh wrote down the contact info.

"Thank you, sir."

O'Malley laid thirty bucks on the table. Josh reached for his wallet. O'Malley held up a hand. "I'm on duty. Can't take freebies. Good luck."

O'Malley left. Josh phoned Jaycee Bushnell. She picked up on the second ring.

"Hello?"

"Mrs. Bushnell, my name is Josh Pratt. I'm a private investigator from Madison. Jerry Bushnell has asked me to look into your husband's death. I got your contact information from Officer O'Malley, who was on duty the night Don died."

Jaycee sighed. "I wish Jerry would let it go. I've accepted Don's death. All he's doing is stirring up memories I'd rather forget."

"I understand, ma'am. I wonder if you would speak to me about it. I might be able to bring a set of fresh eyes."

Long silence.

"I'm sorry. What's your name?"

"Josh Pratt. I'm an investigator."

Another pause.

"All right. I don't buy for one minute that was a random attack, and the cops were worthless. They didn't even pretend to care. Let me give you my address."

Jaycee lived in Delafield on an acre of land, the white and green ranch house attached to a three-car garage. It was one of those semi-rural neighborhoods with a few widely spaced houses for people who valued solitude. Elm and oak shaded the front yard, covered with autumn's stubble. Josh parked at the curb, zipping his jacket as he stepped out. He followed the fieldstone path to the front door. It opened before he got there.

Jaycee looked like she stepped out of the *Real House-wives of Milwaukee*. Attractive, lean, great cheekbones, dark hair drawn back and braided, wearing a green cotton sweater with the sleeves rolled up.

"Mrs. Bushnell, I'm Josh Pratt."

They shook hands. She looked him up and down. She turned around, motioning him to follow.

"You can call me Jaycee. Would you like some coffee?"

"Better not. I already had two cups."

She laughed from the kitchen returning a minute later with a tray bearing cheese and Ritz Crackers. She sat down on a sofa and pulled a pen and pad off the side table. "May I see some identification?"

Josh showed her his driver's license and private investigator's license.

She wrote in her pad.

"All right, Matlock, what do you want to know?"

"Did you go to the waterfront with Don?"

"No. I stayed home with the kids. He really wanted to see Cheap Trick."

"Was he meeting anyone there?"

"He was meeting Butch."

"Who's Butch?"

"Butch Denza. Army buddy. Now he sells insurance and teaches kung fu."

"Do you know how I could get in touch with Mr. Denza?"

She pulled out her phone, poked, handed it over. www.Denzainsurance.com Josh pulled out his pad and pen. "Where were Sam and Max?"

"They were with me. Max was in his room playing video games and Sam was riding her bike up and down the street, probably visiting her friend Rosalie."

"Did your husband have any enemies?"

Big breath.

"Where do I begin?"

CHAPTER 4

BASEMENT MEMORABILIA

"Donnie was in Afghanistan from 2007 to 2009. He was a helicopter mechanic. We lived at Fort McCoy in family housing. Most of the time, the children were with me. My parents were wonderfully supportive during that time period. I don't know how we would have made it without them. Donnie was promoted twice which meant an increase in salary, but it wasn't until he got back and built his own business that we started making money.

"He served under a Lieutenant Randolph Holmes. I guess it's safe to say they hated each other's guts. Holmes was always playing rap music in the mess hall. Donnie went up to him one day and asked him to turn it down. Holmes called him racist."

"Why didn't he ask for a transfer?"

"They were understaffed. Donnie was a very good mechanic. He kept that fleet flying mostly by himself."

"What were they flying?"

"MD 530s and Black Hawks. I thank God every day Donnie got out when he did. Just look at what happened." She bit her lip.

"Do you know what became of Lieutenant Holmes?"

"No idea. Donnie was just glad to be out of there. Holmes stayed in Afghanistan when Donnie mustered out. But honestly, the man was in the Army. I doubt very much he was the murderer, and besides. He wasn't from around here. He was from someplace in the South."

"You said Donnie might have other enemies."

"He did a job for a woman in Brookfield whose basement was flooding. Turns out, she had another plumber in there about a month before to repair a clogged sewer line, and he screwed it all up. Donnie fixed it, explained what happened, and the woman went on a vendetta against the first guy. The plumber's name was John Alston. He worked for some plumbing company, and when the woman posted her experience, she mentioned his company as incompetent and praised Donnie. They fired Alston. He showed up here drunk one night, honking his horn, threatening to beat Donnie up. Well Donnie wasn't afraid of anything. Alston was halfway across the lawn when Donnie took him down and held him in a jiu jitsu lock while I phoned the police. He became homeless and started doing drugs. He sent us threatening emails and we blocked him and reported him to the police. I haven't heard from him in years."

"How would John Alston send an email?"

"Public library."

"Would you happen to still have those emails?"

"No. Why would I? But the library might. It was the Waukesha Public Library. The date sticks in my mind because it was July 4th, 2007."

"Is that why you don't think Donnie's death was random?"

"Partly. Alston struck me as a lunatic. No impulse control. On the other hand, planning to murder Donnie seemed too ambitious for him. There's always a chance he was at the concert, saw Donnie, and waited for his opportunity. But I don't think an anti-social jerk like that would go to a concert."

"Do you know where Alston is now?"

"Of course not. I wouldn't be surprised if he were dead."

Josh wrote in his pad.

A willowy teenage girl blew through the front door holding a skateboard, her brown hair in a ponytail. "Hi, Mom! Hi, guy!"

She headed for the stairs.

"Come back here, young lady."

Sam pivoted on the ball of her foot. She wore denim coveralls over a purple sweatshirt.

"This is Mr. Pratt."

"Hi, Mr. Pratt."

"You can call me Josh."

She looked Josh up and down. "You look like an ex-con."

"Sam!"

"You'd make a good private eye," Josh said. "I served four years in Waupun."

"What for?"

"Sam!"

"Assault. It's all right. It is what it is."

"What's going on?"

"Your uncle has hired Mr. Pratt to look into Dad's death."

Sam rolled her eyes. "As if! We all wish Uncle Jerry would just let it go."

"Got any ideas?"

"No. Somebody killed him. They never found the killer. The end. You look cool. Mom won't let me get a tat."

"You're excused."

Sam went upstairs.

Josh laid his card on the table. "Thank you very much, Mrs. Bushnell. If you can think of anything else, please call me."

"How can Jerry afford you?"

"We worked out a barter."

"What could Jerry possibly have that you would want?"

"A handwritten letter from Ulysses S. Grant."

"What? Where would he get such a thing?"

"He said it was in his family for generations. Do you know anything about that?"

"I never met Donnie's father. Donnie wouldn't speak of him, except once, he said that his father was a Civil War buff, and used to participate in, what do you call them, when they dress up like historical figures and play war."

"A historical reenactment."

"Yes, that's right. His name was Charles. He has a brother who lives in Alabama. Luthor."

"Do you know how I can get hold of Luthor?"

"Hang on a minute."

Jaycee went to a sideboard, opened a drawer, took out a cardboard box and set it on the coffee table. It was filled with cards and pictures. She riffled through them and held up an envelope.

"Here it is. Luthor sent me this when Sam graduated from high school. I was stunned. I don't think I've heard from him before or since."

She handed Josh the envelope. He pulled out a Hallmark card showing a cartoon girl glowing in mortarboard and gown. Inside it said, "Congrats to the girl chile! Your uncle Luthor." The return address was 2195 RR12, Faubus, Georgia. He copied it down.

"Do you know what groups Charles joined?"

"No. But somehow all his stuff ended up in the basement. His wife had him declared dead and they had to clear out the house. It was a rat warren. Donnie agreed to take all this stuff. I think, he didn't want to cut himself off entirely from his father, you know? Would you like to look through it?"

"If you don't mind."

She led him through the kitchen down the steps to a concrete basement, cardboard boxes stacked against one wall, furnace, water heater, and an old armoire in one corner surrounded by plastic bins.

"I'll leave you to it. If you're going to take anything, please show me."

"Thank you."

The armoire contained several replica Union uniforms, boots, belts, hats, a cavalry sword hanging from a peg, and a Spencer M1 lever repeating rifle. A box of modern replica ammo sat on the floor. The uniforms were those of a lieutenant and a captain. The bins contained black and white and color photographs from historical reenactments, complete with cannon belching gray smoke. The players posing, blue on the left, gray on the right. Charles smiling, arm in arm with a friend. Charles had a beard, and a leather holster on his waist.

Josh took out his phone and photographed close-ups of comrades in arms. One was a black-and-white photocopy of an old black-and-white photograph. Matthew Brady stuff. It showed three Confederate soldiers in kepis, standing stiffly in the field with their rifles, hands on hips. They had that Civil War look. Stern faces, handlebar mustaches. Beneath the man on the right someone had written "McCauley."

Another showed two impossibly young West Point attendees arm in arm. Trying to grow facial hair. Someone had written in blue magic marker: Ethan Bushnell on the left, Roderick McCauley on the right.

Footsteps entered the kitchen above.

Josh went through the uniform pockets and found a

card. Burke's Regulars, 2nd and 4th US Infantry, and the National Civil War Association. He wrote the information down in his pad. He examined Charles' US Army Model 1860 revolver, a muzzle-loading six-shooter. The cavalry saber had a wooden sheath. The suits were clean and neatly pressed, the weapons clean and oiled.

Jaycee was in the kitchen loading the dishwasher, a tall, good-looking young man in a varsity sweater seated at a small kitchen table staring at his phone.

"You must be Max. I'm Josh Pratt."

They shook hands. "Mom told me what you're doing. Let me know if there's anything I can do to help."

Josh showed Jaycee the two cards and the photocopy. "May I take these?"

"Sure."

"Thank you for your time."

"I just hope something comes of it. I'll walk you out."

Outside, Josh asked, "Are you aware of anybody in your family or McCauley's dying under suspicious circumstances, prior to Don's murder?"

Jaycee bit her lip and looked up. "Don said something once that one of his father's uncles was killed in the Gulf War by his own men."

"Do you remember his name?"

"No, I'm sorry. I'll ask the kids."

JOSH GOES THROUGH HIS EMAIL

Josh arrived home at five, went across the street. No need to knock. Fig, Gracie and George stood on the other side barking. Louise opened the door.

"Thanks, Louise. You know, if you two ever need me to watch George and Gracie while you're out of town, I'd be happy to do that."

"Thanks, Josh. We usually drop them off with our daughter Sarah."

Fig followed Josh across the street and sat in the kitchen, tail wagging expectantly.

"I'll bet Louise already fed you, and you're trying to con me out of an extra meal."

Fig grinned and thumped the floor with her tail. Josh pulled a pound of chicken breasts from the fridge, went out back and fired up the grill. The temperature was in the fifties as he grilled the breasts, took them back in, waited until they had cooled, and put one in Fig's bowl. She wolfed it down.

"Do you even chew, bro?"

He called Ray.

"Can't talk. Middle of rehearsals. Love you!"

"What rehearsals?"

"Drunk Octopus Wants to Fight. Tomorrow, I promise."

Josh checked his email.

UNITED NATIONS NEW YORK
WORLD BANK ASSISTED PROGRAMME
DIRECTORATE OF INTERNATIONAL
PAYMENT AND TRANSFERS.
10017 WIRE TRANSFER/AUDIT UNIT
Our Ref: WB/NF/UN/XX02x79
ATTN: BENEFICIARY,
IRREVOCABLE RELEASE OF YOUR PAYMENT

We have actually been authorized by the World Bank and international monetary fund (IMF), to investigate the unnecessary delay of your payment. Recommendation and approval of your claims for payment is certified as genuine.

During the course of our investigation, we discovered with dismay that your payment has been unnecessarily Delayed by corrupt officials of the Bank, who are Trying to divert your Fund into their private accounts, to forestall this, security for your funds Was organized in the form of your personal

Identification number (PIN) and your transfer access code (T.A.C), this will enable only you have direct Control over this fund.

We have also agreed with the World Bank and international monetary fund (IMF) that, we will handle this payment in our selves to avoid the hopeless situation created by these corrupt Officials.

We have obtained an irrevocable payment guarantee on your Payment from the World Bank and international monetary Funds (IMF). We are happy to inform you that based on our recommendation/instructions; your Entire contract fund/inheritance claim has been credited in your favour through our paying bank You are therefore advice to contact: MR.DOUGLAS BENSON, of African Development Bank Group the (un)paying bank Liaison Office in Nigeria Lagos with the contact informations stated below: PAYING BANK: AFRICAN DEVELOPMENT BANK GROUP EMAIL: adbg_bankplc@vipmail.hu CONTACT PERSON: MR. DOUGLAS BENSON. Phone Number: +234-9047 7356 69

Make sure that you contact the above-mentioned person to collect your original payment slip with your pin and transfer access code. As soon as you submit these codes and your payment slip to your bank, they will credit your account without any delay.

YOU ARE ADVISED TO RE-COMFIRM YOUR INFORMATION TO AVOID TRANSFER OF THIS FUND INTO A WRONG ACCOUNT.

Your Bank Name:

Your Bank Address:

Your Bank Account No:

Routing No:

Swift Code No:

Account Name:

Age & Occupation:

Your Driving license:

Full Name:

Home Address:

Your Direct Tel, Mobile & Fax No:

NOTE: YOU ARE ADVISE TO CALL MR. DOUGLAS BENSON ON HIS DIRECT TELEPHONE NUMBER +234-9047 7356 69 AS SOON AS YOU RECEIVE THIS MAIL TO CONFIRM THE MAIL TO HIM AND FORWARD YOUR DETAILS FOR THE PAYMENT TO HIM IMMEDIATELY THIS IS DONE.

CONGRATULATIONS.

REV. WILSON P KLERK

Email: rev.wk002@gmail.com

UNITED NATIONS, NEW YORK

He deleted it.

We have video of you pleasuring yourself. You have twenty-four hours to deposit $1000 in Bitcoin in the following bank account, or we will release the video on all channels.

He deleted it.

Hello and how are you doing today and how is the weather condition up there today, handsome? Jennifer Clark.

He deleted it.

Hey Chainsaw!
Your old buddy Bix here. Glad to see you're doing so well. Maybe you can help a brother out. I'm about to be evicted from my apartment. If you could loan me one thousand dollars, I promise I will repay you within a month. I have a classic Jaguar sedan I've been restoring, and pretty sure I can sell it for big bucks.

Your old buddy,
Bix Hemsworth.

He deleted it.

QATAR FOUNDATION
Address: Qatar Foundation Building
Al Wajba Area, P.O. Box 5825 Doha, Qatar.

Qatar Foundation is a government-funded organization here in Qatar, founded 1995 by decree of Sheikh Hamad bin Khalifa Al Thani, Emir of Qatar. Qatar Foundation in conjunction with the European Union(UK), These Donations are freely given to individuals for their business, educational and personal development. Congratulation, You were among the lucky beneficiary selected to receive this donations award sum of £ 1,000,000GBP(One Million Great Britain pounds Sterly)each as charity donations/aid from the Qatar Foundation to promote your business and personal developments.

For more details on how to receive your Donation Bank Draft, please contact the President of Qatar Foundation with your pin numbers(QF-999-9814),Full Names, Sex, Contact Address, country, Nationality, Occupation, date of birth and your Valid Phone Number via contact details below.

YOU HAVE TO REPLAY THIS MAIL BELOW ONLY.

President of Qatar Foundation:
Dr Mohammad Fathy Saoud

Deleted.

At least the White Oaks Homeowners Association had stopped trying to buy him out.

He went to Facebook. His last post had been two years prior, but sometimes old friends tried to contact him, and it was useful in reaching out. He phoned Jaycee.

"Ma'am, I forgot to ask. Do you know what Lieutenant Holmes looked like?"

"Yes. There's a photo of Donnie and the rest of his squad. I should have shown it to you. Let me get it."

"Could you photograph it and send it to me?"

"I can do that."

"Thank you, ma'am."

There was no Butch Denza. There was Denza Insurance with a link to White Dragon Kung Fu. Josh wrote, *"Dear Mr. Denza. My name is Josh Pratt. I'm a private investigator out of Madison. Jerry Bushnell asked me to look into the circumstances surrounding his brother Donnie's death. May I call you?"*

He looked at Donald Bushnell's obituary. It mentioned his service and family, but there were no details about his murder. It barely rated two inches in the *Milwaukee Journal*. There was no description of the assailants. He thought about contacting Jarell Moore. That's where Josh got Fig. Jarell's bitch had a litter. It had been years, but what the hell. He dug out Jarell's email.

Jarell. You want to see how your dog's doing? I'll

*buy you lunch. Meet me in Lake Mills. I'll show you
the pyramids.*

He included his phone number. It was dark out. No
Ray. He thumbed through his collection of DVDs. *Ninja*,
starring Scott Adkins. The complete *Sons of Anarchy*. The
complete *Breaking Bad*. He subscribed to some streaming
services and haunted local pawn shops and used bookstores
for DVDs. He had hundreds, including the complete works
of Charles Bronson and Lee Marvin. He settled on *Man On
Fire*, which he had watched five times. He slipped it in the
DVD player in the living room and sprawled on the sofa
with Fig's head in his lap.

John Creasy was moving into his new digs in Mexico
City when Josh's phone rang. The number had a Milwaukee
area code.

"Josh Pratt."

"Brother Josh. This is Jarell. I would be happy to meet
you in Lake Mills."

CHAPTER

6

JARELL

It was raining Saturday morning as Josh headed east. Lake Mills was a pretty little town of six thousand on the shores or Rock Lake. In nearby Aztalan State Park, Middle Mississippians had built a series of flat-topped pyramids between AD 1000 and 1300. They may have been cannibals. Josh checked their website. The last update was three years ago.

"Visitors are encouraged to practice social distancing, frequent hand washing and to wear a face covering if not yet vaccinated or if social distancing cannot be maintained. For more information, please see: COVID-19 Information."

Josh pulled up in front of the Dolores Café on the square in downtown Lake Mills. It was a different planet inside the diner, warm, moist, and redolent with the smell of coffee and bacon. A slim Black man, buzz cut, sports jacket and gray turtleneck signaled from a booth in the back. Jarell stood and they embraced. The last time Josh had seen Jarell, he'd had a fadeaway, wore a hoodie, and enough gold around his neck to finance the space program. Josh sat. The man across from him had none of the arrogance he'd exhibited six years ago.

"Jarell. What happened?"

"I found Christ, brother. Through the guidance and wisdom of Pastor Paris Goodings, I quit the thug life and have dedicated myself to helping boys get back on the right path."

Josh experienced a moment of gratitude that brought tears to his eyes. "I can't tell you how happy I am to hear that. I came to God in prison. Pastor Michael Dorgan was my guide."

"I heard that. Don't mean I don't like to party, but these days I limit myself to beer and marijuana. How's that pup doin'?"

Josh pulled out his phone and brought up a video he'd shot that morning. Fig sitting, grinning, wagging her tail.

"Are you a good girl?"

"Woof!"

"Who's the greatest band that ever lived?"

"Woof woof!"

"That's right. Tower of Power."

Jarell laughed. "I dig 'em myself. I saw them at Summerfest once."

"That's what I want to talk to you about. I'm investigating the murder of a man named Don Bushnell. He was stabbed to death at Summerfest on June 15, 2012. South end of the park. Cheap Trick was playing."

"Why ask me?"

"Conflicting reports. Some people said it was a gang of Black teenagers in hoodies."

"So naturally I would know about such a thing."

"You were a criminal back in the day."

"That's true, I was."

"You ever go to Summerfest?"

"Ain't missed a show in twenty-two years."

"So you were there in 2012."

"Yeah, but I don't know the exact dates, and I can't remember who I saw. One year it was George Clinton. The Weekend, you know, it might have been Kool and the Gang. Old school. I love old school."

"Were you there on June fifteenth?"

Jarell shrugged. "I have no idea. It ain't like I keep a diary, although maybe I should. Summerfest is three weeks long. You think all Black people know what all other Black people are doing?"

"Look on the bright side. I'll buy you lunch."

On cue, a pert young thing in an orange dress with a white apron and a white cap on her head approached. "Have you gentlemen had a chance to look at the menu?"

Jarell looked up. "Do you have cheeseburgers?"

"We certainly do."

"I would like a cheeseburger, medium, with a side of coleslaw."

"I'll have the same."

The waitress marked in her pad. "Anything to drink?"

"I'll have a Coke," Jarell said.

"Me too."

"What is it you want me to do, exactly?" Jarell said.

"Ask around."

Jarell grinned. "About an incident that took place thirteen years ago because all us Milwaukee Black people know each other?"

"Now I feel bad."

"I cut you some slack because of who you are. I'm here for two reasons. One, because you asked me. Two, because I need your help."

"Whoa."

"One of my things to get kids off the street is teaching martial arts at Grace Baptist. I took a turntable and a load of vinyl over there to bring the kids up to speed with sounds they may have missed. All that rap. It's getting to the point where I'm telling them to pull the fuckin' bass outta their ass and listen to gospel."

"Man, you used to love that stuff!"

"That's before I got my wake-up call. You should meet Paris. You'd like him. One of the records I brought was a vinyl two-fer, *Fathers and Sons*, signed by Muddy Waters, Otis Spann, Paul Butterfield, and Mike Bloomfield."

"Holy shit."

"Yeah. The quadfecta. Someone kuiped it. I'd like it back."

"Do you have video?"

Jarell shook his head. "No. We want the boys to feel comfortable. We're trying to instill an honor system. There's a gymnasium in the basement of the building, and a small office where I keep my vinyl. I brought over five hundred records, stored vertically in alphabetical order, but the ones I play, I just lean against the wall. *Fathers and Sons* was leaning against the wall. My question, how does a seventeen-year-old even know who they were? That record's worth a lot of money."

"That's gonna be tough. How many kids? What do you know about them?"

"Well here's the thing. Some of these kids are hard to turn around. Some are gang members. Vice Lords. Latin Kings. I hope that if I can engage them, I can open their eyes to possibilities beyond the thug life. There are maybe a dozen who could have done it, but the question is, again, how would they know to steal such an arcane item? Most of them don't have fathers. Who's listening to Muddy Waters?"

"Is there someone who stopped coming?"

"Naw, these kids are brazen. They're sociopaths. It takes time to turn 'em around. We got a pretty hardcore group 'cuz who doesn't want to learn martial arts, y'know? You help me, I'll help you."

"Do you teach?"

"Yeah, I teach. I started training in Brazilian Jiu Jitsu fifteen years ago."

"All right. How 'bout I come by next week? I'll be a guest

instructor. I can teach 'em a few things."

"I'll bet you can."

"And you'll ask around?"

The waitress brought their burgers.

Jarell got his in a two-fisted grip. "I'll see what I can do."

CHICKEN PARMESAN

When Josh got home, he went into his office. Butch Denza had responded to his inquiry.

> *I would be happy to discuss it with you. We could do it here on Facebook, if you wish.*
>
> *Dear Mr. Denza: Thank you for your prompt response. I prefer to meet in person. If you would like to suggest a place in Milwaukee, I can meet you there at your convenience sometime next week.*

Denza responded within a minute.

> *Sure. I like Stanley's on North Downer. I'm free Mondays and Tuesdays at four o'clock. I teach on other weekdays, beginning at five. Or we could meet later. I am through teaching at eight and could meet you at eight-thirty.*
>
> *Let me check and I will get back to you.*

Josh wanted to combine his meeting with Denza and his visit to Grace Baptist. He emailed Jarell, asking when would be a good time for him to come by. He looked at cycle pages online. *Easy Riders. American Iron. Bikernet.com. Cycle World.* Harley was going all electric.

"Harley-Davidson is planning to phase out motorcycles powered by its storied internal combustion engines, and will slowly but surely transform into an all-electric brand. Harley CEO Jochen Zeitz tells *Dezeem* that after 120 years of being famous for its big gas-powered models, electrification is the logical next step. That is, if the company plans on sticking around for another 120 years."

Josh shook his head.

Fig thrust her snout in his lap so he love bombed her, went into the garage, turned on a space heater, and worked on the Basket Case, an S&S motor fit into a Thompson Chopper frame. He removed the previous owner's extended front forks, replacing them with a Twisted Choppers springer. He was waiting for Acme Leather to finish his tractor seat. Fig stepped onto a pile of quilts he'd thrown down and minced around, probing with her front paws. Round and round she went, poking with her paws.

"Sit."

Fig paused, looked at him, and continued to circle, plumping up the quilts with her paws.

"Sit!"

She did two more rotations and finally settled down.

"Thank God," Josh murmured. He'd left his phone behind. Bike building was holy. You forgot yourself and concentrated on the task at hand. Josh used to think God rode a Harley, but more and more, he was thinking Indian. Various reasons. It conferred honor on the original inhabitants, never mind that no Native American had anything to do with its founding. George Hendee and Oscar Hegstrom founded Indian in Springfield, Massachusetts. Over the years, the name changed hands more often than a dollar. Some of the Indians were creepy. Some were cool. Compared to the modern Indian, they were barely rideable. God would ride a Super Chief Limited. Josh was thinking of picking up a Scout. One of the new ones. Indian had no plans to go electric. When he looked up it was five o'clock and Fig was snoring.

Josh turned off the heater and went into the kitchen, Fig at his heels. Fig talked. It almost sounded like English. Josh got a can of The Farmer's Dog out of the cupboard, decanted it into Fig's bowl, cut up an apple, threw it in, and swooped the bowl down on its stool while Fig watched, intent. She ate like six sharks.

"How was it? Can you describe the taste?"

Fig looked at him and belched. Josh pulled a California Kitchen Sicilian pizza from the freezer and set the oven to four hundred. He went into his office. Jarell wrote:

What's up? I'm out of touch when I'm on the floor.

Josh wrote back.

Can I call you?

Jarell sent his phone number.

"What's up?" Jarell said.

"When would be a good time for me to check out the

school?"

"What about Tuesday? We have a class at five."

"Great."

Jarell emailed him the address. Grace Baptist, 302 South Newton, between Garfield and North.

Josh retrieved the photocopy of the Confederate soldiers. He was no expert, but he recognized McCauley's chevrons as sergeant stripes. He searched for Sergeant McCauley, Civil War. There was one mention on Wiki of Sergeant McCauley having served under General John Bell Hood at the Battle of Tunnel Hill in Chattanooga.

Fig woofed excitedly. Ray let herself in, one arm gripping a Whole Foods bag. She went into the kitchen.

"Forget the pizza!"

Josh followed and smacked her butt. She whirled into his arms. She pushed away and began removing things from the bag. Grated parmesan cheese. Broccoli. Garlic. Chick-pea linguini, butcher wrapped chicken breasts, pesto.

"Baby, you don't have to cook. I could take you out."

"I'm cooking."

"How did the rehearsal go?"

"We have a lot of work to do."

"What's this about again?"

"*Drunk Octopus Wants To Fight* is about a bitter ex-cop who was fired for excessive use of force. Every night he hangs out at the neighborhood bar getting shit-faced. It's kind of a character study, like *American Buffalo*. He never sees his kids. He owes alimony. His only friend is the bartender. He's played by a woman, Idaho Mongoose, terrific actress."

"Does Idaho have a beer gut?"

Ray laughed. "No, but she's very convincing."

"She'd be more convincing with a gut."

"This has to go in the oven. Give me fifteen minutes to throw it all together and I'll meet you in the bedroom."

"What is it?"

"Chicken parmesan."

"Thank you, Ray, although I was sort of looking forward to that pizza."

"Get out before I throw you out."

Josh took a shower, put on a Wild One sweatshirt and flopped in the living room. Ray came out of the kitchen smacking her hands. She crouched with her dukes up. "C'mon, tough guy. Show me what you got!"

Josh lunged off the sofa, grabbing her around her waist, hoisting her over his shoulder, carried her into the bedroom, and closed the door with his foot. He threw her on the bed. She peeled off her yoga pants. He peeled off his shirt. Fig stood outside the door and whined.

As they lay panting in each other's arms, Josh asked, "Where's Sid?"

"He's at home. Idaho's staying at my place and watching her."

"All of Idaho? Or just parts?"

"Idaho lives in Waunakee. I let her stay at my place."

"Oh that's good. I was worried."

"You miss Sid." Sid Vicious was Ray's cat, who peed on Josh's shirts. Only lately, since she'd been a house guest and bonded with Fig over pork sausage, not so much.

"What's going on?"

Josh told her about sad Jerry Bushnell and his family. "He gave me a handwritten letter signed by Grant as payment. I'm thinking, this will probably go nowhere, and I'll hook him up with a good auction house, if he wants. Guy's living pretty close to the bone. One step up from homeless."

"Grant who?"

"Ulysses Grant, the President."

"Where did he get that?"

"One of his ancestors raided a command post during the Civil War. Maybe it's fake. Omma have it checked out. I'll take it to the university."

"I'm staying here tomorrow."

"The Pack is playing Minnesota!"

"I'll try not to distract you."

AUTHENTICATION BLUES

Monday morning, Josh drove downtown, parked in the Park Street ramp near campus, and headed toward the Wisconsin Historical Department on Library Mall. Grant's letter was enclosed in a mylar sleeve with a backer board, sandwiched between two hard plastic sheets in his backpack. He put on his mask and entered. Inside, the old lobby smelled of books. Josh wasn't much of a reader but he loved the smell. A young woman wearing both a face mask and a clear plexiglass shield sat at the information desk.

"Can I help you?"

"Yes, ma'am. I'm looking for someone to authenticate a Civil War relic."

"What kind of relic?"

"A handwritten letter signed by General Grant."

"You might want the George Mosse Historical Foundation in Humanities, or the Civil War Museum or the

Wisconsin Veterans' Museum, at the head of State Street."

"Do you have any Civil War experts here?"

"Not really. This is more of a library. You're welcome to go through our catalog. It's all online. Have you tried to ascertain its authenticity by comparing the signature to Grant's?"

"Yeah, it looked good to me, but what do I know? Thanks for the advice. I'll try the Mosse next."

It was a brisk sunny day. Taking off his mask, Josh walked down Park Street passing gaggles of backpack-clutching students in down-filled jackets, most of them masked. A group of girls stepped into the street to avoid sharing the sidewalk with him. The Humanities Building was a grotesque Bauhaus-style concrete inverse pyramid swarming like a hive. He put on his mask and entered the lobby. There was no info desk, but a sign directed him to the Mosse Foundation on the fourth floor. A hall gave way to corridors filled with offices, with a large lecture hall in the center. Josh heard a teacher speaking as he passed. A tall, athletic looking student in a Badger sweatshirt headed his way, books under his arm.

"Sir," Josh said, "who do I see about the Civil War?"

The man stopped. "What Civil War?"

"The American Civil War."

"Oh. Hang on a minute." The student pulled out his phone and poked. "You want George Hagenauer, room four fifteen."

"Thank you."

The door to four fifteen was open. Inside, a man sat at a

gunmetal gray desk typing on a keyboard. He had a salt and pepper beard and wore glasses and a tweed jacket. A sign on the corridor wall identified him as George Hagenauer, American History. Josh tapped lightly. Hagenauer looked up. He pushed back from the keyboard.

"How can I help you?"

Josh stepped inside. Hagenauer blinked and pushed minutely against the desk. "Are you a student?"

"Sir, my name is Josh Pratt. I'm a private investigator. I'm seeking to authenticate a letter."

"What kind of letter?"

"A handwritten letter by General Grant. Would you like to see it?"

"By all means. Have a seat."

Josh sat in a wood captain's chair across from the teacher, set his backpack down and removed a zippered vinyl folder containing the letter. He removed the letter, still in its mylar sleeve, and laid it on the desk in front of Hagenauer. Hagenauer stared at it.

"Hmmm." He opened a desk drawer and took out a magnifying glass. He took off his glasses and eyeballed the document. He turned to his computer and brought up examples of Grant's signature. "It certainly looks authentic. It would be helpful if we could carbon date the paper and ink. Would it be possible for you to leave it with me for a couple of days?"

"I don't know. If it is authentic, it's worth a lot of money. How much does a history professor make, anyway?"

"You're not serious."

"I'm not letting it out of my sight."

Hagenauer pulled out his phone. "May I?"

"Knock yourself out."

Hagenauer took several pictures.

Josh cracked his knuckles. He took one of Hagenauer's cards from a card holder on the desk. "Let me think about that, Professor. Here's one of mine."

Hagenauer carefully slid the card toward himself using one finger. "It certainly looks genuine. I will consult a handwriting expert. If it is real, it's worth a great deal of money. Civil War collectibles are a boom market. Next to Lincoln, Grant's signature is the most desired."

"Give me a call if you feel like it."

"I certainly will." Hagenauer perused Josh's card. "You're a private investigator?"

"Yup."

"Oh, a tough guy, eh?" the professor said in a mock Cagney accent. "A dick. A shamus. A gumshoe."

Josh smiled. "That's me." He slid the document back across the desk and put it in his backpack.

"You're welcome to monitor my classes."

Josh stood. "I'll keep that in mind, professor."

He went home and looked up Grant. Grant was in charge of the Union Army from 1863 until the surrender. People were still bitterly divided over the war, and about Grant, in particular. Prior to rejoining the military, he had lived in poverty. He had written hundreds, if not thousands of notes during the war. They ranged in price from two thousand dollars to one hundred thousand. Most of them were housed in museums. The odds of your average Joe finding a genuine Grant signature were slim. What did Josh know? He was fifteen when his father abandoned him. His first foster family enrolled him in an upper middle-class high school where he was in constant trouble. He barely finished the eleventh grade.

He looked outside. Orange leaves everywhere. All his neighbors were out scraping up leaves and stuffing them into plastic bags. Most hired a lawn service. Sometimes Josh half-heartedly raked leaves. What was the point? They weren't a blight and if you just let them lay there, they would rejoin the soil. Nobody gave him shit. For them, it was like having Al Capone for a neighbor. Like that time the Insane Assholes showed up in his front yard and shot it out with the cops.

Once the neighbors got to know him, they liked him. Like Phil Bass, the developer who'd built White Oaks and had been trying to buy Josh out. Lately he'd laid off. Phil shot the psycho Scipio when he broke into Phil's garage and threatened Phil with a knife. And who told Phil to get a pistol and learn how to use it?

Fig sat at his feet woofing. Long, controlled woofs filled with pathos and meaning.

"All right, all right."

Josh grabbed a phosphorescent Frisbee and they went into the backyard. Josh tossed the Frisbee underhanded, snapping the wrist to impart maximum spin. Fig plucked it five feet in the air.

They went inside. Josh took the California Sicilian pizza out of the refrigerator and set the oven to four hundred degrees. He called Ray.

"No can do, buddy! I'm going to be here until late," she yelled over other people yelling.

"Oh, come on."

"*Drunk Octopus Wants To Fight!* I'll call you tomorrow."

Josh took the pizza into the living room. Fig did her thing, thumping and whining.

"Sorry, big guy. This shit's not for dogs."

Fig whined, tilted her head, put her paw on his knee. Josh went into his office and shut the door so he could finish his dinner in peace.

IN THE CELLAR

Stanley's on North Downer was an "All-American Tavern" and neighborhood saloon with upscale pub fare. Josh parked on a ramp and entered the restaurant a few minutes before four. He looked around. Nobody stuck out. A waiter appeared.

"Sir?"

"Lookin' for a guy."

"Are you Mr. Pratt? He said to meet him at a table in the back. I'll take you."

Josh held out a fin. "Thanks, kid. I can find it."

The interior was modeled after late nineteenth century London gentlemen's club, with leather booths, dark green wood with brown highlights, and a stamped tin ceiling. Local art graced the walls. Cubist bebop interpretation of the Pabst Mansion, five thousand dollars. Sitting in the corner, in the dark, Denza looked like a small planet waiting to explode. He wore a white wool sweater under a leather jacket, steel hair crewcut, jumbo mitts. He stepped out of the booth to shake.

"Mr. Pratt? I'm Butch."

They shook.

"Thank you for seeing me, Mr. Denza."

"Call me Butch. Donnie was my best friend. I'll do anything I can to help."

"Jaycee said you ran a martial arts studio."

"I sell insurance, but I teach at the White Dragon in the evening."

"You know about the jiu jitsu at Grace Baptist?"

"I heard someone was teaching."

"Old friend of mine. Jarell Moore. Used to be a gangster, but he had a come to Jesus moment."

"Good to hear."

"You know, with all this kung fu talent, we should make a movie."

Denza studied him.

"Joke."

Denza smiled and nodded his head. "My ex-wife always had to explain jokes to me. I mean, I like to laugh as much as the next guy but let's face it. Jokes are the lowest form of humor. True humor arises out of the absurdity and pain of the human condition."

The waitress came over. "What'll it be, fellas?" "What's on tap?" Josh asked.

Denza picked up a laminated menu. "Try the Regal. It's

very good."

"I'll have a Regal lager, and a cheeseburger, I guess."

Denza ordered a pale ale and fish and chips. The waitress beelined toward the kitchen.

"Nobody's wearing masks," Josh said.

"This ain't the university."

"Sir, do you remember the night Donnie was killed?"

"I think about it every day. We were in front of the Cheap Trick stage—they all have names. I forget which one. May not even be there anymore. I had to visit the john. Every year, festival organizers are shocked and stupefied to learn people need to pee. Every year, they cough up twelve porta potties. Twelve porta potties to serve twenty-five thousand people? I had been standing in line for fifteen minutes when we heard shouting, and people in a frenzy, like piranha, trying to get away from the stage. Then the cops ran in. I had no idea it was Donnie. I finally used the porta potty and headed back. They'd set up a perimeter. Crime scene. Who died? I asked. They told me. I talked to them for forty-five minutes, but I didn't see anything."

"Was there anything odd about that evening? Some detail that just feels out of joint?"

The waitress returned with their food. They salted their food and ate. Josh put ketchup on his burger. After ten minutes of silence, during which Josh was acutely aware how loud was the rest of the café, Denza looked up.

"There was one thing." Denza's forehead wrinkled. He looked upward. "On the way in, we passed a dude dressed like a Confederate soldier. Donnie took my elbow and guided me away. He said he didn't want to be anywhere near that guy."

"Did he say why?"

"No, but he told me that his father, who left him when he was eleven, had been a Civil War buff and participated in historical reenactments."

"Remember what the guy looked like?"

"Not really. It was about eight, still light. He looked slim. And he had that pillbox hat on, you know. He was standing by a bench drinking beer in a plastic cup. Wristband."

"Did he have facial hair?"

Denza examined the ceiling. "Yeah, now that you mention it. Beard, mustache, mutton chops, the whole thing. What's so interesting about this, was the crowd was about half black, and this is a very liberal city. People might not love a Confederate soldier up here the way they would in Birmingham."

"Huh." Josh handed Denza his card. "If you think of anything, please contact me."

"I will."

"What kind of insurance do you sell?"

"Life, home and auto."

The waitress cruised by. "Can I get you guys anything else?"

"Just the bill, please," Josh said.

The waitress removed it from her apron pocket and Denza snatched it out of her hand.

"Hey!"

"Sorry, buddy. You can buy next time."

Grace Baptist on West Atkins was an old-fashioned gray stone church with oak pews, a nave, a bell tower and a chancel. It was just after five as Josh pulled up at the curb around the corner, got out, beeped the car and headed for the front door carrying a massive gym bag and a basketball.

Four teens hung out in front smoking. They wore hoodies and expensive sneakers, and nodded as Josh passed. A handful of parishioners sat in the nave. Josh took the basement stairs off the narthex and found himself in a great room with a twelve-foot ceiling, a half-court hardwood floor, a five-foot pile of interlocking mats, and an aisle in the rear flanked by men and women locker rooms. Two free-standing heavy bags stood close to the wall along with plastic bins filled with sparring equipment and kicking paddles. An American flag hung on one wall.

Two kids were playing b-ball one on one. The kid pressing the action was about five eight, wearing a Bucks jersey that came down to his knees, hair cut short. The defender was over six feet, wearing an XXL flannel shirt with the sleeves rolled up, both in tennies. Josh walked the perimeter and went down the hall to an open office door. Jarell sat inside poking at a keyboard. He looked up, stood, and welcomed Josh with a smack and a bump.

"Thanks for coming. What's with the ball? We got our own."

Josh turned the ball so Jarell could see the signature.

"Is that really LeBron James' autograph?"

"It's the best I could do. Where was the record they stole?"

Jarell pointed to a stack of records leaning against one wall. Otis Rush led the parade.

"So they stole it right out of your office."

"Looks like. I don't know how they got in here. Church has a security system, s'posed to alert ADT if anybody breaks in."

"And that never happened?"

"No. It's possible it was taken during normal operating hours, but that meant someone had to get back here while we were working out. There's a back entrance that goes up into the parking lot, but an alarm sounds if you use it."

Josh removed a small black dot the size of a nickel. "This is a Rainbeo micro-motion-activated camera." He looked around the room. A cluster of framed photographs covered one wall. Jarell arm in arm with four homies back in the day, pants low, flat-brimmed hats, gang signs. Certificates of appreciation from Grace Baptist and the Youth League. Jarell crouching with a part border collie/German shepherd mix. Josh rotated the mini-camera on switch, peeled off the backing and stuck it in the corner of a black-and-white photograph of Ali looming over a fallen Sonny Liston. It was hardly noticeable. He pulled out his phone and activated the app, turning it so that Jarell could see the two of them standing, looking at the phone.

"Ahuh."

"Figure whoever took the record might try again."

"How they gonna know what's back here?"

"'Cause we're going to show them this ball."

Jarell looked at a wall clock. "'Bout that time. You ready for this?"

"I'm ready," Josh sang. "Ready as a man can be."

GRACE BAPTIST

Josh stripped off his clothes in a small bathroom off the office, turned off his phone, put on a cup, and dressed in gray sweatpants and sweatshirt. The big gym bag contained sparring equipment: fifteen-ounce gloves, shin protectors, rib guard, mouthpiece, and foot guards. He carried the bag out on the floor where six kids were warming up, hitting the heavy bag, stretching next to the wall using a barre. They wore sweats, gym clothes, whatever they had on hand. All wore sneakers. They were silent as Jarell stood at the end of the room beneath the hoop and clapped his hands.

The seven boys, ranging in height from five-four to six-four, lined up.

"Class, this is my friend Josh Pratt. Josh is going to school you in some techniques. What techniques you gonna school 'em in?"

"How to throw a punch."

The kids laughed and shuffled their feet.

"Face the flag. Bow. Face front. Bow. What's our motto?"

"I promise to develop self-discipline," half said while the others shuffled and looked at their feet. "To bring out the best in myself and those around me."

Jarell flipped a switch on a boom box. The SOS Band sang "It's a Long Way to the Top."

"Let's shadow box. Move those feet."

Josh moved around the room throwing light jabs, crosses, and uppercuts. A short boy with short hair furiously pummeled the air. Some bobbed and weaved. The tall kid repeatedly threw right hooks followed by right uppercuts.

"Add some elbows and knees," Jarell said. Five minutes later he said, "add some kicks."

For fifteen minutes they juked and shuffled around the floor. Jarell shut off the boom box and clapped his hands. "Gloves and targets. Pair up."

Some of the students had brought their own equipment. The rest helped themselves to gloves and targets in two jumbo plastic bins at the back. The odd number resulted in the tall boy looking around. Josh motioned him over. Josh had brought his own gloves and targets.

"Six punches," Jarell said.

Josh held the pads at shoulder height. "My name's Josh."

"D'artagnan."

"Three Musketeers?"

D'artagnan looked at him funny.

"Begin," Darrell said.

D'artagnan threw the jab followed by the cross, left hook, right hook, left uppercut, right uppercut. Josh met the punches with his pad, slapping down to get a good sound. It felt good to be back in the gym training. It had been too long. D'artagnan was a powerful young man with a lot of snap. After five minutes, Jarell had them switch and it was Josh's turn. Jarell changed it up. Block, one punch counter. Block, two punch counter. Block, three punch counter.

When they'd been at it for twenty minutes, Jarell said, "Put your gear on."

D'artagnan put his on fast and returned to Josh, eager to spar. The bell rang. D'artagnan danced in pumping his jab. He was tall and fast, but Josh kept stepping to the right and going over the jab, beating him to the punch. Light pops on D'artagnan's headgear. D'artagnan smiled.

"How you do that, man?"

"You're dropping your elbow when you punch. Look at this." Josh turned his fist so that the thumb was on the bottom. "Now when I throw the jab, my elbow comes up and blocks your counterpunch."

"Ho shit!"

The bell rang and they changed partners. Josh sparred with kids who had no idea what they were doing and kids who did.

At six-fifteen, Jarell clapped his hands. "Line up."

They lined up.

"Face the flag. Bow. Face front, bow. Let's thank Mr. Pratt for his input."

"Thanks Mr. Pratt!"

"All right. Who's up for a little b-ball? Let's pick up those mats."

The boys folded and stacked the mats. Jarell went down

the corridor and returned with the basketball, which he tossed to D'artagnan. D'artagnan was about to dribble when he saw the signature.

"Ho shit!" he said, displaying the signature to the other boys. "Is this for real?"

"Ask Josh."

"Far as I know. It's still just a ball. Signature doesn't affect the way it bounces."

"Where'd you get it?"

"I won it in a charity raffle. Twenty bucks."

The students formed teams. Three men on a team. Jarell played hip-hop. Josh followed him back to his office.

"Okay, I'm outta here. Thanks for the invite."

"You gonna check on this ball?"

"Yeah. I get an advisory every time the camera is activated, which is gonna be all day every day when you're in here."

"Can you adjust the times?"

"Yeah, I think I can do that. I'll ask my girlfriend. I can barely operate this phone. You want me to send you the app? It's cued to this phone."

"Yes please."

"What time do you close up shop?"

"Around nine."

"Okay. I'll adjust the app so that it operates from nine p.m. to six a.m. That should cover it. No one's gonna sneak in here at dawn's first light to steal that ball. They're gonna do it at night when they can walk out with it without being seen. Donnie Bushnell."

"I'm on it."

"Thanks, mon."

Slap and bump.

It was dark as Josh exited the church parking lot and headed for the interstate. He found a jazz station out of Milwaukee playing Eric Reed. Ex-Jugan Bobby Hines had turned Josh onto Reed. Hines was a two-fisted pianist himself, great-grand-nephew of Earl Hines. Josh pulled into his driveway at eight thirty to a barrage of barks. He'd fed Fig at three but now she wanted more.

"All right, all right!" he said, hands up as he went into the kitchen and tossed Fig some treats. He checked his phone and realized it had been off for several hours. He turned it on. Ray had called, asking him to call her. Jerry Bushnell had called twice. Josh returned the call.

"I haven't heard from you," Jerry said. "What have you found out?"

"Jerry, I promise to report once a week. I usually do that Friday. I met with Jaycee. She told me you have an uncle who lives in Alabama."

"Uncle Luthor. He never liked me. I only met him once or twice before our father abandoned us. He was just loud. And mean. He drove a car with a Confederate flag decal. I haven't heard from him in years. He may be dead."

"I also talked to Donnie's friend Butch Denza. He was there that night, but he was away from the stage and has no idea what happened. I'm making some inquiries. I have a friend who knows people who might have been there. I'll let you know as soon as I learn anything. I'm also having Grant's letter authenticated. If it's real, it could be very valuable. I will only put it up for auction with your permission, and I will only charge you what this case is worth. With any luck, you should be left with a nice nest egg."

"I live in a basement. It has no windows. It has bedbugs."

"Do you have a computer?"

"Yes."

"Look up how to get rid of bedbugs."

"No one cares about me."

"Good night, Jerry."

Josh phoned Ray.

"I'm going to bed, baby. You gonna be around tomorrow?" she asked.

"Yeah. Want to come over?"

"Can I bring Sid? He's going crazy staying here all by himself in the day. Today he shredded my living room curtains."

"What happened to Idaho?"

"She went back to her apartment in Waunakee. Sid was pissing on her shirts."

"All right. Don't bring anything. I'll cook."

Josh signed off and went to bed. Fig got up on the bed and tried to slip him the tongue.

"Not tonight, Fig."

SAINT CHRISTOPHER

Following his morning run, Josh tried to Sid-proof the house. He picked up all the laundry, put it in the laundry room and shut the door. He thought about spreading a motorcycle cover over the sofa, but the sofa was already mauled for life. Tears, burns, stains. Let Sid have the sofa.

He drove to Woodman's, got some hamburger, eggs, and salad fixings. As he carried his groceries to his car, he watched a man roll his empty shopping cart into the parking space next to his truck and open the driver's door. Josh set his bags down. He watched as the man got in his truck and shut the door. Josh walked over and spoke through the open window.

"Sir," he said, pointing. "Would you mind returning your shopping cart to the rack?"

The man whirled, snarling. A big man with a barrel chest and greasy hair.

"Who the fuck are you? The cart narc?"

Josh stood legs slightly apart, hands on his belt buckle, stone-faced. The man took in the dragon's tail crawling up his neck.

"Sure thing."

The man got out and dutifully rolled his shopping cart into the cart corral. It was funny how much appearance and attitude mattered. At home, he used the lettuce spinner Ray had given him, set his cell phone on the microwave, and went to work.

Fig's interest was intense as Josh prepared meatloaf, mixing the ground beef with onions, crushed pretzels, Liquid Smoke, and barbecue sauce. He put the finished loaf in a baking pan in the refrigerator. The salad could wait. His phone rang.

"Pratt."

"Mr. Pratt, this is George Hagenauer. Several experts have examined your letter and determined that it is probably genuine. There's no way to know for certain, of course, unless we analyze the paper and the ink."

"Thanks, professor. Suppose the owner wanted to sell it. Where would he go?"

"Well, I'm no expert on these things. Some big auction house specializing in memorabilia, I imagine. One thinks of Sotheby's, of course."

"What do you know of the Battle of Tunnel Hill?"

"Not one of the significant battles, but certainly of interest. Why do you ask?"

"Guy who gave me the letter, his great-grandfather fought there. And his father was a Civil War nut. I mean buff."

"It happened toward the end of the war. As I recall, General Hood was trying to bring his men north to Tennessee. I'd have to brush up."

"I'll buy you lunch if you'll talk me through it."

"Well I would be delighted to meet you for lunch."

Josh looked at his calendar. "Can you meet me Saturday at the Student Union?"

"The Student Union? Let's go to the Madison Club. It will be my treat."

"Deal."

Fig barked.

"It's only three o'clock, Fig. You have an hour to go."

Fig rolled on her back, paws meekly folded and whined.

"It didn't work before, Fig. It's not working now."

Fig got up and barked furiously. She ran to a wicker bin by the back door and grabbed a Frisbee.

"All right all right."

They went in the back yard and Josh skimmed the Frisbee on a gentle incline. Fig snatched it five feet off the ground. When they went inside, Josh found that Jaycee Bushnell had phoned.

He phoned her back. A man answered in a gruff voice.

"Delafield Police Department. Who is this?"

"Sir, this is Josh Pratt. I'm a private investigator from Madison."

"I know who you are. What do you want?"

"I'm returning Mrs. Bushnell's call. Do I have the wrong number?"

"Mrs. Bushnell can't come to the phone right now."

"Can you tell me what's going on?"

The cop breathed heavily. "Her son Max is in a coma from smoking fentanyl-based marijuana."

"Oh my god."

"Did you know him?"

"No."

"Mrs. Bushnell told us about your visit. Sounds like you picked a bad time to show up."

"Who's this?"

"Malcolm Portier."

"How do you know what happened?"

"One of his friends found him unconscious in a park and called an ambulance."

"Can you tell me who called it in?"

"Listen, I gotta go. You'll have to ask someone else. That's all I know."

"Let me know if there's anything I can do to help."

"I don't know yet, but thanks for the offer. I might get in touch with you."

Josh phoned O'Malley and left a message. Ten minutes later O'Malley called back.

"Thanks for returning my call, sir. Did you hear about Max Bushnell?"

"Yes. Milwaukee is on track to beat its all-time best for

overdoses. We've seen an uptick in drugs on the streets."

"Fentanyl, or what?"

"Mostly fentanyl. It's the workhorse of drugs. You can put it in anything. All we know now is that Max got the marijuana from one of his high school friends."

"Max is twenty-one."

"He was working as a teaching assistant at Saint Christopher's. He planned to enlist in the spring."

Josh thanked him, went into his office and looked up the Battle of Tunnel Hill. Tunnel Hill, now a suburb of Chattanooga, had been a small town through which General Hood planned to march. Upon arriving, he found the town protected by four thousand Union troops under Brigadier General Robert S. Granger. Their entrenched line included two forts. Hood suffered unexpected casualties before pulling back and heading further west, to find a path across the Tennessee River. The delay of four days shortened the war.

He looked up Saint Christopher's.

"St. Christopher's Military Academy educates and develops young men to be responsible citizens as well as moral and ethical leaders inspired to take full advantage of life's opportunities. We achieve this goal through academic excellence, spiritual and character development, a vigorous athletic program, and leadership training in a secure, nurturing, and inclusive environment.

"Saint Christopher's Northwest Academy admits students of any gender, race, color, national and ethnic origin to all of the rights, privileges and activities generally accorded or made available to students.

"We believe character is learned behavior, shaped by beliefs. Spiritual and character development at St. Christopher's Northwestern is built on our Episcopalian roots and extends to respect every student's faith tradition. We help students articulate what they believe and why they believe it, because that knowledge empowers them to lead a life of purpose and service."

The chapel looked warm and inviting.

Pictures of young men lined up in sharp blue uniforms wearing polished black stovepipe hats. Pictures of young men in identical white shirts and blue shorts on a soccer field. Pictures of young men in their best uniforms dancing chastely with willowy young women in gowns in a hardwood floored ballroom.

Josh found Max's class picture, a smiling young man with an almost white crew cut. Josh had no idea if Max's overdose had anything to do with the death of his father. Maybe it was just bad luck. Maybe not. Something seethed beneath the bland surface of an unlucky suburbanite stabbed to death by random thugs, and Max's misfortune. Something serpent-like and ugly.

Josh returned to the kitchen and made the salad, adding cherry tomatoes, hearts of palm, and green onions. He put the meatloaf in the oven.

At six, Ray squeezed through the front door with Sid in one arm and a cloth bag of groceries in the other. Fig went crazy. Ray dropped Sid and knelt to let Fig lick her face.

"Don't let him lick your face!"

"Don't worry! I'll wash my face."

Fig lay on the sofa as Sid licked his face.

"What are you cooking? It smells delicious."

"Meatloaf."

Ray picked up the grocery bag. "I brought champagne."

"What are we celebrating?"

"Champagne."

SECURITY DEPOSIT

Ray and Sid left in the morning. It was raining. Josh wanted to call Jaycee Bushnell, but was reluctant to pierce her capsule of grief. It was too soon. He called O'Malley.

"O'Malley."

"Officer, it's Josh Pratt. Do you have an update on Max Bushnell?"

"He's out of intensive care and it looks like he'll survive."

"What was it, exactly?"

"Cardiac arrest. They got him on the Narcan right away. Probably saved his life."

"Can you tell me where he's staying?"

"Why?"

"I might bring him some comic books."

O'Malley laughed. "He's at Waukesha Memorial on American Avenue. Doubtful you'll get in the room. He's still in intensive care."

"Any idea where the fentanyl came from?"

"It's not my case. But you can bet it originally entered the country through Mexico."

"Thank you, sir."

Josh phoned Jarell. "Who distributes fentanyl in Milwaukee?"

"You got two gangs. Latin Kings and Vice Lords. I lost two students to fentanyl this year. Only reason I know this is because I'm low to the ground. I don't ask questions. I start asking questions, I attract attention and lose students. I'm here to do God's will and help these boys."

"I understand."

"Why?"

Josh told him about Max Bushnell.

"That there is some sad shit. As if that family didn't have enough to deal with."

"I know."

"Anything pop up on the camera?"

"Not yet."

"You let me know."

"You pull that bad boy out tonight. You'll know as soon as I do. It's on your phone."

Josh found a statement from the Milwaukee City Council chairperson.

"Like much of the nation, Wisconsin continues to battle a heroin and opiate epidemic that is placing an increased burden on communities to better understand the local challenges associated with addiction and its public health implications. Milwaukee County alone has seen an 800 percent increase in fentanyl-related deaths between 2014-2021. These deaths, together with other opiate-related overdoses, have exceeded injury-related deaths such as motor vehicle fatalities and homicides. Seventy-five percent of these deaths occurred due to fentanyl, either by itself, or mixed with cocaine, heroin, and marijuana."

Josh emailed Steve Fleiss, the criminal lawyer for whom he delivered summons, with a copy of Grant's letter.

"Steve, how do I find out what this is worth, assuming it's authentic?"

Jerry Bushnell phoned. "I'm being evicted."

"Why?"

"I'm late on my rent, and the landlord hates me."

"Why does he hate you?"

"I don't know. Everybody hates me. I don't know what to do."

Bushnell was halfway to homeless. From what Josh had observed, Bushnell suffered from some cognitive disorder. Asperger's. Who knew. Josh felt sorry for the guy and wanted to help, but didn't know what to do beyond giving him money to find a place to live until they sold the letter. Providing the letter was worth something.

"Do you have any place to go? What about your kids?"

"They hate me."

"Family is family. Reach out to them."

"They won't take my calls."

"Send me their contact info. I'll talk to them."

"Everybody thinks family is so great, but it's really fucked up, for some of us."

Josh thought about his own father who abandoned him when he was fifteen, only to return decades later to beg for money. Josh still didn't know who his mother was.

"Will you send me their contact info?"

"I don't know if it's up to date. We haven't spoken in years."

"What are their names and birthdays?"

"Ron and Shelby. I'll have to look up their birthdays."

"All right. Listen. I'll pick you up and we'll get you settled somewhere until we can sell that letter."

If we can sell that letter.

"Then you'll have a nest egg so you can afford to rent."

"Please hurry. I have to be out of here by the end of the day or the landlord is calling the cops."

"I'll be there in two hours."

Josh looked at Fig, snout on his thigh. "I gotta go. I'll be back in plenty of time for dinner. Do not bring any dead squirrels or rabbits into the house."

Josh checked his tires, gassed up, and hit the interstate. It was raining. Pastor Dorgan had taught him attitude was everything. This was true, unless you were being eaten by a shark, in which case it was useless. Jerry had a bad attitude. Josh had seen enough to know there was no talking Jerry out of his self-pity and malignant worldview. Therapy wouldn't help, even if Jerry could get into a veterans' program. Josh wondered how much of Jerry's story was true. He would have to look into that. Josh felt sorry for the guy. After he took care of Jerry, he would go to the hospital and try to talk to Jaycee.

Josh pulled up to Jerry's brownstone at eleven. The rain had receded to a light drizzle that added to the chill of the late November air. Josh went into the unlocked lobby, which smelled of disinfectant and cigarette smoke. Several of the brass postal boxes were broken. The building contained twenty-two units. Eight of those units had no name next to the button. Bushnell had no button.

Josh went outside, down the basement steps to an open door. A stout Black man in carpenter pants and white shirt, hands on hips, his back to Josh yelled, "You're goddamn lucky I don't call the police on your cracker ass!"

"Fuck you!" Jerry responded through a haze of cigarette smoke. "I want my security deposit back! This place has bed bugs! There are drug dealers on every floor! I'm going to sue and I'm going to tell the police!"

"You tell 'em whatever you want, Bushnell. I've had enough of your abuse. I'll help you carry your shit out to the sidewalk. After that, you're on your own."

"Excuse me," Josh said.

The man turned, frowning. "Who the fuck are you?"

"Josh Pratt, sir. I'm here to help Jerry move."

The custodian turned back to Jerry. "Who the fuck is this?"

"That's my friend Josh. You'd better not fuck with him or he'll lay you out like a beach blanket."

The man turned, hands at his sides. "Is that so?"

"No, sir. I'm here to help Jerry move. That's all."

"He's got to be out of here no later than five p.m. I wouldn't be down here if he weren't going floor to floor telling lies."

"They're not lies! I'm not the only one with bed bugs! And cockroaches! And fucking rats the size of cats! This place is a shit hole. I won't be sorry to get out of here, but you'd better pay me back my security deposit, and give me what's left for the rest of the month 'cause I done paid the fucking rent."

"How much was the security deposit?"

"Eight hundred dollars!"

Josh turned to the custodian. "Why not give his security deposit back?"

"This guy's been nothing but a pain in the ass since he got here. All he does is complain."

"You want him out? Give him back the security deposit. Otherwise it's going to get messy. I work for a lawyer who specializes in rental cases. Jerry, what proof do you have that there are bedbugs?"

Jerry stripped off his shirt revealing a pasty white body covered with tiny red bite marks. Josh took a picture. He moved and took another picture of Jerry's back, including the custodian.

"What's your name?"

"His name is Hal Davis," Jerry said.

The custodian grimaced. "I'll talk to the landlord. Where do I send the check?"

Josh handed him a card.

WEEKLY RENTAL

Jerry's boxes filled the back seat and the trunk. The car wasn't big enough to haul his thrift store metal bed frame and the mattress was a goner. Jerry smelled of body odor and cigarette smoke.

"Do you mind if I smoke?"

"Just open the window."

Jerry fumbled with a worn pack of American Spirits, stuck one in his mouth, lit it with a Bic. "I have no place to go. My children hate me."

"Knock it off, Jerry. We'll find you a place to go. Can you hold a job?"

"What do you mean?"

"What do you think I mean? Do you have any special skills?"

"I was a helicopter mechanic in the Army."

Josh tried to imagine Jerry working on complicated mechanics. Jerry was not positioned to apply for such a job. Josh had researched weekly hotels.

"Do you want to be in the city or in the suburbs?"

"What do you mean?"

"I'm going to put you up at one of those hotels with a kitchenette where you pay weekly or monthly."

"I don't have any money."

"Don't worry about it, Jerry. I'll take care of it. You can pay me back when we sell the letter."

"I was working from home for Brasstech Kinetic but they fired me."

"What were you doing?"

"Customer service. I took a three-week training course. I passed. They said I couldn't do the job."

"Jerry, I know this is a sore point with you, but family is family. Have you reached out to your boys?

"They hate me."

"When's the last time you talked to either of them?"

"It was years ago."

"What are their names again?"

"Ron and Shelby."

"That's right. Why don't you give me their contact info. I'll speak to them."

"If I can find it."

Josh felt like he was trapped in a hall of mirrors.

"City or suburbs?"

"Well I don't have a car, so city I guess."

Josh drove to Davenport Suites, a national chain specializing in business meetings, on West Juneau Avenue, just west of the river, down the street from Calvary Baptist Church. Josh parked on the street.

"Jerry, wait here a minute. I'll see if they have vacancies."

Davenport Suites was a Soviet-style block with glass walls. Inside, the decor was abstract bland, with framed abstract paintings in bright colors. A bored Hispanic woman sat behind the desk scrolling through her phone. She put it down and smiled as Josh approached.

"Hello. How can I help you?"

"I have a friend who needs a place to stay. I'd like to pay two weeks in advance, if that's all right."

Her smile looked a little frozen. "Where is your friend? Why doesn't he apply himself?"

"He's a little down on his luck. He was just evicted."

"Does he have a criminal record?"

"No. His name is Jerry Bushnell. You can check that out."

"We have rules. No overnight guests, drug use, smoking in the rooms."

"That won't be a problem."

"And you are?"

Josh slid his card across the desk. "My friend is a veteran. He served in Afghanistan. He may be suffering from PTS, do you know what I mean?"

The woman nodded sympathetically, her lips open.

"He's perfectly harmless. He just needs a place to stay until we can find a more permanent situation."

"I understand," she nodded.

"If you have any problems with him, call me. But I don't think you will. Will you take my credit card? Two weeks."

"Of course."

"Thank you. I'll tell Jerry the good news and we'll be back shortly."

Jerry leaned against the car smoking, phone in hand. "I emailed you the last email addresses I have for Ron and Shelby. They never responded."

"All right, you're all set. I paid for two weeks. If I haven't cracked the case in two weeks, I'll pay for another two weeks."

"Why are you doing this?"

"Just my way of showing appreciation for your service."

Jerry barked mirthlessly. "My service. They won't even see me at the VA. I told them about the bedbugs. They didn't care."

"How's your health?"

"I feel tired all the time. I haven't been able to sleep because of the bedbugs."

"There's no smoking here. You'll have to go outside to smoke unless you have a balcony."

It took several trips to haul Jerry's cardboard boxes to his third-floor enclave. It wasn't bad. It was clean, had a view of the street, a kitchenette, a tiny bathroom, and a balcony just big enough for a folding chair and a Weber.

Josh looked in the stoop-down fridge. "Got any money?"

"No."

Josh gave him a hundred-dollar bill. "Get some food. Is your cell phone paid up?"

"Yeah. I paid six months in advance. I had a little money from my last job."

"Okay. You have my phone number. But do me a favor. Don't call if you're just gonna bitch. Only call if it's something important. I'll be in touch."

"You promised to call on Friday."

"I will."

Waukesha Memorial was a modern structure with a curving facade on a residential street, far removed from the riots that had swept the city three years previously. Josh parked in the visitors' parking lot. The front door was plastered with warnings. WEAR A MASK. MASK REQUIRED BEYOND THIS POINT.

Josh pulled one of numerous free light cotton masks from his jacket pocket and entered. The receptionists all wore masks. He went to the window. A matronly woman wearing a mask, her glasses lightly fogged, looked up.

"Can I help you?"

"I'm looking for Max Bushnell."

She consulted the computer. "Mr. Bushnell is in intensive care on the fourth floor. It's unlikely they'll let you see him. Are you a family member?"

"No, ma'am. I'm working for Jaycee Bushnell. It's her I want to see."

"Well you're welcome to go look. She came in this morning, but I haven't seen her leave."

"Thank you."

Josh took the elevator to the fourth floor along with a doctor and a nurse, both wearing surgical face masks. The desk pointed him to a waiting room at the end of the corridor, where he found Jaycee seated by herself staring at her phone.

"Mrs. Bushnell?"

She looked up, startled, relaxed when she recognized him. "Josh. What are you doing here?"

Josh sat. "I came to see about Max."

"Well that's very thoughtful. I thought of something."

Josh sat next to her.

"Several years ago, I got a threatening note in the mail."

"What do you mean?"

"It was so peculiar. It was a greeting card, but so peculiar. It had that orange car with the Confederate flag on the roof. Some old sitcom."

"Dukes of Hazzard?"

"Yes. That's it. Inside it said, soon there will be no more Bushnells. Something like that. It creeped me out."

"Do you still have it?"

"I threw it away. I didn't want it in the house."

"Do you recall where it came from?"

"Yeah. Because it was so peculiar. It was postmarked some little town in Alabama."

"Anything like that ever happen again? Are you on social media?"

"Hardly." She chuckled. "I have too much to do. Sam

is."

"Has she ever mentioned something like that to you?"

"No.

"This may be important."

"You think my son smoking fentanyl-laced marijuana has something to do with Don?"

"I'm a little OC. Do you know where he got the reefer?"

"All I know is that he and his friends went to Axe to Grind last night."

"Axe to Grind. What is that?"

"It's a bar where you throw axes at a target."

"They serve alcohol and you throw axes?"

Jaycee laughed. "I know. Great idea, right? It's very popular with young people."

"Do you know who he went with, who he met there?"

"No, but it's a popular bar."

"Did you know Max smoked dope?"

"Yes. We talked about it. I smoked dope too when I was his age. I wasn't crazy about it, but it's practically legal now. Max has always had common sense. He only smoked it on weekends. He would never go to school or a job high."

"Would you send me several photos of Max?"

"I'll do it right now."

"Where is Axe to Grind?"

Jaycee poked at her phone. "Sixteen seventeen Summit Avenue. They should be open now."

"Thank you."

AXE TO GRIND

The rain had slowed to a light drizzle as Josh pulled up in front of the bar at two o'clock. He got out of the car, pulling a ball cap low on his forehead, pushed open the door and smelled beer and sawdust. The bar ran halfway back on his left. The back third of the room was devoted to axe throwing, with a series of paper targets taped to wooden planks, a selection of axes on a shelf to the right. A wooden rail divided the axe throwing from the rest of the bar. There was one patron, an old man sitting at the bar near the door nursing a beer. The bartender was a big, knobby guy with an Adam's apple. Flat-screen televisions hung from the ceiling, none visible from the axe range. There were four discreet cameras, two in the front top corners looking back and two in the rear top corners looking forward.

Josh sat on a stool. The bartender came over.

"What can I do you for?"

"Sir, I'm a private investigator from Madison." He slid his card across the table. The bartender picked it up.

"And?"

"Do you know about the patron who was taken to the hospital yesterday from having ingested fentanyl?"

"Oh, for Chrissake. The police questioned me for two hours. I'll tell you what I told them. I don't know a thing about it. We don't tolerate any smoking in here. If he was in here, it was just coincidence. Lotta kids come in here. They want to smoke, they go outside. They want to smoke reefer, they go to their cars or that park across the street. What's your involvement?"

"The boy's father was murdered. I'm looking into it."

"That's too bad."

Josh brought up a picture of Max and held it out. "Do you recognize him?"

"That's Max. He's in here all the time. Good guy. Told me he plans on enlisting. I was in the Army."

"They say he ingested fentanyl-laced marijuana and went into a coma. He's at Waukesha Memorial."

"I know. I was here."

"One of his friends found him unconscious in the park across the street and called an ambulance. Do you know who it was?"

"Harv Dennison. He's in here all the time too. He came in here after the ambulance arrived."

Josh wrote it down on his pad. "Would it be possible for me to look at your security footage from last night?"

"I don't know what you're going to find."

"Did the police look?"

"No. They don't have the manpower. There was a mass exodus three years ago during the riots."

"I can devote more time to this than the police."

"I don't get it. I thought you told me you were looking into his father's death."

"I'm concerned about his family."

"Sure, why not. Hey Bill," he said to the lone customer. "I'll be right back."

"No prob."

Josh followed the bartender to the back of the rear, through a corridor containing men's and women's bathrooms, through a door to a warehouse stacked with boxes with a desk in the corner on which two monitors sat.

"What's your name?" Josh said.

"I'm Murray."

"Josh Pratt."

They shook. Murray sat and stroked. "Okay, you can sit here and scroll through the videos. Use this key to advance, this key to rewind, and this key to freeze frame. You can print those out by keying up the printer."

"What time was Max in here?"

"He came in around eight-thirty and left around nine."

"Thank you, sir."

The black-and-white footage was sharp. Josh spotted Max as soon as he entered, watched him order a drink from the bar and join two other young men at a table between the bar and the booths. Behind them, young men and women stepped up to the line and hurled axes end over end at the targets. Some stuck. Most fell to the ground. The video was silent but Josh saw revelry in their happy faces, arms raised in triumph, and laughter. At nine-fifteen, two men entered, got beers, and went to Max's table. They wore hoodies, concealing their faces.

Josh paused the feed and switched to the cameras at the back of the bar pointing forward. The newcomers pulled up chairs and sat, facing the targets. Josh zoomed in on their faces, young White men with buzz cuts. One had a GI Joe beard. He froze the frame and printed both men.

After a few minutes, Max and the guy with the beard stood. Max shrugged into a jacket and left through the front door. Josh watched for forty-five minutes but neither returned. According to the police report, Max was found unresponsive at ten forty-five by his friend Harv.

When Josh reentered the bar, there were five new patrons and a college girl taking orders. He went to the bar where Murray was pouring taps. Josh waited until the mugs were filled, showed Murray the pictures.

"Do you know these guys?"

Murray held the prints, lower lip protruding. He pointed to the beard. "I think I've seen him in here before, but I don't know his name. Never seen the other one."

"Lemme ask you something."

"Ha ha."

"How is this place possible? How can you afford insurance? How come drunks don't start swingin' on each other?"

Murray shrugged. "I saw a need. I filled it. I'm not the only one. Go online. Google axe-throwing bars. You'll be surprised."

"How much to throw the axe?"

"On the house. Knock yourself out."

Josh went to the back, grabbed an axe, hefted it, stepped up to the line, and flicked it end over end at the target. It stuck with a satisfying thunk. He headed for the front.

"Thanks for your help."

"You bet. Hope you get him."

Josh returned to the hospital. Jaycee sat in the fourth-floor lounge working on her tablet. She looked up as Josh entered. "Find anything?"

Josh took the chair next to hers and showed her the print-outs. "Can you identify either of these young men?"

"No, but maybe Sam can. She should be here soon. She was coming over after her last class. She's studying business at UW Milwaukee. You know, Josh, you don't really have to do this. This is a matter for the police."

"Do you think they're doing a good job?"

Jaycee stared off into the distance. She started to sob. Josh put his arm around her, and she leaned into him. A nurse passed, eyes averted. Josh felt uncomfortable but he didn't know what else to do. After a while the sobs subsided and she pulled back. She pulled a tissue from her purse, lowered her mask, and dabbed. An orderly glared. Josh looked at him. He moved on.

"I'm sorry."

"It's okay. As far as I'm concerned, looking into Donnie's death, finding out who gave Max the fentanyl, it's all one to me. This is what I do. I have nothing better to do."

"I can't pay you."

"Give me a dollar."

"Why?"

"You are officially employing me to look into the circumstances of Max's overdose."

Jaycee opened her purse and handed Josh a dollar.

They sat in silence. Sam strode toward them wearing sweats, tennies, and a fleece-lined jacket, swinging her backpack.

"Mom, are you okay?"

"I'm fine. Have a seat. Josh wants to ask you a question."

Sam pulled up a chair facing them. Josh handed her the print-outs. "Can you identify those men?"

Her face darkened. She pointed to the one with the beard. "That's Darren Olsen. He's a high school buddy. I don't know the other one."

"Do you know where I can find Darren Olsen?"

"He should be in Max's cell phone."

Jaycee shrugged helplessly. "The police took it."

CHAPTER 15

RABBITS

Josh phoned O'Malley and left a message. He hit the road. The rain had tapered off, and he drove beneath a gray blanket of clouds, pulling into his driveway at six-thirty. Fig was all over him.

"Yeah, yeah, just let me get into the kitchen."

Fig capered about while Josh decanted a can of Castor and Pollux grain-free butcher and bushel organic chicken into a bowl. Fig savored the rich aroma, dipped her snout and inhaled it all in five seconds.

"How did it taste?"

O'Malley phoned back. "What?"

"The Waukesha PD has Max Bushnell's phone. I'd like to look at it."

"Why?"

"Samantha Bushnell identified one of the men with Max the night he OD'd as Darren Olsen, a childhood friend."

"So?"

"I'd like to talk to him."

"Pratt, I think you're a good guy but this isn't your case. The Waukesha police have it."

"Sir, you know as well as I do that they're understaffed and this case is a low priority for them."

"I know a guy. I'll talk to him."

"Thank you."

The phone book was no longer a useful tool. The phone book was extinct. Josh went online and looked for a Harvey Dennison. Facebook had five Dennisons, but only one was in his early twenties, lived in Waukesha, and liked to mountain bike. Josh sent him a friend request. They had two friends in common, Sam and Max Bushnell. He called Jaycee. Sam answered.

"Hello?"

"Sam, this is Josh Pratt. Is your mom there?"

"No, she's in with Max. He's conscious!"

"He's awake?"

"Yes! The doctors say he'll have to stay overnight, but he may be ready to come home in the morning."

"Sam, that's wonderful news. Maybe you can help me. Are you Facebook friends with Harvey Dennison?"

"Yes."

"I just sent him a friend request. Would you tell him why?"

"Why?"

"I'm trying to learn where your brother got the dope."

"I thought you were working on who killed Dad."

"I have a feeling they're connected."

"That's crazy. They have nothing to do with each other. Dad died ten years ago."

"What's the worst that could happen?"

"Yeah, I'll do it. I don't know why I was being such a little shit. Is this your number?"

"That's it. Are you friends with Darren Olson?"

"No," she said emphatically.

"What's wrong with Darren?"

"He's a creep, okay? He asked me out. That's just creepy. I was fourteen. I didn't even have boobs."

"Did Max know about it?"

"No way. And neither does Mom. So don't tell her."

"You'll tell Harvey?"

"Yeah, I'll tell him. I already told the cops."

"Thank you."

He phoned Ray. "You want to come over? I'll grill brats."

"I would love to come over, but Ida is throwing a tantrum. I have to talk her down off the ledge, or we have no show."

"Doesn't she have an understudy?"

"The understudy is a man."

"I see. All right. How about tomorrow? I could make a reservation at the Hoity Toity."

"I'm listening."

"That's it. We go to the Hoity Toity, we come back here, and we boink."

"You talked me into it, you silver-tongued devil."

Harvey had confirmed Josh's request. Harvey was online.

Harvey, I'm a private investigator looking into Max's overdose. Can we talk?

Yeah, dude. You seem legit.

Can I call you right now through Facebook?

Sure.

Josh put on a headset he'd bought at Walmart for eight dollars and hit the phone icon. Harvey picked right up. Harvey had a pale round face covered with stubble, a Beatles cut, and pink lips. He squinted.

"Whoa, dude."

"Hello, Harvey. Thank you for taking my call."

"No prob."

"How'd you find Max."

"I was stuntin' at the skateboard park. I walked off to smoke a joint. Max was in the bushes. I got down, felt for his breath, y'know, tried to bring him out of it. I called nine-one-one right away. I stayed with him until they came, then I went into Axe to Grind. I needed a drink."

"Did you know Max before?"

"We were friends in high school."

"Do you know where he got the reefer?"

"No idea."

"Where do you get yours?"

"Does Chevy tell Toyota?"

Josh laughed. "Any ideas?"

"That park, Owen Park. It's always been a dealer's hangout. Reefer, blow, smack, whatever. There's a different crew on every corner. They had it pretty much cleaned up before the pandemic hit, and then the Rittenhouse thing, and then that crazy motherfucker in the SUV…a lot of cops have quit. They didn't want to get the jab, and they felt like they were in the crosshairs, y'know? I mean all this defund the police shit. I may smoke reefer, but I'm not stupid enough to think we can get along without cops."

"Do you think Max may have scored there?"

"It's possible, but I don't think so. Max is a pretty standup dude. Sure he likes to smoke a little reefer. Don't we all? But he's not the kind of guy to approach some scumbag in a park."

"Do you know Darren Olsen?"

"Nope."

"I'm PMing you my phone number. If you learn anything, or have any ideas, give me a call."

"Hey, man. Do you carry a gun?"

"No. I'm a convicted felon. I'm not allowed to own guns."

"You're a what?"

"I was pardoned by the governor."

"What did you do?"

"I cut off a man's arm with a chainsaw."

"Holy shit."

"Then I found Jesus. Want to hear about it?"

"Ah, no thanks, man. I'll call you if I hear anything."

"Thank you, Harvey."

Josh pushed back from the terminal, stretched, went into the living room. Fig lay on the hardwood floor chewing on a dead rabbit.

"For fuck's sake!"

Fig looked at him sheepishly, picked up the dead rabbit and left through the doggy door.

O'Malley called. "What's up?"

"Sir, Max's sister Sam identified one of the friends he was with the other night at Axe to Grind as Darren Olsen. She doesn't know how to contact him, but she said his phone number is in Max's phone, which the Waukesha PD have. I'd like to talk to Darren."

"Don't you think you should leave this to the Waukesha PD?"

"Normally I would, but I understand they are understaffed and that this case is not a high priority."

"Look. Here's what I'll do. I will ask them to return the phone to the family. How is Max?"

"He's regained consciousness, and it's possible they will release him tomorrow."

"That's great news."

Josh cleaned a spot of blood off the living room floor, sat on the sofa and turned on the television. Fig joined him as if nothing had happened. After scrolling for fifteen minutes, he settled on an old Disney film, *Iron Will*, about a boy who enters a Canadian dog sled race to save the family farm. The dog was good. Fig slept through it. If it wasn't there in the room with her, if she couldn't smell it, it didn't exist.

They went to bed. In the middle of the night, Fig started running in her sleep, paws paddling the air, emitting strange blips. Josh shook her awake.

"I don't want you to even dream about rabbits."

HOITY TOITY

Sam phoned Josh at noon Thursday.

"They gave us Max's phone back. Darren's phone number is 262 417 8831."

Josh wrote it down. "Thank you. How's Max doing?"

"He's weak, but happy to be home. There was a detective here at ten, asked him where he got the marijuana. He told them Darren. I gave them Darren's phone number too. They called, but nobody answered."

"How did Max know Darren?"

"High school."

"What high school?"

"Sojourner Truth High School in Hartland."

"Thank you."

Sojourner Truth opened in 1959 near Nagawicka Lake. It had been named Patrick Henry High School until 2014 when the School Board voted to change the name. It had three hundred and fourteen pupils from kindergarten through twelfth grade. Josh found their website. Muriel Wyziluski was their principal. Josh wrote her a letter.

Dear Principal Wyziluski. I am a licensed private investigator from Madison. A member of the Bushnell family has retained me to investigate the circumstances of Max Bushnell's seizure. Would it be possible for us to speak? Please contact Steven Fleiss, Attorney at Law, or retired Madison Police Detective Heinz Calloway for references. Thank you. Yours sincerely, Josh Pratt.

He included his phone. He didn't have a website. Seemed like something he ought to have. While Pratt had been serving time, the world leapfrogged ahead. Now he had to deal with passwords, log-ins, cookies, and bizarre correspondence. He checked his email.

Am Christine, I'm searching for an attractive guy to smash my hot pussy and huge booty. A lust is killing me, just a one-time-shag is will satisfy me. Am so idyllic so the guy should be set for a lip service and all styles of bang all night, hoping this will remain secret. If possible, I will like a guy to host, am available the whole weekend. It's basically for an experience with an older guy. No tokens but he should host me.

He deleted it. His phone rang.

"Pratt."

"Mr. Pratt, this is Muriel Wyziluski. What do you know about Max Bushnell?"

"I met him briefly at his home. His uncle Jerry hired me to find out who killed Max's father, Donnie."

"Such a terrible tragedy. I have prayed that his family will know peace. And now this. Give me a day to check your references. We can get together tomorrow. We can do a Zoom call."

"I don't mind driving over."

"From Madison?"

"I get mileage."

"Let's tentatively say five p.m. tomorrow."

"Thank you, ma'am."

Josh had made reservations at the Hoity Toity, on the west side overlooking the university golf course. He showered, changed into gray Dockers, boots, and striped cotton pullover that covered his ink. At five, Ray entered, pumping elbows, fingers outstretched.

"What a bitch!"

"Mongoose?"

"She doesn't want anyone to look her in the eye! Who does she think she is? Ellen DeGeneres?"

"There's always that understudy."

"He's a man!"

Josh grabbed her around the waist. "So am I!"

The sharp angles went away. She kissed him hard.

A half-hour later, they left for the Hoity Toity. It was just around the corner. They could have walked to it. The Hoity Toity had been built into a berm using stained native lumber. It looked like a series of low shelves with grass growing on top. Josh pulled into the parking lot, found a place between a Tesla and a Fiat that looked like he could crush it with his hands.

Ray wore hip-hugging blue jeans and a man's shirt with the sleeves rolled up. She was a big girl. Not an ounce of fat.

Inside the candle-lit dark wood lobby, a beaming black-haired gentleman in a black vest, white shirt, and black bow tie looked up from behind the desk. He wore a pin that said Fernando.

"Good evening! Do you have a reservation?"

"Pratt."

"Right this way."

They followed the waiter through the long, low bar looking out on the golf course. to the dining area. Floor-to-ceiling windows, hardwood floors, Navajo rugs, a black baby grand. They slid into a booth opposite each other. The host handed them heavy menus.

"Your server will be right over. Her name is Veeblefetzer."

"Huh?" Josh said.

"Veeblefetzer."

"Great!"

Veeblefetzer looked like a gypsy with her jet black hair and kohled eyes. Her arms were sleeved with ink.

"Would you like to start with a drink?"

"What kind of Chardonnay do you have?"

Josh zoned out.

"And for the gentleman?"

"I'll have a shot of Jack and whatever ale you have on draft."

"Very good. Would you like me to tell you about our specials?"

"By all means."

"Tonight, we're featuring barbecued buffalo ribs…"

Josh held up his hand. "Go no further."

Ray ordered a quail in a nest of ancient grains. They looked out through the horizontal windows through a curtain of evergreens at the golf course. The die-hards headed for the clubhouse in their golf carts.

Ray poked his thigh with a stockinged foot.

"Stop it."

"What's up with the cold case murder?"

Josh brought her up to speed.

"Wow," Ray said. "That's awful. That poor family. Well at least that's good news about the boy, right? Max?"

"Yes, as long as there wasn't permanent damage. Fuckin' fentanyl is everywhere now."

"I'm always afraid you're going to put a skull on your chest and go full Punisher."

Josh frowned and swiped with his hand. "Not me, babe. I try to keep a low profile. You know anything about the Civil War?"

"Huh?"

"Civil War."

"Iron Brigade."

"What's that?"

"Wisconsin's most famous Civil War unit. It was composed of the 2nd, 6th, and 7th infantry regiments. They saw action at Bull Run, Antietam, Gettysburg, and Tunnel Hill."

"How do you even know that?"

"I took a course in college."

"If I wanted to know which Wisconsinites fought, where would I go?"

"You should try the Civil War Museum."

"What Civil War Museum?"

"The one at the top of State Street. But there's a better one in Waukesha."

Veeblefetzer brought their drinks. A high school basketball game played silently on a flat screen at the end of the bar.

"What are you looking for?"

"I don't know. Wisconsin soldiers named Bushnell who fought at the Battle of Tunnel Hill."

"You should try Camp Randall. They have that arch and I think it has most of the names of Wisconsin volunteers."

"You're so smart."

She thrust her toe in his crotch.

WAR MEMORIAL

Ray left in the morning. Josh and Fig ran. He showered and went online to look for the Camp Randall monument. The monument was still there, but seven years ago, Madison Mayor For Life Saul Brogden prevailed on the city council to remove the great bronze plaque listing the names of Confederate War dead who had perished in the POW camp. He also removed a monument to Confederate War dead from Forest Hill Cemetery. Both monuments were locked away, never to be seen again, in Wisconsin Veterans Museum storage, in a warehouse in what was formerly the Gisholt Machine Works on East Washington, not far from the High Noon Saloon.

Josh sent a follow-up note to Principal Wyziluski saying he looked forward to meeting with her. He checked his email. Jerry Bushnell sent him a friend request on Facebook. He accepted. He went to Jerry's page.

I'll be homeless soon. No money for storage
There is nothing affordable here. I will be dead or in
the homeless shelter
Clearly I am waiting for nothing. I waited all my life
for things to get better.
My brother was murdered. Nobody did anything.
I have hired a private detective to find who killed
my brother.
Thank you, Josh Pratt, for taking my case.
I have no friends.

Josh felt a leaden sensation in his gut. How could Jerry even afford an internet connection? He would ask his client to remove any mention of him. What was he thinking? Plastering private business all over the net. He called Jerry.

"Hello."

"Jerry, it's Josh. I was looking at your Facebook page. I would like you to take down any mention of me, or the case."

"Why?"

"There are many reasons, but first and foremost, I don't like seeing my name plastered about on social media. I keep a low profile. Can you take that shit down?"

Pause.

"I guess."

Jerry sounded sullen.

"Somebody sees that, they get the wrong idea, they think they know something, they interfere, makes it harder to proceed. Do you understand?"

"No, not really."

"Did you reach out to your sons?"

"They hate me."

"I know. You've told me five times. You've told the world. The whole world knows your children hate you. How's it going?"

"This place is okay, I guess. They're looking for a maintenance man. I told them I'd like the job."

"What did they say?"

"They told me to submit an application. But I'm just going to go around fixing things."

"Good idea."

"I need a microwave."

"I'll bring you one."

"Have you found anything? It's Friday."

"I'm making progress."

"Well, okay I guess."

"Talk to you soon."

Fig whined.

"You will survive. No dead rabbits please. I will be back to feed you a late lunch."

Josh drove through the city and parked on Baldwin near the Veterans Museum storage. The big, two-story blond brick structure crowned with solar panels and had been subdivided into offices housing twenty-six businesses, including designers, architects, legal, advertising, and numerous sole proprietors including artists and sculptors.

The steel door to the basement storage unit was locked. Out back, angled steel doors in the parking lot were also locked. Josh roamed the halls until he encountered a custodian changing a light bulb in one of several entrances.

"Sir, can you let me into the War Veterans storage area?"

The custodian, an oval-shaped man with thinning hair wearing gray coveralls over a blue workshirt, and a tool belt, turned.

"Are you from the historical society?"

"No, sir. My name is Josh Pratt. I'm a private investigator." He showed the custodian his license and handed him a card. "I just want to take a look at those Confederate War memorials that were removed several years ago."

The man shook his head in disgust. "I call bullshit on that. History is history. You don't cover it up because it might offend someone." He stuck out his hand. "Frank."

Frank unlocked the door and turned on a light. Josh followed him down the metal stairs to a broad open area lined with wooden crates, except where metal doors led to private storage. Fifty feet down, they came to a door with "Wisconsin Veterans Museum" stenciled in white.

Frank unlocked the door and turned on the light. "Just turn off the light and shut the door when you're finished."

"Thank you, sir."

The room had a nine-foot ceiling and was packed with wooden crates, many of them labeled, forming a corridor to the rear, where a concrete ramp rose toward the parking lot. It was here Josh found the Confederate monuments. The memorial from Forest Hills was a five-foot stone cenotaph inscribed with the names of deceased Confederate soldiers from Wisconsin.

"Erected in loving memory by United Daughters of the Confederacy to Alice Whiting Waterman and her boys."

A framed poster read, "Michael Telzrow, director of the Wisconsin Veterans Museum, said they accepted the monument for a specific reason."

"Based on its connection to Civil War history and, more importantly, the role in which some Wisconsin Union veterans played in raising money for the memorial, we accepted its acquisition," said Telzrow.

Telzrow said two Wisconsinites who fought with the Union's Iron Brigade, Frank W. Oakley and Hugh Louis, assisted in fundraising and participated in the cenotaph's unveiling.

The monument, then, is an artifact of reconciliation—a period in the late nineteenth century when white residents from the north and south diminished slavery to romanticize the war and come together.

Over the nearly year-long period when Madison residents and council members debated what to do about the now-removed monument, they dealt with complex questions of history, symbolism and preservation. Telzrow said museums have an important role to play here; they can preserve complicated materials while society grapples with their history.

"Rather than come out with a definitive declaration on what should be done and how we should do it, I think it's prudent in this case—as much as they can be, if they are removed and they have historical value beyond a memorial to a particular cause—that they be preserved until we can come to an agreement about what their place is on the cultural landscape," said Telzrow.

The museum has no current plans to interpret or display the monument.

The bronze plaque listing Confederate soldiers who had died in the prisoner of war camp was behind it, leaning against the wall. Dim light from the overhead fixtures was insufficient. Josh used his pen light.

"Unsung heroes, far from their homes in Alabama, Tennessee, Mississippi, Alabama and Arkansas."

Branford McCauley appeared near the end. Josh wrote it down. Turning off the lights and shutting the door behind him, he left the warehouse and drove to Walmart, where he purchased a microwave oven for sixty bucks. He put it in the trunk, drove home, and fed Fig.

CHAPTER
18

JENNIFER

Sojourner Truth High School was a two-story red brick Federalist structure with an athletic field and a big parking lot in which sat a few widely spaced sedans and a yellow school bus. Josh entered the building just before five, inhaling the scent of books, cleaning solution, and dust. He went into the visitor's office where a young man with a fadeaway looked up from his computer.

"Yes, sir."

"Josh Pratt for Muriel Wyziluski."

"I'll tell her you're here, sir. Have a seat."

Josh sat on a wood bench and looked at the wall, covered with framed class photographs, two dozen to a class. The earliest class pictured was 2014. The clerk looked up from his phone.

"Ms. Wyziluski will come down to meet you."

A bird-like middle-aged woman, gray hair drawn back in

a severe bun with pince-nez around her neck entered. "Mr. Pratt?"

Josh stood. "Thank you for seeing me, Ms. Wyziluski."

"Let's go to the faculty lounge."

She turned smartly on sensible shoes and headed down a corridor past several offices to a break room overlooking the athletic field, containing a counter, refrigerator, coffee machine, big Formica table, plastic chairs, and a couple of sofas that looked like they'd been left behind on student moving day.

"Would you like coffee?"

"Please."

She went to the counter. "Why don't you mix it yourself."

She poured herself a cup and waited for Josh, who mixed in cream and sugar. The principal took hers black. She gestured to one of the sprung sofas.

"Have a seat. What is this about?"

"You know about Max Bushnell."

"Yes. We were shocked. Max is an outstanding young man."

"You'll be happy to know that he's regained consciousness and is recovering at home. Max's uncle hired me to look into his father's death."

"That was at least ten years ago."

"His mother Jaycee has asked me to find out where Max got the marijuana."

Wyziluski put the pince-nez on her nose and looked at

him with renewed interest.

"Have you met Max's uncle Jerry?"

"I didn't even know he had an uncle."

"Yes. Apparently, it's been eating at him. I met Max. The cops are a skeleton crew. They don't have the resources to look into this. I understand Max had a classmate named Darren Olsen."

"They were an odd couple. Max athletic, accomplished, straight A's, Darren kind of a hanger-on. He worshipped Max."

"Did you know they smoked marijuana?"

"First I heard about it was the news about Max. But I'm not surprised to learn that Darren smoked weed."

"Do you know how I can get in touch with Darren?"

"Mr. Pratt, you may very well be a saint, but we don't release information about students or former students. I'm sorry. May I see some identification, please?"

Josh showed her his license and gave her a card.

"You would if it were the police asking."

"Of course."

She sat back, chin in hand. "Hmmm. I'll tell you what I can do. I can point you to his parents. I met them on several occasions when Darren misbehaved."

"Was he ever caught with marijuana at school?"

"Yes. You can contact the parents. They may tell you to go to hell, but I would prefer not to talk about former students without their permission. I would like to call them and ask their permission. Do you mind?"

"Not at all."

Wyziluski pulled out her phone. She poked, listened, set it down. "That number is no longer in service."

"Do you have an address for them?"

She turned to her phone. "In 2014 it was 615 Holyoke Drive, Hartland. I'm not sure they're still there."

Josh wrote it down. "Thank you, ma'am."

"I'm not going to regret this, am I?"

"No, ma'am. You can call Steve Fleiss, retired Madison Police Detective Heinz Calloway, or Milwaukee police officer Shawn O'Malley for references."

She wrote on a legal pad. Josh slid one of Fleiss's cards across the table.

Wyziluski smiled. "You're not how I pictured a private investigator."

"I go where God sends me."

"You look more like a biker."

Josh smiled. "You are correct, ma'am."

"Keep me in the loop. Here's my card."

Josh took the white rectangle and stuck it in his biker's wallet, connected to his pants by a chain. "Will do."

He brought Holyoke Drive up on Google Maps. Four miles, in the country. Josh drove past fields filled with stubble, red barns in the distance. The address was a ranch-style house on a large lot backing up against a golf course. There was a Subaru Outback in the driveway. No sidewalks out here, but plenty of lawn. He parked on the two-lane blacktop and walked up the red brick path to the front door, a front porch big enough for a couple chairs beneath a peaked overhang. He rang the doorbell.

Moments later, a young woman holding a baby, wearing an apron, her cheek smudged with flour opened the door. She stepped back.

"What do you want?"

"Sorry to trouble you, ma'am. I'm looking for Jennifer and Martin Owen. I was given this address."

"Oh. No, they haven't been here in years. We bought this house in 2016."

"Do you know how I can get in touch with them?"

"Mr. Olsen was having cognitive issues. Jennifer said they were looking to move into a retired living facility."

"Do you happen to know which one?"

"I'm sorry, what is this about?"

"My name is Josh Pratt. I'm a private investigator from Madison." He showed her his license. "I'm not at liberty to reveal, but I assure you, it is above board."

"You know, they sent us a Christmas card a couple years ago. I save all my Christmas cards in a box. My husband says I'm a hoarder. Wait here. Give me a minute. I'll be right back."

She gently closed the door behind her. Josh looked around. There was a two-story red brick Colonial across the road with a turn-around drive that came up to the front door. The countryside seemed muted, drowsy, waiting for sleep.

The door opened. The woman handed Josh a white envelope with a printed label.

Jennifer and Martin Owen, Prairie Rest, 216 MacArthur Blvd., Oconomowoc. Josh looked it up. Twelve miles. It was dusk as he pulled into the parking lot. Prairie West was stylish red brick in the universal nursing home style, expanded eaves and double-glass doors.

He entered through the sliding glass doors. A woman looked up from behind the receptionist's desk and smiled. "Good evening."

"Ma'am, I'd like to visit Jennifer and Martin Owen."

Her smile froze. "Are you a family member?"

"No, ma'am. I'm a private investigator from Madison." He showed her his license.

"Well this is a first. Can you tell me why?"

"I'm looking for their son Darren. Do you know about the young man who smoked fentanyl and went into a coma?"

"Yes. Terrible. It was all over the news."

"I'm trying to find out where he got the marijuana."

"Are you working for the family?"

"Yes."

"I have to tell you that Martin is not doing well and sometimes doesn't know where he is. Jennifer's still sharp but unable to get around on her own. Why don't you sign in there and I'll walk you back. This won't upset her, will it?"

"I hope not, ma'am. I try to be discreet."

"You don't look like a private investigator."

"I hear that a lot."

"Well they've just finished dinner. They're most likely in the dining area. Come with me."

She led the way down a carpeted corridor redolent of the smell of age, a hint of urine, and cafeteria food. The dining room was a large carpeted area with a dozen round tables, sliding glass doors looking out on the verdant patio, and beyond that a pine windbreak. Silverware clinked, servers wheeled carts. Most of the tables were deserted. The receptionist led Josh to a table near the back where two senior citizens sat in wheelchairs. They looked more like a twenty-year-old's grandparents than parents.

"Jennifer, you have a visitor."

The woman looked up, smiling brightly. "Hello."

CHAPTER 19

ATTITUDE

Josh pulled up a chair. Jennifer Olsen was everybody's idea of a plump, cheerful grandmother with pink cheeks and a swirl of white hair.

"Ma'am, my name is Josh Pratt. I'm a private investigator from Madison."

An attendant came up. "Mind if I borrow your husband?"

"You go right ahead," Jennifer Olsen said. The attendant wheeled Martin away.

"Like a shamus?"

"Exactly."

"Do you carry a gun?"

Josh laughed. "No. You're Darren's mother?"

A cloud crossed across her face. "Oh dear."

"Did you know Max Bushnell?"

"Oh yes. Lovely boy. How is Max doing?"

"You haven't heard?"

"Oh dear."

"Max nearly overdosed smoking fentanyl-laced marijuana."

"I don't even know what that is. I do know Darren likes to smoke pot. We tried to stop him, but what can you do? He was an only child. We spoiled him."

"When was the last time Darren came to visit?"

"Oh, I don't know. I'd have to ask the registration desk."

"Over a month?"

"Oh yes."

"Mrs. Olsen, here's my card. If you think of anything, or I can help you, please call."

Mrs. Olsen took the card and tucked it into a brocade purse on her lap.

"Does anybody visit?"

"My niece, Laura."

"When was the last time she came?"

"Last week. She brought me some crafting magazines. I like to make cards."

"Mrs. Olsen, would you allow me to look at the sign-in sheet?"

"Certainly."

"May I wheel you out to the receptionist's desk? I'll bring you back."

"Let's go!"

Josh wheeled her down the hushed corridor to the atrium, up to the receptionist.

"How are you, Mrs. Olsen?"

"I'm fine. Would you let Mr. Pratt look through the sign-in book?"

"We normally don't allow that."

"Oh, do make an exception, Jean. He's trying to find my son Darren. I haven't heard from Darren in ages. I don't even remember the last time."

"It was back in July."

"I would appreciate it."

With a smile, Jean lifted a heavy, leather-bound volume onto the counter.

"Wow," Josh said. "No electronics?"

"Our residents and visitors prefer the old-fashioned way."

"Thank you, ma'am."

Josh quickly thumbed through the pages until he came to last July. Visitors signed the resident's name on the left, their own on the right. It did not take long for Josh to find Darren Olsen's signature, accompanied by a friend. Brandon McCauley. He made a note. The receptionist watched him write it down.

"I remember him."

"Darren?"

"No. His creepy friend."

"What made him creepy?"

She touched her upper lip. "His nose ring. It was big enough for a door knocker. And he had a pentagram tattoo on the back of his hand."

"I don't suppose you have video."

"All our video is purged every month."

"Thank you, ma'am."

At Mrs. Olsen's direction, he wheeled her down a residential corridor to the suite she shared with her husband. The door was ajar. Wheeling her inside, he saw a nurse in a green uniform taking Mr. Olsen's vital signs.

"Well hello, Gail," Mrs. Olsen said.

"Hello, Jennifer. Who's your friend?"

"Josh Pratt, ma'am. I was just leaving."

It was six-thirty by the time he returned to his car. It would take another hour to deliver Jerry's microwave. Fig would survive. She had water, toys, and a doggie door. Josh drove east toward Davenport Suites. There was plenty of street parking as commuters headed home. He hefted the boxed microwave from the back seat and carried it into the building. The same bored clerk sat scrolling through her phone.

She looked up. She looked down. Josh took the elevator to the third floor. As he got off, he heard sounds of a scuffle, flesh on flesh, a man bleating in pain. Jerry. The door to Jerry's unit was ajar. Josh set the microwave in the hall and pushed open the door. Two men in cheap jackets were beating and kicking Jerry, hunched over in a corner. Josh dug his fingers into the closest man's mandible from behind, grabbed the back of his collar and threw him to the floor, stomping on his sternum, while the other, oblivious, continued to rain down punches. Josh grabbed him by the back of his collar and kicked his knee forward, throwing him down, and stomping on his groin.

The first man with close-set eyes, pocked skin and a pronounced Adam's apple shrimped on his side, struggling for breath. The second, with a shaved skull and plump lips, squeezed tears from his eyes as he held his crotch.

"Fuck's goin' on, Jerry?"

"That motherfucker…" Pockmark groaned. "He stands in the fucking door yelling that nobody likes him. I asked him to shut up."

Shielding his head with his arms, Jerry got tentatively to his feet, kicked Pockmark in the head. Josh grabbed him by the arm and led him away.

"That's enough, Jerry. Who the fuck are these guys?"

"We live here too," Pockmark gasped.

"Get out."

The two men staggered out. Josh retrieved the box and shut the door.

"I brought you a microwave."

"I have no friends."

"Excuse me, I just brought you a microwave."

"You're my only friend."

Sighing, Josh collapsed on the cloth sofa. "Nobody likes a whiner. You ever think the reason you don't have any friends is because you do nothing but complain?"

"Nobody likes me."

Josh wondered if Jerry was developmentally disabled. The Army had taken him. Perhaps they were sucking air for recruits at the time. Josh could see where Jerry might not have received an honorable discharge.

"All right it's Friday, so here's your report. Have you heard of Branford McCauley?"

"McCauley's the name of my great-great-grandfather's best friend. They went to West Point together. They fought each other at the Battle of Tunnel Hill."

"Well McCauley's a common name. What about Darren Olsen?"

"No. What does this have to do with my brother's murder?"

"I don't know. I just pull strings 'til something falls out. I found a Civil War photo of three Confederate soldiers in your grandfather's Civil War collection and someone had written 'McCauley' underneath one man."

"What did he look like?"

Josh pulled out his phone and brought up the picture.

Jerry stared, lower lip protruding. "I don't know."

"How do you pay for your internet connection?"

"Donnie left me some money in his will. It's almost gone now."

"How do I get in touch with Ron and Shelby?"

"They hate me."

"Do you have their phone numbers?"

"Yeah. They're in my phone."

"Give them to me."

Jerry read the numbers. Josh wrote them down.

"I gotta split. Remember what I said. Nobody likes a whiner. Attitude is everything."

"How'm I supposed to have a good attitude? I have no friends, no job. Everybody hates me."

Josh sighed. "Listen. There's a church down the street. Go talk to the pastor."

"I'm not very religious."

"Do as I say. Tell him what you told me."

"Why? He won't give a shit."

"You came to me, right? You want me to find who killed your brother? Do as I say. All right?"

Jerry stared at the floor, arms on knees. "All right."

Josh couldn't wait to get out of there. He got home at eight-thirty, parked in the garage and entered through the kitchen. Fig was there to greet him. He walked into the living room. A headless rabbit lay on the sofa.

RON AND SHELBY

Dear Ron and Shelby: I'm a private investigator from Madison. Your father Jerry has asked me to look into his brother Don's death. I don't know if you are aware of this, but Jerry isn't doing too well. He was recently evicted from his basement apartment in Milwaukee and is unemployed. He is currently living at Davenport Suites in Milwaukee. His phone is: --- --- ----. His email is -------@---.com.

He has confessed he was not a good father. I understand your reluctance to communicate. My own father abandoned me when I was fifteen. However, in the long run, family is all we have, and your father needs your love and support. The Bible asks us to "Honor your father and mother, so that you may live long in the land the Lord your God is giving you."

If you have any questions, you have my contact information. Thank you. Yours sincerely, Josh Pratt.

Darren Olsen was all over social media. Facebook. Twitter. TikTok. Reddit. Darren's FB friends included Branford McCauley. Branford's FB page featured pictures of the lovable cut-up posing with guns, smoking a blunt, soaring off a ledge on his board, posing in front of a statue of Bathomet, flashing demonic horns. His tongue was split like a serpent's. Several entries had been covered with WARNING: EXPLICIT CONTENT. Josh clicked the buttons to see Branford mooning a statue of Abraham Lincoln, wiping his butt with a face mask, and urinating on a gravestone. Rufus King, 1814 - 1876. The tombstone was in Jamaica, New York. It was a long way to go to piss on a tombstone. He recognized Bathomet from the Illinois State House.

The last picture was Branford in a karate gi, black belt, facing off with a tall black man. In the background, White Dragon was painted on the wall next to a stylized dragon.

'Branford's curriculum vitae said he was a self-employed freelance graphic artist specializing in urban sticker, poster, and stencil art. The pictures gallery reminded Josh of every freight train he'd ever seen. Giant, nearly illegible scrawls of fat letters in vivid colors. Pentagrams. "SEVENTH SON" in enormous, bulging letters. The only way Josh could figure Branford made a living was when people paid him not to deface their walls. "Graffiti removal" was a sideline.

Nice little business you got here.

Branford's last post had been in July. No nose ring.

Among his photos was a picture of a rustic cabin surrounded by woods with an old Toyota pickup parked on the dirt drive. Josh enlarged the photo. The Georgia license plate read VFF 763. He wrote it down.

Josh switched to Brandford's Twitter page.

So are we supposed to just not ask questions about the last 2+ years and how globalist leaders turned free countries into totalitarian states for "public health and safety?"

Don't challenge me. You won't like what you get.

On fleek, my dude.

I'm a hoochie-coochie man. Yes I am.

TikTok was mostly videos of Branford stunting on his board making faces, flipping the bird at a bust of JFK, or humping an inflatable sex doll while looking up and sticking out his tongue.

Josh called Ninja.

"The number you have reached is no longer in service."

Josh scrolled on, expecting Ninja to return his call. An hour later, no call. Josh wasn't worried. Ninja could take care of himself. But it wasn't like him to ignore a call, unless he was on the run. Josh needed help. It was an hour earlier in Denver. He phoned Randall Kleiser.

"The number you have reached is no longer in service."

Josh drummed his fingers on Fig's head. His phone rang. Number unknown.

"Pratt."

"Kleiser. What's going on?"

"Randall, I wonder if you would help me with a case. I will be happy to compensate you."

"Don't worry about it. What do you need?"

"Can you track down a Georgia license plate? Tell me where it lives and if it's still active?"

"Sure. What's the number?"

Josh told him.

"I'll have something for you tomorrow."

"Thanks, Randall. Send me an invoice."

"Forget about it."

Josh phoned Denza.

"What can I do for you, Josh?"

"Do you recall a student named Branford McCauley?"

"He's been training with me for four years."

"When was the last time you saw him?"

"About a week ago. What's this about?"

"He may have been the person who supplied Max Bushnell with the fentanyl."

Beat.

"Did you know Branford knew any Bushnells?"

"No I did not. And Branford never mentioned it. That's quite a coincidence. I find it hard to believe."

"Does he have a nose ring?"

Denza laughed. "No, but it left a big hole in his septum. He wasn't fooling anybody."

Josh was about to go to bed when he decided to check his email one more time. He despised himself for it. He'd lived most of his life without the internet and he resented the hold it had on him and everyone. One thing about smartphones. They'd revolutionized standing in line. Now you could stand in line compulsively checking your email, Facebook, Twitter, TikTok, Reddit, the news, the sports, sexy single women of Hungary, whatever you like.

A non-Hodgkins settlement offer. Andersen had windows for him. The real reason Fig licked her paws.

"Hello Dear, I have sent you two emails and you did not respond, I even sent another message a few days ago with more details still no response from you. Please are you still using this email address? I am VERY SORRY if sincerely you did not receive those emails, I will resend it now as soon as you confirm you never received them. Regards, Susan Yu-chen"

He deleted it.

Digital investment funding within 72 hours without stress.
Please write back if interested in the offer.
Upon Response, you'll be emailed with more details
We are here to demonstrate a better way to financial freedom!

Note: We do not charge any upfront fees for our services.

Sincerely
Trust Funds Capital.
Luis Osorio

Deleted.

Dear Sir: I am the widow of the late General Antonio Gubuza, who died recently, leaving an estate of some fifteen million American dollars. I have determined that you are a person of character and probity, and the right person to oversee the transfer of his wealth, which is currently held in a Swiss bank, to the United States, where I will be moving with my five children…

Deleted.

"Dear Mr. Pratt: I was surprised to receive your letter regarding my father. I have not heard from him in years. This has been my choice. Our upbringing was not ideal, but I'm sorry to hear that he has fallen on bad times and I would be interested in offering him some assistance. I would like to hear your perspective. I live in Madison. We could meet, if you like. Yours, Ron Bushnell."

Josh wrote back,

"Ron, I would be happy to meet with you at your convenience, if you would care to name a place and time. I am free much of the time, which is not to say I'm not working. I set my own hours. Yours, Josh Pratt."

Josh looked at Fig. "Now what?"

Fig woofed.

Josh picked up the remote his provider had sent him. You could speak into it and find any show you wanted. He picked it up.

"Paul Butterfield Blues Band."

For a moment there was nothing. A series of images appeared on screen. Butterfield at Newport Folk Festival. Butterfield at Howlin' Wolf's club. Butterfield at the Factory in Madison, Wisconsin, 1970. *Horn From the Heart*, the Paul Butterfield story.

Josh turned to Fig. "Should we watch this movie?"

"Woof!"

They watched the movie. A lot of people talking. Elvin Bishop. Paul's brother. But not much in the way of performance. Josh went back and saw that there was one live recording after another, so he chose one at random. Butterfield in some smoky blues club playing "Born In Chicago."

Fig whined and scratched behind her ear.

"You don't like this?"

"Woof!"

"All right, all right, let me see if I can find a dog movie where the dog doesn't die."

CHAPTER
21

RON

Josh agreed to meet Ron Bushnell at one p.m. at the Hubbard Avenue Diner in Middleton. It was a gray, overcast day as he parked on a side street and walked around the corner to the Hubbard, which was characteristically busy. As he entered, a man of about thirty with wavy brown hair, wearing a brown wool suit and white shirt, stood and motioned him over. Josh saw the resemblance. They shook hands.

"Thank you for seeing me, Mr. Bushnell."

"Call me Ron. Have a seat. I'm buying."

The waitress came over. Josh ordered a BLT, Ron a chef's salad. Hubbub clacked around the room, bouncing off the hard surfaces. Cooking odors emanated from the kitchen.

"How's Dad doing?"

"He's not doing too well. He was evicted from his basement apartment. I put him up in Davenport Suites. We'll take it a week at a time."

"You? You put him up?"

"Your dad's in a tough place. I respect his service to our country."

Ron barked humorously. "He's lucky he wasn't court-martialed."

"Why would he be court-martialed?"

"One of the helos he worked on crashed, killing a crew of four. They later determined it was due to faulty maintenance. Honestly, it's a mystery to me how he ever landed a job as a mechanic."

"How many helos did he work on that didn't crash?"

"I don't know. I've been reluctant to get in touch with him because, well, you've met him."

"I understand."

"You say he hired you to look into our uncle's death?"

"That's correct."

"Look. It's none of my business, but how does he expect to pay you?"

"He gave me what appears to be a handwritten letter by Ulysses S. Grant."

"Oh that. I thought it was just a family legend. No one else has ever seen it."

Josh brought up a picture of the document on his phone and handed it to Ron.

"Send that to me, would you?"

"Certainly. I understand where you're coming from. My father abandoned me when I was fifteen. He's currently serving a life sentence for murder."

"Sorry to hear it."

"I don't know Jerry that well, but I suspect he suffers from some form of cognitive dissidence. Does that make sense?"

"Yeah, in retrospect. The problem is, when you're just a kid, like me and Shelby, you don't understand those things. All we knew was that he was never there for us. Our mother Connie had her hands full. We were five and six when Jerry joined the Air Force and he just wasn't a factor after that. And he didn't really support the family. Every now and then he'd send a few bucks home, but it was mostly Connie who worked like a dog to pay the bills, which made her tense."

"Where's your mother now?"

"We had to put her in a home. She's only sixty, but she began breaking down around the time Uncle Don was killed. She'd sit and stare for hours, started hitting the Chardonnay every afternoon, then every morning, unable to accomplish simple tasks. By rights, Shelby and I should be on the street or in prison. But we made a pact. We weren't going to end up like our parents. I went to work right out of high school. Anything I could do. I went to college at night, studying business. I got my Masters from UW Milwaukee and joined Dunnigan Financial Services. At first I was just a clerk, but I worked hard and bit by bit, I made headway. Now I'm a vice president. Shelby's the manager of an auto supply chain. He's in charge of six stores. It wasn't an easy decision to put Connie in a home, but we both have families of our own. We visit her weekly, one of us. Sometimes both. We take her out on her birthday and the holidays. She loves her grandchildren. We think it's bringing her back a little bit."

"How many kids?"

"Two. Alex and Marie, five and three."

"I assume Shelby got the same message as you."

Ron sighed. "Shelby hates our father. I'm afraid he's a lost cause."

"What about you?"

"I've been a bad son. It doesn't matter how he treated us, family is family. I regret that we've neglected him all these years and I'm willing to step up. What did you pay to the hotel where he's staying?"

"Don't worry about it. I'll email you the particulars, and you can take over the payments. Do you have his phone number?"

"Text it to me." Ron pulled out a business card. Dunnigan Financial Services. He turned it over and wrote with a ballpoint pen. "This is my personal number."

Josh put it in his wallet and gave Ron one of his.

"Do you think the letter is real?"

"I'm trying to get it verified. I showed it to the experts, but they want to borrow it for God knows how long, to do carbon dating. I prefer to keep it where I know it's safe. I did a little research on my own and original Grant letters go for anywhere from a couple hundred to a hundred thousand, depending on length and importance."

"That's a lot of money."

"We'll see. If it's real, I hope to get it to an auction house."

"So how do you make money off this deal?"

Josh laughed. "I don't think I'm gonna make any money off this deal."

"So why are you doing it?"

Josh shrugged. "It's what I do. I'm glad you're willing to step up. Will you call him?"

"I'll call him today."

As Josh got in his car, his phone rang. Unknown number. He answered. "Pratt."

"Kleiser. I got some info. The license is current and is registered to a Luthor Bushnell of Rural Route Fourteen, Faubus, Georgia."

"That's it? No street number?"

"That's it. Don't ask me how he got away with it. I don't know."

"What about a phone number?"

"The number he gave motor vehicle registration is no longer in service. I looked for a Luthor Bushnell, but I couldn't find him."

"What about Branford McCauley?"

"What can you tell me about him?"

"Young man from Milwaukee area, about thirty. I'll send you some pics."

"I'll get on it."

"Thanks, Randall. Is this a good number for you?"

"Nope. This one's going in the trash. That number you called before, use it if you need to get in touch and I'll get back to you."

"And they can't trace it?"

"Not the way I've got it set up."

LUDDITE

When he got home, Josh sent Kleiser every picture of Branford McCauley he could find. At least a dozen pics. Branford in shades holding a black automatic. Brandford in shades and swim trunks, arm around a smiling redhead. Branford in shades looking up from a mirror covered with white lines. Branford with an arm draped around the statue of Baphomet.

Josh phoned Jaycee. "How's he doing?"

"He's up and talking, thank God. He got the joint from Darren. I told the police."

"Good. With any luck, they'll pick him up. I'm leaving for Georgia tomorrow. I'll check in with you."

"What's in Georgia?"

"Following up a lead. Are you familiar with anybody named McCauley?"

"McCauley? No, I don't think so."

"Are you aware of Bushnell involvement in the Civil War?"

"Donnie may have said something. He rarely mentioned his father. Why?"

"I don't know. I just pull strings."

"Well have a safe drive, and thank you."

"You're welcome."

Ray phoned. "Can I come over? Mongoose is driving me crazy."

"Sure."

"I'll be there in an hour. I'll bring dinner."

"Okay."

Ray brought Mo' Betta Gumbo in a bag. Josh dragged her into the bedroom. They ate in the living room watching Tower of Power Live in Copenhagen.

"They sure are great," Ray said with a mouth full of chicken.

"It's hard to believe they've been at it since 1968. Some of the original members have died, but they keep coming back."

"They're the most syncopated band I've ever heard."

"Yup."

"What's in Georgia?"

"Dude sold fentanyl-laced marijuana to a friend of mine."

"Oh Josh, I don't want you to go. It's not your problem. Are they paying you?"

"Boy's uncle. I'm looking into his brother's murder."

"Oh yeah, you told me about that. But how does that extend to this kid?"

Josh shrugged. "My client's a real sad sack. I feel sorry for him. The mom's a peach and both kids are great. A man can't just sit around."

"Are you going alone?"

"That's the plan."

"Are you taking a gun?"

"You know I'm not allowed to own guns. You hate the Second Amendment."

"I'm wrestling with it."

"What's with Mongoose?"

"She wants hash brownies. She wants a bowl of M&M's, with the green ones removed. She thinks she's Angelina Jolie. And I can't fire her because I'd get canceled."

"I could rough her up a little."

Ray laughed. "As if. My folks want to know when we're going to tie the knot."

"Huh?"

"You heard me. I'm not saying anything. I'm just telling you what they told me."

Here it comes. Love and marriage, love and marriage. The kid, the yard, the whole nine yards. On the other hand, was he not a good Christian? Did not the Lord God intend for man and woman to marry and be one? Who was he to defy the word of Christ? He could do it. He could do it. But first he played for time.

"Let me think about that."

Ray pulled back. "Well don't take too long."

He reached for her. "Come here, baby. You know I love you. It's a big step, but I'm willing to take it."

"Is this a proposal?"

"Kinda."

Ray grinned and threw her arms around him. "I'll take it."

"We'll have an old-fashioned biker wedding."

"Wait a minute."

"Everybody will arrive on bikes and get shit-faced. We'll have ladies mud wrestling and a blues band. I'll invite my friends and you invite your friends. The whole Rise Up colony. Dancing."

"Mongoose may not be invited, if she doesn't straighten up and fly right."

"You know what? Give me the script. I'll do it."

"You're a man."

"So's drunk octopus, right? A cynical old beat cop."

"The whole point of the play is to use surrealistic tropes to turn gender expectations on their head. It's called neuro-queering."

"Neuroqueering."

"Neuroqueering is a rejection of able-hetero assimilation and counter-identification, in favor of disidentification."

"Let me chew on that."

Ray went to the bathroom. Josh checked his email. There was an encrypted message from Kleiser. Josh went into his office and brought it up on his computer. Using his phone felt like looking at the world through a screen the size of a postage stamp. He followed the link and entered the password Kleiser had given him. Two still images filled the screen, harsh, sodium lamp lighting showing a young man with a shaved skull fueling his car at a Loaf & Jug, and the same young man paying at the counter inside. A silver earring caught the light.

"Check your text."

Josh checked his text.

"Brandon McCauley at four seventeen Bakerton Avenue, Nashville, last night at ten ten."

McCauley was driving a decommissioned police Dodge Charger, white body, black hood, and greenhouse.

Josh phoned Kleiser. "That number is not in service at this time."

Five minutes later, Kleiser called back. "Does that help?"

"It sure does, Randall. Thank you. What about credit cards?"

"I watched the video. Dude's paying cash."

"Did you trace that car?"

"Belongs to Branford McCauley, seven thirty-seven Highlander Lane, unit forty-two, Brookfield, Wisconsin. It's a 2014 Dodge Charger, used to belong to Wisconsin State Patrol. McCauley has no outstanding warrants. He was busted for speeding three years ago, paid a fine. I checked his social media. He's all over Facebook. I have no idea what he does for a living. That's a nice apartment building."

"I got those pictures from his Facebook page."

"Well it's gone now. No Twitter, no LinkedIn, nothin'."

"That must all have come down in the last twenty-four hours. And he's on the run."

"You spooked him."

"He doesn't know I exist."

"Well something spooked him. I think we both know where he's going."

"Could you pinpoint that on a satellite or something?"

"Yes. Don't you have Google Earth?"

"I don't know."

"Ask any teenager."

"I'll find it. Hey, do me a favor."

"What?"

"Don't vex me, don't text me."

"Don't text you?"

"That is correct, Randall. I never think to look at my texts."

"Luddite."

"Yeah thanks."

Josh signed off and looked up Luddite.

"A member of any of the bands of English workers who destroyed machinery, especially in cotton and woolen mills, that they believed was threatening their job."

Ray was curled up on the sofa wearing flannel nighties with cats, Fig's head in her lap.

"Randall says I'm a Luddite."

"Who's Randall?"

"Friend of mine. Do you think I'm a Luddite?"

She looked him up and down. "I would say so."

"I don't destroy machinery."

"What do you mean?"

"I looked it up. It says a Luddite is an English worker who destroys machinery. I don't destroy machinery. Except for that knucklehead."

"What knucklehead?"

"It's a type of Harley."

"It means someone who shuns modern technology and prefers to do everything the hard way. That's you."

"What are you watching?"

"*The Real Housewives of Miami.* Fig likes it, don't you girl?"

Fig thumped her tail.

CHAPTER 23

EASY PEAZY

Ray left Sunday morning. After his run, Josh spoke with Max Bushnell.

"Mom tells me you're after Darren."

"Did he sell you the reefer?"

"He gave me the reefer. It was a blunt. That's what we call these professionally rolled, cone-shaped joints you get from medical marijuana joints. It came in a plastic tube like a prescription drug."

"Do you still have that tube?"

"No. I tossed it."

"I'm not really after Darren, although I did pass that information on to the police."

"Fine with me."

"So where did Darren get the dope?"

"No idea."

"Tell me about it. How did he come to offer you that

joint?"

"Gerry invited me out for a puff. He had a roach that was maybe a half-inch long. It was ditch weed. We were hanging out on the bandstand not getting high. Gerry says, 'This shit is bogus' and flipped it on the ground. Darren comes up and hands me the cylinder. 'Have one on me,' he said. I thanked him. He waved it off and went away. I knew him from high school but we never hung out. I was a jock. He was a stoner."

"And you've never met Brandon McCauley."

"Nope."

"You know your great-great-grandfather and Brandon's great-great-great-grandfather were in the same class at West Point?"

"Really? That seems awfully coincidental."

"You've never heard that?"

"Uncle Jerry might have mentioned it, but half the shit he says is totally made-up."

"Such as?"

"Like that story about his Purple Heart. He was a chopper mechanic. He was never even in combat."

"Huh." Josh could have kicked himself around the block for not checking Jerry's bonafides.

"What are you going to do now?"

"I'm going to find Brandon."

He went across the street. Dave Lowry answered the door.

"Come in, Josh."

Josh followed Dave into the rec room with the sliding glass door looking out on the patio.

"Would you like a cup of coffee?"

"Sure."

"Cream and sugar?"

"Sure."

Dave returned with two mugs.

"Dave, I hate to ask this of you…"

Dave laughed. "Of course we'll look after Fig. We're glad to have her. How long will you be gone?"

"Not sure. Maybe a week."

"George and Gracie will be glad to have the company. Where you off to?"

"Georgia."

"Beautiful country."

"I'll bring her over before noon."

"Great."

Josh thanked him and returned to his house. He was no internet whiz, but he knew enough to dig up Jerry's military records. Dishonorable discharge. Insubordination and failure to perform basic duties.

Josh threw clothes in a gym bag. Fresh socks, underwear, shirts. He'd wear the same pair of jeans for a month. Two burner phones Kleiser gave him. An Autel Robotics EVO II Pro 6K HDR Drone Quadcopter. A used Apple laptop Ninja had reconfigured. Three Apple Air Tags.

He took Fig across the street at eleven and drove counterclockwise around the city heading for ninety. He'd take ninety-four to Chicago, sixty-five to Tennessee, twenty-four to Faubus. Faubus was in the northeast corner of the state. The drive would take two days. He found a blues station out of Chicago and headed east. He pulled into Louisville at eight p.m. and called Ray.

"Hey Ray, I'm in Kentucky."

"Can't talk right now. I'm dealing with a crazy woman."

"Idaho Mongoose."

"Love you, baby! I'll call you tomorrow."

He crossed the Georgia state line Monday at two-thirty, heading east toward Faubus through the Blue Ridge mountains. He pulled over at two look-outs, inhaled and took pictures. He pulled out a burner and tried to call Randall but there were no bars. The Wi-Fi returned at Gunnip, twenty-two miles from Faubus. Josh parked at the town square, heavy with oak and willow trees, built around a statue of John Bell Hood.

Josh sat on a slatted bench looking inward as two boys stunted on the steps and iron rail in the center. He called Kleiser.

"The number you have reached is not in service at this time."

Pigeons approached cooing. He spread his hands. "Sorry, boys."

Josh watched a young mother pushing her baby in a stroller, a businessman across the street in dark blue with red tie hustle out of a four-story office building. A church fronted another side. All the stores were personal. No JCPenney or Target. No Olive Garden or Applebees. The town was quiet, the only sound was the murmur of tires on the street, jacked-up pickups bellowing and belching, or friends calling to one another.

Josh's burner rang. "Randall, have you connected that license plate to a property yet?"

"Yeah, hold on. I hacked Starlink and matched that car's overhead profile with Faubus. I got two hits. These are big files. I don't think you can download them on your phone. Do you have access to a computer?"

"I'll try a motel."

"Yeah. They're satellite images with coordinates and they appear to show McCauley's Charger in a rural setting."

"Rural?"

"Yeah. I see what looks like a still."

"That's funny."

"Give me a call when you get where you're going."

"Is this phone still good?"

"You should be good."

"Thanks, Randall."

Josh drove a half hour to Faubus and the Violet Estates Motel, an ancient string of rooms extending from a one-story office. Josh parked in front and entered. An old dude the color of café *au lait* who looked like Santa Claus, white beard, sat behind the desk reading a book. A bulletin board behind him on the wall listed local estate shows, various business cards, and a poster:

BATTLE OF TUNNEL HILL
REENACTMENT NOV. 30 FEATURING
TUNNEL HILL CIVIL WAR PARK
CHATTANOOGA

The proprietor looked up.

"He'p you?"

A black-and-white photograph on the back wall showed six Black bikers standing around their chops, drinks in hand, grinning, flipping the bird, doing the Chuck Berry duck walk. Josh pointed and looked at the old man.

"That you?"

The old man chuckled. "You got a good eye. You ride?"

"Oh yeah. I'd ride down here but the weather's iffy."

"What's your business?"

"I'm a private investigator."

"Seriously?"

"I'm no Rockford."

The old man laughed, stood, held out his hand. "Leonard Murtagh, but my friends call me Easy Peazy."

"Josh Pratt. What's the name of your club?"

"Outcasts. Mostly veterans. How long you stayin'?"

"Don't know how long I'll be here. Long enough to get the job done."

"Well it's sixty-five a night, cash up front."

Josh pulled out his Harley wallet.

"What do you ride?" Easy Peazy said.

"Modified Road King."

"What'dja do to it?"

Josh took a deep breath. "Engine: 88 with oil cooler. Changed the cams to S&S gear drives with 510 lift. Took out the fuel injection and replaced it with an S&S Super E, Yost Power Tube, S&S manifold and Pingle High Flow petcock. S&S Tear Drop air cleaner cover with a K&N filter. Screaming Eagle Hi Performance ignition unit with a 6200 rpm rev limiter. Accell Super Coil, Fire Wire plug wires and spiral wound metal core wires. Accell Platinum tip plugs. Five-speed tranny with Barnett Kevlar clutch, self-adjusting hydraulic chain tensioner. Screaming Eagle dualies. Progressive springs in front with higher viscosity, Progressives in back. Changed the rear swing arm bushings to "STA BOW" nylon high density. SBS semi-metallic disc brake pads and the brake lines are stainless steel braids. Went to tubeless wheels. What do you ride?"

Easy shook his head. "I had to get a goddamn trike last year."

"Hopefully, that's still a ways off. This town have police?"

"Nah. We're too small for the police. Used ta be, nothin' ever happened. But lately, lotta drug activity. We rely on the sheriff's department. Sheriff Tom Woolery. He ain't so bad."

Josh peeled off some bills. "That's for three nights. If I'm done before, you can keep the change. Oh yeah. Can I use your computer and your printer?"

BONAFIDES

Faubus was an intersection with a church, a gas station, a
Piggly Wiggly, a hardware store, a Carnegie Library, Moon-
rise Distillery, Goats on the Roof, and Grace's Restaurant
on the ground floor of a two-story brick structure. Popu-
lation: five thousand six hundred and seventy-two. The retired Dodge police cruiser was parked at the Piggly Wiggly.
Wisconsin plates, check. Hula dancer glued to dash, check.
Radar detector, check. Josh couldn't believe his luck. He
pulled the tracker disc from his pocket, super glue from the
glove compartment, laid down a dime of glue, and sauntered toward the store. He paused at the back of McCauley's
Dodge and stooped as if tying his shoe. He slapped the Apple tracker to the underside of the chassis.

The town nestled in a valley, the hills covered with ash,
birch, and box elder. As Josh ambled back to his car, his
phone rang. Not the burner. It was Jarell.

"What up?"

"Got him."

"Got who?"

"The thief. I got a message on my phone at two-thirty in the morning about activity in my office, signed in, and saw McTelvin Bobinmoyer lifting the ball. With that infrared, it was bright as day. I'll lay odds he took my Muddy Waters LP too."

"That's great, Jarell. Listen, I can't talk right now. I'm on a stakeout. I'll call you tonight."

"Stakeout?"

Josh laughed. "Weird, huh? Oh oh, here he comes."

Brandon McCauley pushed a cart containing a cardboard crate and four plastic bags. He used a lot of real estate when he walked, arms akimbo, legs bowed, like Connor McGregor entering the ring. Josh watched him put everything in his back seat, leave the shopping cart in a parking space, and head south. Josh waited for a pickup truck to get between them and followed.

McCauley turned south on Hayward Road, winding through narrow valleys. It was beautiful country with trash in the ditch. He lost sight of McCauley in a coulee and when he emerged, the road ran straight for a mile. No McCauley. Josh drove slowly down the road, past rural mailboxes and dirt roads, some barred with aluminum gates. A flicker of white caught his attention. An old sign said Briar Valley Road, more like a trail with tire tracks. Josh recognized the Piggly Wiggly bag as he passed. He pulled off into a gated field entrance, walked a hundred yards back, and picked up the bag. Inside was a receipt: beer, vitamins, butter, apples.

The old tin mailbox was off-kilter, the result of drive-by bashes. The lane disappeared in the cottonwood and willow. Josh wore gray slacks and a taupe shirt, not bad for creeping through the woods. He was not prepared to survey the house by day. He walked back to his car. His phone buzzed. Jaycee.

"Josh, I asked Max which uncle got killed in Iraq and he said it was Steven Bushnell, from Boston."

Josh wrote it down. "Thanks, Jaycee."

Josh drove back to town and pulled into a park with a swing set and a jungle gym. He stopped in the gravel lot, big enough for twenty cars, and phoned Kleiser.

"The number you have reached is not in service at this time."

Five minutes later, Kleiser called back. "Yeah."

"McCauley pulled off on Briar Valley Road. Can you do a sky grab for me?"

"I can, but it's gonna cost."

"No problem." Josh pulled out the card with Easy Peazy's email. "Send it to this address."

The red brick Carnegie Library had white columns and a domed roof like a pocket Monticello. Josh parked on the street behind a jacked-up Dodge Ram with Alabama plates and went inside. That smell of books. He looked around. The wood floor and walls were buffed to a high sheen, shelf after shelf of books. A Gettysburg panorama occupied the center of the big room, tiny Union and Confederate forces reenacting Pickett's Charge. Each figure had been lovingly hand-painted. Josh gazed at it for long seconds before approaching an elderly woman at a desk typing on a manual. Clack clack. She looked up smiling.

"How can I help you?"

"Yes, ma'am. I'm looking for histories of local families that fought in the Civil War, especially the Battle of Tunnel Hill."

The woman beamed, her rouged cheeks puffing. "You know, you're the second person today to ask me about that. I'll tell you what I told the other gentlemen. We have a shelf devoted to local Civil War history. You just go straight down that aisle and you'll find it against the back wall next to the window. Which families in particular are you interested in?"

"The Bushnells and the McCauleys."

"That's where you'll find them. The book you want is *McCauleys in the War Between the States*. Let me give you the number." She wrote it out on a slip of paper.

"Thank you, ma'am."

Josh passed a young girl sitting in an alcove reading. At the end of the corridor was a floor-to-ceiling wooden bookcase with a hand-lettered sign: "Local Civil War History." Josh went down the shelf. He'd never heard of most of the books, but he was no history buff. A gap between books indicated where the McCauley history had rested. To his right, a big man sat in an alcove, pouring over a heavy, leather-bound book. Josh walked over.

"Is that the McCauley book?"

The big man looked up. He was the size of a bulldozer with close-cropped hair and a trim GI Joe beard. "Yes."

"You gonna be at it for a while?"

The big man looked down. "As long as it takes."

"You interested in the McCauleys?"

The big man looked up. "Maybe. Why do you ask?"

"Business."

"What kind of business?"

"I'm a PI. My client's brother was murdered. His name was Don Bushnell. His great-great-grandfather attended West Point. His best friend was Roderick McCauley. Don's son nearly died from fentanyl-laced marijuana. I believe it was supplied by Brandon McCauley. 'Brandon's just outside of town visiting his uncle."

The big man closed the book and stood. "Let's go outside."

As they passed through the foyer, the librarian looked up. "Sir, that book doesn't leave the library."

The big man paused and laid the book on her desk. "I'll be right back."

It was warm. They sat on a bench beneath a willow tree in the library yard. "Levon Cade," the big man said. "Tell me about the fentanyl."

Josh told him about Jerry Bushnell and how he got involved. He pulled out his phone. "This is a picture from before the Civil War. That guy on the left is Ethan Bushnell. The guy on the right is Roderick McCauley. An eyewitness reported a man dressed as a Confederate soldier at Summerfest the night Don was killed."

"How old is Brandon?"

"Thirty. He would have been eighteen in 2010. What's your interest?"

"I need time to check your bonafides. Let's meet later. In the meantime, I'm almost done with the book. For now, the book is yours."

Josh handed him his card. "Thank you, sir."

THE MUTILATED BOOK

Josh sat in the alcove and went to the index. *McCauley Family History* by Richard McCauley, copyright 1989, years before Brandon was born. Leather bound with gilt trim. Nice book. Heavy. It was over four hundred pages long with an index and a list of illustrations. Josh flipped through the illustrations. The earliest was a black-and-white photograph of a painting showing Lord Shawn McCauley, the fifth Baron of Dunston. He moved to the computer.

"The Baron is the fifth and lowest rank in the Scottish Peerage and is not a seat in Parliament. A Baron has landholdings or property worth more than £0.25 million. More than 160 Barons in the Scottish Peerage: the Baron of Balnagown, the Baron of Balfour, the Baron of Elphinstone, etc. They have privileges and responsibilities similar to those of a Viscount."

Back to the book. The McCauleys emigrated from Scotland in 1819 and purchased farmland in rural Georgia. Patriarch Archibald had raised cattle and brought with him prized Angus stock. By 1830 he had built a thriving business, his beef much prized in Georgia, and New Orleans, of all places, where a consortium representing several restaurants transported the cattle overland to Natchez, down the Mississippi to New Orleans where they were butchered and the meat whisked away within the hour. One restaurant, Le Grande Maison, had briefly employed Marie Laveau, the Voodoo Queen of New Orleans, as a sous chef. Dining at Le Grande Maison, Archibald praised Laveau's cooking and asked to meet her. He later hired her and her hand-picked crew to host a party at his plantation.

Archibald's first son, Roderick, was born in 1820 and attended West Point from 1838 to 1842. Archibald's wife died in childbirth. He would never marry again. At West Point, Roderick met Ethan Bushnell, of Mineral Point, Wisconsin. Josh looked at the pictures he'd taken at the Museum warehouse in Madison.

In 1845, Roderick married Isabel Morel of New Orleans, who gave birth nine months later to their first son, Archibald. Six more boys followed, the last being Jules. In 1856. Roderick settled in Colby, Alabama, where he bought a cotton plantation with family money. He and Ethan Bushnell maintained a friendly correspondence over the years.

July 17, 1859.

My Dear Roderick: I am writing to express my delight at the birth of your seventh son Jules. I hope it is not too much to hope that he will follow in our footsteps, and that of your sons Lemuel and Carlton, and pursue a military career. If you would like for me to write a letter of recommendation when the time comes I would only be too delighted. I am grateful to the Lord for the continued health of our own two children, Terrence, seventeen, and his sister Samantha, fifteen. It is my heartfelt desire that you would come to visit us here in Wisconsin and meet our family. I talk about you so much, Ruth feels as if she already knows you.

My great fear is the growing division between North and South will drive a wedge into our friendship. While I understand your need to employ slaves to harvest your cotton, you must understand that those of us north of the Mason Dixon Line view the world through a different lens than those in the agrarian south.

I am also compelled to inform you that a Corporal Malcolm Gutilia, of the First Regiment of Dragoons, has been spreading scurrilous rumors that an ancestor of yours, Eisenthorp McCauley, of Caithness County, was alleged to have been burned alive as a witch in 1628. I searched for this fellow when I was in Pennsylvania at the same time as the Dragoons, to give him some advice. Alas, I was unable to locate him and some weeks later I heard from a friend of a friend that learning I was looking for him, he deserted his post and decamped for points west. I just thought you ought to know. Whether the rumor is true or not is no concern of mine, and in any case, would have no effect on our friendship. You are not responsible for the sins of your ancestors.

I trust this letter finds you well, and I look forward to visiting sometime this year, the Good Lord willing, and our differences settled by a wise and compassionate Congress.

Your lifelong friend, Ethan Bushnell.

The signature was decorative and legible.

"After the first Battle of Bull Run in 1861, Ethan Bushnell was recalled to the Union Army with the rank of major and assigned to the 4th Army of the Potomac under General George McLellan. Roderick McCauley joined the Army of the Confederacy under General James Longstreet as a major. Major McCauley commanded ten thousand men of Lee's Army of Northern Virginia...

"Following the Battle of Gettysburg, McCauley retreated to his plantation outside of Colby, badly shaken. He had no illusion that the Confederacy would recover from their massive loss. He understood the north's advantages not only in manpower, but in industrialization, which was ushering in a new age for which the South was ill prepared. The invention of the cotton gin had revolutionized the textile industry. While the South relied on rifle musket-making machinery salvaged from the destruction of the federal Harper's Ferry Armory during the first weeks of the war, the North had five times the lumber of armories, including Colt and Remington, whose small arms were technologically superior to the south's.

"Dr. Richard Gatling was so distraught by the carnage of the war that he invented the world's first successful rapid fire gun, the Gatling Gun, in an effort to create a weapon so horrible that it would stop the Civil War in its tracks and prevent any future conflict from arising. Although the gun was only used once, during the Siege of Petersburg, McCauley saw the handwriting on the wall. In July 1863, he traveled alone to New Orleans to ask Marie Laveau to intervene on behalf of the South. Whatever possessed McCauley to seek supernatural help, we do not know. The precedent may have been with his seventeenth-century ancestor Eisenthorp McCauley.

"It was at the Battle of Tunnel Hill that Major Roderick McCauley faced his one-time best friend, Colonel Ethan Bushnell. Bushnell had been appointed a brevet colonel by General Grant at the Battle of Fort Henry in 1862. Colonel Bushnell distinguished himself through bravery under fire and initiative, in leading his troops in an unexpected charge that punctured the Confederate defense. That battle took place on November 25, resulting in seventy-four Confederate casualties, and only sixteen Union casualties. General Grant later said it was the key to their success. After that, all communications between the one-time best friends ceased."

"Marie Laveau declined to participate, fearing a backlash should the North win the war, which seemed likely. McCauley learned of another practitioner of the dark arts, Aleksander Mendeleev, a recent Russian émigré. Mendeleev referred McCauley to Vodou Houngan Jean-Jacques Serenop, a Haitian émigré. No record exists of this meeting, but when McCauley returned to his plantation, he was a different man. Gone was his youthful optimism and faith in the Republic. To the dismay of his wife Muriel, he began bedding his female slaves like a man possessed, siring child after child. All boys. He lost all interest after the birth of his seventh son, Christophe. Alone among his half-siblings, Christophe was allowed into the main house and given an education. He was light-skinned enough to pass for Creole.

"Although no written record exists of what the Houngan told McCauley, it is believed he told the Major about the power of the seventh son."

The seventh son of a seventh son is a concept from Vodou legend regarding special powers given to, or held by, such a son. To qualify as 'the seventh son of a seventh son' one must be the seventh male child born in an unbroken line with no female siblings born between, to a father who himself is the seventh male child born in an unbroken line with no female

siblings born between. In some beliefs, the special
powers are inborn, inherited simply by virtue of his
birth order; in others the powers are granted to him
by God or the gods because of his birth order.

"We will never know how or why Major McCauley became enamored of this concept. If he hoped that his off-spring would somehow affect the outcome of the war, he also had to know that by the time Christophe achieved his majority, the war would have long since passed. Christophe was a gifted horseman, a handsome and able young man with a likable personality. In 1886, he hired on with the Sylvester Ranch in Arizona Territory as a horse wrangler and married an Apache woman with whom he had three children. In 1889, his only son Joseph was born. In 1919, Joseph begat Jedediah, who did not marry until he was thirty. Jedediah sired his only son Bartholomew in Sioux Falls, South Dakota, in 1949. I was born in 1969. I am Bartholomew's third son. I have four brothers. Matthew and Martin came before me. Richard and Lester came after. As of this writing, Martin's wife Elizabeth is pregnant with twins.

"This is one reason I have chosen to write the McCauley family history.

"On April 14, 1934, Nicholas McCauley was shot and killed outside Jeremiah's Tavern in Quiller, Georgia. He was not robbed. The motive and perpetrator remain a mystery to this day."

The rest of the book was torn out.

Josh closed it, returned to the computer station and searched for Levon Cade. Nada. He returned to the stacks and phoned Kleiser.

"The number you have called is no longer in service."

Josh looked around. He was the only visitor. Sleepy little town. Deep in the stacks, he saw books in every direction except the narrow aisle to the center line. His phone buzzed.

"Randall, can you find out everything you can of a Levon Cade of Colby, Alabama?"

"I'll call you. You might as well toss that phone. Do me a favor, would ya? Take out the battery. Smash the phone and dump it in a creek."

Josh went to the front desk. The librarian looked up.

"Ma'am, did you know someone tore pages out of this book?" He showed it to her.

"Oh my. Oh my. No, I did not know. That's terrible. This book is very rare. This may be the only one in existence. It was published privately and bequeathed to the library. Who would do such a thing?"

GETTING TO KNOW YOU

The library closed at six. Josh walked down the street to Elmo's BBQ, a homespun café in a two-story red brick office block that featured a certified tax accountant, a second-hand store, and an insurance agency. Josh pushed open Elmo's door and stepped into blessed low humidity and cool temperatures. The smell of barbecue made Josh's stomach rumble. A Formica counter ran the length of the back, with red soda fountain stools. One wall was covered with testimonials.

"Best BBQ in the South" – CC Riders MC

"We always eat here" – Greg Allman

A framed black-and-white photo of a man in coveralls wearing a Confederate kepi at a big outdoor grill. "Archie Haas, founder, 1990."

A series of booths fronted Main Street. Josh spotted the big man who'd given him the book. He walked down.

"Mind if I join you?"

The big man looked up from his phone. "Have a seat."

Josh slid in. "What's good?"

"Don't know. I'm new to this town."

"Yeah, me too."

A young waitress in shorts and halter top, shoulders and arms fully inked, flowers, parrots, paisleys, Chinese lettering, handed Josh a worn menu. Her tag said Jillian.

Josh looked up. "What's good?"

"We got the best brisket sandwich in the south."

"Yeah, I'll have that."

"Me too," said the big man, without looking up.

"Y'all want it fatty or lean?"

"Lean," both men said.

"Pickles and onions?"

"Yes, please," the big man said.

"Me too."

"Somethin' to drink?"

"You got Pepsi?" Josh said.

"We got RC. It's better."

"I'll have one of those."

"Me too."

"I told you why I'm here," Josh said. "Why are you here?"

Cade folded his hands on the tabletop and regarded Josh with ice-blue eyes. "Same reason. Two kids died where I come from. Colby, Alabama. Fentanyl. Only instead of a joint, it was cut with their heroin. I know their folks. Good people."

"Are you law enforcement?"

"I'm just a concerned citizen."

"I'm looking for Brandon McCauley. He's thirty. He's the one who gave the fentanyl-laced joint to my client's son."

"You saw the book."

"Yeah. Did you know someone ripped out a bunch of pages toward the back?"

"I saw that. I've heard the name McCauley before."

"Where?"

"Paul Kuhner. Afghanistan. Ran into him at the Piggly Wiggly in Colby several months ago. His girl Jasmine died from fentanyl. She died across the street. They found her at the base of the Confederate statue, holding her lipstick. She'd circled McCauley on the list of Confederate War dead. I found out about the book after. I don't know what I expected to find. I'd like to talk to Brandon."

The waitress brought their meals. Cade held up a finger, gripped his sandwich in both hands and went to work. They ate in silence for a few minutes hearing the clatter of coffee cups and silverware, murmurs of conversation, outside traffic.

Josh wiped his mouth with a paper towel from a roll on a metal tube. "What's in it for you?"

Cade spread his hands. "Something to do."

"What are you gonna do if we find him?"

Cade shrugged. "I'll talk to him."

"Yeah, right. Listen. I got a drone. Infrared. We can take

a look at the place without them knowing."

"What place?"

"Briar Valley Road. I tracked him."

"Tracked him how?"

"Apple Air Tag."

"What if it's him? What are you gonna do? Turn him over to the police?"

"Well yeah."

Cade looked out the window. He looked back. "You served time."

"You checked me out."

"For assault."

"That's right."

"What if I were to tell you that I'll take care of it on my own? You have my word justice will be done."

"You're gonna handle this all by yourself? How you going to get in there?"

"I'll watch. I'll wait."

"Yeah? So?"

Cade sighed like he was dealing with a fool.

"Who's your client?" Josh asked.

"The boy's mother."

"How much is she paying you?"

"That's none of your business."

"What if I paid you more to leave it to me? You have my word. Justice will be done." Cade's face was placid.

"I tried to look you up. I couldn't find jack shit."

Cade shrugged. "I try to keep a low profile."

"More like no profile. You want to get a drink?"

"Sure."

The waitress returned with the bill. They both reached for it, but Cade got it first. "You can buy the first round."

It was dark and cool by the time they left the diner and walked a half block to Carlton's, a smoky red brick bar with a neon Dixie sign in the window. The jukebox was the brightest thing in the dim interior. Hardwood floor, stamped tin roof, feral hog mounted over the bar on the left. A couple trucker types at the bar, two black bikers playing pool. Outcasts. Two leathery women in a booth. Lynyrd Skynyrd on the juke. The buck-toothed blond waitress wore her men's shirt with the sleeves torn off and the tail wrapped around her taut middle.

"What'll you boys have?"

"Whatever's on tap and Maker's Mark chaser," Cade said.

"Me too," Josh said. They watched her return to the bar.

"I feel like I stepped back in time," Josh said.

"Yeah, lotta that around here."

The song ended. Josh went to the juke and put in a buck. B.B. King's "Every Day I Have the Blues."

The pool players looked up. One gave Josh the thumbs up and turned back to the game.

The waitress brought their drinks on a tin Coca-Cola tray.

"Mah name's Vanessa. You want to start a tab?"

Josh gave her a ten. "Yes, please. That's for you."

They watched her go.

Josh held up his whiskey. Cade clinked. They tossed them down and reached for their beers.

Cade set his glass on the hardwood table. "We have a certain way of doing things in the South."

"I can appreciate that, but I still gotta answer to my client."

The song ended. One of the bikers went to the juke. "Very Superstitious."

Cade waved Vanessa over and ordered another round.

"All right," Cade said, watching her go. "There are at least three people on that property plus your boy Brandon. It may be that I could use some help."

"How do you know?"

"I looked."

"What's the plan? What's the goal?"

"You said you had a drone."

"Yup. Let's take a look. I'll drive."

Cade smiled tightly. "Let's get the drone and I'll drive."

"You want to drive?"

"I got a pick-up."

Cade drove a new Dodge Ram with a cracked windshield. They headed southeast on Briar Valley Road, passing another pickup on its way into town. Cade reached under the dash and turned on a police scanner.

"Burt, where are you?" Crackly voice.

"Haines's Coulee. Somebody dumped a load of chemicals in the ditch. Lord, I can smell the acetone. I ain't touchin' this shit."

"I'm on my way."

Cade switched it off, turned on the radio. Soft jazz played over the speakers.

"Cedar Walton," Josh said.

Cade grunted. "You like blues."

"I like all kinds of music. Except rap."

"Amen, brother."

"We just passed the turn-off."

Cade drove a quarter mile down the road and pulled off into a rutted access road that rolled over a bump jouncing them in the air. They got out. Cade pissed in the woods while Josh opened the carbon fiber drone case, removing the four-rotor, X-shaped device. He set his laptop in the bed, turned it on, and linked it up with the drone. Cade returned. It was a bright night, half-moon, stars gleaming. Josh turned on the drone, controlling it from the laptop.

It rose fifty feet and scooted northwest, transmitting images of the glowing green forest below.

WHAT THE DRONE SAW

The woods creaked and rustled. Frogs croaked. Something ripped through the shrubs like a freight train.

"Feral hog, most likely," Cade observed.

Josh sent the drone up a hundred feet. It picked up the glow from a farmhouse. As the drone headed toward the farm, they saw a two-story wood building with a porch, separate two-car garage, and a pole barn in back. McCauley's Dodge sat in the yard next to an old Chevy C-10, and a rat chopper with ape hangers and a sissy bar. Lights on, faint fiddle music via the drone's directional mic.

Cade sounded out of place, an intrusion. "Can you bring it in closer?"

"What do you want to see?"

"See that tree out front? That's a bottle tree."

Josh brought the drone down to fifty feet. It could hover over the house and no one would notice. He zoomed in on the tree. It appeared dead, each branch broken off with an empty bottle on the stub. Mostly beer and booze bottles.

"What's a bottle tree?"

"They put the bottles on the branches of a crepe myrtle in hopes of capturing spirits." Cade was barely audible. "Supposed to bring good luck."

Josh brought the drone around from the back in a big U, holding it above a juniper with a view of the front yard. Through the open drapes they saw a bearded, bare-chested man rise, grinning, tree-trunk arms flailing at something beneath him. A woman's naked leg flashed. The directional mic picked up a faint scream followed by laughter.

"Shit," Josh said. "Maybe we ought to go in there."

"Wait a minute. Keep an eye on that window."

Another man appeared, joining the first in holding something down. Neither was Brandon. The woman screamed and cursed. The newcomer smacked her hard. The slap of flesh on flesh.

"All right," Cade said. "Let's get in there. I'm going around the back. I find the circuit box, don't be surprised if everything goes dark."

Josh laid his laptop in the truck's bed, felt for the tactical flashlight in his pocket. "The drone will return to the truck."

Cade leaped in the bed, unlocked a steel toolbox and pulled out a heavy revolver. "You got a gun?"

"No. I'm a convicted felon."

"Take a look in here."

Josh joined him in the bed. The toolbox held a Sig Sauer nine and a Taurus Judge, chambered for .410 shotgun shells. Josh picked up a wood-handled axe in a leather sheath, hefting it in his hand.

"Take this too." Cade handed him a can of bear repellent. They got in the cab. The drone clinked down in the bed. Josh jammed the bear repellent in the pocket next to the flashlight. Cade turned the truck around and they jounced back to Hayward and headed north. A chain stretched across the entrance. A red and white sign read NO TRES-PASSING. The chain snapped like a thread as the big Ford headed for the farmhouse, gleaming faintly through the trees. As they entered the yard, a man came out on the front porch carrying a shotgun, shouted something, brought the gun to his shoulder and fired. Cade and Josh bailed. Pellets peppered the windshield. Cade rolled and came up behind a massive tire—something off an earth-moving machine, drew a bead on the shotgun and squeezed off two shots. The man staggered back as a slug struck a shoulder. He whirled, nursing a dead arm to run into the house.

Cade made a circular motion. Josh split to the right, ducking behind a steel waste disposal bin. Cade ran the perimeter clockwise. Josh hung back. Dim light showed through the door. Seconds later, it went dark. Josh leaped to the porch, around the corner to a bedroom, smashed the glass with the axe, ran it around the perimeter to remove jags, crawled in and ran into the living room. A bare-chested hillbilly had a woman, little more than a girl, pinned on a filthy mattress. The man with the shotgun leaned against the wall panting, staring at the blood running between the fingers of the hand clasped to his shoulder. He wore a denim vest with Quantrill's Raiders stitched in red. He had knobby wrists and an Adam's apple like a toilet bowl float. Blood streamed down his front and pooled on the hardwood floor.

"Fuck me!"

"Hey!" said the guy bending over the woman, rising. He looked to be in his thirties with brillo pad stubble, his torso covered in blue ink. Skulls, naked women, guitars, daggers. He pulled a foot-long Bowie from a leather sheath strapped to his leg like a gunslinger, gripped it in his right hand and charged. Josh threw the axe. It made a half turn and struck the man flat on the forehead. He dropped to the ground. The knife skittered across the floor. The third person was Brandon McCauley. He'd been sitting on a threadbare sofa bending over white lines on a mirror. He reached down into the sofa's cushions.

Cade appeared in the entrance to the kitchen behind and aimed a tactical flashlight alongside the big-bore revolver. The shotgunner ran out the front door. McCauley grabbed a backpack and followed. The girl crawled into a corner, hugging her knees and crying. Seconds later, the Dodge roared to life, spewed dirt, and disappeared.

Cade nudged the man on the floor. He lay still. "Anybody else?"

"Lights on in the pole barn. Maybe someone there."

Cade picked a blanket up from a rocking chair and threw it over the girl. "You okay?"

She ran a finger under her nose. "No I'm not okay. That motherfucker right there raped me."

She pointed to the unconscious man.

"How many men here?"

"These three motherfuckers and two more in the barn. You don't want to go in there without a hazmat suit."

"They got masks?" Josh said.

"In the dining room. Hazmat suits in the lab."

Cade put his knee in the fallen man's back and secured his feet and ankles with zip ties.

"Hey, man. Don't leave me here," the girl said, eyes wide.

Cade kicked the zip-tied man in the head.

"You'll be all right."

Josh went out the back, found the fuse box attached to the outer wall and flipped a switch. Yellow light shone from a ceiling fixture in the kitchen, dead flies at the bottom. The dining room table was heaped with Patriot Survival Meals, guns, boxes of ammo, body armor, and a plastic bag of pastel-colored pills. Josh picked up a respirator-type mask.

"You stay with the girl," Cade said. "I'll check the barn."

From the back of the house they heard a truck start up and drive away, opposite the way they'd come in. Hefting an automatic he'd drawn from the holster secured against the small of his back, Cade turned to the girl.

"You know how to use one of these?"

"Fuck yeah." Drawing the blanket around her, she held out her hand. Cade checked the magazine, jammed it back in, jacked one in the chamber.

"Don't shoot us."

"Who the fuck are you guys?"

Cade headed for the front door. "Come on. We'll come at 'em from different angles."

Josh looked at the guns. Fuck it. He picked up a revolver from where it lay on the cushion of a sagging armchair, checked the cylinder, held up a finger and winked. "What's your name?"

"Maybelline."

"Maybelline what?"

"Ward."

Josh followed Cade out the front door. Cade headed counterclockwise. Josh went clockwise. They came wide around the farmhouse and faced the pole barn fifty feet apart. Josh ran to the back. The door was open. He saw through to the front as Cade pushed the door inward without showing himself. Silence. A whiff of acrid chemicals. Cade switched on overhead fluorescent lights illuminating two buffet tables, end to end, covered with canisters, scales, plastic bags, and a pill-making machine.

MAYBELLINE

At the truck, Cade held up a hand. "Listen."

Josh opened his ears. The forest thrummed with the sound of crickets, an owl, things rustling through the undergrowth.

"I don't hear sirens," Cade said. "People pop off a few rounds out here, nobody notices. I think we have a little time."

"Whatcha got in mind?"

"We'll split and call the cops."

"Good idea."

While Cade poked his phone. Josh looked in the rear seat. Maybelline was curled up in the back hugging a camo backpack. She'd put on some clothes. She could have been anywhere from seventeen to thirty, with wavy brunette hair, a butterfly tat peeking out from beneath denim cut-offs, fully inked sleeves, and red-rimmed nostrils. She looked a little Latina. She'd left his Colt on the front passenger seat.

"You okay?"

"Yeahhh," she drawled.

"You need to see a doctor? Police?"

"Not likely!"

"Okay, who were they?"

Maybelline looked at Josh as if seeing him for the first time. "Who are you?"

"Josh Pratt."

"Who's the big guy?"

"Jones," Cade lied. He jammed his phone in his pocket. "Wait for me. There's something I got to do." He headed for the house.

"Who was in that room? Who's that guy I dropped?"

"Horace Garney."

"Who were the guys in the lab?"

"Cartel guys."

"What were you doing out here?"

"Garney hired me to give him a blow job. I get out there he wants me to give everyone a blow job. I didn't feel like it. I got mouth sores. I told him. He threw me down on that mattress and fucked me up the ass. Then he wanted everyone else to do it. Guy who lives there said that one guy with the shaved head was his cousin."

"McCauley?"

"That's right."

"Who lives here?"

"Ed McCauley. His cousin gave me the creeps. He started babbling in some foreign language."

Cade loped up to the truck. "They had a landline. I phoned Waldrop County. We gotta move. Where can we drop you?"

Maybelline clasped herself. "I better not go home. Those boys are mean. They're gonna blame me."

Josh looked at her in the rearview. "You didn't do anything wrong."

"Tell them that. They're killers."

"I'm staying at Violet Estates. I'll put you up for the night. Where you headed, Cade?"

"I'm not going anywhere until I find who's passing that shit. This motel cool?"

"It's cool. Proprietor's a biker. You ever hear of the Outcasts?"

"Man, that brings back memories. They were a thing when I was growing up. They still around?"

"At least one."

As they neared town, they heard sirens approaching.

It was ten-thirty when they returned to the motel. The office lights were on. Maybelline stayed in the truck. Murtaugh was in a recliner sawing logs, an empty bottle of Johnny Walker on the counter. His eyes popped open and for an instant he looked confused, as if he'd wandered onto a stage. Placing his hands on the armrests, he heaved himself to his feet and stood behind the counter.

"Mr. Pratt."

"Mr. Murtaugh. We need two more rooms."

Murtaugh looked Cade up and down. "Who's this?"

"That's not important right now," Cade said.

"Who's the third room for?"

"Friend of ours. She's hiding from her abusive ex. She's cool."

"How you wanna pay?"

Cade pulled out a leather wallet. "How much?"

"How many nights?"

"Let's take this day by day."

"Sixty-five a night."

Cade laid two hundred-dollar bills on the counter. Murtaugh opened a drawer beneath the counter and made change. He handed Cade two keys. "You and your friend are in five and six."

They walked to their rooms. Maybelline took the middle room. She paused outside her door. "You boys got any blow?"

"No."

"Not me," Cade said. "I'd like to know a few things."

Maybelline opened her door. "Come on in."

The room was spare but clean, with a painting of a duck hunter crouching in a blind.

Maybelline headed for the bathroom. "Gimme a mo."

She turned on the fan. They heard the toilet flush and water running. She came out looking fresher and sat on the bed.

"What can I tell you?"

"Do you know Brandon McCauley?"

"The punk?"

"Yeah. The guy with the fadeaway. Drives a Dodge police cruiser."

"Oh, that little shit. He was talking in tongues. Creeped me out. Something about Baphomet. Who the fuck is Baphomet?"

Josh pulled out his phone. "Baphomet is a deity allegedly

worshipped by the Knights Templar that subsequently became incorporated into various occult and Western esoteric traditions. The name Baphomet appeared in trial transcripts for the Inquisition of the Knights Templar starting in 1307."

"Knights Templar Cartel," Cade said. "Remnants of La Familia Michoacana drug cartel based in Michoacán. 'Fight and die' was their motto."

"Yeah. He wanted a blow job too. Mort demanded fifty bucks and they started arguing. That's when Garney grabbed me. He threw me on that mattress and did his thing. Then you guys showed up. He didn't get to shoot his wad, poor baby. I told Mort ahead of time I was only doing hand jobs. I'm tryin' to get over an infection."

"Mort who?" Josh said.

"Mort Lyman. He's the Raiders' Sergeant at arms, whatever the fuck that means. Pushes smack and blow out of his garage. Mort's Garage. He's the guy you shot."

"Who brings the fentanyl?" Cade said.

"Baby, I don't mess with that shit. I like reefer, blow, and whiskey."

"You don't know the source?"

"Wha'd I say?"

Josh took out a pen and pad. "Please give me the names of everyone at the house."

"Are you trying to get me killed?"

"We're trying to save your life," Josh said.

"Y'all ain't narcs, are you? You gotta say so if you are."

"Nope."

She sucked her lips. "Mort Lyman. Known him for years. He's my blow connection. We always got along fine, 'til tonight."

"You ever been to that house before?"

"Couple times. It's Ed McCauley's house."

"Who's the dude tried to rape you?"

"Garney. I seen him around but we never partied. I got to know someone before I let 'em inside."

"Who else?"

"Ed McCauley. Another Raider."

"Could he be the fentanyl source?"

"For the town, sure. But he's too stupid to be some kind of mastermind. You got any downers? I could use something to take the edge off."

"A minute ago, you asked if we had any blow."

"All right, all right. I appreciate what you boys done for me. But sure as shit, they're gonna think I'm squealing."

"Why would they think that?" Cade said.

"'Cause you was there. That's how they think. Anybody shows up, it ain't an accident."

Cade yawned. "You think of anything, where they live, what they do, criminal record, write that down for me."

"I ain't writin' shit. I'll tell you and you can write it."

Josh looked at his pad. "So, we got Ed and Brandon McCauley, Mort Lyman, and Horace Garney. They got day jobs?"

Maybelline snorted. "Mort's the only one who has a visible means of support. Lyman and Garney deal drugs. I didn't know that was Ed's nephew. I ain't never seen him before."

"Do you know where Mort and Horace live?"

"I been to Mort's place. Garage on East Sixteenth Street.

Yard's dead with a couple old tire tractors set up like raised flower beds only there's nothing in 'em but weeds."

"Do you have the address?"

Maybelline shrugged her shoulders and held out her hands.

Cade yawned again. "Let's call it a night. I been at it since four o'clock this morning."

"Yesterday," Josh said, looking at the clock on the table.

Cade leaned forward. "You gonna be here in the morning?"

"Yup," Maybelline said.

"No family?"

"My old man's in Walker doin' a nine-year stint for homicide. My sister won't speak to me. She's married to an insurance salesman in Athens. My brother Ricky disappeared six years ago. He's probably dead. My mother lives in Lavonia. I see her sometimes. Look, let's go over this in the morning. I gotta crash."

Josh and Cade stepped outside, walked across the parking lot to a copse of elm crowding the road.

"She'll be gone in the morning," Cade said.

IN THE SHITTER

Maybelline didn't answer Josh's knock. He went to the office. Murtagh sat behind the counter, feet aimed at a flat screen on a side wall. He muted the TV.

"Don't you sleep?" Josh said.

"I sleep fine rightchere. What can I do you for?"

"You know who deals fentanyl around here?"

Murtagh used a lever to lower his feet. "I ain't smoked a joint in twenty years. I seen too many of my buddies go down. We didn't have no fentanyl back then, but smack and blow will get 'er done."

"Where's a good place to get breakfast?"

Murtagh pointed. "Dolly's Diner. Right across the street."

"Thanks." Josh headed for the door.

"Your friends stayin'?"

"Five is vacant. Don't know about six. Think he's stayin'."

Josh went outside.

Cade stood next to Josh's 300, wearing carpenter pants and a leather jacket over a crew neck shirt. "This your ride?"

"Yeah. Let's get breakfast."

"Where at?"

Josh pointed. "Dolly's Diner."

They waited as light morning traffic buzzed by, pickups bellowing.

"You like that car?"

"It's all right. Been drivin' it for five years. Probably the last car I'll ever own."

"Why's that?"

"No electronics."

"Ed McCauley's been in and out of trouble for twenty-five years. D&D, DUI, possession with intent to distribute."

"Did he serve any time?"

"No. He must have a good lawyer."

They took a booth in the diner and ordered omelets and coffee. Outside, old pickups parked diagonally to the curb. A young man rode by on his ten-speed wearing a helmet.

"That book."

Cade looked out the window. "What about it?"

"My client's name is Bushnell. He said that his great-great-great-grandfather had a feud going with Roderick McCauley. My client's husband was stabbed to death at an outdoor festival. His brother was murdered in Iraq."

"How do you know he was murdered?"

"They called it a fragging. I'm no genius, but I looked it up and Second Lieutenant Stephen Bushnell broke up a drug ring in Karbala. Grunts planning on smuggling heroin back. That much was in the newspapers. You gotta be hooked up to the military to find out who they were or what happened."

"Write it down for me." Cade took out his pad.

"It might be a feud, like the Hatfields and McCoys."

"A feud going back to the Civil War?"

"And still going on today. That could be the reason somebody ripped out those pages."

"Colby's a small town. I have friends whose son died from fentanyl. Kid thought it was MDMA. He went to my daughter's school. Other kids told her he was waiting for a Brandon McCauley to bring some primo ecstasy. I've known that family since I was twelve. We went to high school together. I was overseas when the boy graduated high school. He got a science scholarship to Creighton University. Good-looking kid. I only met him a couple times, but he had everything going for him. His death left my daughter's school devastated and my friends depressed. The police listed it as an accidental overdose, even when they found out it was fentanyl."

"Brandon's the kid with the fadeaway. I put an air tag on his car."

"Let's see it."

Josh pulled out his laptop, set it on the table and poked.

A Google map of Waldrop County, Georgia showing McCauley's location in the Chattahoochee Oconee State Forest off Highway 60. Josh rotated the screen toward Cade.

"That's in the Blue Ridge mountains. There's folks up there who still haven't forgiven the Union. They still make shine, but fentanyl's changed the game. Anything you pop, snort, or ingest'll take it. It's pouring in from Florida and Alabama."

They finished eating. Josh picked up the tab. As they returned to the motel, Josh stopped at a kiosk containing *The Atlanta Journal* as the delivery truck pulled away from the curb. Inserting four quarters, he snagged a copy of the morning edition. It was on page three.

WALDROP COUNTY SHERIFF'S DEPUTIES BUST METH LAB

Responding to a tip, Waldrop County Sheriff's Deputies raided a rural farmhouse late last night, seizing two kilos of meth and a kilo of fentanyl in pill form. Sheriff Tom Woolery says the tip was likely the result of a falling out between thieves. The body of convicted trafficker Horace Garney was found in the living room, hands and feet secured by zip ties. His throat had been cut.

Josh handed it to Cade. Cade read it and handed it back. "You cut the dude's throat?" Josh said.

"I looked you up, Josh. You must have had some kind of help because there's hardly anything, but they couldn't bury your rap sheet. That guy whose arm you cut off with a chainsaw. Did he die?"

Josh felt a deep sense of shame. "I'm not proud of that. I'm no longer that person."

"So, you haven't killed anyone since you got out?"

Josh handled his memories. *I deserve this.* "No one who…" He had been about to say didn't have it coming, but who was he to judge? *Lord Jesus Christ forgive me.*

Cade watched him silently, eyes flat as nickel. "Didn't have it coming? I tell myself that too. I killed my first man in Iraq. I was a Marine."

"But that was war."

"That was war. We're in a kind of war here. Fentanyl's been pouring in from Mexico for three years. It's a war on the young."

"We catch up to whoever was in that cabin, are you gonna kill 'em?"

"That's up to them."

"Don't kill Brandon McCauley before I ask him a few questions."

Cade sighed. "Come on. We'll take my truck."

"Let me get my backpack."

They drove northwest past a sign that said Chattahoochee State Forest. Josh turned on his tracker app.

Cade drove with his elbow in the wind. "Tell me about your client."

Josh told Cade about Jerry, Don, Jaycee, Max and Sam.

"You don't strike me as the PI type," Cade said.

"What's the type?"

"A fortyish cat lady who works from home. Everything's online. You don't even have to get dressed. Dial up Google Earth. Zoom right in on any location."

"You ain't wrong, but sometimes people need someone practical. I also do security."

"You still ride?"

"Yes."

"What do you ride?"

"Ninety-five Road King. You?"

"I ride horses. My daughter likes them."

Josh looked up. "Nine miles, state forest access road on the right. No markings."

They rode in silence for twenty minutes until they came to the turn-off. Cade put the truck in four-wheel drive and they jounced uphill.

"There's a parking lot at the end, where the trail starts."

Cade opened the center bin. "You want that Ruger?"

A Ruger lay on top of two boxes of nine mm.

"Still got that axe?"

Cade snorted. Josh suspected it was as near to laugh as this guy ever got. "Omma pull over here and we'll walk the rest of the way in."

The road followed a creek coming down off Mt. Wiley. They pulled off into a copse of spruce, beech, and hemlock. Cade reached into his toolbox and handed Josh the axe. "I'd feel better if you took that Ruger."

"Oh fuck. Hand it over."

Josh tucked the axe in the back of his pants and carried the Ruger down at his side. They stepped on a boulder to cross the stream. They headed uphill through the trees. The big man moved like a shadow, stepping on hard surfaces, hands in front, Colt tucked into the front of his pants. Ten minutes later, Cade held up his hand and pointed. Through the trees Josh spotted a vehicle. Not McCauley's. Cade circled counterclockwise while Josh headed straight for it. He paused at the tree line, standing in shadow.

A green Subaru station wagon was parked in the gravel lot. It was the only vehicle. Josh watched for long seconds. Across the lot, Cade stepped from the trees, twenty feet behind a carbon fiber outhouse, door shut.

Cade gestured, palms out. Josh knelt, took out his laptop and set it on a rock. There was no reception, but the object they were tracking was somewhere on the lot. The program pinned it down to within an inch. The signal was coming from the outhouse.

Cade padded silently to the outhouse, came around and yanked the door open. He motioned Josh forward.

Josh stood outside the outhouse looking at his laptop. "It's in the shitter."

CHAPTER 30

IN THE BARN

Brandon McCauley inhaled the aroma of hay, horses, and leather, standing one-legged on the hardwood floor of a barn wearing only GI pants, his taut body covered in ink. The goat face of Baphomet covered his back. Skull and crossbones on his left bicep, pentagram on his right. White terry cloth around his head. A Confederate flag hung on one wall, the Polk flag opposite.

McCauley placed his hands together and inhaled deeply, as Sensei Denza had taught. He sank on one leg and sprang into the air, explosively expelling air. McCauley seized a chin-up pole nine feet off the ground and yo-yoed up and down. He dropped silently, like a cat. He sank into a cat stance and flowed through a Uechi-ryu kata. He went through nine more katas and sank to the floor, legs folded, palms together.

"Ommmm."

Last night Darren had phoned. "Fuckin' Bushnells hired a fucking private investigator, man."

"Tell me about it," McCauley said.

McCauley looked Pratt up. All he got was that Pratt was a licensed PI in Wisconsin, and had served four years for assault. Whoever hit his uncle's house killed Garney. McCauley had grabbed eight pounds of fentanyl and three keys of smack on his way out the door and took it to Luthor's place. Once there, he got on his back and slid beneath his car, searching for the transmitter. It was there, glued to the frame. He used a hammer and chisel to bust it loose. He left Luthor's at midnight, returning at four in the morning after depositing the tracker in an outhouse in Chattahoochee State Park.

When McCauley was seventeen, Luthor had reached out to him via Facebook. At that time McCauley was aware of the long-running feud between their families, but didn't take it seriously. That was about to change. Luther drove up from Georgia to meet him. Luther brought primo blow. Luther was the opposite of the historical Bushnells, patriots, veterans, hard-working family men. Except for Jerry. Every family had a loser.

Brandon's breathing was rhythmic and deep. Until it wasn't. His eyes opened, face contorted in anger. "Who the fuck are these fucking *fucks*, and why the *fuck* are they on my case?"

Luther entered the barn in worn coveralls, an off-color cotton pullover, pockmarked face and mullet. "You're back.

When'dja get back?"

"Four. Hope I didn't wake you up."

"No, man. Nothing wakes me up. Whered'dja get those drugs?"

"Ed's."

"What are you gonna do with them?"

"I'm gonna move 'em. You're gonna help."

"Wait a minute. Wait a minute. Since when are we moving weight?"

"Man, how long you been sleeping? Two cowboys raided the farm last night, killed Garney, shot Mort and phoned it in. That bag's all that remains of the last shipment."

"What? What?"

McCauley grabbed a towel off a horse stall and draped it around his shoulders. It was fifty degrees in the barn. "Don Bushnell's family hired an investigator. He trailed me to the farm. That's how they found us."

"Jesus fucking Christ! How?"

"Air tag glued to my chassis. Left it in an outhouse in the Blue Ridge. I have no idea how they got on to me."

"How did you know where to look?"

McCauley spread his hands. "DUH."

"Hired an investigator to find what?"

"Find out who gave their kid a fentanyl-laced joint."

"Did you?"

"Wasn't me, hoss. It may have come from me, but I don't do retail. You knew that, right?"

"What kid?"

"Max."

"Aw shit. How's he doing?"

"He'll live. We gotta move that fentanyl. Diego signed off on it. In fact, he's gonna meet me up there."

"How much?"

"Two keys. We cut it into three keys with the smack. I can move that in Milwaukee in a day. Diego wants me to rep the cartel. But we gotta move fast."

"What's the rush? Who knows you have it?"

"Come on. El Gorila's got informants everywhere. He'll know exactly what the cops copped, and he'll know what's missing. It's only a matter of time before he tracks us down. He'll start with Ed, 'cause it was his op. Ed will give me up in a minute. I want to get that shit to Milwaukee, make the score, and get back here for the battle."

"You got people up there?"

"Yeah I got people."

"What people?"

McCauley smiled. "Need to know, bro. Need to know."

"Are you dealing with a Black gang?"

"Wha'd I say? Why? What do you care?"

"Those motherfuckers are just as bad as the cartels."

"You want to handle it?"

Luthor put his hands up. "That ain't my thing."

"I know what I'm doing."

"You've got eight days before Tunnel Hill. You gonna make it?"

"Piece of cake. I'll leave tomorrow. Right now I gotta

crash. Then I got to mix the shit. Then I'm outta here. All right if I take your car?"

"How'm I gonna get around?"

McCauley reached into his gym bag and tossed Luthor his car keys.

"I ain't gonna get in trouble driving it, am I?"

"What're they gonna do? Give you a ticket? There's no paper on the vehicle. Who's gonna give you shit? The county? They're too busy chasing down illegals. Car's clean. I'll vacuum the floor just to make sure."

"I'll just ride my bike."

McCauley left the barn. The one-story wood frame farmhouse had two bedrooms and one bath. Luthor had filled one bedroom with his Civil War memorabilia which covered the floor. McCauley had to shift a hundred pounds of shit off the bed in order to sleep. He went into the bathroom and showered in the rust-stained tub, toweled off, back to the spare bedroom and threw himself down. He looked in the mirror. He removed the sterling silver skull from his left ear and set it on the counter. In case he was stopped. The investigator bothered him. He was getting weird vibes off the guy. And fuck that motherfucker Jerry. It had never occurred to him that Don's idiot bastard brother, who couldn't even hold a job, had hired a PI. How could he afford it? McCauley had concluded several years ago that there was no point in taking out Jerry. He'd be doing the family a favor.

CHAPTER 31

WAITING FOR A GUY TO GO

Mort's Garage on E. 16th Street had a Confederate flag over the door. A couple derelict cars sat in the dirt yard including a Pinto with a backward flame job. Cade drove around the block and parked on a side street. Faubus seemed exhausted. Calling it working class was being generous. Aside from the bars, hardware, liquor, and convenience stores, it had no industry. Most yards were untended. A woman screamed at her children as they passed a house with a Big Wheels overturned in the front yard. Two Black preteens hung on a porch playing mumblety peg, taking turns tossing a pocketknife at the desiccated wood deck. They looked up once, returned to their game.

An old man wearing coveralls mowed his crabgrass with a push mower. They turned the corner onto 16th. A willow tree shrouded the yard. The garage was closed. They went around to the back, shielded from its neighbors by an abundance of willow, beech, and holly. Two ropes hung from a low-hanging branch, one connected to an ancient plastic swing seat dangling down. The back door was locked. Josh peered in the window. A cot set up next to an industrial sink, a dorm fridge, and a hot plate on the counter. Cade looked around for cameras. He picked a rock up off the ground and smashed the rear window, reached in and unlatched the door. The linoleum floor had turned yellow. The linoleum countertops were covered with smeared detritus attended by flies that buzzed and bumped at the window over the sink, filled with dirty dishes. An empty bottle of Ron Rico sat on the floor next to the cot. The chairs were so old the vinyl had cracked.

Josh opened the refrigerator. Half carton of eggs, a yoke of Dixie beer, old Styrofoam containers. Cade entered the garage whistling "Dixie."

Josh followed. There were two bays, one occupied by an ancient SS 396, the other by a Hyundai sedan. A replica Confederate sword hung on the wall next to a hand-carved sign. "THE SOUTH SHALL RISE AGAIN." A framed denim vest with QUANTRILL'S RAIDERS the top rocker, PROSPECT at the bottom. In between was a skull superimposed on the Confederate flag.

"Mort's in the wind," Josh said.

"Yeah, let's go."

"Wait a minute." Josh reached into his backpack and pulled out another Rainbeo mini cam, which he glued to the back wall next to a wrench hanging from a peg board, indistinguishable among the tools and stains. He turned it on and checked his phone, turning it so that Cade saw the view.

"Nice." Cade nodded.

They went back to Elmo's for dinner. The same waitress took their orders. Josh ordered the pulled pork. Cade ordered the brisket sandwich. Cade reached inside his barn coat and pulled out a white envelope addressed to Morton Lyman. It was from the AAA.

"Morton Lyman served four years in Arrendale for dealing. He got out in 2020, just before the shitstorm hit. Seems he's back to his old tricks."

"What are you gonna do?"

"I'm going to find him, put him out of business."

"You've put a lot of guys out of business. I asked my guy to do a background. There are eighteen unsolved killings in and around Colby, Alabama, going back seven years. All child predators, dealers, or both. You've been a busy boy."

"I wouldn't know."

"What branch of the service were you in?"

"I started as a Marine. I moved around a lot. I was attached to various hunter/killer teams from different branches. Never rose above the rank of private."

"What do you do for a living?"

"You're kinda nosy."

"Comes with the territory."

"I raise horses. I'm trying to talk my uncle into going legitimate with his whiskey."

"There's money in that."

"Always has been. But it's past time he went legal."

"How we gonna find Lyman?"

"We?"

"I just keep pulling at threads. It's what I do."

Cade shrugged. "That's fine. You seem competent. I like the way you used that axe."

"I've been practicing. How we gonna find Lyman?"

"He rides a 2011 Fat Bob, registered to that garage."

"Do you have a picture?"

Cade brought up a black-and-white photo on his phone, Civil War reenactors. He'd circled Lyman with a black felt tip, a gangly guy with a big Adam's apple, knobby wrists showing between his hands and the gray sleeve of his Confederate uniform posing with three other reenactors.

"Your theory may be right. I believe these good ol' boys have been going at it for one hundred and eighty years. Eight years ago, Ed McCauley's sister Emma was the victim of a hit and run. In 1934, Nicholas McCauley was shot and killed in Quiller, Georgia"

"You think a Bushnell did it?"

Cade shrugged. "I don't care. That's not why I'm here. My goals are more short-term."

"Send me that photo. I got a guy who can put it in a program and see if anything pops up. He's got video at every 7-Eleven in America."

"Can he do criminal records?"

"Yeah. I'll call him when we get back to the motel."

"Can he access police data systems?"

"Probably."

Their food came. Conversation ceased. Other customers talked among themselves, A basketball game hung from the ceiling. A jacked-up pickup was the loudest thing in town.

Cade wiped his mouth on a paper towel. "How soon can you get in touch with your friend?"

"I'll call him. He usually calls back after a few minutes."

"Your phone safe?"

"It's a burner he gave me. I should probably ditch it and take out the next one."

"Are you on any lists?"

"Dubious."

"How do you know you're not on any lists?"

"'Cuz my guy sweeps once a week."

"Really. I might like an introduction."

"He'll check you out."

"Good luck. What I'll need him to do is break into the State of Georgia Highway Department and see if McCauley used a toll road recently. Video automatically records every license, and if you don't have a Peach Pass, they send you a bill. I'll send you the details and that pic."

Cade pulled out Josh's card and texted Josh. "Now you have mine."

When the bill came, Josh reached for it. Cade closed a vise-like hand around his wrist.

"Are you using a credit card?"

"Yeah."

"I'll get it."

Cade left a twenty-dollar tip and they went across the street to the little town square with the band cupola in the center, and a monument to Confederate War dead, a Johnny Reb in ragged uniform helping a wounded comrade, holding a flagstaff in the other hand. You could see where the stars and bars had been removed.

Cade took pics while Josh phoned Kleiser.

"The number you have reached is not in service at this time."

Five minutes passed. Josh walked around the park, admiring the Confederate statue, walking around the block. A bronze statue of John Bell Hood. Cade came up, read the plaque affixed to the marble base.

Born in Owingsville, Kentucky in 1831 and a West Point Graduate at the age of 22, John Bell Hood was one of the most rapidly promoted leaders in the Confederate history of the Civil War. He joined the Confederacy as a cavalry captain in 1861. He was soon promoted to colonel of the Texas 4th Infantry. He distinguished himself in the Peninsula Campaign and at Second Manassas. At the Battle of Gaines's Mill on June 27, he led his brigade in a charge that broke the Union line—arguably the most successful Confederate performance in the Seven Days Battles. While Hood escaped the battle without an injury, every officer in his brigade was killed or wounded.

Promoted to lieutenant general under J.E Johnston, Hood launched four major offensives trying to break Sherman's siege of Atlanta. They all failed with significant Confederate casualties. Finally, on September 2, 1864, Hood evacuated the city of Atlanta, burning as many military supplies and installations as possible.

Hood marched his army into Tennessee where his forces were crippled trying to break through Union breastworks at the Battle of Franklin. His army suffered again at the Battle of Nashville from Union forces led by General Thomas. Hood was relieved of his rank (at his own request) in January of 1865 and returned to his post as lieutenant general. In May 1865, Hood gave himself up to Union forces in Natchez, Mississippi. After the war, Hood moved to New Orleans and lived there with his wife and children until he died in 1879 of yellow fever.

The two men stared at the plaque in silence. Josh's phone rang.

"Yeah?"

"What do you need?"

Josh told him. "I'm sending you the pictures."

"Wait wait wait."

"What?"

"Let me give you a different email address. Ready?"

"Shoot."

"Fasteddy19@upchuck.net."

"Seriously?"

"Don't worry about it. I'm trying out some new shit."

Josh sent the data. He gave Cade the thumbs up.

Cade gestured. "Let's walk around the neighborhood. These old neighborhoods in the Deep South feel like home."

They crossed the street and headed west on Arcadia Street, lined with willow, elm, oak and distinguished two-story southern houses with wrap-around porches, many on the second floor. It was a quiet neighborhood. They passed a young mother wheeling her child in a carriage. Cade touched his forehead.

"Ma'am," Josh said. They stopped to admire a red stone antebellum mansion with a porte cochere over a circular red brick drive. Josh's phone rang.

"Your vehicle entered a parking garage at 457 Mickelson St. in St. Evans. That's fifteen miles from your present location."

"Thanks, Randall."

Josh snapped his phone shut. "Let's go. Four fifty-seven Mickelson in St. Evans."

Twenty minutes later, they cruised past the four-level concrete parking garage adjacent to St. Evans State Bank. St. Evans was twice the size of Faubus, big enough to throw down the roadside sentinels that stand at every city's gates. McDonald's. Arby's. Popeye's Chicken. Taco John.

Cade turned into the ramp and headed down to the basement. And there, on the bottom level, parked in a corner by itself was an old Toyota pickup. Cade backed into a space a hundred feet away. A video cam covered the level.

"I have another air tag."

Cade looked around. "Let's sit on him and follow him. There's only one entrance."

They pulled out and parked facing the garage a half block down.

AN IRRESISTIBLE OFFER

Brandon pulled into the parking lot of Belgravia, the upscale condominium development on the outskirts of Gainesville, his beaten Corolla looking out of place next to an electric Mercedes. Shouldering his backpack, he entered the elegant foyer and pushed the button for Guttierez. Seconds later, the door buzzed and he entered, taking the stairs two steps at a time to the second floor, down the carpeted hallway, roses and chrysanthemums on green, to unit two-forty-seven. The door was unlocked.

Brandon went in and saw that the patio door was open. Diego sat on the deck smoking a Cohiba and gazing out at the woods that came up to the tennis courts.

"Out here," he said through clenched teeth.

Brandon went out on the patio and sat in a wrought iron chair angled toward the trees and toward Diego. In his mid-forties, Diego was fit as a marathoner, his black hair cut short except for the bushy mustache. Diego had purchased the unit at the start of the pandemic, anticipating what was to come. The cartel had eyes and ears in Washington and was well aware of its plans for the border.

They owned the property on Briar Valley Road. They made Ed an offer he couldn't refuse. Now that Ed's place was compromised, they would move their activity to Briar Valley.

Diego offered Brandon a cigar.

"No thanks."

Diego grinned. "Cocaine si, tobacco no. Whatchoo got?"

Brandon unzipped the backpack and dumped eight pounds of fentanyl and three keys of smack on the glass tabletop.

"Good boy! I thought those pendejos would get everything."

"They didn't take anything. They called the fucking cops."

Diego put his hands behind his head and stretched. "Who are they? Why would they do that?"

"Vigilantes."

"How they find out?"

"Fuck if I know."

Diego leaned forward and aimed the cigar at Brandon. "You have no idea?"

"There was some trouble in Milwaukee. Some choir boy ended up in the hospital and his mother hired a private detective to find out where he got the fentanyl-laced marijuana."

"Fentanyl-laced marijuana," Diego said carefully. "Who would do such a thing? Hmmm?"

"I know a guy. He said he could move weight."

"What guy?"

Brandon leaned forward to match Diego's posture. "Have you heard of the Vice Lords?"

"So you are saying he got the fentanyl from you?"

"It's possible. I gave an ounce to a friend. I've known him since grade school."

Diego sighed. "You know, Brandon, I respect you. That thing with the hand…" He threw hands like Elvis Presley in a concert. "You one tough hombre. You smart. But maybe not that smart. Where is your friend now?"

"I don't know. I had to get out of town, but I'm heading back, and I have a buyer."

"Is it your friend?"

"No. I'm not stupid. I'll have a little talk with him."

"Who is it?"

"Vice Lords."

"A little talk. Maybe he needs something stronger."

"That's not the message we wish to send."

"No? What message should we send?"

"This woman who hired the detective. She's a zealot. She won't quit until she traces that fentanyl back to the source. That is the message we need to send. I want to make a statement."

"Milwaukee is far from the border."

"Not that far. I'm not the only one running drugs. Mexican Posse, Surenos, La Raza all have a piece of the pie. If we send a message, it will also serve to put these other groups on notice."

"Yes, but those groups you mentioned. Mexican Posse and those other two. Those are Latino groups and Vice Lords are black. Why would we not wish to align ourselves with other groups who might prove more simpatico?"

Brandon rubbed his forefinger and thumb together. "Vice Lords are bigger, stronger, more fearless. There's nothing they won't do. They can handle the weight. Come with me. See for yourself."

Diego blew a smoke ring.

"When are you leaving?"

"This morning."

"I would like to join you but I have business here first. Why don't you go ahead, meet with your Vice Lords, let me know what happened, and perhaps by then, I will be free to join you."

"I could pick you up at the airport."

Diego laughed. "No. If I come, I will drive. I'm very curious about what happens in Milwaukee. I've been meaning to go up and there and see for myself."

"It would be great if you'd help deliver the message."

Diego spread his hands. "We'll see what we shall see."

"Now's the time. The cops are stretched paper thin. We'll be in and out before they can say boo."

"Have you ever killed a man?"

"Yup."

Diego gazed without blinking. "I believe you. I would even believe you did it with your bare hands."

"I used a knife."

"Aye, caramba! Maybe I come up to see how you do things."

"I'll show you a good time. I'll get you laid."

Diego laughed. "I never have no problem. Where's that girl Maybelline you talked about? Can you send her over here?"

"Uh, I think she's outta the picture. She had a bad experience with Garney."

"Horace Garney? The man they found?"

"Yeah. He wasn't exactly gentle."

"You got to know how to treat the ladies. You know how to treat the ladies, Brandon?"

"I never had a problem."

"You have someone in your life?"

"I got two or three. Well listen. Thanks for the cigar. I gotta get going. I got two days to drive eight hundred miles."

"You should be able to do that in a day, amigo."

"I gotta get my eight. I'm no good when I don't have enough rest. I'll call you when I get there."

"Wait here."

Diego went into the condo and returned a minute late with a black phone. "Use this. Use the prerecorded number under recents. You can use this maybe nine or ten times before anybody notices. You want me to bring anything?"

"Maybe some hardware."

"I'll bring hardware. You send me details. I want to know the address, I want to know who lives there, and I want to know who else is involved."

"Thanks for the stogie."

Brandon stopped for gas at a Loaf & Jug on the way out of town. Three sixty-three a gallon. Thirty-five bucks to top it off, half what he paid to fill the Dodge with premium. Luthor's piece of shit Corolla was so old it had a cassette player. Brandon dug around in the center console and pulled out *Workingman's Dead*. It could have been worse. He slipped it in the deck, drove through town and hit the interstate.

CHAPTER

33

ELVIS

Lyman's truck emerged twenty minutes later. They followed at a discreet distance southeast on State Highway 27. A half mile ahead, the truck turned left onto Davis Drive, winding blacktop with the consistency of dried cheese. Lyman was out of sight around the bend. The ditches were filled with trash. Discarded cans and bottles, ripped plastic trash bags, in contrast to the trees that rose on either side.

Josh rode shotgun with his elbow in the wind. "What's with all the trash?"

"It's a hillbilly thing," Levon said from behind the wheel.

"What do you know about the Evans State Bank?"

"Nothing, yet."

Around the corner, four vultures picked at roadkill. It looked like it was a raccoon once. They passed an aluminum gate on a dirt road. TRESPASSERS WILL BE VIOLAT-ED. A mile on, Josh glimpsed something gleaming through the trees.

"Wait a minute."

Cade stopped. "What?"

"Back up to that dirt road."

Cade put the truck in reverse and pulled onto the shoulder. A chain hung between two pipe stanchions buried in concrete. The dirt road twisted out of sight but as the wind blew they heard the clink of glass on glass.

"Pull ahead a quarter mile. Let's take a look."

Cade stopped at a roadside clearing heaped with trash. Josh got the drone out of the truck bed, set up his laptop and put on the control goggles. "You'll see what I see on the laptop. It's just easier for me to control when I wear the headset."

The drone rose silently and scraped treetops toward the northwest, the view showing the rolling hills. From above, they looked like fields of broccoli. A clearing appeared, a sharecropper's shack with an overflowing dumpster in the yard, four chops, a Toyota pickup parked next to last year's Corvette, and a black Denali.

"That's money," Cade said. "See if you can get the license plate."

Josh dropped the drone to six feet, sticking close to the woods, and zeroed in on the Vette's license. Cade wrote it down. They did the same for the Denali. Pops like firecrackers. Cade pointed to his ears.

"You hear that?"

Josh brought the drone to a hundred feet and trained the camera on the backyard. Three men, backs to the house, plinking at a row of bottles balanced on a two-by-four between two saw horses. Three bottles remained intact. The ground behind was littered with broken glass. One of the men wore a white bandage on his left arm.

"Can you get a frontal view?"

"If they don't look up."

Josh brought the drone around in a curve hovering a hundred feet beyond the bottles, zooming in on the three men. Left to right: Lyman, arm bandaged, wearing a dirty wife beater and a Braves cap, a swarthy man with a shaggy black mustache in a leather vest, cig stuck to his lip, and a slim, colorless man wearing carpenter pants, a button-down short-sleeved shirt, glasses, with a bad comb-over. Lyman pulled out a pint bottle of whiskey, took a drag, passed it around.

Mustache gripped his automatic in both hands, took aim and fired, missing the bottle. Josh heard tinny laughter over the drone's directional speaker. The man at the end, who looked like he'd wandered out of an accounting office, pointed at the drone and said something. The others stared. They raised their weapons and fired.

The feed stopped, replaced by a flat gray screen.

"Shit! They shot my drone!"

"Lucky shot," Cade said. "Maybe we should go."

They headed back toward town. "Can they trace you through that drone?"

"I had to enter a hard-drive connection but they won't be able to trace that laptop, even if they get the address. I'm its fifth owner. Each time it got swiped and encrypted."

"Ask your tech guy."

"I will when we stop. No bars out here."

They rode in silence. Cade braked for a doe and two

fawns. It was four fifteen when Cade pulled around to the back of the Laurel Pub and Tavern on East Main Street. The street right in front of the bar was marked in red paint. RESERVED FOR CYCLES. Cade went around the block and parked on the opposite side in a residential area. Josh grabbed his backpack. As they walked around the block, they passed old wooden houses with porches. People spoke softly and looked at the stars. Main Street glowed. They walked past Hern Mortgages, around the corner, and in through the front. On the left, the bar with two flat screens at either end, red vinyl stools, and five booths on the right. There was a pool table in back next to a short hall leading to the restrooms.

They took a booth, table carved with initials. The Laurel had a high ceiling crisscrossed with ducts and an old juke-box mercifully silent. A skinny, long-haired blond sashayed over in cut-offs and a Laurel T.

"What'll it be, boys?"

"You got Hellbender?"

"Yup."

"Shot of Hellbender and an Orpheus chaser."

She looked at Josh. "I'll have the same."

At this hour, there were only two other customers, two men seated at opposite ends of the bar bending over their drinks. The bartender was a bald fire hydrant with a black arm garter. His expression never changed.

"Getting back to your job," Cade said, "you think these families have been going at it since the Civil War?"

Josh shrugged. "I've known people to kill for less. This Brandon McCauley. I spoke to his kung fu instructor. Says the kid's crazier than a shithouse rat. Into Aleister Crowley, Kenneth Anger, Gurdjieff. Pentagram and devil tats."

"Kung fu instructor?"

"Yeah. The instructor's cool."

"You read that shit about the McCauleys trying to hire Marie Laveau?"

"Yeah, ended up with some Haitian voudou shaman."

"You remember when the Misfits tried to break into her tomb?"

"Huh?"

"Nineteen eighty-four. Punk rock musicians arrested in a cemetery."

"Crazy shit."

"Nothing surprises me anymore," Cade said.

The waitress brought their drinks. "You have a chance to look at the menu?"

"We're just drinking," Cade said. She went away.

Five minutes passed in silence. A basketball game played above the bar.

"Did your ancestors fight in the Civil War?" Josh asked.

Cade gazed into infinity. "My great-great-great-grandfather fought for the Confederacy. My great-great-grandfather fought in World War One. My great-grandfather fought in World War Two. My grandfather fought in Korea and my father fought in Vietnam."

"You should write a book."

Cade shook his head. "I'm not a writer."

"You could tell it to a writer, he could write it down and you could split the profits."

A rare grin from Cade. "You want another?"

"Sure."

Cade signaled for two more shots and chasers. They sat in companionable silence while a slender woman in hip-hugging jeans and high hair pushed coins in the juke. "Sweet Home Alabama" started to play.

"I could have predicted that one," Cade said.

"You go out for live music?"

"Nope."

"I do. The pastor played a lot of jazz and blues."

"Well this is the country for it."

"Elvis played Madison. It was before my time. While he's cruising through town, he sees a teenager on the ground, being attacked by two punks. Elvis's limo swerves in, Elvis leaps out. He's wearing a blue leather jumpsuit with sequins and fringe on the arms. He sinks into a karate stance. Does a few moves, you know. Like toward the end. 'I'll take you all on,' he snarls.

"The two punks look at each other, kid on the ground gets up. They're gob-smacked. 'Are you Elvis?' Tosses off a few more moves. 'What do you think?'

"Story in the paper next day says he was overweight and had jet black hair."

Cade gazed, bemused. "Ahuh."

Josh pulled out his phone. "I'll show ya." Seconds later, he handed the phone to Cade. Picture of an engraved marble block: "On this site on June 4, 1977, Elvis Presley was riding in the second of two limousines. Elvis noticed a youth being beaten by two other youths at the Skylar Service Station..."

The corner of Cade's mouth twitched. He slid the phone

back across the table. Motorcycles roar from outside filled the air. Josh leaned and looked out the window where several bikers were backing their bikes to the curb. The thin girl was bopping next to the juke, hands up, hair swirling. Four men entered, dense and gnarly. They went to the bar. Two stood, two sat. Their denim vests showed a skull on top of the Stars 'n' Bars. The top rocker said QUANTRILL'S RAIDERS. The bottom said FAUBUS. One of the men stared at them in the mirror. Ed McCauley.

They ordered drinks. A man in denims, leather vest, boots, buzzcut and beard, spun on his stool, back to the bar, and pulled out his phone. He scrolled. He looked up and met Josh's gaze, holding it longer than necessary.

Cade reached into his jacket pocket. He put the brass knuckles on beneath the table, folding his hands when he'd finished. The brass was too dull to reflect light. Josh looked around for a weapon. All he had was a folding knife, and two beer bottles.

He put his laptop away.

CHAPTER 34

A FRANK AND HONEST EXCHANGE OF IDEAS

The bikers stared at Josh and Cade in the mirror. The bartender lined up shots. The bikers threw back. They grabbed their beer chasers. The leader swiveled back to the bar.

"Hey Mel," Ed said to the fire hydrant.

"Hey Ed."

McCauley leaned over the bar and spoke softly. Mel glanced over.

Josh motioned to the door. Cade shook his head.

"You know anything about seventh sons?"

"Isn't that an old blues song?" Cade said, keeping his eyes on the bar.

"Some people take it literally. I think Brandon McCauley thinks he's the seventh son of a seventh son. He's into voodoo."

Cade gazed placidly at Josh. "Really."

"Yeah. You read that in the book, didn't you? And that

bit with Marie Laveau and the voodoo hougan?"

"People down here believe all sorts of things. That doesn't make them true."

"I'm thinking maybe we can use that against him."

"It would be simpler to just kill him."

The Raiders sauntered over, arms akimbo, big steps, McCauley in charge.

"Was that you in my house last night?"

Cade raised his eyebrows. "Me? I don't think so. Why? What happened?"

McCauley reached behind him. Cade swiveled and planted his size fourteen boot in McCauley's gut. McCauley flew backward, knocking down the guy behind him. An automatic pistol clattered to the floor. Josh catapulted himself out of the booth, grabbed the nearest Raider by the neck and pulled him into a knee.

The table was bolted to the floor. Cade gripped the back end and ripped it loose, swinging it like a bat, striking the skinhead in the forehead.

"GODDAMMIT, McCAULEY!" the bartender said. "What did I tell you?"

Josh grabbed a Raider with Juice stitched on the vest, swung him into a booth-mounted hat rack.

Shotgun blast. Everybody froze. The Raiders turned to see the bartender standing in front cradling a twelve-gauge Remington. Drywall dribbled to the floor. McCauley straightened up, flicked dust off his shoulders, and smiled. "We'll see you boys later."

The Raiders left, the last one dancing backward on bent legs flipping them the bird. Engines roared, growled into the street, receding until there was silence.

"Thanks," Josh said.

"I heard about you," Mel said. "Some kind of detective from up north."

"Nailed it."

Mel turned to Cade, who leaned against the wall with his arms crossed. "You, I don't know."

"And you don't want to."

The barrel drooped toward the floor. Mel turned to Josh. "What's your story?"

Josh handed him one of his cards.

"Well if that don't beat all. You're the first private eye I ever met."

"I'm sure there will be others."

"Can you talk about those good ol' boys?" Cade said.

"Nope. Not 'til I know what you're doin' here."

"Boy I know from Milwaukee. Scholar. Athlete. Smoked a fentanyl-laced joint and nearly died. His mother asked me to find out where he got the dope."

Mel went behind the bar, drew two beers and set them on the table. "That's our dirty little secret. Faubus where they mix that shit with other shit. You obviously know all about it. Let me give you a piece of advice. The QRs don't mess around. There are five guys they killed I know about."

Cade lifted the amber glass and glugged half. He set the glass down. "Have they done time?"

"Yeah, McCauley served four years for distributing along with his pals Lyman and Garney."

"It bother you?" Josh said.

"Does what bother me?"

"Surrounded by drug dealers, no cops."

Mel rested his chin in his hand. "Not me. I'm ready for it. I ain't the only one. I don't mess in their business, they don't mess in mine."

"Law ever come?"

Mel poured himself a shot of bourbon. "Last year. Couple boys drag-racing. They collided right out in the town square. Wasn't enough left to fill a tobacco pouch."

"Sheriff's department?" Josh said.

"That's right. Sheriff Woolery. You don't mess with the sheriff. He used to be Georgia State Amateur Heavyweight, two years in a row."

"What about our friends? They waiting to jump us when we leave?"

"I wouldn't put it past them. You can always leave through the alley."

"What do you know about those guys?"

"I think I've said enough. I got to live here."

Cade shrugged. "Fair enough. We're not police. We just want to find whoever's responsible."

"I understand."

A guy in a yellow shirt with a bandanna tied around his head pushed through the door, saluted.

"Hey Bri."

"Hey Mel. Sorry it took so long."

"You missed all the excitement."

Bri looked around. "What happened?"

"McCauley and his gang started a fight with these guys. I stopped it with this." He hefted the shotgun.

Everyone looked at the hole in the ceiling.

"This here's Bri. Bri-Dog. I'm goin' home to watch football. Roll Tide."

Bri shook hands.

"We'd better go," Cade said, walking around the bar.

Through a dimly lit storeroom out the steel door. Lights glowed in a corrugated Quonset hut backed up to the alley. Oily pools of water reflected rainbow colors. They walked in silence. They turned left at the end of the alley and walked away from Main Street down Kuhner Road. Cade had parked a half block away and around the corner. A family sat in silence, the mother feeding her newborn formula, the father chewing tobacco.

They got in the truck.

Cade started the engine. "Maybe we shouldn't go back to the motel. It's the only motel within ten miles."

"Where?"

"Let's go to Haspierre and talk to the sheriff. You can buy whatever you need there."

They drove out of town on Tabasco Road. They passed a couple vehicles in the winding wooded hills. Five minutes passed quietly, wind whistling through the open windows.

"So what do you want with these dealers? I mean, I know

what I want. But what do you want."

"I want them gone."

"Aren't you worried someone's gonna notice?"

"I didn't say I was *going* to kill them. I said I *wanted* to. We'll get together and see how it goes."

"Nice truck."

"Thanks."

"What other guns you got?"

THE REGISTRY

The Raiders roared down Highway 27 turning off at the entrance to Lyman's place. Lyman got off his bike and unlocked the chain. After the others had passed, he rolled through and relocked the chain. They kicked out in the dirt yard before the porch. Lyman and McCauley tossed paint lids on the ground for their kickstands.

They went inside. Lester flopped on the sprung sofa and put his Red Wings on the telephone spool table. The hand-blown bong wobbled and would have fallen but Ed caught it. Meth made him fast. It also made him mean. Ed went into the kitchen and returned with a clear gallon jug of shine. The boys grabbed their Dixie cups and filled up. The skinhead flopped in a thrift store recliner, pulled out a vial of white powder and dumped it on a smeared face mirror. Dukey was stitched on his vest. Ed went back into the kitchen and returned with the remains of the blasted drone. Half the body had torn off leaving two rotors and a lens.

"Anybody know anything about this shit?"

Lyman picked it up, turned it around, tossed it on the spool. "You might ask Guttierez."

"That's fuckin' brilliant, Lester. Ask the fuckin' boss if he can help find the dudes who been spying on us. What are we gonna tell him about the product we lost?"

Lester lit a cigarette with a Bic. "As if he doesn't already know."

"Lester right," Ed said. "We should think about our next move. We should think about buggin' out."

Ed tossed back his Dixie cup. "Fuck that, man. We're the Raiders. We don't run."

Lester leaned forward, forearms on knees. "Dude. This is the fuckin' cartel. We do not want to mess with them. They're not impressed by our colors."

Dukie sucked blow through a straw, snorked, ran a finger. "I'm with Ed. We got a reputation to uphold."

Ed reached for the mirror. "You got an idea?"

"Yeah. We find those fuckin' rednecks and get it back."

"How we gonna do that?"

"Y'know that old motel on the north end of town? I think I saw that pickup in there."

"Violet Estates? Yeah, I know it. Owner's a biker."

"He's a nigger," Dukie said.

"Jesus, Dukie. Get your head straight. He's a biker first and black second."

Ed's phone buzzed. He pulled it out. He went outside.

He came back in. "Guttierez is coming tomorrow. He wants his money and he's dropping off five keys."

"Shit," Drake said. "SHIT! What are we gonna do?"

Ed stuck his hands in his belt. "Maybe it's time we cut ties with him."

Lyman shook his head. "You been smokin' too much marijuana. We can't stand up to the cartel."

Dukie did another line. "I don't know."

"I been thinking about this a lot," Ed said. "Since before last night's clusterfuck. There are three hundred Raiders. We all have guns and know how to use 'em. Fuckin' cartels operate in this country like they own it. We'd be heroes."

"How many men do the cartels have?" Lyman said.

"This is the fuckin' US of A. We have home field advantage. Guttierez's gonna have four or five sicarios. We hit 'em, leave the bodies with Confederate flags pinned to their chests, they'll get the message."

"And next time," Lester said, "they'll bring fifty."

"I'm counting on that. We set a trap. We know they'll come. We can get twice as many Raiders to meet 'em."

"Then we'll have local authorities on our ass as well. They leave us alone 'cuz we stay under the radar."

"Are you fuckin' kidding me? Show some cojones. Our ancestors fought at Shiloh and Gettysburg."

"This is dope talkin'," Lyman said.

Ed got in his face. "You call yourself a war counselor?"

"I need time to think about it."

"Well don't take too long. Guttierez is gonna be here

tomorrow, and what then? We only got half the money, and half the dope."

"We outta cruise by that motel, see if those rednecks got it," Lyman said.

Ed poured more shine. "Fuck that. They're fuckin' Boy Scouts. They called the pigs to raid the farm. That's how we lost it in the first place. Cops said they recovered two keys."

"Yeah," Lester said. "But there were five keys. Maybe ask your nephew."

"My nephew?" Ed sneered. "That boy is down. He wouldn't take our shit."

"Maybe ask him?" Lester said.

Ed snorted and pulled out his phone. He waited. "Brandon. It's Ed. Call me." He looked at his watch. Ten-twenty. "Let's cruise that motel. Maybe we'll catch a break."

They roared through town. The Violet Estates sign glowed neon purple by the side of the road. A couple of widely spaced beaters in the parking lot, no truck. The Raiders kicked out in front of the office. The lights were on. Inside, Easy Peazy turned from the TV, where he'd been watching the Bulldogs/Gators game, and put his feet on the floor. Ed, Lyman, Nelson, and Dukie swept in bringing the scent of marijuana and unwashed bodies. Easy stood.

"What's up?"

Ed extended his fist. "Ed McCauley. We met at Maxwell Street Days in 2010."

Easy extended his fist. "Oh yeah. I remember. What can I do for you?"

"Lookin' for two guys. One's a Yankee, thirty-something, buzz cut, scar here." McCauley traced a line from his left eyebrow to his chin. "Other's a big ol' good ol' boy. Six-two or three, dark hair, GI Joe beard, drives a truck."

Easy shrugged. "Can't help you."

"Mind if I look at your registry?"

"Yeah."

"Yeah what? I can, or you mind?"

"I mind. This here's a private business."

"Give you a hunnert bucks."

"Sorry."

Lyman leaned on the counter. "How 'bout you just leave the room for a minute?"

"I ain't goin' anywhere."

Ed grimaced. "You think you can stop us?"

Easy looked at Dukie. "What happened to you?"

"I forgot to duck."

"How bout it, Easy?"

Easy reached under the counter and pulled out a .357 magnum. He placed it on the counter then held it by his side.

"I'm getting the impression you might be lying," Ed said.

"Ain't told a lie yet. I said I can't help you."

"You as much as admitting you know these men."

"How do you get that? Maybe I'm just ethical and don't show private records to anyone who walks through the door."

"Do you know how many Raiders we got?"

"Do you know how many Outcasts there are?" Easy gestured with his thumb to the picture on the wall.

Dukie snorted. "We're s'posed to be scared about a bunch of geriatric n—spades?"

Easy fixed him with a stare.

Ed turned. "Let's go."

Easy watched them go. Their bikes made the windows rattle. Gradually the sound faded. Easy picked up his phone and hit the button on a familiar number.

"Whatchoo need, old man?" a man answered.

"May be nothin'. May be somethin'. May need your help."

"Want me to stop by?"

"If you would be so kind."

DARREN

It was just past midnight as Darren strolled through City Park, sucking on his vape. That shit he got from Mulgrew was heinous. Hash oil that was fifty-five percent pure THC. Darren couldn't have been higher if he were an astronaut. Every now and then he'd put the vape away and snorted coke through another little device he'd purchased at a head shop in Madison.

It was a crisp, clear November night and Darren wore his black leather jacket, Doc Martens, blue jeans, and snap-brimmed fedora like the gangster he imagined himself to be. He'd seen a young woman seated on a bench sketching in a pad six hours earlier. He didn't suppose she was still around. Of course not. A proper young woman didn't go out alone after dark. If she was smart, she didn't go out at all. Crime flooded the burbs. Darren rode the wave. He'd started shop-lifting when he was ten years old. When a shopkeeper finally put his hand on Darren's shoulder, reached into his jacket pocket and removed a pack of batteries in their hard plastic case, Darren bolted like a rabbit and never went back.

Man, what wouldn't he give to fuck her socks off. Or any nubile female. Darren did a decent impression of a normal guy when he was straight. You know who he'd really like to fuck? Sam Bushnell. Darren knew his friend Brandon was obsessed with the Bushnells, but it had nothing to do with Sam. Brandon would get high and babble incoherently for hours. Sometimes he spoke in tongues, quoted Aleister Crowley, or prayed to Baphomet. He told Darren he sacrificed animals. Dogs and cats, mostly. He lured them treats, shove them in a bag, and hang them in the park. He quit when it started to garner national attention.

Darren worked for a landscaping company but who knew how long that would last. He'd already kuiped enough electric drills, paint and tools to open his own store. Didn't know how much longer it would last. He'd overheard a manager and a bossman talking about the thefts last week and it was only a matter of time before they zeroed in on him. It certainly wasn't his work. Darren's carpentry was top-notch. He'd learned from his father, who left one night to go visit some friends and never returned. Darren was thirteen. His mother started hitting the bottle and was still hard at it, but she'd added oxy and blow to the menu. It was a miracle she was still alive. In addition to her post office pension, she was on disability, living alone in the little stone cottage where he'd been raised, not a mile from where he walked. He'd thought about taking out a fat life insurance policy, but the dope made her mean and suspicious.

The last time he'd dropped by, she couldn't answer the phone. He found her lying face down in the living room, a pool of drool beneath her chin. Disgusted, he'd dragged her into the bathroom, stripped her repulsive body and washed her like he'd wash a dog. He toweled her off, put her in bed and drew the covers. He rifled through the fridge. Bitch had nothin'. Darren didn't know how she survived. He rifled through her purse. Sixty bucks. Fat city. He took forty. She'd need the twenty to take the cab to the psychiatrist who gave her the oxy.

Darren walked close to the hedge, blending in with the dark. He'd been that way his whole life. Move in darkness. Try not to be noticed. One day he noticed a whacko doing martial arts in the park. Whacko had a shaved head and tats all over his torso and arms.

Darren stopped and pulled out his phone. "Yo! Mind if I take a picture?"

The guy strode right at him like a locomotive. Darren backed up, holding up his hands placatingly. "Whoa, buddy! That's why I ask! I wouldn't take a picture without permission!"

Darren would have turned and run had anyone else noticed. The guy got in his face. He wasn't much older than Darren. He suddenly smiled and relaxed.

"It's cool, bro. It's cool."

"What was that you were doing?"

"Mantis style kung fu."

"That is some cool shit. You can probably take me out with one blow, right?"

"I could. I'm Brandon McCauley."

They shook.

"McCauley?"

"That's right."

"Are you related to McCauleys who fought in the Civil War?"

"How do you know about that?"

"I got a friend talks about it all the time. His uncle is like, whack. His father got murdered ten years ago and my friend says it may have something to do with a curse."

Brandon rubbed his hands together. "I'm all about the curse."

"Cool cool."

"Is your friend Max Bushnell?"

"Yeah. How'd you know?"

"Being a McCauley, I learned all about how the Bushnells ditched them as soon as the war began. How the Bushnells raided his farm, killed a six-year-old and a woman. It's part of my tribal memory. It's in my DNA. It's all my kin would talk about at the dinner table."

"Weird. Yeah, Max and I have been tight since junior high. I'd like to fuck his sister."

"Is she cute?"

"Man, she's at that age. Just right."

"Have you asked her out?"

"Yeah. Fuck no. Those were her exact words. Fuck no."

"Why not?"

"Thanks for asking. Because I'm a creep and a loser. Her words, not mine."

"Got any reefer?"

Darren led Brandon into a dense copse, pulled out a joint and lit up. Soon they were seeing dinosaurs. Brandon laid down on the mossy ground staring up through the trees.

"Check it out. The view's different from down here."

Darren lay down and looked up. It was June and the trees throbbed and flashed like Steve Ditko hyper space. Darren felt a weight on his thigh. It was Brandon, tentatively running his hand. Darren bounced up.

"I'm not that way, dude! Not that there's anything wrong with it."

"Yeah, 's cool. Just checkin' you out."

"Well don't check me out!"

Brandon sat up. "I get it, man! You're straight! No problem. Where'd you get that weed?"

"Some guy I know works construction."

"Yeah, it's good."

"You want a line?"

The sudden tinkle of tin yanked him out of his reverie. He was alone in a park after midnight. Darren grabbed his balisong from his pocket and flipped it open. The blade was black. He was eager to use it.

"Hey man," said an adolescent voice. "You got any reefer?"

"What the fuck."

A wan kid with a mop of blond hair stepped out of the shrubs. Leaves and straw lay in his hair. He looked like he might have been sleeping, and Darren bet that if he looked, he'd find a sleeping bag and maybe a supermarket shopping cart filled with goods. "I can get you high, I guess. Who the fuck are you?"

"Lewis. I'm Lewis. Thanks, man. A little reefer goes a long way toward easing the pain."

Darren drew a reefer from his inside jacket pocket. "What pain?"

"The pain of this meaningless existence in a world built by fools."

"The fuck. H'old are you?"

Lewis grinned, revealing a gap front and center. "I'm twenty-two, but I look younger. I been on the street since I was eighteen. But I got mad skills. I'm a tattoo artist, man. You got any ink?"

"Yeah. As a matter of fact, but it's too cold to take off my jacket. You look cold."

Lewis wore only a torn T-shirt, ripped jeans, and worn-out loafers. He hugged himself.

"Come on back here, man," Lewis said, backing into the woods.

Darren had been right. Sleeping bag. Shopping cart. Lewis patted a flat rock and sat down.

"Let's see that reefer'."

Darren put it in his mouth and lit it with a Bic, drawing

the smoke deep into his lungs and slowly exhaling in a luxurious cloud. He handed the joint to Lewis. It reminded him of that night a year ago when he'd met Brandon. He sat on Lewis's right, balisong in shadow. Lewis toked up, blinked, grinned, blew smoke out through the gap.

"Ahhhh. I needed that. Helps me sleep."

"You prob'ly don't want any blow then."

"Oh mannnn, how can I say no to that?"

Darren pulled out the unit, stuck the tube in his nose, pushed the button and inhaled. He handed it to Lewis.

"Oh man, you really help a brother out."

"No prob. I got reefer and blow, if you're interested."

"Well I'm kinda tapped out, if you know what I mean. But I can think of another way to pay for it."

"Like what?"

Lewis placed his hand on Darren's thigh. Darren slammed the black, four-and-a-half-inch blade into Lewis's chest.

CHAPTER
37

THE SHERIFF

On Sunday they checked into Austin's Motel on the outskirts of Haspierre, a town of thirty thousand and Waldrop
County Seat. They paid cash. Across the street was Bas-
comb's Roadhouse, a beat-up brick building with green
furze on the roof. They sat in a corner booth and reviewed
the drone video before it was shot. Infrared lit the house
green. Two chops, the Toyota pickup and the Corvette.

Josh fed a still shot into Google Earth and came up with
an address. Two four two six State Highway Twenty-seven.
He sent the address to Kleiser.

"I asked my tech guy to find out the owner of that property."

"Are you confident your messaging is secure?" Levon
asked.

"I can barely operate my phone. I know a couple tech
guys that are two steps ahead of the government. Couple

years ago, one got in trouble for hacking into the Pentagon's database. He ducked out, changed his identity, removed his fingerprints from the internet and is back in business. He's the reason there's very little about me on the internet. Unfortunately, I rely on the internet for my business so I can't disappear like he can. You got the dark web and all this shit."

"I try not to use the internet."

"I carry two phones. My own, and the burners my tech guy sends me."

Josh's phone beeped. Ray. He stood. "Gotta take this. I'll be right back."

Josh went out front. At five p.m., the roadhouse was busy. Josh spotted license plates from Kentucky, Tennessee, and Rhode Island.

"Hiya, babe."

"Ooooh, I miss you. When are you coming back?"

"I don't know. It's fucking complicated. How's the play going?"

"Idaho is being a prima donna, as usual, but she's nailing the part. *Isthmus* gave us a write-up. We open next Friday. Can you be here?"

"Planning on it."

"Are you in any danger?"

"I don't think so."

"What will you do if you find the guy?"

"Call the cops. It's beautiful down here. Except there's a lot of trash."

"Are there a lot of hillbillies?"

"More'n Madison, that's for sure."

"Watch yourself. Don't take any chances."

"You know me, babe."

"Yeah, I do. That's why I said it. Can't wait to see you again. Gonna fuck your socks off."

"All the girls say that."

Ray laughed. Josh went back inside.

"Girlfriend," he said, sitting. "You married?"

"Nope. Got a girlfriend. Gonna move in with her."

"Got kids?"

"Got a daughter named Merry. Adopted daughter named Hope."

"Yeah, I got a dog. I should check up on her."

"What do you do with him when you're gone?"

"I got great neighbors. They have two schnauzers and a fenced-in yard."

"Nice of them."

A patrol car pulled up in front of Waldrop County Sheriff's Dept. on the doors. A stocky man with a beard got out and entered the café.

The middle-aged waitress, who wore a sky-blue dress with an apron, looked up from the counter. "Evening, Sheriff."

"How you, Darlene?"

Darlene poured coffee into a ceramic mug and set it on the counter. The sheriff sat with his elbows on the counter. He appeared to be in his mid-fifties and looked fit, even with a paunch.

"I'm gonna go talk to him," Josh said.

"Wait 'til I leave. I'll be back at the motel."

"This was your idea."

"I'm not stopping you. But you're licensed, I'm not."

Cade slipped out of the booth and left. Josh watched him cross the highway, waited a bit, then went to the counter, sitting a stool away.

"Sheriff, I'm Josh Pratt. I'm a private investigator from Madison, Wisconsin."

The sheriff turned startling blue eyes on him. "What can I do for you?"

"A week ago in Milwaukee, someone gave a fentanyl-laced marijuana cigarette to a twenty-one-year-old man. He nearly died. His mother hired me to find out who gave it to him."

"May I see some identification?"

Josh showed him his driver's and private investigator licenses.

"Like every county south of the Mason Dixon line, we are dealing with a full-blown fentanyl crisis. County recorded sixty-eight fentanyl deaths last year, that's a one hundred percent increase over the previous year. And that's just one little county. Also, like every other county, we are understaffed and pressed to the limits. What brings you here?"

"I'm looking for a Brandon McCauley. His association with my client is third-party, but I believe him to be the source of the fentanyl. His uncle lives down here."

"That would be Ed McCauley. I'm not surprised. He's

been on our radar, him and some other good ol' boys. A hunnert years ago, they used to make moonshine. Now they're dealing this shit, mixing it in with everything except their oatmeal."

"I heard something about a bust."

"We raided Ed's place a couple days ago acting on a tip. Had enough fentanyl to kill everyone in the state twice over. We're looking for him, but so far, he's under the radar. We're understaffed, and most of the good ol' boys don't want to get involved."

"You know anything about Brandon?"

"Nope. First I've heard of him."

"He lives in the Milwaukee area. Into martial arts and voodoo."

"Sounds like a TV show."

"I know."

"Was that you phoned it in?"

"No sir."

Woolery gave him the hairy eyeball. "Well you do what you gotta, long's as it's in the law. You come across anything, you let me know."

"Thanks, Sheriff. Here's my card."

Woolery pulled out his wallet, gave Josh one of his. "These crackers don't make fentanyl. They get it from the Sinaloa Cartel. Ever since they opened the border..."

"They've flooded the entire country. It's all over Wisconsin. Any sign of cartel activity around here?"

"We are waiting for that blow to fall. We haven't seen

any actual cartel members, but we feel their presence. It may be these boys are going down to the border to pick it up, but I'm thinking the cartel's running it up here on their own. With the help of American citizens."

A half block down was a package store. Josh bought a bottle of Johnny Walker. With the bourbon in his pocket, he crossed the highway to the motel. He knocked on Cade's door. Cade opened the door and looked at the drone.

"Well?"

"I got some Johnny Walker too."

"Put it away. Leave your phone. We're hitting the distribution center."

DRIVE SAFE

Brandon headed north in Luthor's twelve-year-old piece of shit Toyota, anonymous as a potato, Bathory blasting on the stereo. It was his own cassette. He had a cardboard box full of them in the passenger seat, including Open and Amon Amarth. All Scandinavian. No Western bands could touch the Finnish and Swedish. Black Sabbath? They made him laugh. He drove back roads to avoid detection, a fuzz buster mounted on the dash. He took State Highway Seventy through Kentucky. It was wooded. Lots of squirrels. Rounding a bend near Lewiston, he spotted a squirrel enter the highway from the east and pause. He hit the gas, swerving at the last instant to catch the bolting squirrel. Ka-thud.

"Hail Sobo. Grant me the strength to fulfill my mission."

His count since leaving Luthor's place: four squirrels, two rabbits, and an opossum. The opossum sacrifice was more powerful than all the others combined.

Without voodoo, I am nothing.

Brandon had stumbled upon the pagan religion while researching satanism. He came across Tambor of Mina, which originated in Brazil. It spoke to him with its worship of vodums, orixas, and entities. These were forces of nature as powerful as the wind and the tides. The five families of voduns were his guides and messengers. Through his worship and sacrifices, they empowered him to become a demi-god, walking among unsuspecting mortals. Had they known of his power, they would have tried to kill him, for such was human nature. His faith exalted him and blessed his enterprise. First, to gather wealth. Next, to establish his own church. Eventually, to rule over a vast territory. Although he was born in Milwaukee, he felt a kinship with the Deep South and the voodoo favored by Haitians.

There were many branches of voodoo. He planned to visit Brazil in a couple months, vodum willing. The fentanyl would be mixed with heroin, cocaine, and meth. Brandon made damn sure his supply of meth was pure. He got it from the Vice Lords who'd been cooking their own meth for ten years, long before the fentanyl flood. With Brandon's help, they soon discovered they could triple their profits by adding fentanyl. Dozens had died from this enterprise, but thus far the police hadn't caught up. They had too much to do.

He'd met McTelvin Bobinmoyer at White Dragon. Shortly thereafter, sensei threw McTelvin out for unnecessary brutality. McTelvin didn't care. McTelvin was a vicious street fighter before he began training and didn't need

White Dragon Kung Fu. Brandon stuck it out, believing with his whole being in Denza's semi-mystical instruction and meditation. Brandon was thirsty for knowledge. He was fascinated by man's capacity for cruelty which led him down dark paths. He was particularly fascinated by Nazi interest in the occult and Ariosophy. He'd read *Black Sun* and *The Occult Roots of Nazism*.

"The true value of this study," he recited, "therefore, lies in its painstaking elucidation of an intrinsically fascinating subculture which helped color rather than cause aspects of Nazism. In this context, it also leaves us pondering a central issue: why on earth were Austrian and German occultists, just like the Nazi leadership, quite so susceptible to, indeed obsessed by, specifically aggressive racist beliefs anyway?"

He believed Hitler was possessed by demons. He pulled into a roadside to relieve himself and snort meth. As nine p.m. neared, he approached Bloomington, Indiana, turned toward Smithville and parked in a lot at Fairfax State Park. Even at this late date there were campers visible through the trees. Brandon knew he needed sleep but he was too wired. He put on his running shoes and ran through the park, passing mobile homes with lights gleaming, a few tents. Dogs barked. When he returned, he thought the workout would enable him to sleep. He lowered the passenger seat all the way and spread out between the first and back seats, tossing and turning at an angle waiting for sleep to come. He stank of sweat.

He drifted off. A persistent tapping woke him. A sheriff's

deputy stood by the car tapping on the window with his flashlight. Brandon opened the door and swung his legs out.

"Sir," the deputy said, "may I see some identification?"

Brandon was thirsty and had to take a piss. "What? What's this about?"

"Sir, this park is permit only. There was a sign by the entrance. Do you have a permit?"

Brandon thought about the pistol under the front seat. That would wake campers. He had to defuse the situation and fast. "I'm sorry, officer. I was too zonked to notice."

"License and registration."

He reached between the seats and opened the center console, pulling out his wallet. He stretched to the glove compartment and pulled out Luthor's registration, handing it and his license over.

"Wait here," the deputy said, returning to his vehicle.

Brandon's pulse raced. He had a clean record, but the cop was certain to try and match his identity to the license plate. He wanted to call Luthor but it would be better if the cop woke him up and got an honest reaction. He could see the deputy in the patrol car's light speaking into his phone. It seemed to take forever.

"On the seventh hour, On the seventh day," he sang softly to himself. "On the seventh month.

The seven doctors said, He was born for good luck, And that you'll see. I got seven hundred dollars

And don't you mess with me..."

The deputy talked on. Brandon could grab the pistol and

plug him when he returned. He'd be fifty miles down the road before anyone found out. The temptation was over-whelming, yet some small part of him whispered, have faith. The hougan will guide you through.

After what seemed an eternity, the deputy returned and handed Brandon his license and Luthor's registration. "I spoke with your friend. He wasn't happy about being wo-ken up at four in the morning, but he told me he had in fact loaned you his vehicle. The sun will be up soon. You can either buy a license or move on."

"Thank you, officer. I have to get going anyway."

"Where you headed?"

"Milwaukee. Meeting some friends."

"Drive safe."

CHAPTER 39

EXECUTIVE ACTION

Cade and Josh headed south on Skellar Road, a crumbling blacktop that wound between hills next to a stream. Litter lined the road.

"Turns out I have a friend in the Waldrop County Sheriff's Department. They got a tip last night of unusual activity at a farm outside Bellevue. Black SUVs entering and leaving. I wrote the address on a slip of paper in the console. See if you can bring it up on Google Earth."

Josh pulled out the slip of paper. Eighteen ninety-two Fergus Way. He brought up Google Earth. "I only got one bar."

"This is why I don't rely on the internet."

"Hang on." Josh poked and stroked. The map showed the address at the end of a winding mountain road. "Can't zoom in. What you see is what you get. What did you have in mind?"

"Find a place to leave the truck where no one can see it.

Take a look around. I come in the front, you come in the back. Anybody tries to stop us, we find any drugs, we take 'em out."

"Excuse me?"

"Look. If some nice housewife comes out the front door we got the wrong place. But if some cartel soldier with an AK comes out, we got the right place. What would you do? Call it in?"

"I would."

Cade pulled off onto one of those roadside clearings where people dumped their trash. "Cops can't do shit. You've seen yourself there's virtually no law enforcement out here. They're not equipped to take on professional killers."

"And we are?"

"Don't know about you. You want to excuse yourself, I'll take you back to town. You can keep searching for that McCauley kid. Maybe this isn't your kind of fight."

Josh looked out the window at the trees marching uphill. He'd always thought of himself as a cowboy. Keeper of the cowboy code. Many bikers did. He made his living as a PI and this wasn't on the agenda. On the other hand, the shit had spread to Wisconsin. It was all over Madison by now. In 2021, one hundred and fifty people died from ODs in Dane County. What were the chances their raid could go wrong? What were the chances the police would show? He clasped his hands together and bowed his head.

Cade watched. "You a believer?"

"I'm a Christian."

"What does He tell you?"

"Let's do it."

"All right. Let me show you what I got." Cade got out and boosted himself into the bed. He unlocked the galvanized steel tool chest behind the cab and pulled out another 1911 and a Sig. "Which do you prefer?"

Josh pointed at the 1911. Cade handed it to him. Josh released the magazine, saw that it was full, and jammed it back up. "What's the plan?"

Cade handed Josh a suppressor. "Put that on." He attached one to his own Colt.

"Let's take a look."

The sun had already begun to set, casting the woods in shadow. They crept northwest watching where they stepped. Cade wore faded jeans and his dun-colored farm coat. Josh wore tan cargo pants and a dark gray hoodie. They hiked for twenty minutes when lights appeared through the trees. A jumbo house trailer that had seen better days. Faint laughter and salsa music. A GMC Denali and a Cadillac SUV were parked out front. Two cholos sat on a wood bench backed against the trailer, which rested on cinder blocks, drinking from red Solo cups and smoking cigarettes.

Judging from the sound through the open window there were more inside. The cholos spoke Spanish. Josh copied the vehicles' license plates into his pad, stuck it in the hoodie's pocket.

"Now what?"

"Let's just wait and see what happens."

Fifteen minutes later, another vehicle approached, bouncing and rocking on the rough dirt road. A Toyota mini-pickup pulled into the front yard. A skinny man wearing khakis and a rumpled campaign hat got out, saluted the two on the bench.

"Rodrigo!"

"You got the shit?"

"I got it," Rodrigo said, reaching into the pickup's bed and pulling out a green duffle bag. The front door opened, filled by a fat man with greasy black hair and a beard in blue coveralls. He motioned for Rodrigo to give him the bag. Rodrigo handed it over. The fat man sat on the entrance, feet on a wood plank, and opened the bag. He nodded.

Cade nudged Josh, motioning with his eyes.

"You sure? This is all circumstantial."

Cade gave him a look, eyes narrowed to take stock of another man.

A fusillade of barks erupted from the trailer. The fat man stood and a doberman shot out the door nearly knocking him down. The dog made a beeline for Cade and Josh's position. Josh instinctively moved away. Cade drew his pistol, waited until the dog was five feet away and shot it through the skull. The stifled report was lost in the wind.

"Pecos!" the fat man cried, drawing an automatic and coming at them like a freight train, arms extended. Rodrigo and the men on the bench drew weapons and spread out.

Cade crouched behind a bush, aimed with both hands and squeezed. The fat man went down. Center shot. Josh felt he'd passed through some time warp into an alternate dimension. One minute they were talking about finding a cartel warehouse, the next he was in a firefight. He automatically raised his pistol, tracked Rodrigo, and squeezed. The shot took Rodrigo in the thigh, bringing him down.

The two from the bench separated, firing as they parted. Josh heard the bullets pass through leaves on the trees. A short, wiry man with a furze of black hair came out of the trailer holding a full auto, maybe an H&K, and sprayed bullets in an arc. He hit one of the men from the bench who threw up his arms and fell face forward.

They heard the shooter cursing under his breath. Kneeling, Cade drew a bead and drilled the shooter through the thorax. All was quiet for long seconds as their hearing returned and the insects resumed fiddling. Cade rose to walk to where Rodrigo lay, hissing as he clutched high on his leg to stop the bleeding. Cade put two rounds in his head.

"Jesus," Josh said.

"Let's see what we got. Grab wallets, IDs. Then we'll check the trailer."

Josh trailed Cade to the trailer, waited while Cade threw a rock through a window. There was no reaction.

"Anybody in there come out now."

Silence. Cade entered the trailer pistol first.

"All clear. Take a look."

With a final scan of the clearing, Josh followed Cade inside. The kitchen light cast a seedy yellow glow on a Formica-topped table containing an electronic scale, two plastic-wrapped bricks of white powder, and a big plastic bag of Skittles-colored pills. Cade went methodically through the drawers, and the prefab living room shelves, gathering several manila files and jamming them in a paper bag.

"You get those IDs?"

Josh cursed himself. "I'll get 'em." He went out to the yard and went through the dead men's pockets. Two of them had Georgia driver's licenses. The other three had Mexican driver's licenses. He gathered all the cell phones.

Cade came out, grabbed the duffel bag, went inside. He returned and tossed the empty bag to Josh. "Put everything in there. See if there's a gas can in any of these vehicles."

There wasn't, but there was a full can behind the trailer next to a D2 Cat Dozer. Cade took it into the trailer.

"Awright. Get in the truck. I'll be right with you," Cade called from inside.

Josh got in the truck. It all had happened so quickly he didn't have time to process. It certainly looked like a cartel hideout. Seconds later, Cade stepped out, turned around, lit a book of matches and tossed it through the door and ran. The trailer exploded in flames.

Cade got in the truck.

"Look," Josh said. "Maybe this wasn't such a good idea.

"I'm getting results."

"Your results make me wonder if you don't own shares in a bodybag company."

"You're telling me you'd like to go on without my help?"

"You're a liability, brother.

"This isn't a job anymore anyway."

They didn't speak on the way to the motel.

SWEET HOME WISCONSIN

Josh had left his phone at the motel. It was nine-thirty when they returned. He turned it on. Jerry Bushnell had called four times.

Cade frightened him. He couldn't just leave. He knocked on Cade's door. Cade opened it.

"You want to bring me that bourbon?"

"Yeah. Wait a minute." Josh returned with the bourbon. Cade poured it into two plastic bathroom cups and saluted each other. Cade tossed his back.

"I'm taking off in the morning," Josh said.

"Getting out while the getting is good."

"It's not what I'm here for. I have clients."

"I understand."

"You know how to reach me."

"It's been short but intense."

"Yeah. We'll have to do this again sometime."

Cade laughed. It was the first time he'd cracked a true

smile. "I'll sort through that shit, but hopefully, my job here is finished. There's just one loose end."

"McCauley?"

"Yeah."

"You know about Ed McCauley. You gonna pay him a visit?"

"Maybe. Him and Luthor Bushnell."

"Ask them where Brandon got the fentanyl before you kill him."

Cade raised his cup. "Salud."

Josh stood. "Keep the bottle. I want to get an early start."

"Good luck."

Josh slept fitfully, was on the road by six. He drove through a McDonald's in Chatsworth before heading north on the four-one-one-one, mechanically chewing his Egg McMuffin and drinking corporate coffee. He pulled into a rest stop in Athens and phoned Jaycee.

"Josh. I was beginning to wonder what happened to you."

"I'm sorry I haven't been in touch, ma'am. I traced Brandon to northern Georgia but I didn't have an opportunity to talk to him. By now he's back in Milwaukee. I'm headed your way and will probably arrive sometime tomorrow. I'll call you then."

"What did you find out?"

"Circumstantial evidence strongly suggests it was Brandon who gave the fentanyl-laced marijuana to Darren Olson who gave it to Max."

"Was it intentional? Why would he try to harm my son?"

"I don't know yet. I'll find out."

"Is this about the feud?"

"Maybe."

"I just can't get my head around it. How could someone born in this century bear a grudge over something that happened one hundred and fifty years ago?"

"People are funny. I'll call before I come over."

He called Jerry Bushnell. "Jerry, it's Josh Pratt."

"I was beginning to think you bailed on me too."

"I've been busy. I have a person of interest. How's it going? Did you get the job?"

"I'm working with Friendly Cleaners. We do residential and small businesses. They pick me up at eight in the morning and drop me off at five."

"How's that working out?"

"It's a job. I have a little money. When you sell that letter, I'll pay you for everything you've done for me."

"I'm traveling. I should be home sometime tomorrow. I'll call you then."

Josh pulled into his driveway Sunday evening at nine. Fig barked furiously from across the street. Josh didn't even carry his bag inside. He went across the street and retrieved Fig from the Lowrys.

"I don't know how I can ever repay you, Louise."

"No bother. We're happy to do it. How was your trip?"

"It wasn't a waste."

"What are you working on?"

"I'll tell you once I finish, if I ever finish."

"Will you and Ray be here for Thanksgiving? It's Thursday."

"What day is it?"

"It's Sunday."

"I'll check with Ray. She said something about her parents. If we come, can we bring anything?"

"Just yourselves."

Inside the house, Fig raced around, jumping on the sofa, to the bedroom, to the kitchen and back again. Josh phoned Ray.

"Oh baby, I'm so glad you're back! Can I come stay at your place tomorrow? Mongoose is driving me insane!"

"Are you home? Is she there now?"

"No, she's out clubbing with a friend. She's staying at Foster's house, but I have to work with her. We're opening Friday. I'm getting good vibes from the dress rehearsals, but it all depends on Idaho holding her shit together. I'm beginning to think she's insane."

"Ya think?"

"Can't wait to see you, babe."

"I have to go to Milwaukee tomorrow but I hope to be back by mid-afternoon. You have a key."

"I'll be waiting."

Monday morning was cool and crisp. Josh put on his sweats and took Fig for a five-mile run. Fig grinned the whole way. As he ran toward town, he noticed a middle-aged woman on the other side of the road picking up trash with an extendable claw and putting it in a plastic bag. He waved. She waved back.

Josh showered, fed Fig, ate a hot pocket and called O'Malley.

"What's up?"

"Sir, I have reason to believe that Brandon McCauley

was the source of the fentanyl-laced marijuana that nearly killed Max Bushnell. I saw him briefly in Georgia, and I believe he's headed back, or already in Milwaukee. Do you have time to meet today?"

O'Malley agreed to meet Josh at eleven at a Starbucks on South Water Street. Josh left home at eight. His first stop was Delafield. Jaycee answered the door.

"Come in, Josh. Would you like some coffee?"

They sat in the living room.

"Max is back teaching. It's a miracle. It has renewed my faith in God."

"Amen to that."

"Tell me what you've found."

"I found Brandon McCauley in Faubus, Georgia. Tiny town. No police force. He was consorting with known drug dealers, but I lost him before I could talk to him. I may have located the source of his fentanyl. I turned that information over to the sheriff's department. I have reason to believe he has returned to Milwaukee and is ready to pick up where he left off. I'm trying to find him. I'm meeting with a police officer soon and I'll tell him what I've learned."

"That's so good to hear, Josh. What about Jerry?"

Josh shrugged. "I don't know. I want to speak with McCauley. I'll mention him as a possible suspect."

"How's Jerry doing?"

"He's stable. He's working with a domestic service. Cleaning homes."

"That's good. I'd like to help him but..."

"You have enough problems. I've met him."

"Thank you for your understanding. You really must

allow me to pay you like a regular client."

Josh stood. "Not necessary."

O'Malley was seated near the front of the Starbucks.

"Get you something?" Josh asked. "I promise not to tell."

"Sure. Get me one of those crullers."

Josh returned with a bottled orange juice and two crullers. He sat and told O'Malley what he'd told Jaycee.

O'Malley regarded him with cool brown eyes. "We received a report two days ago of multiple fatalities at a suspected cartel distribution point near Faubus. Know anything about that?"

Josh shrugged. "I got my hands full tracking down McCauley. What happened?"

"Waldrop County responded to a report of gunfire the night of the nineteenth. Four dead at a remote trailer they believe was being used as a meth lab, and for other things. Three of the dead were in the country illegally. The fourth was a known felon who'd served time for distribution."

"No idea who did it?"

"No. They recovered shells in five calibers. Georgia Bureau of Investigation is looking into it. Like most police forces, they are understaffed and overworked."

"Did I tell you my theory about a feud?"

"What feud?"

"The McCauleys and the Bushnells. Roderick McCauley and Ethan Bushnell were best friends at West Point, but when the war broke out, McCauley went back to Alabama, and Bushnell went to Wisconsin. They met at the Battle of Tunnel Hill. I think their fuckin' fathers, excuse my French, taught them to hate the other and they've been at it ever since."

"Are you saying that a McCauley murdered Don Bushnell?"

"It's just a theory, but Brandon McCauley strikes me as capable."

O'Malley made notes. "I'll check him out."

"He drives an ex-police Dodge Charger. Here's the license plate."

"It would make sense if it were a feud. I just find it hard to believe."

"Me too."

Josh was home by three. He checked his email. He made a point of not checking his email while away from home, except for texts, and most of those were from service providers, such as his veterinarian, Calling All Dogs. He'd made an appointment for Fig to get her rabies booster and within minutes of hanging up, Calling All Dogs began texting, phoning, and sending emails.

He fed Fig and took a nap on the living room sofa. Hysterical barking woke him. Ray pushed into his house carrying two cloth bags full of groceries.

DRUNK OCTOPUS WANTS TO FIGHT

Josh grabbed Ray, marched her into the bedroom, and shut the door. Fig stood outside, whined and scratched for a few minutes and went into the living room. Ray peeled off her shirt, but when Josh reached for her black panties, she put out a hand.

"No," she whispered. "We're going to fuck with our underpants on."

She worked his cock out through the flap in his Hanes and pushed her panties aside. When he was about to come, she reached under and grabbed his balls.

Josh lay on his back. "Oh my god."

"I missed you too. Now I'm going to make lasagna."

It was seven-thirty by the time they finished. They sat in the living room with the TV on but the sound off. *The Masked Singer*.

"Dress rehearsal Tuesday night. I'd like you to be there."

"Is Mongoose behaving?"

"She's such a diva. The only time she behaves is when she's actually acting. She takes her acting very seriously. Everything else is just irritating. She was coming on to me and I had to slap her down. 'But Rayyy,' Ray sang in a falsetto, 'have you ever been with a woman?'

"Whatcha tell her?"

"I told her I was all woman and I wasn't confused. I wished her well. There are at least three lesbos in the company she could hook up with."

"But they don't look like you."

"Alegra is very attractive. She's the short redhead."

"Is she gay?"

"Nobody knows. Everybody's afraid to ask."

"What time?"

"Four p.m. We hope to be done in time for dinner. You're coming with me to my parents' house tomorrow night."

"Guess so."

"Try to show a little enthusiasm."

Ray put on clothes and went to make dinner. Seeing her opportunity, Fig bounded into the room, up on the bed and furiously licked Josh's face until he pushed her away. Josh got dressed and went into his office. His phone sat on the wood door resting on two file cabinets he used as a desk. Denza had called.

"Call me back."

Josh phoned back and went straight to voice mail. Denza was probably teaching. "Butch, it's Josh Pratt returning your call."

He checked his email.

Hello,

Did you receive the mail I sent you last week concerning your relatives fund that is about to be confiscated in a bank here in my country?.

Reply urgently so I can give you details on how to secure the release fund.

Best regards.
Hussain Shahid.

He deleted it. Fraida Comintern, who looked like a sex doll and lived in Croatia, wanted to be his friend. Deleted. Lawyer Steve Fleiss asked if he could deliver a summons tomorrow. He wrote back, "Steve, I'm working on a case. I'll let you know in the morning."

Someone using a friend's name wrote, "I've been meaning to send you these pictures for a while. They should stir some memories." No signature. Deleted.

"Dear Mr. Pratt: How much to guard me and my brother Elvin when we go gambling in Las Vegas? We expect to win big and don't want to become a target for robbers. Yours, Darryl Eich."

"Dinner is ready," Ray sang from the kitchen.

Josh went into the kitchen where Fig sat wagging her tail and staring at the countertop. Ray had prepared two salads on the kitchen table made with red lettuce, arugula, red onions, and red peppers. Josh attacked the lasagna brick.

"Delicious. I'll do the dishes."

"I have to do a little cat herding."

Ray went into the living room and pulled out her phone. Fig jumped on the sofa and laid her snout in Ray's lap. Josh did the dishes. Ray was still herding cats when he finished. He went into his office and checked his biker forums. Kawasaki was coming out with a four-cylinder 400 to beat the insurance rates on middleweights. Sales were down because Generation Z was risk-averse and didn't know how to shift gears.

"Cats are all in a row!" Ray exulted. They retired to the bedroom. They watched a movie about Little Richard. Josh overslept. When he woke, Ray was gone. She left a note on her pillow. "See you tonight! XXX!"

It was cold and drizzling so Josh went into the basement and worked the heavy bag for forty-five minutes. He went upstairs, showered, and phoned Steve Fleiss, the lawyer for whom he sometimes worked.

"What's the job, Steve?"

"Summons to appear in court regarding failure to pay child support. Tyler Cooper, lives in Sun Prairie."

"What do we know about Mr. Cooper?"

"Served thirty days for assault two years ago, several DUIs, license currently suspended, rides a Harley."

"On Thanksgiving?"

"It's still a work day for me."

"I'll be there in an hour."

Josh drove downtown, parked in the lot just off the square, and went up the stairs to Fleiss and Associates. Fleiss' receptionist, a new girl named Gail, handed him the summons.

"He's in a meeting right now. He asked you to call him

later to tell him how it went."

"Thanks, Gail."

Cooper lived at 1532 Jasper Circle, a cul-de-sac in Sun Prairie a couple miles from Highway 151. The two-car attached garage door was open. Cooper was working on his Harley, listening to a blues show on WORT. Josh parked at the curb, pulled his hoodie over his head and walked up the drive. Cooper looked up.

"Tyler Cooper?"

"Shit," the man said. He was tall and rangy with thick wrists and narrow eyes, wearing stained blue jeans, work boots, and a nylon jacket. He got off his stool and held out his hand. He knew what was coming. He'd been there before.

Josh handed him the summons. "You've been summoned."

"Yeah, great. Child support?"

Josh nodded. He looked at the Harley. "You like that V-Rod?"

"Best bike they ever made. Why they stopped making them I don't know. You ride?"

"Yeah. I got a '98 Road King." Josh said nothing about Cooper's suspended license. "I also got a Hawk GT."

"Yeah, those are sweet little bikes. That there V-Rod's the last Harley I'll ever buy."

"Why is that?"

"They're going electric, haven't you heard?"

Josh shook his head in disgust. "I don't understand it. Nobody wants that shit. They may as well close their doors."

Josh texted Fleiss that the job was done and headed

back to town. He arrived at Rise Up Dance Studio at four, parked on Williamson Street behind a Chevy Volt, rear covered with stickers. BLM. No Borders No Walls. No One's Treading On You, Sweetie. Vote Democratic. The East Side. Josh entered. A dozen people milled around the lobby, sipping beer from plastic cups and munching on popcorn. Josh recognized a few, said hello. The lights blinked. Ray appeared in the entrance to the theater and clapped her hands.

"Move it, people!"

Fifty people sat on folding chairs, with room for one hundred and fifty more. Josh sat in the third row on the aisle. The lights dimmed and Ray appeared wearing pedal pushers and a man's shirt with the tails tied over her taut belly.

"Folks, you'll find comment cards on the seats. This is a dress rehearsal but we're going to do our darndest to entertain. We would appreciate your filling out the comment cards and dropping them in the box on your way out. Thank you."

Hushed whispering. The lights went down, the curtain went up revealing a bar angled toward the audience at upper left, a tatted, bearded bartender making a drink, and at the end of the bar, back toward the audience, a sullen figure with scraggly white hair staring into his drink. Two thin young men wearing glasses and beards, one with a man bun, enter stage right.

Bartender: "Hey Ralph. Who's your friend?"

The men went to the bar. The thin young man with the man bun says, "Carter, meet Ron, the best bartender on the East Side."

Ron drew the beers. "Whaddaya think? Muskies have a chance this year?"

"Who are the Muskies?" Carter asked.

"Local team."

"In Wisconsin," Ralph said, "we have a saying. Mush your huskies and hush your muskies."

"I don't get it."

Ralph turned to the man with the scraggly hair. "Hey Monty. How they hangin'?"

Without looking, Monty drew his right arm across his body and flipped Ralph the bird.

"What's his problem?" Carter asked.

"They shitcanned his ass for harassing a trans woman."

The man on the right turned to face them. A thin, scowling face, small eyes deep set beneath a black unibrow. Josh couldn't tell if it was a woman.

"I didn't harass shit. I told it to get its ass out of the women's restroom."

Josh's phone dinged. He pulled it out. Text from Butch Denza: "Brandon came to class tonight. Will be here tomorrow night."

"He's always been a good student, but there's another side of Brandon that few of us here see. I've witnessed some questionable behavior over the years, and once, several years ago, he showed up under the influence of something. I spoke to him about it and it hasn't happened since. Look. If you think he's a drug runner, why not leave this to the police?"

Josh was silent. "You know, I'll try that. Thank you. If I'm unable to get through, I'll come myself."

Josh phoned O'Malley. It went to voice mail. "Officer, it's Josh Pratt. Brandon McCauley, whom I believe supplied the fentanyl-laced marijuana that made Max Bushnell ill, will be at White Dragon Kung Fu in Whitefish Bay tomorrow evening. Call me if you have a chance."

Backstage, cast and crew mingled with the audience swilling beer and smoking marijuana. Mayor for Life Saul Brogden was there. Josh spotted Ray holding court, parted the crowd with his palms placed together and kissed her. "Congratulations!"

"Did you like it?"

"Fascinating."

A slight woman with a cap of red hair wearing khaki dungarees sauntered over holding a plastic cup filled with champagne. "So this is the famous biker."

"Josh, Idaho."

They shook hands. "You were great. Very convincing."

"I ride."

"What do you ride?"

"Yamaha Virago 535. I'm short, so I ride a cruiser."

DRESS REHEARSAL

As the dress rehearsal wound on, Josh texted Denza. "I'm at a play. I'll phone you soon."

Drunk Octopus was ninety minutes but seemed interminable. At last the curtain fell and the audience enthusiastically responded, standing, clapping, yelling "Bravo!"

It was seven-thirty when he went out front and phoned White Dragon.

"Josh Pratt for Sensei Denza."

"Hold on, I'll see if he's available."

Five minutes. "This is Denza."

"Butch, it's Josh Pratt. Is McCauley there now?"

"Yes. He's working with some new students. He's a teacher."

"Thanks for the heads-up. I told you I saw him i gia, but I don't think he saw me. He doesn't kno am. He was at a drug distribution spot. I think he'

"Very cool. Do you have a picture?"

Idaho pulled out her phone. The bike was far from stock with moderate ape hangers, a khaki green tank with a five-pointed white star, and sinister pipes wrapped in heat tape. No muffler.

"Holy shit! That's cool. Did you do that yourself?"

"No, I had help. Claudette's Customs in Waukesha. We should go for a ride sometime."

Ray rolled her eyes.

"Yeah. Here's my card."

"The reviewer from *Isthmus* is here!" Ray said.

"I'm sure he loved it."

"It's she," Idaho said.

Ray grabbed Josh by the arm and dragged him behind the curtain.

"You're not really going riding with her."

Josh shrugged. "I feel better about her knowing she rides. I hope you're not jealous! I wouldn't touch that with a nine-foot pole. She'd probably shiv me if I tried."

Ray laughed. "Don't let her bait you. There's nothing she loves more than lecturing dumb White men."

"Me? Dumb?"

"I'm trying to give you her worldview."

"That's okay. I'm fine without it. Listen. I'm gonna split. I gotta go to Milwaukee tomorrow, maybe home late."

"That's okay. Tomorrow we hold the postmortem and I'll be here late. What about Thanksgiving?"

"I'm all yours."

She kissed him. "Groovy, baby!"

Josh circumvented State Street, circling around the capital and heading west on Mineral Point. He turned the radio to WORT and listened to a soft-voiced deejay describe his family, and dreading the upcoming Thanksgiving holiday. He would be forced to eat turkey and his mother-in-law's arid stuffing. He was thinking of bringing his own food.

It was dark by the time Josh hit Ptarmigan Road, soft lights from million-dollar houses gleaming through the trees. There were no sidewalks in White Oaks. The buses didn't run out here. They didn't want buses out here. Except for Josh's modest ranch-style, White Oaks was upscale all the way. As he pulled into his drive, Fig trumpeted through the door.

Josh knelt inside the door to give Fig pets and hugs. He went into his bedroom. A decapitated rabbit lay on the bed. Josh got a plastic bag from the kitchen.

"Have you been watching *The Godfather*?"

He put the corpse in the garbage. Fig's score that year was four rabbits and three squirrels.

Josh pulled a can of Tyranena from the fridge and settled in front of the television. He was working his way through *Yellowstone*. He was on the fourth season. When the episode ended, he switched to YouTube and asked for Tower of Power. He could speak into the remote and the streaming services would find anything that matched. There were at least six months of Tower of Power on YouTube. They'd been touring since 1968, gone through countless personnel and lead singers, but every band was tight as yoga pants and they had fans all over the world. Josh hoped to see them live someday. He watched a live concert in Copenhagen, and a fiftieth-anniversary concert in Oakland.

He asked for Bobby Hines, and four live performance videos of his old friend from the defunct MC Jugans popped up. Bobby playing "Take the A Train." Bobby playing "Nica's Dream." Bobby playing "All the Things You Are." Bobby playing "Caravan," the last shot in Madison's own Edgewater music lounge and bar. When it finished, the screen asked him to rate the performance. He gave it a ten. Bobby had saved his life.

His phone clicked text. Calling All Dogs reminded him of Fig's appointment to get her rabies booster next week. He checked his email. Calling All Dogs warned him not to forget Fig's appointment next week. Calling All Dogs wanted him to fill out a survey on Fig's last visit, a month ago, to repair a torn dew claw. Responding would only encourage them.

At ten, he switched to the local news. Two stolen cars got into burnouts at West Towne Mall, one of them crashing into Buford's Liquors. The thieves abandoned that vehicle but not before stealing hundreds of dollars of liquor. Mayor for Life Saul Brogden cut the ribbon at the renovated Civil War Museum at the top of State Street.

"A Milwaukee police officer was shot and killed this afternoon in what appears to be an ambush. Detective Shawn O'Malley was stopped at a red light on West Clarke Street when an unknown assailant stepped from between parked cars and shot him point blank in the head. Warning. The following video may be too graphic for some viewers."

The grainy black-and-white video showed a man in a hoodie walking calmly across the street to the driver's side, pointing the pistol and shooting. There was no sound but Josh saw the gun hand jump. It could have been anybody.

He got down on his knees and prayed for O'Malley's soul.

WHITE DRAGON

Josh phoned Jerry in the morning.

"How you doing?"

"I'm working. We're cleaning a big house in Waukesha. I work with two Mexican women. They don't like me. They gossip about me in Spanish."

"Really? Maybe they're discussing the weather."

"No. I can tell because they look at me and laugh."

"Jerry, be happy you're working."

"Did you find my brother's killer?"

"Maybe."

"What do you mean?"

"I have a suspect."

"I gotta go. The boss just showed up. She looks like a feral hog."

"Talk to you soon."

Josh grabbed a couple Apple Air Tags and left for Milwaukee at noon. At one-thirty, he pulled into Jaycee's drive-way in Delafield and got out. Jaycee answered the door.

"Come in. You think this McCauley boy gave Max the joint?"

"McCauley gave Darren Olson the joint."

"Would you like coffee?"

"Sure."

Five minutes later Jaycee returned with two mugs filled with coffee, a carton of half and half, and a sugar dispenser. Josh could tell by the sound she was using a Keurig. He'd tried one but it didn't taste the same. Not strong enough.

"Thank you."

Jaycee sat.

"Did you hear about the police officer who was mur-dered yesterday?"

Jaycee's forehead scrunched. "No. Where?"

"Milwaukee. Detective Shawn O'Malley. I knew him. He was helping me with the case."

"You mean finding Donnie's killer?"

"Yes."

"That's terrible. Do they know who did it?"

"No. Let me tell you what I found in Georgia."

Josh described the events, omitting the corpse Cade had left behind and the raid on the cartel warehouse.

"You think this McCauley boy murdered Donnie be-cause of some feud going back to the Civil War?"

"It's as good a reason as any. He's into the Civil War. There's a good chance he'll show up at a reenactment."

"What reenactment?"

"The Battle of Tunnel Hill on November thirtieth."

"That's in one week. What are you doing for Thanksgiving?"

"I have plans. I have a girlfriend."

"Oh Josh. Do you love her?"

"Yes."

"I'm happy for you. I was going to invite you here, with Max and Sam, and maybe some of their stray pals."

"What about Jerry?"

Jaycee sucked her lips. "Why don't we just drink Romilar instead?"

Josh shrugged. He wasn't going to press it.

"You know, you know, Josh? You're right. I will invite Jerry. I'm trying to be a better person. You're a good influence on me."

"I doubt I had anything to do with that, Jaycee."

"Don't sell yourself short. That poor policeman. Does he have a fund for his family or funeral or something?"

"I don't know. Probably."

"I'll find it and donate."

"I will too."

Josh drove downtown, parked on a side street and walked to Lake Park on the Upper East Side. The season was winding down. Only the evergreens were green. Skeletal oak and elm shook their branches in the stiff breeze off the lake. Josh walked to the North Point lighthouse, a magnificent snow-white house built in 1896 to house the lighthouse keepers.

The lighthouse was attached. Inside was a museum, mostly about the Great Lakes. He paid eight bucks and took the tour. The view from the seventy-four-foot tower was awesome. He could see freighters a mile offshore, and close up, sailboats from the McKinley Park Yacht Club.

He sat on a bench overlooking the lake, white seagulls wheeling overhead. It sounded like the ocean. Josh checked. O'Malley's family, meaning his daughter Rebecca, had set up a GoFundMe for a memorial. The funeral was scheduled for Sunday at the Cathedral of St. John the Evangelist.

Josh grabbed a late lunch at a café in Shorewood. By five p.m., it was twilight. White Dragon was part of a strip mall on North Teutonia, including a liquor store and a store that sold reptiles, with REPTILES spelled out in neon orange in the front window. The parking lot was half full, with the area around White Dragon parked up. Josh parked several rows back. No Dodge, but an old Corolla with Georgia plates. Josh took a picture. He grabbed an air tag and super glue. No one noticed as he sank beside the vehicle and glued the air tag to the inside of the right rear wheel well.

He thought about popping the trunk. Chances were it was empty. Passing the drugs would have been the first thing he did upon arrival.

Through the mist-covered window, Josh saw a foyer with a waist-high banister separating it from the dojo. A couple of parents waited in the foyer talking on their phones or roaming the internet. Josh went inside, smiled at the others, and sat with his back to the window. Denza wore a traditional Chinese kung fu uniform, instructing eight students ranging from teens to sixties. They were doing sticky hands. Denza walked from couple to couple offering encouragement or suggestions. He was very low-key. The floor was covered with interlocking foam mats. On the back wall were the American, Korean, Phillipine, and Brazilian flags. No China. China was in the doghouse.

Brandon's partner was an older man with long white hair held in a ponytail, wearing gym pants and a White Dragon sweatshirt. Brandon wore black gi pants and a Bruce Lee T-shirt. The pair were well matched, moving together like a sine wave punctuated with forays probing the other's defense. Denza clapped his hands. Everyone stopped what they were doing and faced him. "Suit up!" he said.

Some filed into a changing room in back, but Denza, McCauley, the man with the ponytail sat on a bench pulling on protective gear. Denza put on shin guards, foot gear, a midriff pad, hand and headgear. He set a timer on the counter in back.

"One-minute rounds." He put his mouthpiece in and pressed the button.

Ding.

They all squared off except for Denza, who didn't have a partner. Skill level was uniformly high. Their control was excellent. McCauley dominated his older partner. The old guy was no slouch, but he couldn't match McCauley's speed or aerial acrobatics. McCauley levitated, twisted in midair and smacked the ponytail in the side of his head with an instep, so lightly as to barely make a sound.

When the buzzer sounded, a tall man with white side-burns bowed out. Denza stepped in, facing a smiling Asian with a Beatles cut poking out from beneath his headgear.

Denza defended himself effortlessly, moving just far enough out of range to make his opponent miss, or swatting down punches and kicks like they were flies. After the next buzzer, Denza went with McCauley. It was a chess match, mostly footwork. McCauley juked left then reversed himself, trying that aerial spinning roundhouse, but Denza saw it coming, crouched and put up a palm. When the buzzer rang, he backed out and white sidewalls stepped back in.

Denza came out and sat with Josh. "There he is."

"I see."

"What are you going to do?"

"I'm just going to talk to him."

"Does he know who you are?"

"I don't think so. I only saw him for a split second down in Georgia and it was dark. He knows someone's after him. He knows he stepped in it."

"I don't know. Brandon exhibits an almost supernatural self-control. I've never seen him angry. I have to close the class. Will you wait here for him? He usually takes a shower and changes."

"I'll catch him outside."

"Good luck."

A HARD RAIN

Denza clapped his hands. The class lined up in two rows.

Josh sat on a bench outside the liquor store, noting two cameras over the liquor store door covering one hundred and eighty degrees of the parking lot. Fifteen minutes later, McCauley came out wearing a leather jacket and creased Dockers, carrying a leather gym bag. Josh stood.

"Mr. McCauley?"

McCauley turned. "Who are you?"

"Josh Pratt. I'm a private investigator from Madison."

McCauley grinned. "What can I do for you?"

"I wonder if I could buy you a cup of coffee and ask you a few questions."

"What kind of questions?"

"My client hired me to find the source of a fentanyl-laced marijuana cigarette that landed her son in the hospital."

The smile froze. "What the fuck. What the fuck, man. Why come to me?"

"I tracked you to Faubus last week. I saw you in your Uncle Ed's house. You didn't see me. We saw the fentanyl. We told the sheriff's department."

McCauley got right in Josh's face. He was the same size. "Who's we?"

"Me and a friend."

McCauley shoved Josh hard. Josh staggered back but didn't fall. "Fuck off."

McCauley strode toward the Corolla. He wheeled around. "You want to try me?"

"No, I just want to ask you a few questions."

"That's what I thought." He got in, slammed the door, and made the front tires chirp. He accelerated on N. Teutonia to over sixty miles per hour without fear of being ticketed. There just weren't enough police.

A few students had watched the exchange but moved on by the time Josh returned to the dojo. Denza came out of the back wearing creased gray slacks and a blue shirt open at the collar, jacket slung over his shoulder. "Did you get what you needed?"

"Mr. McCauley wasn't interested in talking."

"I'm not surprised. You want to tell me what this is all about?"

"I had a hunch about him, so I followed him to Georgia. He was in a house used to process fentanyl into whatever. We went in there because they were raping a woman."

"How do you know that?"

"We could see through the window and she was screaming."

"Who's we?"

"A friend and me. It was dark inside. My friend pulled the breaker box. I recognized McCauley. He left immediately. I don't think I registered, but just now, I told him I was there."

"For God's sake, why did you do that?"

"I wanted him to know that I can place him at a fentanyl distribution center."

"I hope he doesn't come after you."

"He's been training with you all these years and you didn't know he was a thug?"

"He's always been very respectful. He's great with kids. I had him teaching a class for a while."

"You want to get a cup of coffee?"

A light rain had begun to fall. They crossed the street to a Dazbog. Josh bought Denza a medium. They grabbed a table in the back.

"Did you hear about the police officer who was ambushed yesterday?"

Denza stared into his cup. "Yes. They've been bleeding cops since 2018. Then came the summer of 2020. I considered being a cop once. I'm glad I didn't."

"His name was Shawn O'Malley. I knew him."

"I'm sorry."

"He was helping me with my case."

"You don't think…"

"No. Sounds like it was random. I liked him. Were you aware of Brandon's supernatural leanings?"

"Huh?"

"You must have seen the ink. The pyramid with the eye, pentagrams, skulls, Hebrew, voodoo symbols."

"I just thought he liked to cover himself in ink."

Josh took his jacket off and rolled up his sleeve.

Denza took his jacket off and rolled up his sleeve, revealing a Marine tattoo, an American flag, and a skull with a knife through it.

"I don't know what's happening anymore."

"You married?" Josh said.

"I was. We're divorced. Two kids. The girl's in Madison studying to be a doctor. The boy's in New York trying to be an actor."

"An actor?"

Denz laughed. "I know, right? He never had an interest in the martial arts. Now Joan, she's different. She loves it. She's studying krav maga in Madison."

"Why not with you?"

"Oh, I had her in class for nine years. She was teaching when she left. What about you?"

"Well I'm on the cusp."

"What does that mean?"

"I've run out of reasons why I shouldn't marry my girlfriend. Her name is Ray and she's a dancer and theater director."

"Lemme see."

Josh pulled out his phone and brought up a picture of a smiling Ray on the Union Terrace, looking over her shoulder. Denza whistled.

"She's gorgeous."

"She knows. I got to get a ring."

"You don't sound very enthusiastic."

"I love her, but all my life I've been an outsider. I served four years in Waupun. Prior to that my relationship with women was shameful. Every day I ask the Lord for forgiveness."

"What did you do, if you don't mind my asking?"

"I cut off a guy's arm with a chainsaw. I was in a gang. The Bedouins. One percenters. I grew up without a father. Well, I had a father, but he was not a good father. He left when I was fifteen. I bounced from foster family to foster family. I was eighteen when I met the Bedouins and they became my family."

"Jesus. What about your mother?"

Josh shrugged. "No idea."

"Did you ever hear from your father again?"

"My father's in prison for murder."

"You've had it rough."

Josh shrugged. "I'm doing okay. I don't blame anyone. I believe in God. I met a pastor in prison. Frank Dorgan. He brought me around. He opened my ears to jazz."

"You like jazz?"

"Yeah."

"Me too. Well listen. You need any more help from me, don't hesitate to ask."

"Would you let me know if McCauley returns to your school? I have a hunch he's about to go off radar."

"After what you just told me, I doubt I'll see him again. He knows how I feel about drugs. I thought I knew him. Be careful."

"I will. Thanks for listening."

Denza rose. "Anytime."

Josh remained behind. He pulled out his phone and

tracked the air tag. The Toyota was stationary at North Forty-First Street. Vice Lords. They'd formed a partnership with the Black P. Stones primarily to deal drugs. He thought about going down there. He thought about calling Cade. There was no point going down alone, and Cade wasn't about to drop everything and race to Wisconsin, which would take two days. There was no point calling the police. There was nothing he could do. He was halfway to Madison when his phone rang.

Josh let it ring. The rain had increased and required his attention. He passed an SUV in the ditch, lights blinking. It was nine-thirty when he finally pulled in. Fig was there to greet him, leaving muddy paw prints across the floor. He grabbed a towel in the kitchen and gave her a rubdown. He flopped on the sofa and opened his phone.

"Josh, it's Jaycee. Please call me as soon as you can."

"Hey Jaycee. What's up?"

"Josh, it's so terrible," she sobbed.

"What?"

"Jerry's in the hospital. Someone tried to run him down. The police called me because they couldn't reach either of his sons."

HIT AND RUN

It took Josh forever to fall asleep. He tossed and turned until two a.m. Fig whined. Finally he wrapped his arms around her and drifted off into unrestful unconsciousness punctuated by images of severed limbs. He rose, fed Fig and they ran. He showered and phoned Ron Bushnell.

"This is Ron. You know what to do."

"Ron, please phone me as soon as you can. Your father was in an automobile accident."

On his way out the door, he said, "Don't panic. I will be home in plenty of time to feed you. No dead rabbits, please."

He was halfway to Milwaukee when his phone rang. Ron Bushnell.

"Ron, I'm driving. Let me pull over and I'll call you back in a few minutes."

Josh pulled off at Johnson Creek and parked in a park-

and-drive.

"I'm in Belize with my wife and daughter," Ron said. "What's up?"

"Your father was struck by a car last night as he walked home from work."

"Oh my god. What happened?"

"That's really all I know. Jaycee phoned me, and I checked the police reports this morning. I'm on my way to Milwaukee now. I'll find out which hospital he's in and let you know."

"Does Shelby know?"

"I don't know how to reach him."

"I'll tell him. I'll make arrangements to return as soon as possible."

"Do you think he'll come?"

"I don't know. Probably not. He really hates Jerry."

"I'm sorry to be the bearer of bad news."

"Don't be. Thank you for reaching out. I don't think Jaycee has my phone number. We're really not close."

"Let me give you hers."

Ron wrote it down.

"Okay. Give me a call when you get to town."

"Yes sir. And thanks again."

Josh parked in front of the Bushnell residence at eleven. Sam let him in.

"Mom's shopping. She'll be back any minute. Would you like a cup of coffee?"

They sat in the living room. There was a framed color

photo on the wall from before Don's death. Sam and Max were adolescents.

"Do you know Jerry?"

"I only met him a couple times when Dad was alive. Dad always invited him to family events. He only showed on Thanksgiving. I don't remember much about him. He didn't say much. It's not like I loved the guy. I feel terrible about what happened, but we weren't close."

Jaycee pulled into the driveway in a beige Honda van, opened the sliding door and grabbed two cloth bags of groceries. Josh went outside to help.

"Hello, Josh."

"Let me give you a hand."

"Get that cardboard box."

Josh hoisted a cardboard box filled with cans and followed her into the kitchen. She put away the refrigerated items, poured herself a cup of coffee and went into the living room.

"Where's Jerry?"

"Froedtert."

"I should go."

"I'm going there next. I'll call you when I get there."

"Do you think it was deliberate?"

"Maybe. And maybe the party or parties who killed Don are still at it."

Jaycee drew a hand across her face. "I find it hard to believe that anybody would be so sick as to continue a feud that began over a century and a half ago."

"People have killed for less. I can sell Grant's letter to pay for medical expenses."

"That's yours, Josh. You earned it. I can afford to chip in. Don planned well. There's no reason for you to keep working."

"That's not the way I see it. I think I found the person who supplied Max with the fentanyl. He's here in Milwaukee right now. If I stop now, he's going to continue to mule fentanyl up from Georgia killing God knows how many people."

"You're a little OC, you know that?"

Josh shrugged. "I've been told."

"What can I do for you, Josh?"

Sensing he had overstayed his welcome, he stood. "I'll call from the hospital."

She stood. "Josh, thank you for coming. I apologize for being short. I'm just not used to all this drama. Sometimes I wish Jerry had just minded his own business. I can't help but think his reaching out to you may have precipitated Max's poisoning."

"I doubt that very much. My feeling is that if it was deliberate, it had been in the works a long time."

Josh drove downtown to 900 N 92nd Street and parked on a ramp across the street. He went inside, passed through a metal detector and approached the front desk behind which a woman wearing horn-rimmed glasses looked up. A police officer stood by, hands clasped behind his back.

"How can I help you?"

"Ma'am, I'm looking for Jerry Bushnell. He was struck by a car yesterday."

"Are you family?"

"No, ma'am. I'm a friend."

She consulted the computer. "He's in intensive care on the third floor, Room 312."

"Thank you."

Josh took the elevator. The hospital had dropped the mask mandate but there were still people wearing them. He went to room 312 and looked in. Jerry lay in bed with his right leg in a cast and elevated. His head was bandaged.

"How you feeling?"

"I feel okay. They got me on painkillers."

"What happened?"

"I was walking home from work on Thirty-Second Street. I waited for the light. I was halfway across when I got hit. I never saw who did it. The police say they may have camera footage. Someone saw and called nine-one-one."

"What are the damages?"

"Broken leg, broken rib, concussion. Doctor says I'm lucky to be alive. I tripped."

"Huh?"

"Yeah, I tripped on a pothole and lurched forward. That's what saved me. If he'd hit me when I was just walking, I'd be roadkill now."

"You talk to the police?"

"Yeah, a cop was in here when I came out of surgery and asked what happened. That's all I know. Figures this would happen to me."

"Okay. If they can find whoever hit you, you're gonna need a lawyer. You want Steve Fleiss. Lives in Madison. I'll write his number down for you. Wait. You know what? I'll call him myself."

The door opened and a man in a gray suit, white shirt, and red tie entered smelling of cop.

"Mr. Pratt? I'm Detective Anderson. Let's talk."

Josh followed Anderson down the hall to a waiting area.

"Coffee?"

"I'm good."

"Detective O'Malley mentioned you in relation to the Max Bushnell poisoning."

"I'm sorry for your loss. He seemed like a great guy."

"He'll be missed. As you know, we're understaffed." Anderson indicated the room. "I shouldn't even be here with my caseload. You have some information on the Bushnell case?"

"Isn't that Wauwatosa?"

"We're all doing what we can."

"Brandon McCauley. He lives somewhere around here. I believe he supplied Darren Olsen with the joint and Darren gave it to Max."

"What makes you think so?"

"Jaycee Bushnell hired me to find out where that joint came from. I traced Brandon to a drug distribution center outside Faubus, Georgia."

"Lay it out for me."

Josh told Anderson about tracking McCauley to Faubus. "While I was down there, there was some kind of incident at the distribution center. I read about it the next day. The sheriff's department recovered several kilos of fentanyl and heroin."

"I'm aware of that."

"I ascertained that Brandon left Faubus the following day and returned to Milwaukee. Last night I spoke to him."

Anderson steepled his fingers. "Go on."

"I asked him if he was running fentanyl. He told me to fuck off."

Anderson turned to his computer. "He's not in the system. How do you connect him to Max?"

"He's friends of Darren Olsen, who gave Max the joint."

"How do you know that?"

"I visited Darren's grandmother in a nursing home and looked at the sign-in sheet. Last July, Darren visited with his friend Brandon McCauley."

Anderson opened a laptop. He brought up Brandon McCauley's driver's license photo. "This the guy?"

"That's him."

"How did you track him down?"

"He studies Kung Fu at White Dragon in White Fish Bay. He has a Facebook page."

The computer. Anderson turned back. "Not anymore."

"You can't just erase your Facebook page. It doesn't work that way."

"I can have one of our techs try to track it down, but as

I said, we're understaffed. I'll pass this information along. Our drug task force will find it helpful. If you have any other information, please don't hesitate to call me. Here's my card."

"What about Bushnell? Do you have any video?"

"We're looking into that right now."

"If you can identify the vehicle, Bushnell's going to need a lawyer."

"I'll let you know."

CHAPTER

46

LUTHOR

Cade watched the house from the tree line. Luthor Bushnell's relationship with Brandon McCauley was puzzling. They were supposed to hate each other. When Cade accessed the sign-up sheet for the Battle of Tunnel Hill, he found Bushnell had signed up as a Confederate. By rights and tradition, Bushnell should have signed Union.

Why would a man turn against his own family? It puzzled him. Luthor had an extensive rap sheet. Assault. Attempted murder. Rape. He'd served seven years in Arrendale on the latter. He'd been out three years. In prison, he'd joined the Sons of the South, a white supremacist group with a Dixie tint. Among his jail tats was the Confederate flag.

Cade watched as a black SUV pulled up in front of the shack. Two men got out and went in. It was too dark to see them clearly. Cade waited a half hour before inching toward the house. The rear was dark. He approached hiding in the shadows. Gardening shed to evergreen tree. He crouched behind the small porch off the kitchen. The rear window faintly reflected light from the front room. He heard the men talking. He crept along the side until he had a clear view of the SUV. He copied the license plate number and returned to the rear of the house.

A bedroom window was partially open.

"Where's McCauley?" a man said in a Mexican accent.

"Don't know."

"That's his car in your barn."

"We swapped cars."

"Why you do that?"

"That's a cop car. He felt it was a little too conspicuous."

The night reigned. An owl hooted.

Bushnell's scream shattered the silence.

"Now maybe you give us some answers, yes?" said the voice.

Cade cupped his ears. His hearing was excellent despite being subjected to months of bombardment and gunfire.

"Where's our stuff?"

"Brandon took it! He took it to Milwaukee. He's working with some gang up there."

"What gang?"

"I don't know! I swear to God! He didn't tell me!"

Bushnell's scream collapsed into a groan. Cade thought about just sitting there. No. He had his own questions. Bushnell's gasping and shrieking masked the sound of Cade sneaking in through the unlocked kitchen door. He lurked in the shadow, not peering down the corridor to the front until he'd examined his options. He'd thought about slitting their throats but that would leave DNA all over the place. He looked around. Underneath the sink, a plastic pail held two kilos of some white powder wrapped in heavy plastic. A cast iron skillet lay on the counter. He picked it up. He looked around the corner. Two men wearing baggy dungarees, one in a denim jacket, one in leather, backs to Cade, had Bushnell pinned on the sofa. One of them held a hammer. One stood on one leg, the other boot planted hard in Bushnell's gut. Both Mexican. As Bushnell writhed, Cade saw a blue/purple scar growing on his forehead.

"You're gonna tell us..." denim jacket said as Cade walked quickly and silently down the corridor and swung the skillet counterclockwise, catching the man on the temple. He fell like a pole-axed steer. The other turned. Cade kicked him in the nuts hard enough to lift him up off the ground. Cade knelt with a knee on the man's gut, wrapped the man's bolo tie around his neck, yanked him upright and turned one-eighty so they were back to back. Cade squeezed the bolo tight and bent forward. The man struggled violently but Cade had him by sixty pounds and wasn't on drugs. The man on his back struggled hard before collapsing into a dead weight.

He turned to the man he'd brained, who lay still. Cade felt for a pulse. Dead.

Bushnell lay exhausted, bleeding from his nose, arms at his side. "Who are you?"

"Where's McCauley."

"Who?"

Cade brought his right heel down on Bushnell's nearly supine form. The air whooshed out. "Okay," Bushnell croaked, bent over. "Okay."

Cade eyed him. "Try to run and I'll cripple you, understand?"

"Yeah."

Cade went into the kitchen, found two clean glasses in the wood dish rack. One featured Daffy Duck, the other Mickey Mouse. He filled them with water from the sink and returned to the living room where Bushnell sat leaning forward, forearms on thighs, breathing fast. Cade handed him a glass.

"I think I have a concussion."

"I'd bet on it. How come you signed up as a Confederate?"

"Huh?"

"Battle of Tunnel Hill. The reenactment. Your ancestors were all Yanks. What's your story?"

"I always identified with the South."

"Why is that?"

"Nothing to do with slavery. Their heritage and lifestyle are more to my liking. They were gentlemen. The Union was drunks and mercenaries."

"They didn't make that much money."

"The Bushnells got no use for me and I got no use for them."

"Did you kill Don Bushnell?"

Bushnell stared at him.

"You killed your own blood."

"It was a matter of honor."

Cade barked. "You stabbed him to death at a concert."

He reached inside the denim jacket's pockets, pulled out a cell phone, a money clip, a balisong, and a .25 automatic. His name was Yair Cahudo, home address Culiacan. Cade turned to the other, eyes and mouth open, Zapata mustache and slicked back black hair. Emil Condit, Nogales.

"Who are these guys?"

Bushnell turned his head and hawked a loogie over the edge of the sofa. "Sinaloa."

Luthor's face was stippled with pockmarks, deep-set eyes of a mean dullard.

"You dealin'?"

"Me? No! Never!"

"But McCauley was."

"Yeah, he's got connections up north."

"Where up north?"

"Milwaukee."

Cade went into the kitchen and grabbed the plastic bag filled with skag. He threw it at Bushnell's head. Bushnell barely got an arm up in time.

"What's that?"

"I don't know! Where'd you get it?"

Cade snorted. "You're gonna tell me everything I want to know."

"If I do, will you leave?"

"Yeah, I'll leave. Who all's involved in distribution?"

"These cartel guys are new. They're up here because Brandon was stealing from the Raiders."

"Quantrill's Raiders?"

"Yeah."

"Who else?"

Luthor counted fingers. "Garney. It was his house. He's dead. Paul Etteridge. He got blown away two nights ago, him and Wallace, and three cartel guys. I don't know their names."

Cade knew. He had their IDs. "What's McCauley up to?"

"He's movin' shit."

"Tell me."

"Vice Lords are dealin' with the cartels now. Brandon's their boy in Milwaukee."

"What about the Bushnells? Is he going to leave them alone?"

Luthor stared at the floor. "I doubt it. He's crazy about that. Just batshit insane. He says Ethan Bushnell stabbed his great-great-grandfather Roderick in the back and left him to die on the battlefield."

"That didn't happen. I read that book the guy wrote. Roderick returned home and took over the family plantation."

"Brandon thinks that if he wipes out all the Bushnells, it ends the family line, he'll descend into Luciferean hell, which is what he wants, and sit at Baphomet's feet. He's gonna go after them. The Bushnells."

"What Bushnells? Why?"

"I told you he was crazy. I don't get it."

"Does he use?"

"He's the only guy I know who can hoover a gram of blow and act perfectly normal."

"How long has he been supplying the Vice Lords?"

"Six months. Listen. I have money."

Cade picked up the cast iron skillet and stood. "Keep it."

Bushnell looked around like a cornered rat. "You said you'd leave if I answered my questions!"

"I'm leaving. You don't want to see it, turn around."

Bushnell got to his feet and turned to face the night.

CHAPTER 47

WAITING FOR DIEGO

With his horn-rimmed glasses, ear hoops and beard, Darren Olson looked like the type of hipster you saw any afternoon bending over his laptop in a Starbucks. He gingerly turned the pistol over and over in his hands, marveling at its weight, its purpose, its lethal finality. He held it out sideways like a gangsta rapper, rotating through his living room on the fifth floor of Caden Arms Apartments in Wauwatosa. The pistol almost reached Brandon, who reached up and shoved it away hard.

"Listen, you dumb son of a bitch. Don't point the pistol at anyone you don't intend to kill."

Darren abruptly pulled back. "I knew that."

"Are you with me or what?"

"It's a big step."

"Fuck an A it is. That's why I'm paying you the big bucks. As soon as it's done, we're outta here. We can stay with Diego. He's got a house on the beach in Ensenada. We'll live like kings with this score. You can live like a rich man in Mexico for what it takes to live like a starving student in the US. There are collectors in Mexico who will pay a fortune for what they got in their basement."

"Why doesn't your uncle do it himself?"

"Ed's got enough on his plate right now. He's got to deal with the cartel. How'd it feel when you stabbed that fag in the park?"

Darren spread his fingers. "I don't know, man. It felt like power. It felt like god. It felt like I could do whatever I wanted."

"That feeling only gets stronger. How bad do you want that bitch?"

Darren grinned lasciviously. "Bad. I always wanted to fuck her. She always treated me like shit."

"Well there it is." Brandon looked at his watch. "Diego should be here any minute. You get that tequila?"

"Yeah, man."

"The good stuff. Not fucking Jose Cuervo."

"Fifty bucks a bottle." Darren opened the narrow drawer on his coffee table, pulled out a hand mirror, a baggie filled with coke, his balisong and a cut plastic straw. He held up the straw. "Who'da thunk that plastic straws would become illegal? I always saved my straws."

"Well you musta thunk it or you wouldn't save them."

Darren grinned. "No, I just hate to throw anything out."

He shook a chunk of crystallized blow out on the mirror, flipped the balisong open with a flashy double maneuver, and set to work chopping up lines.

THE DARK BEFORE THE STORM

Josh got home at five, fed Fig, had a pepperoni pizza with cauliflower crust and a bottle of New Belgium. He went to bed at seven thirty and he dreamed he was riding Ed Hotchkiss' five-cylinder radial bike, the Hotchkiss. He woke with Fig licking him at first light.

Josh fluffed the dog. "Every day I get to sleep a little later."

It was Wednesday and Ray was coming over. Tomorrow was Thanksgiving. After his morning run and shower, Josh headed to Woodman's to shop for dinner. Quinoa pasta. Fresh asparagus, mushrooms, and onions. Hickory smoked bacon. It started to drizzle. Josh brought his sixteen-gallon Craftsman shop vac in from the garage and went to work. Fig shed her own weight in fur every week. He thought about saving the fur and having a sweater made.

He was scrubbing the toilet bowl when his phone rang.

He didn't recognize the number.

"Pratt."

"Pratt, it's Levon Cade. I talked to Luthor Bushnell last night. He says McCauley's gonna wipe out the Bushnells, starting with Jaycee."

A cold hand squeezed Josh's heart. "When?"

"I don't know but soon. He won't act alone. He's bringing friends."

"What friends?"

"He didn't say."

"Where's Luthor now?"

"He isn't available. Some of these friends. They may be trying to establish a beachhead."

"Shit."

"Some of these friends, they're the same people bringing shit up from Mexico. You helped me. I'd like to return the favor."

"How soon can you be here?"

"I'll be there tonight. I left yesterday."

"Shouldn't we let the police handle this?"

Silence.

"Do you mind if I tell them?"

"You can do what you like, but their total department is forty-eight officers, down from fifty-four prior to the pandemic. And what are you going to tell them? That the Sinaloa Cartel is targeting a suburban family in Wisconsin?"

Josh gave Cade Jaycee's address. It was three p.m. It would be dark by five. He had to get moving. He called Ray.

"Baby, we're gonna have to postpone dinner. Something came up."

"What?"

"Business."

"What business?"

"It's just something I have to do."

"Now I'm gonna spend the whole night worrying about you. Will you call me? When you're done?"

"If I can call, I will."

"What's that supposed to mean?"

"I'll call you."

"Fine."

He knew what that meant. He phoned the Delafield Police Department. A woman answered.

"Sergeant Roney."

"Sergeant, this is Josh Pratt. I'm a private investigator from Madison. You know about Max Bushnell?"

"Yes. What is this about?"

"There's a possibility that someone is going to harm the Bushnells in the next couple of days. Would it be possible for you to keep an eye on them?"

"Could you be more specific?"

"Whoever supplied Max with the fentanyl may not be done. I mentioned this to Detective O'Malley, in Milwaukee. Whoever killed O'Malley may be going after the Bushnells."

"I will report this to our watch commander. Is this a good number for you?"

"Yes."

"Where are you now?"

"Madison."

"Thank you for bringing this to our attention. What makes you think someone is going after the Bushnells?"

"It's a long story. I would be happy to fill you in in person tomorrow."

Josh prepared to leave. If the cartel was involved, they'd bring guns. Josh was not allowed to own guns. He had seven guns in a safe in the basement. Cade would have guns. If Josh used those guns, he would be committing a felony. He grabbed a tactical flashlight. Maybe if he shined it in their face, they'd go away. He grabbed the last of the burners.

It was a curse having the thing in his pocket. It was demonic. The temptation to look was overwhelming. The only thing good about it was that it had revolutionized standing in line.

"Is Mis Zenab. working with Al Rayan Bank Of Britain Plc United Kingdom I got your email from my company email search. I would like to discuss something very important with you about abandoned funds in my bank that I want both of us to benefit from. that is if you don't mind; if you reply I will give you the full details."

Deleted. He hit the road.

He cruised past the Bushnell residence and turned into

a cul-de-sac ending with a circular turnaround crowded by four big houses under construction. He didn't want to advertise his presence. He walked an eighth of a mile back to the Bushnells and rang the doorbell. Sam answered, phone clamped between head and shoulder, wearing sweats.

"Hang on. There's someone here. Hello Josh. Come in."

Josh followed her in. She held up a finger, walked away talking to her friend, and returned.

"What's up?"

Josh dropped his backpack on the table. "Is your mom here?"

"She went to Costco. She'll be back soon. Make yourself at home. Do you have any news on our father?"

"I have a theory. You know your uncle Jerry was hit by a car yesterday."

"No! Oh my god. Is he all right?"

"He'll live. Broke some bones. Where's Max?"

"Max is sleeping at the academy. He's teaching again. Should I call him?"

"No."

"Did you learn who gave him the dope?"

"Darren got the dope from Brandon McCauley. You know him?"

Sam shrugged, her long brown hair dropping a bang across her forehead. "Nope. I guess he's one of the big bad McCauleys. Mom told me your theory. I can't wrap my head around it. I mean, come on people. Get a life. You don't inherit a grudge. Especially for something that happened one hundred and fifty years ago. Would you like some coffee?"

"Sure. I'd like to set a few cameras in here."

Sam wrinkled her nose. "Cameras? What do you mean?"

Josh reached into his backpack and took out a small gray disc. "This is a motion-activated camera."

"Sure."

Josh set one in a brass pot holding a dieffenbachia. He put another at the back of a dark wood bookcase, gluing it high up on the inside wall. It covered the whole room.

Sam went into the kitchen. Josh followed. She popped a canister into the Keurig. "How do you like it?"

"Strong."

She pushed buttons. Minutes later she handed him a steaming white porcelain mug shaped like a Star Wars Empire soldier's helmet. Josh added milk and sugar. Sam made one for herself. They sat at the kitchen table looking out on the backyard, grass gray-green in anticipation of winter. Most of the yard was covered with fallen leaves.

"There are certain cultures," Josh said, "that elevate malice and revenge to holy status." He thought about Polly Furst, the young woman who put out a Muhammad comic, hired him to protect her, and how he blew it. She was dead. He thought about his first serious flame Fig Newton. Dead. He couldn't lose another client. He just couldn't.

"But that's so un-American."

"Tell me about it."

"Like who, for instance?"

"There are still Micks in Ireland who are willing to die to remove any vestige of English rule."

"Oh you're kidding."

"I wish. Have you seen *The Foreigner*? Starring Jackie Chan?"

"Oh I love Jackie Chan! No, I haven't seen it."

"Good movie."

A car pulled into the driveway.

"Here's Mom."

CHAPTER

49

BAPHOMET

Diego Guttierez pulled up in front of Darren's apartment building in a rented Mustang and got out. At six-two and a trim two hundred pounds, he looked like the boxer he'd once been, once ranked in the Top Ten of Mexican middleweights. His thick, wavy black hair concealed beneath a Brewers ball cap, he wore a brown leather aviator jacket, tan cargo pants, and hand-engraved cowboy boots. A thick black mustache clung to his upper lip. He opened the trunk, shouldered a heavy duffel bag and entered the foyer, which smelled of dust and wood polish. He pushed the ivory-colored button for Olsen.

Olsen buzzed him in. Diego bypassed the elevator and took the stairs. He didn't trust elevators ever since he'd torched an apartment building in Vera Cruz when he was a teenager. Manuel Pico had paid him good money to do it, as the owner had refused to sell the property, which Manuel needed to build his Fiat dealership. Twelve people died, including three who'd been trapped in the elevator.

Diego sprinted up the stairs to the fifth floor and pushed out into the carpeted hallway. The door to 515 was open. Inside, Brandon rose from the sofa.

"The man is here."

Brandon and Diego embraced, pounding each other on the back. Brandon introduced Darren. They shook hands. Diego looked at the coffee table. Cava de Oro. White lines on a smeared mirror. Cigarette butts and a fat roach in an amber ashtray.

"Hey, man," Darren said. "Let me pour you a shot of Cava."

Darren decanted the bottle into a red Solo cup and handed it to Diego, who held it up. Darren and Brandon held theirs.

"Cheers," Diego said.

They sat. Darren pushed the mirror across the table toward Diego, who sat in an old wing-backed chair upholstered in rose-colored fabric. Diego pushed the mirror back across the table.

"Hombre. You are in no condition to do what needs to be done. We have business with…" He looked at Brandon. "Who's your friend?"

"McTelvin."

"Yes. I thought we were getting together with McTelvin tonight."

"We are."

"Now you are adding persons. I ask you, how certain are you that this house contains the items you want? How easy will it be to sell them? Objects of such value are usually insured, and that usually sparks a police investigation."

Darren waved his hand. "Nah, man. Max told me they never look at that shit. He was thinking of selling it."

"How do you propose to monetize it? You can't take it to an established auction house."

"Nah, man. We'll find a private collector. It ain't hard. Do you know how many Civil War societies there are on the internet? You could spend all day just looking. The most valuable item is a handwritten letter from General Ulysses S. Grant."

"Did your friend Max ever see it?"

"No. He just talked about it, but he's pretty sure it's there. He always thought that shit was creepy. A lot of that shit is actual stuff they used in the Civil War. The uniforms, saber, all that shit is real."

Diego steepled his fingers. "Even if we were able to get top dollar for it, it cannot begin to compare to the profits we make with drugs. The only reason I am accompanying you is because I value your friendship."

Brandon placed his hands together and bowed. "Sensei."

"What about the cops?"

"Delafield's understaffed. They don't have enough officers to cover traffic."

"A noise like this, they're gonna call in whoever. I suggest a diversion."

Brandon leaned forward, all ears. "What you got in mind?"

"I have an explosive device. We plant it where it'll get attention, maybe a school. Once that happens, they won't have time for anything else."

"I like it," Brandon said. "I'll plant it. I know just where to put it."

Darren blanched. "Come on, man. You want to blow up a bunch of kids?"

"It's not just an explosion. It's tribute."

"Tribute for what?"

"Tribute for Baphomet."

"Fuck you talkin'?" Diego asked.

"Baphomet's the devil," Darren said. "Brandon worships the devil."

"We don't call him the devil."

"That true, ese? You worship the devil?"

"I worship Baphomet."

"Who the fuck?"

"Some scholars believe Baphomet was simply a corruption of 'Mahomet' - the Prophet Muhammad."

Diego stared at Brandon as if seeing him for the first time. "I'm Catholic. I'm not praying to some Muslim pendejo."

"The more who pray, the greater our chances."

"Why'd you even bring this up, Brandon?" Darren whined. "Couldn't you just go off by yourself and pray alone?"

Brandon looked up. "And now, if you don't mind, I'd

like to offer a prayer for our success."

Diego tilted his hand. "Go ahead."

Brandon stared until Darren looked down. "I'm not asking you to join me, but it would help if you did."

"How about I just sit here and keep my mouth shut."

Brandon nodded. "Turn off the lights, wouldya?"

Darren got up and turned off the lights. Brandon reached into his backpack, pulled out a glass candle holder bearing a black Baphomet, billy goat head on a hermaphrodite body, caduceus on its belly, pentagram on its brow. He set the candle on a DVD case: *Fast & Furious VII.*

"Place your palms together."

Darren and Diego placed their hands together. Brandon sat back, hand pointing up, left hand low. "As above, so below. Believe in one God, do we, Satan almighty. The uncreator of heaven and soil...and the unvisible and the visible...and in his son, begotten of Father, by whom all things will be unmade...

"Who for man and his damnation...incarnated, rise up from hell...from sitteth on the left hand of his father...for thence he shall come to judge...out of one substance with Satan...whose kingdom shall haveth no end..."

Diego leaned forward, arms on thighs, grinning like a rabid dog.

"Hear our Satan prayer, our anti-Nicene creed. Hear our Satan prayer for the coming of seed..."

Diego slapped his hands together. Darren started, looking wildly around. "That's enough."

Brandon looked up. "It's not finished. I have to finish the prayer, or our chances of success will diminish."

Diego pointed. "Go the fuck in the back there and finish your fucking prayer."

Brandon rose immediately and left the room without looking at his companions. Diego and Darren looked at each other.

"I mean, what the fuck."

"That shit creeps me out," Darren said. "I don't believe there is a god, certainly not some crazy thing like Baphomet."

Diego shrugged. He looked at his watch. "We're gonna move tonight. You need time to plant those claymores."

"Where'd you get claymores?"

"Knights Templar."

"Huh?"

"Knights Templar. Former Mexican military. Now they work for us. Where is that cabron? How much time does he need?"

Brandon reentered the room. "We're good to go."

"Don't you want to sacrifice a dog or something?" Diego asked.

"That's what the bomb's for."

"Diego says we're going tonight." Darren said.

"Why?"

"Because I say so."

Darren's buzzer rang. He looked up, alarmed.

"Chill. It's McTelvin. He's gonna be joining us." Brandon said.

"Who's McTelvin?"

Brandon got up and buzzed him in. "He's my Vice Lord's connection. He's cool. I met him at kung fu."

Minutes later there was a knock at the door. Brandon opened it admitting a tall Black teenager wearing an XXL Lebron James jersey and baggy cargo pants.

"McTelvin, Diego, Darren."

McTelvin lifted the jersey showing an automatic pistol tucked into his pants. "What's the payoff?"

CHAPTER 50

NO FUN

Sam went upstairs. Jaycee pulled into the driveway in her Honda, got out, opened the rear door and grabbed a cloth bag imprinted with Chili's Home Repair. Josh went outside.

"Hey Jaycee."

"Josh. Thanks for coming."

"Is there someplace you and the kids could go for a couple nights? If money's a problem, I'll be happy to spot you."

She gave him a funny look. "Why?"

"I'd say the chances are one in one hundred, but McCauley may come out here to finish the job."

"Oh you're kidding."

"I don't kid. I told the police. I asked if they could step up patrols, but they've got a manpower problem."

"Tonight?"

"The sooner the better."

"Josh, I'm exhausted. We're not going anywhere tonight."

"Mind if I spend the night?"

"Of course not. You can take Max's room."

"Do you have any firearms?"

Jaycee scrunched her face. "No! Do you?"

"No. I'm not allowed to own firearms."

"Do you think we need guns?"

"I just like to be prepared."

"Have you ever been in a situation like this?"

Josh flashed back to the monster Moon, who'd killed three police officers and Josh's girlfriend Cass before he was killed by his own son.

"It's what I do. I provide security. Says so on my card. You know, I'd feel better if you'd go stay at a friend's house."

"I wouldn't know who to call."

"You'd be safer in a motel. I passed several on my way over."

"Don't be ridiculous."

"What about St. Christopher's? Could you go there?"

"You're not serious."

Sighing, Josh took out his phone and called the last number on "recents," the number Cade had used.

"This number is no longer in service."

As Josh put his phone away, he had a feeling that unlike Ninja and Kleiser, Cade was not about to call him back. What to do, what to do. He had no proof the McCauley clan was about to descend guns blazing. Only Cade's hearsay. Josh's run-in with McCauley should have been sufficient to dissuade McCauley from any further action. But he really didn't know McCauley. Satanic worship indicated he might not be rational.

He muted his phone.

Jaycee went into the kitchen and pulled out her phone. "Max? Where are you?"

Beat.

"No reason. Just checking in. I love you too."

She returned to the living room. "Max has a room at St. Christopher's. He's the dorm monitor. He's got about a dozen kids who look up to him."

Josh rose. "Excuse me one minute." He went outside and phoned the Delafield Police Department.

"Sergeant. Roney."

"Yes, ma'am. This is Josh Pratt. I phoned you yesterday."

"I remember. What can I do for you, Mr. Pratt?"

"I'd like to brief you on the situation."

"What situation?"

"As I said yesterday, the people who slipped Max Bushnell that fentanyl-laced marijuana may want to return and finish the job. This is about a feud that goes back to the Civil War."

"Excuse me?"

"Bushnell and McCauley were best friends at West Point. When the war broke out, Bushnell joined the Union and McCauley the Confederates."

"Mr. Pratt, let me stop you there. We are severely understaffed. If you have knowledge of a crime, by all means, come on in. Right now, I don't need any conspiracy theories."

"Can you do a drive-by?"

"I can't promise you anything, but I'll try."

"Thank you."

He went inside.

"I heard you through the open door," Jaycee said. "What did they say?"

"They'll try. Let me take a look around here. May I go downstairs?"

"Of course. What are you looking for?"

"I don't know yet."

"Knock yourself out. I'm going to take a nap."

Josh went downstairs. The basement was divided between a finished rec room with well windows looking out on the backyard and the concrete-floored utility room. Josh went to the window on the left and cranked it open. It would not be obvious to anybody outside due to the leaf guards. Jaycee and Sam were slim enough to get through. Both well windows opened on the backyard. The utility room held the washer, dryer, furnace, and Civil War artifacts. Across from the armoire was a wood workbench backed up by pegboard containing tools. There was a jigsaw and a lathe. Josh pulled an axe from the pegs, flipped it, caught it by the handle. It was sharp. He jammed it in the back of his pants.

The oak door between rooms felt solid. The lock was the weak part. One solid kick.

"Hey," Sam said.

Josh jumped. "You snuck on me."

"I'm part Indian. What are you doing?"

"I'm looking for a place to dodge bullets."

Sam wrinkled her nose. "Huh?"

"These people you've been feuding with for a hundred and sixty years…"

"I'm not…we're not feuding with anybody."

"All right. They're feuding with you. If they show up, we need a plan."

Sam grinned. "Are you on drugs?"

"Look. You know what happened to Max. Do you think I made that up?"

"No." She frowned. "Now you're freaking me out."

"Which is why it would be a great idea for you and Jaycee to get out of the house. At least for tonight."

"Oh jeez…oh jeez…I'll talk to her."

Josh returned to the artifacts. The pockets yielded six Liberty dimes, forty-five cents Indian pennies, a hundred and ten dollars in greenbacks. He pulled the saber from its sheath. It was dull. He put it back. He picked up the Spencer. He picked up the box of ammo and carried them to the workbench. He checked the Spencer's action, grabbed a bottle of gun oil and went to work.

"We're not going anywhere!" Jaycee yelled. "Get it out of your head."

Josh slid seven cartridges into the Spencer's magazine. Sam came down blowing raspberries.

"Mom wasn't too crazy about your idea."

"I tend to be a little paranoid."

"You know if I told Max what's going on he'd race back here with a half dozen of his buddies."

Josh shook his head. That was the last thing he needed. "Not a good idea."

Sam put her hands on her hips and looked at the axe in Josh's pants. She giggled.

"Are you serious?"

Josh shrugged. He felt stupid.

"And these guys are gonna have guns?"

"If they come."

"You know, I have a black belt in karate."

She sank like Elvis and threw hands, shouting. "HAI! HOO! HA! DIE YANKEE DOG!"

"Seriously?"

"Yes. Salick's Karate right here in Delafield."

"Good to know, but you don't want to see these guys, and you certainly don't want them to see you. So if they should come tonight, it would be great if you'd take Jaycee out the back door and go to your nearest neighbor."

"No, I want to help! What can I do?"

"Just get out of here. And take your mom with you."

Sam pouted. "You're no fun!"

CHAPTER 51

AFGHANISTAN

Cade hissed a near-silent curse as he came up on a clusterfuck on Highway 87, traffic backed up as far as the eye could see. At ten o'clock at night, the road looked like a zipper of red lights. Cade made an illegal U-turn across the dividing strip and drove to the first exit, Dousman Road heading west through rolling farm country. Ten minutes later he drove around a bend. Silence enveloped him as he pulled over and turned off the engine. Seconds later, the cicadas began their nightly concert. Cade opened the glove compartment and pulled out the State Farm Insurance Road Atlas and looked up Waukesha County. He'd have to circle clockwise, adding seventy miles to the trip.

He headed west, windows open, inhaling moist soil, pine, a hint of cow manure. Cold air rushed past him through the open windows. It smelled different up here. Alabama smelled of moonshine and honeysuckle. Plus the garbage everybody dumped by the side of the road. Lights glowed from farmhouses.

McCauley had supplied the fentanyl that killed Charles Howley's boy Ruther, and Amos DuWayne's daughter Cynthia. He'd watched Ruther play football for Colby twice, when he'd gone to watch Merry cheerlead for the Colby Cougars. Cade wasn't close with the Howleys and DuWaynes. They were friendly acquaintances, good people who worked the land and paid their taxes. Cade wasn't looking to set out on a lifelong crusade to clear the earth of predators. But there were times he couldn't turn away, couldn't let it all just slide to hell like that. He was not alone. Vigilantes had sprung up all over the country. Phoenix Jones in Seattle. That dude in Texas. Cade didn't kid himself he was on any kind of holy crusade. He only went to church back when his wife was alive to drag him. He wanted to believe. He wished he could believe.

The men of faith he knew had an inner tranquility he envied. *It is God's will. Inshalla.* Faith was a gift. You either had it or you didn't. He wondered if his folks had been more religious, and took him to church more often whether he would become a God-fearing man. He might have been a man shaped by faith rather than a weapon forged by other men.

He was coming up on a small hamlet. "Griffin, Pop: 1243." He cruised slowly down Main Street, past the Herbivore Vegan Restaurant, Jake's Tavern, Ace Hardware, and Gold Real Estate. Two kids rolled down the sidewalk on one-wheeled skateboards. Two guys on Harleys burbled by heading east. Cade pulled into a 7/11 on the west end to gas up and hit the head. Three kids wearing hoodies stood in the shadow of the side wall, smoking a joint. He could smell it. It cost $110.00 to fill the tank. He added Slim Jims and a ginger ale and paid in cash.

As he walked toward his truck, the teens lit a Roman candle. The sudden flare of light sent a ripple down Cade's spine and he was instantly transported to a shithole north of Kandahar where the Taliban had set off a bomb in an open-air market, killing four people and maiming dozens. Cade was down the street, looking at fruit on a card table. Raisins, figs, apricots, dates, and cherries. Cade used a wooden spoon to ladle cherries into a cardboard cup.

He saw dust and splinters a split second before the shock wave hit him, combusting the air and making his ears pop. Instinctively he dropped to the ground as debris rained. His hearing gone, he got to his feet and looked for survivors. He carried an old woman out of the carnage and lay her on a rug in the shade before emergency responders arrived.

When he returned to the base, they told him that the explosion was a diversion while the Taliban slaughtered a family tending their sheep. Cade inhaled deeply and let it out in a controlled stream through his nose. *Let it out. Let it out. Don't let it take root.*

Cade got in his truck and booked. Thirty seconds and he was through town, fast food joint trailing off into a lumber-yard, trailing off into a tractor supply store. Light receded.

Millions of stars showed in the sky. He drove in silence, save for the rumble of his tires on asphalt. Cade would have preferred to retire to the ranch and raise horses but the world wouldn't leave him alone. The flow of refugees and drugs only got worse. Over ten thousand child predators had entered the country illegally. Not a day went by that the news didn't announce multiple arrests of convicted felons who'd been deported many times. He'd considered going down there and seeing for himself, but that would only cause trouble. Trouble for him, trouble for Merry, Jessie, and Hope.

One man could only do so much. When it came to your front door, it was too late. And here it was, at his front door. It had killed Charles Howley's boy Ruther, and Amos Du-Wayne's daughter, Cynthia. They didn't play poker or golf together but they were part of his community.

And here I am, he thought, *a thousand miles north*. He normally didn't pursue people. But he couldn't stand by while McCauley spread his filth in Wisconsin.

Cade had done due diligence on Pratt. There wasn't much to find. His criminal record up to the year he went to prison. He was polite and forthright and that carried weight with Cade. Cade was a loner by nature. He hoped he hadn't made a mistake. Milwaukee wasn't like rural Alabama or Georgia. For one thing, it was the fifth most segregated city in the US. Detroit was number one. The police department was understaffed, overworked, and reluctant to take action even while witnessing assaults. The whole country was on the verge of barbarism. Cade had never imagined such a thing while he was serving overseas. He'd grown up reciting the Pledge of Allegiance and saluting the flag. Even those his family didn't always live by the strict letter of the law, Cade appreciated the country he lived in.

It may be, in the near future, neighborhoods would have to set up their own police, as they had back in medieval times. The nation would dissolve into territories. Tribes. The Socialist Peoples' Republic of Minnesota. The Free State of Texas. The silver lining was that when civilization finally collapsed, the tapeworms who'd taken over would be useless. Their bodyguards and best friends would turn on them as they had on Caesar.

Cade was the best guy to recruit and train a neighborhood militia, but it went against his nature. He just wanted to be left alone. Raise horses, love Merry, Jessie, and Hope. But the world wouldn't let him do that. For a second he yearned to be back home in Alabama, riding with Merry. Images of his friends' dead children intruded. The poison had found its way to Colby.

Lights appeared just north as he approached the intersection of Oconomowoc and Ninety-Four. He got in line at the access lane behind a Tesla and a van waiting for the green light. Traffic swooshed by. It was just past eleven. The light changed and he hit the interstate heading east. Lights appeared on both sides of the road. Scattered farms, tiny villages. The closer he got to Milwaukee the denser the lights became. It came to a standstill a few miles outside of Delafield. Cade was stuck in traffic and there was a patrol car parked in the median so he couldn't make a U-turn.

He'd passed the last exit fifteen minutes ago.

He turned on AM, flipped around until he came to KDKP Milwaukee, all news all the time. Bodies found at South Shore Park believed to have OD'd. A flash mob invaded Chesterton's Sporting Goods at a mall in Racine making off with eighty thousand dollars in merchandise. The police were unable to respond because most of them were at the waterfront trying to control a mob demanding reparations not only for Blacks but for transgenders as well. A seven-car pileup caused by fog had snarled traffic on the interstate.

Cade looked over the roofs of the cars ahead of him to see police funneling traffic off at the Delafield exit. Red and blue flashing lights winked in the distance. Cade felt no sense of urgency, only annoyance that he was struck in traffic. He couldn't remember the last time. He stayed away from urban centers mostly.

Finally, it was Cade's turn. The cop waved him up the exit ramp. Left was Delafield. Right were farms. Cade turned left, driving slowly through Delafield's genteel apron of commerce, State Farm, Wendy's, Lacklove Law, and Kroger. The Busnhells lived on West Shore Drive. He was crossing Gennessee Street when light flared to his right, the buildings lit as if a nuclear bomb had detonated. A split second later, the concussion hit. He was far enough that it didn't deafen him. He could still hear. His first instinct was to head for the disaster and see if he could help. Then he remembered Afghanistan.

INVASION

Josh lay on the sofa, window cracked an inch, one ear cocked, listening to distant dogs, an occasional moo, and coyote yelps. He didn't expect anything to happen but you never knew. McCauley wasn't rational. Josh had met Satan worshippers in prison. Just as Reverend Dorgan had taken Josh under his wing, there was a dude named Iggy Lustig who declared himself the lord high of darkness and damnation and recruited disciples. He looked the part. At six-four, two hundred and eighty pounds, filed teeth and enough ink for the Gutenberg Bible, Lustig was a formidable figure. There were holes where corrections had removed his nose and earrings and piercings.

Lustig was a ferocious brawler. The Gangster Disciples and Aryan Nation gave him a wide berth. His Satanists weren't the biggest gang in prison, but they were feared because they didn't give a shit. Life, death, all the same to them when it came to upholding their honor. The prison library dutifully ordered *The Lesser Key of Solomon*, *The Book of Lies*, and *The Book of the Law* on their behalf. These volumes were perpetually checked out, passed from Satanist to Satanist until they could recite passages by rote. They had a smack franchise that even the Gangster Disciples left alone.

If McCauley ever went to prison, and Josh hoped he would, he'd fit right in. Josh was ninety percent certain Brandon had murdered Don Bushnell. He hoped to ask him. Josh couldn't sleep. He got up, went to the bathroom off the kitchen and returned to the living room as a black SUV passed the house, lights off. Josh's warning meter went off. He froze, listening through the open window for the SUV to stop, the slam of car doors. It cruised on until it was no longer audible. He phoned the Delafield Police Department and got a recording.

"We are experiencing a heavier-than-usual volume of calls at this time. If you have an emergency, please hang up and dial 9-1-1."

Josh stared at the phone.

"What's going on?" Sam asked from the top of the stairs.

Josh jumped.

"I didn't mean to startle you."

"It could be nothing, it could be something. If I told you to go out the back door and hide in the woods, would you do it?"

"You're freaking me out, Josh."

"Would you?"

"I guess. What about Mom?"

"Maybe. I don't know. It could be nothing. A black SUV passed the house with its lights off. Do any of your neighbors have a black SUV?"

"Probably."

"Do me a favor. Go wake your mom."

"Who can sleep with you two skulking around?" Jaycee said from the balcony overlooking the living room. "What's going on?"

"Josh thinks we're about to be attacked. He thinks we should run out the back and hide in the woods."

"That's ridiculous. This is Delafield."

"Could I convince you ladies to at least go hide in the basement? I opened a window in case you have to bolt."

Jaycee's mouth was a slit. "Come on. We can sleep on the sofas in the rec room."

"I can't sleep."

"Listen. I passed a Best Western on my way over. How about I just run you guys over there for the night? My treat."

"Well we're not going to get any sleep here," Sam said. "That's for sure. You don't have to drive us. We'll take my car. Let me pack a few things."

Sam and Jaycee went upstairs. When they reappeared, Jaycee had an overnight bag, Sam a backpack. Josh stood in the kitchen door as they entered the garage, turned on the light, and got in Sam's banged-up Sentra. She lowered the window.

"Josh hit that button, wouldya?"

Josh pushed the garage door opener. It rumbled and began to open. A dark shape rose from behind matched plastic garbage bins and leveled a pistol at his head.

"Back in the house," an unfamiliar voice hissed.

Josh froze. The garbage cans stood between him and the intruder. He stepped back. From the opposite corner, a man spoke. "Everybody back in the house."

Josh looked around wildly. How had they gotten in? His eyes fell on the rear door that opened on the backyard.

"Hands on your head."

Josh put his hands on his head, went into the kitchen and turned around. The garage door closed. A tall young Black man wearing an oversized hoodie holding an MP5 machine pistol. He looked familiar. He grinned.

"Hey. You a bad muthafucka."

"Grace Baptist."

"That's right. You got a good memory. Brandon, watch this cat. He knows some shit."

Jaycee and Sam entered followed by Brandon McCauley. "Let's go in the living room."

A Latino in a muscle shirt and Zapata mustache relaxed on the sofa. A young man in a hoodie with a shaved head pointed a revolver.

"Darren!" Sam spat. "You fucking creep. What are you doing?"

Darren grinned. "What I always wanted, Sweet Samantha."

Josh turned to Brandon. "Is this about the feud?"

"Sit down. Keep your hands where I can see them."

Josh sat on the sofa, the axe in his belt pressing into his back. "Did you kill Donnie?"

"You're the private dick. You were at Ed's house."

"I told the Delafield Police you might drop by. They'll be making a house check shortly."

Brandon grinned. "They've got their hands full with the explosion down at the mall. We won't be seeing any cops tonight."

"Why?" Sam said. "Why are you doing this?"

"You wouldn't understand. You live a nice, suburban life and you're studying some bullshit at college and you don't even know where you came from. It's in my *blood*!"

Josh leaned forward. Darren waved his gun. "What's in your blood, Brandon?"

"Bad blood. The bad blood caused by the Bushnells when Ethan betrayed Broderick at the Battle of Tunnel Hill."

"How did he betray your great-great-grandfather?"

"They had sworn blood oath at West Point that they would always have each other's backs no matter what. You didn't know that, did you? None of you knew it because you don't give a shit about history."

"Why'd you tear those pages out of the McCauley book?"

"Because they were lies. You people. You people have no idea what it's like to have an ancestral memory, do you?"

"Hey," Darren said. "Omma take this bitch upstairs and leave you to it." He pointed the gun. "Let's go."

"Fuck you."

Darren took three strides and smacked Sam across the face with the back of his left hand. "I said let's go." He poked her with the gun. She trudged toward the stairs.

Josh breathed carefully to keep from freaking out. He had an axe in the back of his pants, against four men with guns. The dangerous-looking Latino and the kid from Grace Baptist looked like killers. Brandon almost certainly was. He only had the one play. He might get one but the others would drill him. Out here in the country, shots fired inside a house would sound like firecrackers.

The lights went out.

UNDER SIEGE

A rock shattered the window in the kitchen. Brandon, the Black kid and the cartel guy sprang to their feet, weapons pointed. Josh pulled the axe and hurled it at the Black kid. The top of the blade hit him on the temple.

"Ow!" He whirled and squeezed the trigger, not really pointing, as Josh threw himself into a forward somersault, kicking out with both legs, catching the shooter in the gut, causing him to grunt, lurch back and fall on the sofa. Brandon ran through the kitchen into the backyard. The cartel guy tracked Josh in the dark squeezing off shots. The third shot grazed Josh's left shoulder like a white-hot poker. Josh rolled behind the sofa and reached for his tactical flashlight. He switched it to high and shined it in the cartel guy's face, blinding him, turned it on the Black kid who put a hand to his eyes and raised his pistol.

Josh ran into the front yard, looked around wildly. He

sprinted for the gorse bushes that lined the driveway. Shots cracked from the backyard. Three sharp. Two barely audible. Chuffs of air. Josh circled the house clockwise, staying in shadow. The thugs' eyesight was returning. Josh hunkered at the rear corner of the garage. At first he saw no one. A slight movement on his right revealed Brandon, moon reflecting on his pale face as he knelt behind a brick barbecue. Holding his pistol at an angle, he squeezed off two shots, the flare lighting the patio. There was no response. Josh looked but saw nothing resembling the big man from Alabama.

He waited. Brandon slipped back into the house and slid the patio door shut. Josh waited. He gave a low whistle. Someone whistled back from the woods. Josh gave the house a wide berth as he circled around to the woods. He was ten feet in when Cade whispered, "Over here."

Cade crouched behind a spreading juniper clutching a .45 with suppressor, infrared binocs clinging to his head like an oil platform.

"Thanks for coming."

"I'm here for McCauley. The others are a bonus."

"He just went back in the house."

"You have any experience clearing a house?"

"Not really."

"Who's in there?"

"Jaycee Bushnell and her daughter Sam. Four thugs. Brandon, cartel guy, Vice Lords guy, and Brandon's friend Darren. He's the guy who handed the fentanyl-laced reefer to Max Bushnell."

"Okay. Here's what we're gonna do. I'm going round to the front and take a look. If I get a clear shot, I'll take it. You watch the back in case they try to get out that way."

"What about the women?"

"I can tell the difference. You got a piece?"

"No."

"It would help if you had a piece."

"I know where I can get one."

"Right now?"

"Yeah. It's in the basement. I think I can get down there without them noticing."

"How you gonna do that?"

"Basement window. I cased it out."

Cade gave him the thumbs up. "I'll ping you on your phone when I'm in position."

"Then what?"

"Where's the basement entrance?"

"In the kitchen."

"I pulled the plug and stripped the lever. The only light they got is what they brought with them. If I see a shot, I'll ping you. You come up from the basement and take out whoever you can."

"I can't shoot someone in the back."

"Don't be a Boy Scout. Those women's lives are at stake. What's with the piece?"

"It's an antique. I'm not sure it will work."

"We don't have time to go back to my truck. I parked about an eighth of a mile down the road next to your car. If

McCauley's intent on killing those women, we have to act now."

"Okay."

Cade disappeared. Josh bowed his head. "Dear Lord, please look after Jaycee and Sam. And Cade too, what the hell."

Josh approached the house from the garage side. Creeping along the baseboard reminded him of the time he'd attended ninja training school. He reached the window well and carefully pried loose the leaf guard, slid down on his ass, turned so that he hung inside the basement and lowered himself to the concrete floor. The basement door was open.

Josh felt his way to the workbench, barely illuminated by soft light coming through the window well. He picked up the Spencer and slowly jacked a cartridge into the chamber. Holding the rifle at port arms, he stood at the bottom of the stairs.

"Fuck we do now, man?" the Black kid said.

"These are the same motherfuckers that hit us at my uncle's place," Brandon said calmly. "There are only two of them. We've got them outnumbered and outgunned. Diego. Go upstairs and see if you can spot 'em in the front yard."

"You talk like you know what you're doing."

"I've been a student of tactics my whole life."

"Why don't you go upstairs?"

Beat.

"This is my turf."

"How many men have you shot?"

"I don't need a gun to kill someone. I can kill someone with my bare hands."

"You go upstairs."

Beat.

Josh heard the creak of tread on the stairs. He heard SPACK as the front living room window absorbed a bullet. Gripping the Spencer in both hands, he ran up the stairs and whirled into the living room where Darren held a gun on Jaycee and Sam, seated on the sofa. Darren turned as Josh brought the rifle to his shoulder and fired center mass. The sound cracked the night open. Darren lurched back and fell, striking his head on the coffee table.

Josh jacked another shell and whirled. Someone had run out the kitchen door and forced the garage door open by hand. Automatic gunfire stitched the night, then stopped. Josh turned toward the stairs to the second floor. He didn't know who was up there. Brandon or the cartel guy. He grabbed Darren's gun, a nine-millimeter Colt, and tossed it on the sofa next to Sam. She picked it up.

"You know how to work that?"

"Yeah." She cleared the breech, jacking a cartridge into the chamber.

"Get behind the sofa."

It was a heavy leather sofa. Jaycee took one end and Sam the other. They shoved it away from the wall and hunkered beneath a *Bye Bye Birdie* poster. Sam pointed. Josh whirled. A body lay on the ground between two wing-backed chairs and a table backed up to the picture window, which had a neat hole in the center radiating cracks. The Black kid with the MP5 lay on his side, mouth open, blood pooling. Josh stayed away from the window, waiting for Cade to ping.

Cade pinged. "What's your situation?"

"Two down. Darren and a Vice Lord. Cartel guy and Brandon still at large."

"I think they took off. Someone ran into the woods. Could have been either. Heard a vehicle start up and take off. Didn't come this way. Let me look around and then I'll come in."

Josh picked up the MP5 and went upstairs, checking each room. The window in the master bedroom was wide open. Brandon had scaled down the shingles extending over the family room, dropped to the ground and booked.

The Bushnells were safe for now.

CHAPTER
54

THANKSGIVING

Jaycee and Sam clutched each other on the sofa.

"Would you ladies mind going upstairs while Cade and I remove the bodies?"

Jaycee and Sam went upstairs.

Josh and Cade stood in the driveway. It was two o'clock in the morning.

"I'll take care of the bodies," Cade said.

"What are you gonna do with them?"

"Not your problem."

"Thank you for doing this."

"I'm not done. I want McCauley and the cartel guy."

"McCauley's driving an '04 Corolla with Georgia plates. Hang on." Josh took out his phone. "I just sent you a picture. I don't think he's gonna stick around. He's gonna head back to Georgia."

"I wish I had your tech support."

"You're an Army guy. Don't you have contacts?"

"Marine. My favor bank's about empty."

"How can I reach you?"

Cade made a face. "I'll text you."

Josh watched until the truck's taillights disappeared around a curve. He went inside.

Josh stared at the bloodstains in the living room. The floor was synthetic wood. You could bleach and scrub it without doing damage. They'd have to toss the carpets.

"Who was your friend?" Jaycee asked.

"You don't want to know."

"Should I call the police?"

"No. And don't talk about this to anyone. You hear me, Sam? Ever."

"I hear you."

"Why do you say that? They could come back at any time."

"No they won't, and if you get the police involved, it becomes a big deal. Reporters, spots on the evening news, stories in newspapers, all of a sudden, you're a freak show."

"Should we call the police?"

"To do what? Be grateful they're not here. I'm surprised nobody reported the shots. Or maybe they did and the police are just too busy."

Jaycee hugged her daughter. "Now I don't want to stay here. Sam, let's go to that motel in Hartland."

"Do you think they'll come back?"

"They'll never come back," Josh said. "This was a once-in-a-lifetime deal. Now they know what they're up against."

"You think this Brandon McCauley killed Don?"

"There's a chance. He was eighteen at the time. Prime time for sociopaths, and he hasn't gotten any better."

"What are you going to do? I mean, as far as I'm concerned, you've more than fulfilled your assignment. And Darren's dead."

"McCauley gave him the drug. We're not quite through with him."

"Who's we?"

"You don't want to know. I can hang around while you pack if you like."

"Josh, you've done enough. Send me a bill."

"I'll get back to you. It's been a long night. You ladies mind if I head out?"

"Of course not. You've done more than anyone could expect. We will always be grateful to you for what you've done. Please tell your friend."

"Okay. If by chance the cops show up and want to know what the hell happened, don't speak to them without an attorney. If you need a good criminal attorney, I can recommend one."

It was frigid as Josh walked to his car on the cul-de-sac, houses under construction across from a fallow field. Picked clean. Josh cut west toward the interstate. At four in the morning, traffic was sparse. It was still dark when he pulled into his driveway at five thirty. Fig barked him into the house. He gruntled her, took a shower, and lay in bed staring at the ceiling. Sleep wouldn't come. He'd saved Jaycee and Sam but he felt empty. Unsatisfied. The biker code demanded that Brandon die for his crimes. But Brandon was no longer his problem. Cade would almost certainly kill him. He got up with the sun, put on his sweats, and went for a run. By the time he'd showered and eaten breakfast, the workaday world had risen. Cars rolled by heading toward the city.

Tomorrow was Thanksgiving. He was not looking forward to dinner with Ray's parents, Hal and Marianne. Both college professors. After he showered, he picked up his phone to call Ray and realized it had been off since yesterday. He turned it back on. Jerry had phoned three times. He called back.

"Where were you? I thought you'd abandoned me like everybody else."

"Jesus Christ, Jerry. Is this the thanks I get?"

He was instantly angry with himself. *Dear Lord, please forgive me for taking Thy name in vain.*

"Cop told me they had video of the car striking me. They said I was in a crosswalk and the driver ran a red light. You can read the license plate. They said they're so busy right now they don't know when they'll get to it, if ever."

"What cop? Did you get his contact info?"

"It was a woman. Yeah. She gave me her card. Diane Hirschfeld." He read the phone number and email account.

"I'm glad you're okay. You should sue the driver. For that, you'll need an attorney. You need Steve Fleiss. He's in

Madison. I'll tell him what happened and put him in touch with you. When are you getting out?"

"Today. Ron's picking me up."

"Your son, Ron?"

"Yeah. I was very surprised when he showed up yesterday. He actually seemed glad to see me. He's taking me to his place in Brookfield. Jaycee called too but I'd already agreed to go with Ron."

"That's great, Jerry. I hope you'll take this opportunity to tell him how much you love him and what this means to you."

"Yeah."

"I'll talk to Fleiss and have him get in touch with you."

"Thanks. Did you find out what that letter's worth?"

"It's kind of on the back burner for now. But I'll get to it."

Ray phoned. "I'll meet you at the folks and then I'll drive to your place."

"How's the play going?"

"Great! We've had standing room only for the premier, and we're going to add more next week."

"Did your folks see it?"

"They were here last night."

"I'll bring a nice Cabernet."

"Don't dress like a slob. Wear something nice."

"I have clean blue jeans and a plaid lumberjack shirt."

"Wear a jacket."

Thanksgiving Day was gray and overcast. Josh riffled

through his closet. Most of it was empty. He had two jackets, one belonging to a blue business suit he'd bought in case he ever had to testify in court and a gray tweed with leather buttons. He wore a pair of gray Dockers pants, a plain light-blue shirt, the blue jacket, and lace-up black shoes he'd bought at JCPenney before they closed their doors due to rampant shoplifting.

The McRaneys lived in a two-story red brick colonial in University Heights, down the street from Frank Lloyd Wright's famous "Airplane House."

Josh pulled his Chrysler into the driveway and parked behind Ray's Prius. At least a dozen stickers adorned the Prius' ass.

JESUS WAS A LIBERAL

FARNSWORTH IS A PATHOLOGICAL LIAR

BE KIND

COEXIST

THIS IS A SAFE SPACE: RACISM BIGOTRY
SEXISM AND DISCRIMINATION WILL NOT BE
TOLERATED

At least the McRaneys had removed their WE BELIEVE sign.

As Josh reached the front door it opened on a radiant Ray, wearing a scooped sky-blue sweater over a short navy-blue skirt, her long black hair brushed to shine. Behind her, her mother Marianne, still svelte in her sixties wearing a black dress with orange pumpkins gestured from the dining room.

"Come in, Josh. Welcome. Would you like a drink?"

"Yes, please."

She came forward and embraced him. "What would you like?"

"Bourbon on the rocks."

"Hal, do we have any bourbon?"

"Look in the cabinet."

Marianne found a bottle of Maker's Mark. She handed Josh the drink and led the way into the living room which looked out on the perfect lawn shaded by fir trees, hunkered down for the winter, concrete birdbath empty.

They sat in a semi-circle facing the large brick fireplace, burning natural gas. Hal came in with a drink and sat next to Marianne on the sofa. He raised his glass.

"Another turn around the sun, another opportunity for gratitude."

Josh raised his glass. "Amen."

CHAPTER 55

THE COMEDIAN

"What did you think of Ray's play, Josh?" Hal asked.

"Brilliant."

"Yes," Marianne added. "The trope of having a woman play the man accentuates the move from a structuralist account in which capital is understood to structure social relations in relatively homologous ways to a view of hegemony in which power relations are subject to repetition, convergence, and rearticulation."

Josh's forehead scrunched. "Huh?"

Marianne's laughter tinkled like ice in a glass. "Oh Josh. That's just academe talk. You know I teach a course in how the question of temporality into thinking structure marks a shift from Althusserian theory that takes structural tonalities as theoretical objects to one in which the insights into the contingent possibility of structure inaugurate a renewed conception of hegemony as bound up with the contingent sites and strategies of the rearticulation of power."

"Thanks for clearing that up."

Ray slapped him on the knee. "She's joking."

Josh squinted at Marianne. "Seriously?"

"No, dear. I said exactly what I meant. Ray's joking."

Josh looked at Ray. Butter wouldn't melt in her mouth. He burst out laughing and pointed at Marianne. "You're funny."

She leaned forward, smiling. "What do you mean I'm funny?

"Just, ya know…you're funny."

"You mean, let me understand this cause, ya know, maybe it's me, I'm a little fucked up maybe, but I'm funny how, I mean funny like I'm a clown, I amuse you? I make you laugh, I'm here to fuckin' amuse you? What do you mean funny, funny how? How am I funny?"

Josh looked at Ray in astonishment. "She's gotta go to the comedy club."

Hal looked back and forth confused. "What are you talking about?"

"Mom's quoting Goodfellas, Dad," Ray said.

"My god, you're funny," Josh said. "Seriously. You gotta get onstage."

"I'm thinking about it."

"You can use Rise Up! I'll sponsor a comedy night!"

The McRaneys served turkey, stuffing, cranberry, salads. Josh agonized whether to offer a prayer. Oh what the hell.

"Folks, do you mind if I pray?"

Hal and Marianne exchanged glances. Ray kicked him under the table.

"By all means," Hal said.

Josh bowed his hands. "Dear Lord, for this food we are about to receive, thank you. I'd like to put in a word for the McRaneys...they're good people."

"Amens."

Josh wondered where Brandon was. He could be right outside. Freaky motherfucker. Josh had another bourbon and put Brandon behind him. Marianne had just demolished his preconceived conceptions. He was tempted to ask what happened to the WE BELIEVE sign. Was it possible Marianne had a come to Jesus moment? What were the odds? A billion to one? He forced down a slice of lemon pie.

"Sir," Josh said to Hal. "What do you teach?"

"Clinical psychology. Postgraduate."

Josh bit his tongue.

"Josh," Ray said. "Do you have something to tell my folks?"

Josh drew a blank. Ray kicked him under the table. Hard.

"Sir, I'd like to ask for your daughter's hand in marriage."

"Well this is a surprise."

"Josh, that's wonderful!" Marianne said.

"How do you propose to support her?"

"Daddy! This isn't the antebellum South! Josh owns his own business. I own my own business. Together, we pull in a six-figure income."

Josh arrived home at nine. Fifteen minutes later, Ray

pulled into the driveway. She set a big Tupperware container on the kitchen counter.

"Leftovers."

Josh looked at Fig, who sat at his feet, lightly paddling her front paws, tail thumping.

"Don't worry. You'll get yours. Your mother's hilarious."

"I know! She was always very funny."

"I can't believe she saw Goodfellas."

"I know! I can't either!"

Josh made a tiny gesture with thumb and forefinger. "We should watch it sometime."

"If you're gonna force me to watch a movie, I get to choose."

"Fine. Just not the Punisher."

"That's not on my radar."

"But here's the problem. The funnier Mom gets, the wider her social circle. Now she's hanging out with beatniks and poets, and Dad's worried."

"What's he worried about?"

"That he'll be left behind."

After they had made love, they lay in bed in Josh's room, Fig between them.

"Success has made Idaho more obnoxious."

Josh stared at the ceiling.

Ray looked over. "Did you hear what I said?"

"Huh?"

She waved a hand in front of his face. "Earth to Josh."

"Sorry. I was thinking about that guy."

"What guy?"

"Brandon McCauley. He killed Don Bushnell and ten years later, he poisons his son."

"Why is that your job? Where are the cops?"

"It is my job. I'm getting paid."

"Well don't you think you've done enough? Just turn him over to the cops."

"Cops ain't gonna do shit. He's no longer in Wisconsin."

"Good. Forget it, then. No longer your problem."

"Well he tried to kill me."

She wrapped her arms around him. "Consider yourself lucky. He's gone. Not your problem."

But it was his problem. It was his obsessive compulsion. He couldn't help it. He couldn't just leave it to Cade. It was his problem.

Fig rolled belly up.

"The dog has capsized," Ray said.

"She gets plenty of attention."

"Is that your phone?"

Josh heard chiming from the other room. "Shit." He swung his legs out of bed.

Ray put a hand on his arm. "Ignore it."

"Can't, baby. It might be a guy I know."

He went into the living room where he'd left his phone on the coffee table. Unknown number.

"This is Pratt."

"It's Cade. Hope I'm not too late."

"Nah. What's up?"

"You know that Civil War reenactment they got going on?"

"Tunnel Hill?"

"Guess where our friend Brandon's going as well as Quantrill's Raiders?"

"No shit."

"Not only that, our friend Easy Peazy's gonna fight for the Confederacy."

"That doesn't make any sense."

"Between five and ten thousand Blacks fought for the Confederacy. Where else is he gonna fight? Easy's ancestors came over on a slave ship."

"What do you want to do?"

"I'm gonna be there. I'm going to take care of business. I just thought you'd like to know."

"Do you need me to help take care of business?"

"Hell no. I just thought you'd like to know."

"Hmmm."

"It's not for three days. Let me know if you're coming down."

"I will." He sat on the sofa staring at the blank flat screen. Brandon McCauley was a serial killer.

"Hey!" Ray called.

"I'll be right in."

"Fig is licking the blanket."

Josh got into bed. "Where's Sid Vicious?"

"He's at home. He'll survive."

Fifteen minutes later, Ray was snoring, the only light

cast by a clock/radio. Josh lay awake staring at the ceiling, hand on Fig's head. Fig struggled to roll over on her back, working against two sets of thighs. She finally made it. Josh dutifully laid his hand on her belly.

Maybe Ray was right. He should let it go. It was Thanksgiving, a time for gratitude.

"Dear Lord," he whispered. "Thank you for my blessings. Thank you for the love of this good woman, even if she is an atheist. I will try to be a better person."

He didn't promise not to go after Brandon.

JOSH ENLISTS

Josh waited until nine to call Murtaugh. "Easy, it's Josh Pratt."

"Mr. Pratt. What can I do for you?"

"I understand you're doing the Battle of Tunnel Hill."

"That's right. So are some brothers."

"Is it too late for me to sign up?"

"I don't know. They got a website. Battleoftunnelhill dot org. You have to have the uniform. North or the South?"

"North, I guess."

"You a Yankee."

"I guess."

"You got a uniform?"

Don Bushnell's would fit. "Yeah."

"Well the cut-off date for registration is Monday. I didn't figure you for a Civil War buff."

"Well let's just say my interest has been kindled. I hope

you don't mind me asking, why would a Black man fight for the Confederacy?"

"Many reasons. Cultural. Heritage. Between fifty and a hundred thousand Blacks fought for the Confederacy, but the South only started training them as soldiers a few months before the war was over. Just 'cuz we fight don't mean we endorse slavery. Quite the opposite. A lotta Blacks thought that if they fought for the South they would be emancipated. I look on it as a cultural and historical event."

"You know how many Quantrill's Raiders have signed up?"

"I don't give a fuck. I'd better not see any of those crackers, or I might be tempted to show 'em a little rough justice. After you left, some of 'em came by the office and tried to intimidate me. That didn't work. I got a gang too. At least six Outcasts have signed up. We're all gonna be in the same company."

"You got a room for me?"

"Well now. I got a full house, but one couple's leaving tomorrow and the rest are just passing through. I'll hold one for you."

"I appreciate it."

Josh called Jaycee. "How you doing?"

"I'm more freaked out than Sam. You know, we have a cabin in Door County."

"Can't hurt. Listen. I got a favor to ask."

"Anything."

"Can I borrow Donnie's Civil War gear? The uniform,

the rifle, stuff like that?"

"Well sure, but why would you want it? Do you think it's worth money?"

"No, I'm gonna participate in a historical reenactment. Gotta have a hat if you're gonna play in the band."

"When?"

"I'll be there by noon."

"I'll be here."

"Thanks, Jaycee."

Josh called Fleiss.

"What? I got five minutes."

"I have a friend who was struck while using a crosswalk in Milwaukee. We got video to track the driver down. It's a personal injury case."

"Send me the video. I'm due in court."

"Thanks, Steve."

Josh went online and registered as a lieutenant in the army of General Joseph Hooker. He went downstairs and opened the safe. He dug around in one of his plastic bins and pulled out the last burner phone.

He drove east. He turned on news radio. Two hundred and five murders in Milwaukee and they still had a month to go. Most were gang related. The overworked police had only been able to clear forty-three percent. He switched to a jazz station out of Kenosha. Sarah Vaughan. As he drove through Delafield he saw a boarded-up storefront with orange police sawhorses. Someone planned ahead. Josh bet it was the cartel guy. They'd been at it long enough. He parked in front of the house. The picture window was covered with plywood. He phoned Cade.

"That number is not in service at this time."

"Fuck me," Josh muttered. He was about to get out when his phone rang.

"Pratt." Cade said. "What do you need?"

"The cartel guy. Can you ID him?"

"Diego Guttierez. Knights Templar. Former Mexican military gone rogue. He's plugged into the Sinaloa Cartel."

"I'm coming down."

"Why?"

"I want Brandon."

"Don't. I'll take care of him for you."

"You shouldn't take that on by yourself. I'll be there tomorrow. I'm leaving as soon as I'm done here. I'm at the Bushnell's."

"How they doing?"

"They're hanging in there. Are you in Faubus?"

"No. Don't look for me."

Sam came out and stood with her hands on her hips looking at him.

Josh went inside. "How you doing?"

"Mom's freaked out. We're going up to our cabin for a couple days."

"You got anyone to look after this place?"

"The Rosenbergs. They live across the street."

The Rosenbergs house was concealed behind a wall of blue spruce. He could see it was a big place made from fieldstone and had a three-car garage. "They can't see shit."

"I'll ask them to get the mail and keep an eye on the place. Mom said you wanted to borrow Dad's stuff?"

Josh went into the basement, pulled out the uniform. A captain's uniform with a double-breasted dark-blue wool coat with brass buttons, dark-blue wool trousers, gold collar and cuffs, a wide leather belt, a saber in a scabbard, leather boots. He hefted the rifle, grabbed the box of ammo. He had just put them in his trunk when Jaycee arrived in her VW sedan, opened the garage door, and rolled in.

"Did you get what you needed?"

"Yup. Thank you, ma'am. I'll try to return it in the condition in which I found it."

"Oh please. It's been sitting down there for years. Do with it as you please."

"You sure?"

"I'm sure."

"When you leaving for Door County?"

"As soon as we can pack. I think Sam's already packed. Come on in, Josh."

Josh followed her into the house. Sam slouched in front of the TV in the rec room watching Judge Judy.

"You ready, kiddo?"

"Yup. It'll take us like two hours to get there."

"We'll stop to get groceries. Josh, would you like a cup of coffee?"

"Sure."

Jaycee went into the kitchen. "You want French roast or

Ethiopian?"

"French."

She returned with a tray holding two mugs of coffee, a silver cream container, and a restaurant-style sugar dispenser. He mixed and sipped. Keurig.

"You talk to Jerry?"

"I called him this morning. They said they were going to release him Monday but Ron had come pick him up, and he's going to have trouble getting around while he heals. He has a cracked rib and a broken femur. They put a titanium socket in his hip."

"You gonna be back by then?"

"Yes. We're only planning on spending two nights at the cabin."

"Did you talk to Ron?"

"I did. I'll be taking Jerry when we get back."

"I gotta get going. I'm heading back to Georgia."

"You must love to drive," Sam said without taking her eyes off the plaintiff, whom the TV identified as Le'bastognian DeFranchesse of New Orleans.

"I love riding my bike. I couldn't care less about a car. Welp, gotta go."

Jaycee put her arms around him and laid her head on his shoulder. "Thank you."

"You ain't seen the bill yet."

Jaycee laughed. Josh got in his car and headed south.

TEXAS HOLD 'EM

Josh spent Friday night at a motel in Louisville, Indiana, and was on the road by six. It was five-thirty by the time he pulled into Violet Estates. The nine-room motel was almost full. Six cars in the parking lot. Florida, Missouri, South Carolina, Michigan and New York. Josh pulled up in front of the end room. Number nine.

It was a cool crisp day with a hint of fall, not the icy wind of the Upper Midwest, but the genteel change in seasons of the Old South. Inside, Easy handed a key to a tall, white-haired man in beige slacks and a leather jacket.

"Thank you kindly," the man said.

Easy put both hands on the counter. "Welcome, traveler!"

"Thanks for holding that room for me, Easy."

"Us bikers got to stick together. The reenactment's Saturday and Sunday. Outcasts are gonna meet at the Pancake House out on Rte. Five before headin' on over. They call muster at ten, and the reenactment's at noon."

Josh pulled out a folded paper from his jacket and spread it out on the counter. "I'm with Hooker's Brigade. I just got in under the wire."

"Well that's the big'un. I'm Army of the Cumberland. We'll be on opposite sides. Rossiter's Creek in the middle. Johnny Reb at the tree line."

"Have you heard from the Raiders?"

"They got better things to do."

Josh brought up a picture of McCauley on his phone. "You know this guy?"

Easy squinted. "Looks familiar, but I just can't place him. Who he?"

"He's the guy I'm after. He'll be with the South."

"What's the beef?"

"He gave fentanyl to a friend of mine. He nearly died."

"You gettin' paid?"

"Yup."

"Huh. Wish I was younger. I could have made good money whoopin' ass. Are you gonna kill him?"

"No, I'm gonna drag his ass to the cops."

"Lotsa luck with that. Only time I see a cop's when I ride into Haspierre."

"No cops in the park?"

"The only cops are those takin' part. They got a whole cop platoon."

"Has the big guy been back?"

"Nope."

"All right. See you tomorrow."

With its worn flannel blankets, paper cups, and faded

rose wallpaper, his room was depressing. The flat-screen TV was the brightest thing in it. He brought in his overnighter and Union equipment. Josh showered, went across the street to Dolly's Diner and sat in a window booth. There were six other customers. A slim, sparkling Black girl wearing a Hello Kitty shirt and a white apron came up.

"Where you from?"

"Wisconsin."

"How was the drive?"

"Boring."

Josh ordered a cheeseburger and took out his phone. He'd turned it off for the drive. When he turned it on, he saw that Ray had called.

"Hey baby."

"How was the drive?"

"I listened to a lot of country."

"Call me tomorrow and tell me you're all right. Don't get shot or bayoneted."

"I'll try not to."

"Love you."

"Love you."

He phoned Cade. Five minutes later, Cade phoned back. "Yeah?"

"I'm at the Violet Motel. I'll be at the reenactment tomorrow."

"I told you not to come."

"Do you know where he is?"

"What are you doing here, Pratt? I told you I'd take care of it. Are you looking for trouble?"

"I'm doing my job. Will you be there?"

"I'll be there but you won't see me. If you were smart, you'd stay away."

"I never said I was smart."

Josh went to sleep early, rose at six, grabbed breakfast across the street, and put on his Union uniform. It felt like stolen valor. He was play-acting. He'd never considered enlisting. By the time he was of age, he'd fallen in with the Bedouins, a one percent gang that flipped the bird to all those square institutions. The church. Schools. Cops. Soldiers. It took four years in Waupun and the help of Pastor Dorgan to turn his head around. He'd had plenty of time to think about it. Everybody in the joint had plenty of time to think about everything. Few came to the right conclusions. Josh was lucky. He bowed his head.

"Thank you, Jesus."

Two and a half hours later, he drove around Chattanooga to the battle site, one of the few recreations that took place on the actual grounds. A sixty-foot tower held a giant red-on-white banner: BATTLE OF TUNNEL HILL, NOVEMBER 29/30, 1864. He pulled into a field that had been turned into a parking lot and stopped for a man wearing a Union kepi.

"Five dollars. Park anywhere."

Josh gave him a fin. "Where's registration?"

The man pointed to a roofed picnic table with three lines snaking back.

"You expect a big crowd?"

The man gestured at the parked upfield. "It's only nine thirty, and the lot is almost full."

Josh parked and walked through the throng toward the

picnic table. He stood in line behind a Confederate corporal. A woman with an open laptop looked up. "Name?"

"Josh Pratt."

She scrolled through her laptop. "Okay. You're good to go. You know where you're going?"

"No."

"Says here you'll be with the Sixteenth Wisconsin volunteers. You see that big oak with all the blue coats? Go over there."

"I'm looking for a friend of mine. Brandon McCauley?"

The woman scrolled. "Can't help you."

A man stood on a plastic milk crate wearing a general's uniform talking to the crowd.

"All right, you know the drill! Any newbies out there, ask the veterans. The battle begins in one hour. If you don't have a copy of the itinerary, you can pick one up at the registration desk. Platoon leaders have this blue and gray ribbon on their tunics." He pointed to his chest. "If you haven't already, you will draw straws to see who gets shot and when. Are there any questions?"

Josh raised his hand. The general pointed at him. "You."

"Anyone from Wisconsin here?"

A man wearing a blue kepi with the crossed swords turned toward him. "Over here."

They separated from the throng. The man was short, chunky, with a bushy mustache. "Bill Archerd. Oconomowoc."

"Josh Pratt. Madison."

They shook hands.

"What do we do now?"

"We wait for the order to advance. This your first battle?"

"Yes, sir."

"You picked a good one. Come on. I'll introduce you to the boys."

"Are they all from Wisconsin?"

"Heck no. They're from all over. We needed volunteers to fill out the roster."

Josh followed Archerd to a group of soldiers sitting and standing around a picnic table with an open box of doughnuts. There were only a handful left. Josh plucked a raspberry. Archerd introduced the other re-enactors. Most were middle-aged. They came from all over. Maine. Michigan. California.

Archerd pointed across the valley, through which ran the railroad tracks, at a steep wooded hill crowned by a rock anvil looking out over the city. "That's Missionary Ridge. The rebels are dug in from that gap in the trees all the way to the tunnel."

"What do we do until then?"

A private in wool pants, suspenders and a plaid shirt pulled a box of cards from his pocket. "Texas Hold 'em. Who's in?"

CHAPTER 58

THE BATTLE BEGINS

Josh was up two hundred when a bugler blasted "The Battle Hymn of the Republic." Members of the Sixteenth Wisconsin volunteers buckled on their sabers and belts, grabbed their rifles and headed toward the big oak.

Archerd walked alongside. "Okay. Here's where we entered the fray. A company under Champion charges the rebels on Buzzard's Tooth Gap."

"Wherezat?"

Archerd pointed at a notch on top of the ridge overlooking the railroad, elevation over eight hundred feet. "Are you a survivor or a casualty?"

Josh shrugged. "I don't know."

"They didn't give you a number?"

"Shit."

"Well don't worry about it. Do what you feel is right."

"How do I know when I get shot?"

Archerd grinned. "That's what the numbers are for. They'll be shootin', and some of us have been pre-selected as casualties. I'm not, but Dane Thiassin is. He's from Oconomowoc too. This is our third reenactment."

"What do you do in real life?"

"Home, health, and life."

Ahead, a buff man in a colonel's uniform grabbed soldiers by the arm and pointed to them. Josh and Archerd came up.

"Where..." Josh said.

"You and you," the colonel spat, pointing. "You're with Walker's Brigade. That tall guy with the blumped hat, that's Major Walker. You're with him. Now go. Go go go. This is war, goddamnit."

Archerd jogged toward Walker, Josh at his heels.

Walker motioned. "Over here. Archerd, you're in charge of Glade's Platoon. Who are you?"

Josh stuck out his hand. "Josh Pratt, sir. From Wisconsin."

"This your first battle?"

"Yes, sir."

"Welcome. Have a good time." He turned toward stragglers.

Glade's Platoon hunkered behind an ancient stone wall clutching their rifles.

Archerd pointed at the Spencer. "Beautiful. May I see?"

Josh checked the chamber, then remembered they weren't using live ammo. Blanks were off-limits. They were too dangerous. Most of the soldiers loaded their own muskets with black powder and a plug of cardboard or, in some cases, tobacco.

What the fuck am I doing? I'm supposed to be looking for McCauley!

The battle's allure was too great. Josh didn't remember having this much fun since water skiing in Lake Monona. They faced the sun. Some wore sunglasses.

"Did they even have sunglasses?"

Archerd spoke out of the side of his mouth. "No, and those aren't very good reenactors. The whole point is to live it as it was lived. It's like method acting. We think about this stuff all the time. What if McIntosh got lost on the way to the battle? What if the rebels had been able to sink the Pontiac."

"They talk about alternate histories…uh oh, here we go."

Glade stood and motioned toward the ridge with his saber. "CHARGE!" A mostly blue wave flexed and charged, running across the narrow valley, leaping the rails, and running uphill into the forest, slowing as the grade increased, finally coming to a crawl as they clung to ridges of sheer rock breathing hard. Reports echoed from every direction. Gray smoke whiffed away. Josh heard grunts from hand-to-hand combat but when he looked around, he didn't see anyone. Josh followed Archerd up a narrow defile that reached the top. Archerd stopped at the tree line beyond which lay the Confederate encampment. Neat lines of tents. Many had spent the night there. Something flattened Josh's hat against his head. A split second later, he heard the report. He looked up. A familiar face sat in a tree about ten feet off the ground, holding an old muzzle-loading pistol. Grinning like Huckleberry Finn with a gold tooth.

"You're dead, Yankee dog," Easy said.

"Easy! What are you doing in a tree?"

"I'm part of a guerrilla group that formed just before the battle. All former slaves whose owners granted their freedom if they'd join the fight. Here I am."

"Where's the rest of your company?"

"More like a platoon." He gestured broadly. He wore well-patched woolen trousers, leather suspenders, a leather Union holster at his belt, and Red Wings. "George and Terribone are over there somewhere with Lieutenant Sanders. Sanders is a White man. We never did make it beyond sergeant."

"What about the Raiders?"

"They ain't showed their redneck faces. Hope to keep it that way. This here's the best attended event in nine years."

"I can't believe Union troops made it up this slope. It's a fucking mountain!"

"I know. Used to climb it when I was a kid. My old man was a truck driver and I'd ride with him when he come up here. He'd drop me off at the base. '"See you at the top, kid.' Then he'd go off and visit a hooker."

"Where was your mom?"

"She walked out on him. She had it up to here. He didn't even bother to hide the evidence. Did you know hookers are named after General Joe Hooker? Fought for the Union. Used to throw wild parties. He was famous for wild parties and debauchery. Ladies of the night who followed him from camp to camp came to be known as hookers."

"I did not know that."

"I just shot you. Why ain't you down?"

"Anybody asks, I'll tell 'em. I'm looking for McCauley. He'd be with the rebels."

Easy pointed up. "They're on the ridge. You got some climbin' to do."

"Where will you be after the battle?"

"Me and the boys usually repair to Roy's Place, road-house in Chickamauga. Come on by, you've a mind."

"What time?"

"Eight."

Josh saluted. "Later!"

He picked up the pace. Thirty minutes later, he slipped behind a neat line of a half dozen tents. Standard Army issue, square with peaked roof, pop tents. Most were made from synthetics. One was original issue. Patches all over. A reb stepped out between two tents and pointed a revolver.

"Where do you think you're going?"

"I'm dead. I'm just looking for a place to sit down."

The man lowered his pistol. "Keep moving."

Josh was passing the last tent when he smelled brimstone and shit. He stopped, looked around. The latrine was fifty feet away. He backtracked. It was coming from the last tent in line, a nylon pop-up dome. Josh walked around front and gazed through the open flaps. Brandon McCauley sat on the vinyl floor, stripped to the waist and covered with satanic symbols, wig, glued-on sideburns and mustache, cross-legged, head bowed, fingers intertwined, muttering to himself.

CHAPTER 59

SKIRMISH

Josh whistled once, softly. McCauley looked up. He was in a trance, eyes unfocused, mouth open. A tendril of drool ran down his neck. His eyes snapped into focus like laser dots.

Josh stepped inside. McCauley popped to his feet.

"What the fuck?" he spat.

Josh swung the Spencer like a bat. McCauley jerked back and grabbed something off the cot. There was no room to maneuver. McCauley thrust a Confederate saber. Josh backed outside and waited, tight to the tent where he couldn't be seen, holding his rifle like a bat.

"McCauley! Come on out here."

"Or what?"

"Or I'll come in and get you."

A battering ram struck Josh's left rib. McCauley had kicked him through the fabric. Air swooshed out of him and he dropped the rifle. He sank to his knees. He'd never been

kicked so hard in his life. His rib was fractured. Instinctively, his hand went to the big Bowie knife on his belt.

McCauley sprang from the tent, pivoted on the ball of
his foot and kicked Josh in the head with the leather instep.
Ears ringing, Josh fell sideways.

McCauley sank into a stance. He looked like a cobra
about to strike. His hands whipped before settling into position, left arm extended, fingers tightly curled, right hand
beneath his chin.

"Whoooo—EEEeeeEEEYAH!" A roc's screech.

Josh's throat was dry. His skin crawled. They were alone.
Sounds of battle drifted up. Gunfire. Cannon. Dense gray
clouds dissolved into wind-blown streaks. Men bellowed
incoherently.

"Die, Yankee motherfucker!"

"Eat shit, traitor!"

"I will say this," McCauley said. "You are one determined
motherfucker. What is it you want?"

"Did you give Darren the shit that Max smoked?"

"So what? What are you, some kind of Boy Scout?
You're just another ex-con with a stick up his ass, delivering
summons for an ambulance chaser. Oh yeah. Steve Fleiss.
Good Jew name. You know, I was praying you'd show up.
And here you are. Fuckin' vodou works."

"You ever think about God, Brandon?"

McCauley's face went slack. "Huh?"

"Have you read the Bible? Ever go to church?"

McCauley barked in delight. "Are you for real? My god

is greater than your god. We've already established that. You a Catholic? A Mormon? Wait a minute. Let me guess. A good Presbyterian."

"Did you give him the fentanyl?"

"So what? You gonna try and convert me? You work for a Jew. Maybe you're a Jew."

"What if I was?"

McCauley grinned. "I knew it."

"I'm a follower of our Lord Jesus Christ."

"What's he done for you lately?"

Josh put his hand on his chest. "Peace."

"You want peace? Omma give you peace."

McCauley was a blur. He moved so fast that he left speed lines. Josh grabbed the Bowie knife and got to his knees. The pain was excruciating.

McCauley put his hands on his hips. "Nice."

Josh lunged, slashing at McCauley's thigh. McCauley stepped back, sank, and exploded. "YEEEEEEEEEEE-HA!"

Josh slashed a figure eight. McCauley whipped his right foot into Josh's hand. The knife flew. Josh grabbed the rifle and levered himself up and held the bat over his shoulder. Babe Ruth. He could barely stand. McCauley ducked low as Josh swung the rifle, grabbed Josh by the waist and drove him to the ground. Pain radiated from Josh's ribs to the top of his skull.

McCauley stepped back smiling. "All right." He morphed into a cartoon Tasmanian Devil, leaping, spinning, striking Josh in the side of his neck with the edge of his hand. Josh fell to his knees, choking. He was getting old. He'd been stupid to goad the younger man. Should have put him in a chokehold from behind. Should have brained him with a rock. Too late now.

Foam flecked McCauley's lips. Josh grabbed a handful of dirt and threw it in McCauley's face. McCauley stepped back, wiping as Josh surged, catching him with a right hook to the liver. McCauley grinned and pointed a finger.

Shots echoed up and down the valley. Josh and McCauley were alone in a narrow rock defile. twenty feet on it ended in a point sticking out over the valley below. Battle raged all around them. Not a real battle. A play battle for overgrown adolescents.

McCauley kicked Josh in the same spot. Effortlessly. Disdainfully. Josh went down, gritting his teeth and holding his busted ribs. He held up a hand.

McCauley slapped his hand away.

"Where's Jesus now, you goddamn Yankee?"

McCauley picked up the dropped Spencer, touched the tip of the bayonet. He jabbed the bayonet at Josh, breaking the skin on his right arm. He gestured at the promontory sticking out over the river. "Let's go. That way. Crawl."

Josh faced the cliff face, twenty feet away. McCauley jabbed him in his lower back. "Crawl."

Josh crawled, looking for a weapon. A rock. A stick. Anything.

Shots echoed up and down the mountain. The pop of pistols. The boom of cannon. McCauley kicked Josh in the

ass sending him sprawling on his chin, inches from the prec-
ipice. Josh could see troops maneuvering through the trees.
He saw the picnic kiosk in the distance. He saw the field of
cars across the street. He inhaled deeply, loving life despite
his pain, savoring one last breath of the world.

McCauley jabbed him in the back of his leg. "Leap! Aw
fuck. You can't leap. I'll just push you off."

Across the valley, a sharp crack. It didn't sound like the
others. Josh rolled sideways as McCauley fell on his face, a
red hole in his right temple.

RIBS AGAIN

Josh stared up at the cerulean blue sky. It was a beautiful day. Sounds of battle continued. A lull and then it would resume. Josh had no idea how long he lay there in a trance. He could see himself lying on the ground as if he were a disembodied spirit looking down.

"Thank you, Lord!"

Cade. How had he known where McCauley was?

Josh slowly levered himself with his back to a tree. His ribs blazed. Bluecoats moved through the forest to his left, across a gap.

"Medic," he gasped. "MEDIC."

Josh heard men scrambling, the ding of a canteen on a belt.

Eazy appeared. He'd tied a Confederate bandanna around his head.

"What happened?"

"I found my man." Josh breathed hard.

Eazy kneeled next to him, took his arm and felt his pulse. "Take it easy. Breath deep. Go on."

Josh inhaled. "Ouch. It hurts to breathe. My ribs are busted."

"How'd it happen?"

"I found my man. He's lying over there with a bullet in his head."

Eazy looked up. "Whoa. Seriously?"

"Yeah. Someone shot him from the other side of the ridge. A sniper."

"Well shit. We'd better let someone know."

"I'm sorry I told you. I didn't mean to rope you into this. Look. Just forget I said anything. They'll find the body. Don't say anything, okay?"

"We'd better get you off this mountain. Best thing is to carry you up to the park at the top. Paved road going all the way into town. Omma call nine-one-one."

He pulled out his phone. "Need an ambulance. Dude's got busted ribs."

Easy listened. "Up on Lookout Mountain. We're about a hundred feet below the Cleburne Monument."

Easy put the phone away, handed Josh his canteen.

Josh tilted the period accurate canteen up and glugged until Easy pulled it away.

"Take it easy."

"I'm a little hyped up," Josh said.

"I guess. Need a hand? Or you want to wait for a stretcher?" Easy looked upslope, gauging the difficulty.

"I can walk."

Easy reached down and pulled him up like a bucket. He put Josh's left arm around his shoulders and supported him as they did an awkward three-step up the mountain. It was painful and slow. Josh had to stop to breathe. As they reached a ledge just below, several rebels looked down.

"Need a hand?"

"Wouldn't mind," Easy said.

Two guys slithered down the slope and grabbed Josh under his arms. By the time they reached the top, an ambulance was waiting.

"I can walk," he said.

"Sorry, sir. Regulations. We gotta put you in a stretcher."

They strapped him in.

"Name?"

"Josh Pratt."

"I'm Ron and this is Harry." Ron was the color of café au lait, with a tight crown of black hair. Harry was a young man with a fade away, name razored onto his skull, with earrings. They slid him into the ambulance and drove down the mountain. Josh was admitted to CHI. Insurance information, X-rays, bandaging. The doctor was a young Indian named Patel in a blinding white smock.

"Your left seventh rib is fractured and the sixth has a hairline crack. Ribs heal fast. It will take about seven weeks before the pain vanishes. I'm subscribing hydrocodone. Which pharmacy do you use?"

"I'm from Madison, Wisconsin, doc. I'll be heading back there. Can I get by with over-the-counter drugs?"

"Well of course that's up to you, and depends on your tolerance level. Do you have someone who can pick you up?"

He could call Easy. Spend a night or two at the motel before heading out. He had to retrieve his car. "I'll be fine. Do you know where my uniform is?"

Patel pointed to a chair on which Josh's uniform lay neatly folded.

"Where's the rifle?"

"I have no idea."

Cade stood in the door wearing his barn coat over jeans with grass stains on the knees. "How you doing?"

Patel stood. "I'll have a nurse deliver the prescription. If you can walk, you're free to go after you sign your discharge papers." He left.

"Discharge papers," Josh said, slowly shaking his head.

"What's wrong with that?"

"How'd you find me?"

Cade hooked a chair and sat down. "It's all over the news."

"Did they run my name?"

"No. Unnamed Union soldier rushed to hospital after falling and breaking ribs."

"They took my rifle."

"Who took your rifle?"

"Whoever found it."

"That's tough." Cade reached into his pocket and pulled out an Air Tag. "Found this on my chassis."

Josh flushed. "Damn."

Cade grinned. He leaned forward and thrust a finger into Josh's bandaged ribs.

"Ouch."

"Don't do it again."

"How did you locate McCauley?"

"You wouldn't believe me."

"Try me."

Cade leaned forward, arms on his thighs. "Do you believe in voodoo?"

"No."

Cade held out a silver skull earring. "McCauley left this at Luthor's. Took it to a friend of mine. She told me when and where."

"Come on. Really."

Cade smiled. "Maybe I got lucky."

"You're not gonna tell me."

Cade shrugged.

"Get me outta here."

Cade shut the door and waited while Josh gingerly put on his shirt, pants, and shoes. Very slowly, he rose from the bed, gripping the aluminum rail.

"Ouch."

"Need a hand?"

The door opened. A tall nurse, her hair in a bob, came in. "What are you doing, Mr. Pratt?"

"I'm outta here."

"The doctor has to release you."

"He just did. He said I have to sign some papers."

"Wait here. I'll get a wheelchair."

"I don't need a wheelchair."

"It's hospital policy."

"Take the wheelchair," Cade said. "I'll get the truck."

An orderly brought a wheelchair. On the way through the lobby, a clerk rushed up with a clipboard and a pen. "Sign here, here, and here."

Josh looked at the forms. Standard boilerplate about insurance and liability. He signed.

Cade pulled up outside the main entrance as the orderly wheeled Josh out the door. Cade watched as Josh slowly got to his feet, limped up and used the pillar grip to get in the truck. They drove through town toward the battlefield, crossing the Tennessee River on a steel bridge.

"They say anything about McCauley?"

"Investigating possible homicide. Identity not revealed until they locate next-of-kin."

"Good luck with that."

"Oh his name will come out eventually."

"What about Diego?"

"Don't worry about Diego."

Fifteen minutes later, they turned into the flattened field that had served as a car park during the reenactment. Josh's car was the only vehicle. It was covered with dust and bird droppings. Josh got gingerly out, beeped the locks, slid in behind the wheel and turned the key. The Chrysler started. Cade stood by the open driver's door.

"It's been real."

"Got any ibuprofen?"

"Hang on." Cade opened his glove compartment, handed Josh a bottle of aspirin.

"Thanks, buddy."

They bumped fists.

Cade booked. Josh turned the car around and headed for the exit, feeling every dip and mound in the field. Twenty minutes later, he headed north on the Twenty-Four.

TRAMPOLINE

Josh was wired and his ribs hurt. He drove straight through, reaching Madison Monday at four a.m. Somehow, Fig divined his arrival and barked from across the street. Josh staggered slowly across the street and opened the gate, taking care not to let George and Gracie out. Fig gamboled around him across the street barking despite Josh's attempts to hush her. He let himself into the house, hit the head, gulped ibuprofen and collapsed on his bed.

The next thing he knew, the sun was shining and Fig was licking his face. Ever so slowly, Josh sat up, put his hand on the nightstand and got to his feet.

"No run today, bud."

He stank. He drew a bath and gingerly levered himself down, feeling bone on bone, soaking in the hot water, washing as best he could. He got out of the tub like an old man, hanging onto the towel rack and sitting on the toilet to dry himself off. He reached for the towel rack to get up and it came off in his hand. He left it on the floor, fed Fig, nuked a Jimmy Dean breakfast sandwich, chewed slowly, and waited until eight before phoning Ray.

"You're back! You're back!" she squealed. "Want me to come over?"

"Yeah. Would you mind stopping on the way and picking up a few things?"

"Whatcha need?"

"Milk, bananas, almonds, boneless chicken breasts, apples, and ibuprofen."

"Why do you need ibuprofen?"

"I busted a rib."

"Oh no! What happened? Are you all right?"

"I fell off a cliff and broke some ribs, but other than that, peachy keen."

"I'm coming right over."

Josh phoned Jaycee.

"Josh, I'm so glad you called. We're back in the house. Max is with us. How was your trip?"

"I found Brandon McCauley. He'll never trouble you again."

"Oh no. What happened?"

"He was shot during the reenactment. No one knows who did it. The police are investigating."

"Shot? How did it happen? I thought the guns all shot blanks."

"He was killed by a sniper using a modern rifle. It may

have been some random nut. We may never know who did it."

"Oh my god. Are you all right?"

"I fell off a cliff and broke some ribs, but other than that, peachy keen."

"Oh my god."

"It sounds worse than it is. It only hurts when I laugh."

"Do you have people to take care of you?"

"My fiancée's coming over."

"Did you say fiancée?"

"Yes."

"Why Josh! Why didn't you tell me?"

"I can hardly believe it myself."

"Who is she?"

"You'll meet her. She's a dancer."

"Okay. I won't keep you. Anything you need. I'll call you tomorrow," Steve Fleiss called. "I got the video. The driver is Cory Wagner of the Milwaukee Bucks."

"Are you shitting me?"

"Slam dunk. I'm visiting your client tomorrow. Want to come?"

"I'll drive."

"Whatcha do in Chattanooga?"

"We reenacted the Civil War."

"You can tell me when you see me."

Josh phoned Jerry.

"Helloo," Jerry answered forlornly.

"It's Josh. Fleiss is taking your case. It's a slam dunk."

"What's that mean?"

"It means you'll never have to work again."

"I just got fired."

Josh laughed. It hurt. "Fleiss and I will be there tomorrow. Where are you?"

"I'm at Ron's place."

"Ron's place! That's great! You got family."

"Yeah, it's weird being here, but I'm in a guest house. It's like this tiny house he put in addition to the big house."

"What's the address?"

"Just a minute." Josh heard Jerry shout. "Hey Ron! What's your address here?"

"Five nineteen Woodland in Brookfield."

"When's a good time to come by?"

"Give me that," someone said. Ron took the phone. "Anytime after two p.m. I want to be here."

"Okay. Mind if I bring a lawyer?"

"Why?"

"'Cause I got no place else to dump him."

"The lawyer?"

Josh laughed. It hurt. "You'll like him."

"Did they find the guy who hit Jerry?"

"Yeah."

"Who was it?"

"I'll tell you when we get there."

He went into his office, gingerly lowering himself into the oak captain's chair, and checked his email. A Zulu chieftain wished to bequeath him fifteen million dollars to make up for past transgressions. Princess Bacteria of Monaco needed his bank number to transfer twelve million for his help in transferring her late father's estate into any small bank. Several pornographic messages. He didn't know how to block them. He was afraid to ask Ray.

It was ten a.m. A car door slammed in his driveway. Seconds later, Ray let herself in and stooped to hug Fig. Josh grabbed a cane from an umbrella stand and hobbled into the living room.

"Oh my god," Ray said, rising. "Are you all right?"

"It only hurts when I laugh."

"Sit down. What can I get you?"

"Did you get me ibuprofen?"

She dug around in a cavernous purse. She handed him a plastic bottle of ibuprofen.

"Poor baby! Sit down. I'll get you something to drink."

"Water's fine."

Josh sat. Fig sat next to him. Ray returned with a glass of water. Josh tried to open the bottle with his hands, but it hurt too much. Raye grabbed it and wrenched it open. Josh swallowed four.

"What are you doing? You can't take four ibuprofen at a time."

"Why not?"

"Look at the bottle. There's a warning right on the bottle." She squinted. "Don't take it if you've had three or more alcoholic drinks."

"Why don't you put Fig in the backyard."

"You sure you're up to this?"

Josh grinned and spread his arms.

"All right. Give me a minute."

She went into the kitchen and then the bathroom. She got a beef-flavored biscuit and lured Fig out of the bedroom. She pulled Josh to his feet and they went into the bedroom and shut the door. Ray forced Josh down on his back and pulled down his pants. Hands on his chest Ray straddled him and rocked side to side.

"Don't move a muscle, mister. One false move, you could break something."

Fig whined and scratched at the door.

They lay arm in arm, panting.

Ray pointed at herself. "Look. I'm drooling."

"Nice."

Ray went into the bathroom. She came out and let Fig in. Fig jumped on the bed and tried to settle on Josh's torso.

"Yah!" he cried. Fig squealed and pulled back.

"Now look! You've frightened her! Poor thing."

"I'm just supposed to let her use me as a trampoline?"

"Why not? I did."

"I have to go to Milwaukee tomorrow. I'm taking Steve to meet Jerry Bushnell."

"How is the dear boy?"

"Miserable. I hope a couple mil will cheer him up."

"Huh?"

"Steve found out who hit him. He'll pay up to avoid publicity."

"Who is it?"

"Can't tell ya. What are you doing?"

"Some stringer for *Variety* saw Drunk Octopus and has set up a video call with an agent who wants to represent me!"

"That's great, Ray! Will Idaho continue as the Octopus?"

"They said they were looking at Michael Shannon."

"Never heard of him. What will Idaho say?"

"She ain't gonna be happy if it happens. Not one word of this to anyone! Capisce?"

"I swear."

Ray kissed him on the mouth. "Love you! Call me later."

"Will do."

"And think about a date, will you? Maybe June?"

"A date? For what?"

Ray opened her mouth and rolled her eyes. It wasn't until the front door slammed that he figured it out.

FAT CITY

Ron Bushnell's split level in Brookfield occupied a half-acre. A boy of about twelve was raking leaves when Josh pulled into the driveway at eleven on Tuesday. A prim woman with a red pageboy answered the door in sweatpants and a Packer hoodie.

"Mrs. Bushnell, I'm Josh Pratt, and this is Steve Fleiss."

"Come in. Call me Alma. Jerry's in the living room."

Jerry sat in a recliner, his leg in a cast on the extended footrest, watching *Judge Judy*. He muted the show when Josh and Fleiss entered.

"Jerry, this is Steve Fleiss."

They shook hands. "Thanks for coming," Jerry said.

Josh wondered if being in a regular household had affected Jerry's outlook. Josh and Fleiss sat on a sofa, half facing Jerry.

"Would you boys like coffee?" Alma said.

"Yes, please," Josh said.

"Thank you," Fleiss said.

Fleiss set his leather briefcase on the coffee table. "Love Judge Judy."

"Yeah, she don't take any shit."

"Jerry, I have good news. After reviewing the video from the traffic camera, we were able to identify the driver who hit you. The video clearly shows he had a red light, and even if he didn't, his driving was negligent. You have a very good case here if you want to go after him for damages."

"Fuck an A I do. Who was it?"

"Before I tell you, you have to understand this is privileged information and you can't tell anybody, or it could jeopardize your case."

"Yeah, I got it. I won't tell anyone."

"Cory Wagner of the Milwaukee Bucks."

Jerry's eyes popped. "Are you shitting me?"

"I have not yet contacted Mr. Wagner. First we have to have an agreement. I've prepared a contract for you." He reached into his briefcase and brought out a sheath of papers. "Take your time reviewing it. I will take thirty percent of damages as my fee. You will get the rest."

"How much we talking?"

"I don't like to speculate, but in cases like this, where there's a celebrity involved, seven figures isn't out of the question?"

"How much is that?"

"You'll never have to work again."

"Seriously?"

"I believe so."

"How soon before I get the money?"

"Let me reach out to Mr. Wagner and see if he's willing to settle with you before we involve the courts."

Jerry threw his hands in the air. "WHOO-HOOO!"

It was the happiest Josh had ever seen him. He felt happy for Jerry, but deep down inside he knew that the money was a curse, that Jerry would run through it in record time, and he would find himself worse off than ever before. He would have no one to blame but himself. Josh would talk to Ron about it. Maybe there was something he could do. Have Jerry declared non compus mentis. And of course if Ron tried to do that, Jerry would accuse his son of trying to seize control of his windfall for personal reasons, never mind that Ron was obviously upper middle class and had no real spending concerns.

Fleiss reached in his briefcase and brought out a sheath of papers. "Here is a contract stipulating our agreement. I have agreed to take this case on a contingency basis, which means my fee will be thirty percent of whatever you recover. You can check with other lawyers. This is pretty standard. You don't have to sign it now. Feel free to contact another attorney or legal expert, but also take a look at my track record. I have a seventy-eight percent recovery record. The document stipulates that you have contracted me to represent you for damages."

"Do the cops know?" Josh said.

"This is probably in the system as Jerry needed an ambulance, but my guess is, if they do know, this is pretty far down the list of things they need to do. As you know, Milwaukee is experiencing staff shortages and prioritizes only the most pressing problems.

"The contract includes a confidentiality agreement. You mustn't talk about this to anyone, and please do not mention the defendant to anyone."

"Hell. Gimme a pen."

"No rush, Jerry," Alma said. "At least wait until Ron gets home and has a chance to read this."

"What would Ron know about it?" Jerry said.

"He's familiar with contracts. He's a financial manager."

"Where's Ron?" Josh asked.

"He had to go to work. Some emergency. He'll be back shortly."

"Couldn't hurt," Fleiss said.

"I want to sign it now. Give me a pen."

Fleiss shrugged and handed him a pen.

"Everything this guy has done for me he done out of the goodness of his heart. I can't imagine he'd steer me wrong now."

"What guy?" Alma asked.

Jerry pointed the pen at Josh.

Josh dropped Fleiss off at his office and got home at two-thirty. A headless squirrel lay on the living room floor.

"You're acting out," Josh told the dog. "You're upset because I haven't been around much. I understand. But bringing dismembered animals into the house isn't the way."

He went online and found O'Malley's funeral Friday at Christ the Good Shepherd in Lincoln Park. He pulled his funeral suit out of the closet. He only got the suit to go to funerals. It was black narrow lapels and looked like something an undertaker would wear. Fig got her leash and sat in front of Josh thumping.

"Can't do it, girl. Gonna be awhile."

Marriage.

The Big M.

You're not a kid anymore. You've gone from chaos to semi-respectability. He thought about Ray, how he yearned for her. He could smell her now. Josh wouldn't repeat the mistakes he'd made in the past. Before prison. He had not been a nice guy. Things he'd done wormed into his brain, that feeling you get when you've been doing blow all night and just want to crash but your skin is crawling. Some of the things he'd done he'd never confided in anyone. And never would. Not even Pastor Dorgan. He was getting better, wasn't he? He truly believed in the deity and a life of penance for his past sins.

He wondered about Ray's friends. People with pronouns who eat keto. He didn't know how to talk to those people. His phone rang.

"Mr. Pratt, this is Professor Hagenauer! I haven't forgotten our little chat. How would you like to join me tomorrow at the Madison Club? I have some exciting news regarding your letter."

"What time?"

"One p.m."

"See you there, Prof."

CHAPTER 63

THE MADISON CLUB

Josh woke Thursday to clear skies, showered, dressed, tossed back a couple ibuprofen and grabbed his backpack. He drove downtown and parked in Fleiss' lot. Josh walked two blocks uphill toward the capitol and the club. By the time he arrived his ribs were killing him and he was panting. He wore a blue wool sports jacket with gold buttons, pleated navy-blue trousers, black leather loafers. The Madison Club was a three-story red brick Georgian just off the Square at 5 East Wilson, looking out on Olin Terrace and Lake Monona. It had been there since 1909. He'd thought about a tie but couldn't decide between Rat Fink or the Roadrunner. His white shirt was open at the throat.

A blond babe in a burgundy dress greeted him in the foyer, with its checkerboard tiles and Arab rugs. "Follow me, sir."

She led him through a great dining room with an arced

ceiling, round tables covered in white tablecloths, ninety percent taken, mostly men speaking intensely, laughing, drinking as college coed waitresses passed among them.

Hagenauer was sitting at a window seat looking out on Lake Monona. He rose as Josh approached, wearing a gray houndstooth jacket with leather elbow patches, looking professorial in his gray hair and beard. Horn-rimmed glasses poked from a jacket pocket.

"So glad you could make it, Mr. Pratt!" Handshake like a vise grip. They sat.

The waitress handed them heavy white menus with gold script. "May I tell you about today's specials?"

"Oh I think this calls for a drink first. Vodka martini, straight up with an olive."

"And for you, sir?"

"You got Capital Autumnal Fire?"

"We have it on tap."

Josh held up a finger.

They watched her go.

"Did you bring the letter?"

Josh reached into his backpack and removed the eight-and-a-half by-eleven rigid plastic sleeve holding the letter.

"May I see it?"

Josh handed it over. Hagenauer put on his glasses. He held it close like an explosive-sniffing dog. He looked up beaming, like a kid who'd got a new bike for Christmas. "The good news is, my associates believe it to be genuine and a collector is interested."

"It's not mine to sell."

"You told me someone had given it to you as payment for services rendered."

"Yeah, but now he's in the money so I can give him a bill."

"Why would you want to do that? My associate is willing to pay eighty thousand dollars."

Josh whistled. "That's a lot of jack. I'll ask him."

"That's all I ask."

The waitress returned with their drinks. Hagenauer held his up. "Cheers!"

Josh clinked and they drank.

"Would you like to hear about our specials?"

"Sure," Josh said.

"We have Moroccan-fried chicken, Barolo braised short ribs, parmesan creamy polenta, foraged mushrooms, and grilled Colorado lamb lollipops with chimichurri sauce."

"Do you have a cheeseburger?"

"Our cheeseburger is raised from one hundred percent grass-fed beef right here in Wisconsin."

"I'll have a cheeseburger."

"Perfect. How would you like it done?"

"Medium."

She turned to Hagenauer who'd stared at her the whole time. "And you, sir?"

"Do you still have the Maine lobster roll?"

"I'm sorry, sir. We're out of lobsters."

"I'll have the Moroccan chicken."

"Perfect. That comes with a dinner salad. And you, sir. Would you like fries with your burger?"

"Got coleslaw?"

"Yes, sir. I'll put these in right away."

Hagenauer stared at her ass as she walked away. Josh looked at Hagenauer's wedding ring.

"Of course, we'll need to verify its authenticity. We can do that via carbon dating and chemical analysis of the ink. I would need to have access for several hours."

"I'll let you know."

"It's an extraordinary offer. Very few Grant letters are worth that much."

"I'll ask the owner."

"Did you resolve your case to his satisfaction?"

"I did."

"Can you tell me about it?"

"No, sir. Most of my cases are really very boring."

"You're too modest, Mr. Pratt. Several years ago there was a shoot-out on your front lawn."

"Oh that. It was all a misunderstanding."

Hagenauer peered at Josh from beneath his shaggy brows. "I'm sure that's not the case. I'm sure your life has been fascinating. Have you ever thought about writing a book?"

Josh laughed. "I can barely sign my name."

"You could work with a collaborator."

"Professor, I know some professional writers. They all have day jobs. Besides. I like what I do. I'm my own boss,

I work my own hours, and I meet all kinds of interesting people."

"Do you do divorce work?"

"In all the years I've been a PI, I have yet to take a divorce case."

"Would you if it were offered?"

"I don't know. I'd have to think about it."

"Why the reticence?"

Josh couldn't tell this stranger about his own upbringing, the interaction his father had had with a long string of hookers, drug addicts, and losers, his problems with intimacy, his reluctance to listen to sordid details. He never knew his mother. He had no desire to find her. He was a detective, and he had no desire to track her down for fear of the heartbreak it would bring. There was no way it could work out well.

She was probably dead.

For all he knew, Duane killed her. He was a convicted murderer. He'd exterminated a family of four because the children were too loud.

"Doesn't really interest me. I've been pretty lucky. Most of my cases have been pretty interesting."

"What's your most interesting case?"

"Probably the time a woman hired me to prove that she was the rightful owner of the song 'Marissa' by Cretaceous."

"Are you kidding me? I know that song!"

"Everybody knows that song."

"Did you do it?"

"I did. Then Wes Magnum popped up and ruined everything."

"'I thought he was dead."

"Most people did. But it all ended happily. Wes confirmed that Marissa was the rightful owner and signed a new document."

"Why did he give her the song?"

"They were lovers. Cretaceous hadn't yet hit the big time. That happened within a year and he ended the relationship. But he gave her the song. She was able to move out of her trailer park."

"Glad to hear it." Hagenauer looked at his Tag Heuer. "I have to go. I have a faculty meeting in forty-five minutes."

"Thanks for the lunch."

Hagenauer signaled the waitress. "Any time."

CHAPTER 64

SID AND FIG

"How does June sixth sound?" Ray said over the phone.

"Pick another date. That's the anniversary of D-Day."

"What's D-Day?"

"The day the allies invaded France. World War II."

"So what?"

"It's bad juju. Trust me."

"Okay. What about June eighth? That's a Saturday."

"Okay."

"Wonderful! My friends and I will plan the wedding!"

"I thought we were going to have a biker wedding."

"What would that entail?"

"We hire a band. Maybe the White Trash Blues Band. We have it outdoors, maybe at a park. We arrive by bike. I know a great pastor who will do the ceremony. We all get shit-faced, and then you and I ride off into the sunset."

"You're joking."

"Maybe a little."

Ray laughed. "Give me a list of who you want to invite and leave it to me. I'll take care of everything."

"Who's gonna pay for this wedding?"

"Are you kidding? My dad! He's been waiting for this his whole life!"

"You coming over?"

"I'll be over tonight. I have a conference call this afternoon with the agent."

"How's Idaho taking it?"

"We're not talking. She may not finish the run."

"What will you do?"

"I'm in talks with another actress. Can I bring Sid?"

"Sure."

"I don't have time to shop, so could you feed me?"

"I'll take you to the Hoity Toity."

"Oh I love that place!"

"Wait until you try the diplodocus medallions."

"What's diplodocus?"

"It's the longest dinosaur on record. It lived during the Jurassic Period."

"So how we gonna eat it?"

"They found some in Siberia frozen in ice for millions of years."

"Oh Josh! I'll see you around seven."

Fig barked and ran at the door.

"No can do," Josh said. "I'm all busted up! Maybe in a week or two."

Josh phoned Jerry.

"Hey, man!" Jerry answered. "What's shakin'?"

Josh stared at his phone. "You feeling good?"

"Are you shitting me? I've been waiting all my life for the big score! Fat City! I'm on Easy Street!"

Did you ever think about working?

Josh was disgusted with himself for the thought. Jerry had been dealt a bad hand. *Lord, forgive me.*

"Don't tell me Fleiss got back to you already."

"No, but today, he sent a letter to Cory Wagner. He's got to pay up. This could ruin his career."

A natural skeptic, Josh held his tongue. "Hope it works out for you. Listen. I met with this professor today and he says he's got a buyer for the letter."

"What letter?"

"General Grant's letter."

"Oh yeah."

"He's offering eighty thousand dollars. I can put you in touch with him if you like."

"Hell no, man. I told you that letter was yours. You want to sell it, go ahead."

"I like to keep things legal. How about I have Fleiss draw up a document which says you're giving me the letter?"

"That's fine. I meant it. You've been a real friend, Josh, a better friend to me that my own family."

"What about Ron?"

"Ron really surprised me. He must feel guilty for all the years he shunned me."

"Did you reach out to him?"

"Nahh. I knew how he felt about me. But now we're getting to know each other."

"Are you still staying at their house?"

"I'm back at the Davenport. I still have two weeks left on that apartment you got me."

"How's Max doing?"

"Honestly, you'd never know he OD'd."

"I'm going to be in Milwaukee Sunday for a funeral. I'll drop by."

"Who died?"

"A police detective. Shawn O'Malley. He was a good guy."

"How'd he die?"

"Some scumbag shot him in his car. No reason. 'Cept they hate cops. Lot of that going around."

"Thank God it's not like that in Madison."

Josh bit his tongue. Fig paddled backward.

"Forget it! Go play outside."

Fig barked.

"Go on!"

Fig went through the doggie door.

Just thinking about Ray aroused him. That perfume she wore. Her lingerie carefully chosen for him. He sniffed his pits. He took a shower, laying on the Axe body armor. He smelled like absinthe mixed with a Thermador. Too much? He took another shower, washing off the Axe. He didn't need no stinkin' Axe. She loved him. He forbade himself from thinking past the honeymoon. Speaking of which, what could they do? He'd never been to Hawaii. He'd take her to Hawaii.

He looked around the house. The place was a sty. Fig had got in the garbage and chewed up an empty Archer grass-fed jerky pack. Then she'd jumped on the desk in his office and got hold of a bag of salted almonds. She went dumpster diving in the office, spreading advertisements, used tissues, napkins, paper plates, discarded pens, and four apple cores. Dog hair covered the sofa and the floor. He got out the twenty-gallon Craftsman. It was the only thing that worked, but only if he got down on his ass and worked the narrow nozzle, going over every inch of the floor. He dragged it into the kitchen and sucked up all the dog hair. He did the dirty dishes, stashing them in the dishwasher he never used.

Fig came back in and sat at his feet thumping her tail and whining. Josh looked at the clock on the microwave. It was five-thirty. He dug out a bag of shredded chicken from Woodman's and dumped it in her bowl with a cut of apple and some cherry tomatoes. Fig went to work.

Josh had just put on a new shirt when he heard Ray fumbling at the door. He opened the door and she fell into his arms. His ribs creaked and groaned. He sucked it up, bent her over backward, and kissed her on the lips.

"Wow! What's going on?"

"You're here. That's what."

"I was going to take a shower and change here."

"We got time."

Rolling her eyes, she tossed her overnight bag over her shoulder. "All right! Wait a minute. I have to get Sid."

"Can't he wait in the car?"

"Don't be silly. We'll close the door so he can play with Fig."

She pushed away, went outside, returning with the slinky Siamese in her arms. Fig thumped her tail. Ray dropped the cat on the sofa. Sid leaped to the ground and barrel raced around Fig's legs.

Ray fell dramatically on Josh, arms on his shoulders. He grunted softly and put a hand to his ribs.

"Oh my poor darling! I am so sorry."

"Don't worry about it. Come with me." He took her hands. They barely got the door shut in time.

CHAPTER 65

O'MALLEY'S FUNERAL

Sunday, Josh woke to overcast skies. Ray had already left. He found a note on the nightstand.

"Dear Heart! Last night was magical. The dinosaur was divine. I'll call you tonight. Yours everlastingly, Ray."

O'Malley's funeral was set for eleven. Josh showered, got his funeral suit out of the closet and put it on. Put on the matching Homburg and a pair of dark glasses, he could have been a Blues Brother.

Josh arrived at the church at a quarter of. He parked near the art museum and walked two blocks to the church. The bell tower aimed at the heavens framed by the Plaza and Prudential to the North. Cathedral Square Park was ringed with cars. There wasn't a space to be had. A Cadillac hearse waited near the main entrance. Mourners mounted the steps softly murmuring. Four police vehicles were parked on Kilbourn, for the honor guard. Josh kept his head down and went inside, standing at the rear of the nave with a handful of broad-shouldered tattooed men. Most of them were fifties and up, but a couple were in their thirties.

The pews were filled with O'Malley's friends and family, consisting of his eighty-year-old mother, his daughter Francine, but not her mother Penelope. Josh walked toward the front and slid into the sixth row, next to three couples. Across the aisle sat O'Malley's friends in the force, active and retired. One dude wore a sky-blue suit and sat in the back row.

Shuffling as the priest walked out, accompanied by a man in a wide-lapel black suit, gray hair to his shoulders, who sat behind the pipe organ and tentatively hit High C. The priest took the pulpit.

"Thank you for coming. Shawn O'Malley was a great cop, someone who made a difference in the lives of those with whom he came in contact. He was loyal to his family and friends, fair-minded and civic-minded, and he loved white-eyed soul. Shawn's friend Arthur Siebecker would like to say something."

Siebecker stood. "Shawn was a true believer. Don't be sad, this is a joyous occasion, for Shawn has joined Our Savior in Heaven and I'll tell you something that's not generally known, Jesus was a soul freak. He loved the Temptations, The Main Ingredient, Ashford and Simpson, and Tower of Power. He particularly loved Kevin Rowland, a.k.a. Dexys Midnight Runners."

Siebecker sat and played "The Teams That Meet In

Caffs."

There were hushed murmurs of encouragement. "Beautiful." "Thank you, Arthur."

The priest stood at the podium beneath a massive crown of thorns. It looked like a medieval weapon. "Shawn O'Malley was a good cop. There are people who hate cops, and some have good reason, but Shawn was not that kind of cop. He was warm, compassionate, generous with his time. He volunteered for youth baseball and could often be found weekends umping a Little League game anywhere from River Hills to the Town of Lake. Shawn was more than a member of this flock. He was a friend. I saw him most Sundays. He'd come back after the service to give confession.

"He has a lot of friends here and some of them would like to share their fondest memories of Shawn. Bill?"

A heavy-set Black man with white hair and mutton chops wearing a dark-blue suit with gold buttons rolled toward the front like a rodeo cowboy. He shook hands with the priest, gripped the podium and looked out.

"I retired two years ago. I saw the writing on the wall back then. After the craziness of summer 2020 and what followed, I realized I had no future in police work, at least not here. If any one of us could have found greener pastures, it was Shawn. Cop of the Year twice, once for saving a little girl's life as she was flushed down a sewer. He told me he wanted to join the Marines but he'd tested positive for grass!"

People laughed with abandon as if they'd been holding

it in.

"I ain't sayin' that was true or not. The Good Lord knows I smoked my share of the devil's weed when I was in high school, and it's only through the grace of God and his Son Jesus Christ that I stand before you here today."

Applause and attaboys.

"Before you fall asleep, omma turn the pulpit over to Jackie Talbot."

A tall, auburn-haired woman in a conservative navy-blue suit stepped up, said something in Bill's ear and faced the congregation. "One night, a bunch of us were down at the Oak drinking. There's this huge thumping bass coming through the wall from the bar next door. It was about eleven and we were shit-faced. Shawn stands up and points a finger up. 'I know!'

"What's that you know, Shawn, I said."

"The Lord was not in the wind, and after this wind an earthquake. But the Lord was in the earthquake. And after the earthquake. But the Lord was not in the earthquake. And after the earthquake, a fire…"

"And he sort of trailed off, and we're all sitting around shit-faced looking at him, and I say, where was the Lord, Shawn?"

"The Lord is next door listening to that blues band!"

Laughter, sobbing.

Josh thought about getting up there. He slunk out. He sat in his car weeping. He headed for Davenport Suites on West Juneau. He parked on the street, took off his tie and jacket and left them in the car. Jerry stood in the foyer, eyes twinkling, with the desk clerk, the same Hispanic woman as when he'd checked in. She was laughing.

"Oh Jerry! You are so funny!"

Jerry turned toward Josh. He wore new gray Wranglers, a tan sports jacket over a blue work shirt, and shiny new boots. "There he is! The man of the hour! I got something for you."

"Where'd you get those duds?"

"Goodwill! Nobody's even worn this jacket. Anyhow, I've decided to move outta here. They said they could only give back half of the unused rent, but I'll make up the rest."

"You don't have to do that, Jerry. What have you got for me?"

He reached inside his jacket and withdrew a white envelope. Josh opened it up. Inside was a handwritten letter.

"Being of sound mind, I hereby bequeath and will this letter by General Ulysses S. Grant that has been in the Bushnell family since 1864 to Josh Pratt, without whom I'd still be living in a shit hole with bed bugs, and has caused a reunion between my in-laws and me and at least one son. Sincerely, Jerry Bushnell."

"This is great, Jer, but it's not a legal document. Besides. I don't want the letter. It's yours. It belongs in the family. It's part of your lore."

"No way! You're taking Grant's letter. If you try to return it, I'll fold it up and mail it back to you."

Josh folded the document and put it inside his funeral

jacket. "I'll ask Fleiss to draw something up."

"If you like."

"We're so sorry to see you go, Jerry!" the clerk said.

"Josh, this is Sonia. Sonia, Josh."

"Oh Mr. Pratt, Jerry has told me so much about you!"

"Pleasure to meet you, ma'am. Jerry, do you want me to take you someplace?"

"No! I called an Uber. I'll be back for my stuff tomorrow."

"Where are you moving?"

"Ron offered me the guest house."

"What are you going to do?"

"I've thought about writing my memoirs."

"Great. You know how to find me."

Josh got home at three.

He was getting married.

He had to get a new suit.

A LOOK AT:

FLORIDA MAN BY MIKE BARON

MIKE BARON DELIVERS A RIOTOUS, HEART-FELT AND ULTIMATELY UPLIFITING STORY IN FLORIDA MAN.

Gary Duba's having a bad day. There's a snake in his toilet, a rabid raccoon in the yard, and his girl Krystal's in jail for getting naked at a Waffle House and licking the manager.

Gary's a redneck living in a trailer by the swamp. But he's got dreams, big dreams. Every time he tries to get ahead, fate deals him a low blow. But then he gets lucky…

With his best friend, Floyd, Gary sets out to sell his prized Barry Bonds rookie card to raise the five hundred needed for bail. But things always find a way of getting out of hand.

"Florida Man will make you laugh out loud. It's sui generis."

AVAILABLE NOW